FIVE HIGHLY ACCLAIMED ⬛⬛⬛ RS
IN ONE MAG⬛⬛⬛⬛N

MARY BALOGH ⬛⬛⬛⬛⬛ er first Onyx Historica⬛⬛⬛ ⬛⬛⬛⬛⬛⬛ *⬛⬛se*. In 1989, she won ⬛⬛⬛⬛⬛⬛ ⬛⬛oks Award for Bestselling Short Historical, as well as a *Romantic Times* Lifetime Achievement Award. She has also won the *Romantic Times* Award for Best New Regency Writer in 1985. She lives in Kipling, Saskatchewan, Canada.

GAYLE BUCK has freelanced for regional publications, worked for a radio station and as a secretary. Until recently she was involved in public relations for a major Texas university. She is currently working on projects in fantasy and romantic suspense. Her most recent book is *The Hidden Heart*.

CHARLOTTE LOUISE DOLAN, author of *The Unofficial Suitor,* has lived throughout the United States and in Montreal, Taiwan, Germany, and the Soviet Union. She is the mother of three children and currently makes her home in Idaho Falls, Idaho, with her husband and daughter.

ANITA MILLS' most recent Onyx Historical Romance is *Winter Roses*. A former teacher of history and English, she has turned a lifelong passion for both into a writing career.

PATRICIA RICE is the author of a number of Onyx Historical Romance novels, including *Touched by Magic* and *Rebel Dreams*. Ms. Rice has a degree in accounting, and her hobbies include history, travel, and antique collecting.

FULL-MOON MAGIC

*Five Enchanting Love Stories
That Will Leave You Spellbound*

by

Gayle Buck

———

Mary Balogh

———

Charlotte Louise Dolan

———

Patricia Rice

———

Anita Mills

A SIGNET BOOK

SIGNET
Published by the Penguin Group
Penguin Books USA Inc., 375 Hudson Street,
New York, New York 10014, U.S.A.
Penguin Books Ltd, 27 Wrights Lane,
London W8 5TZ, England
Penguin Books Australia Ltd, Ringwood,
Victoria, Australia
Penguin Books Canada Ltd, 10 Alcorn Avenue,
Toronto, Ontario, Canada M4V 3B2
Penguin Books (N.Z.) Ltd, 182-190 Wairau Road,
Auckland 10, New Zealand

Penguin Books Ltd, Registered Offices:
Harmondsworth, Middlesex, England

First published by Signet, an imprint of New American Library,
a division of Penguin Books USA Inc.

First Printing, September, 1992
10 9 8 7 6 5 4 3 2 1

Contents

FULL-MOON MAGIC

The Dark Rider

by
Mary Balogh

DINAH RIDDING had her first sight of Malvern by pressing one cheek against the carriage window—she was not wearing her bonnet—and closing the eye that could see only the interior of the conveyance while peering straight ahead with the other. The house was coming into sight around a bend of the tree-shaded driveway. She realized that she was seeing it when it could not possibly be at its best, it being late afternoon with heavy leaden skies bringing on an early dusk. Nevertheless, she felt no doubt at all that it really was a haunted house, as Mama had said it was. It had the look of a haunted house.

"No, not *there*, dearest," Mama had said to Sir Anthony Wilkes, Dinah's stepfather. "We must find Dinah somewhere else more pleasant to go."

Clinton, the youngest of the three children of Mama's second marriage, had been laid low by the measles, a disease that Dinah had never had, and their nurse was quite convinced that the other two would inevitably contract it too. Mama and Sir Anthony were anxious to return to the country to be near them, though they had been planning to spend a whole month in town. But where was Dinah to go? London was rather sparsely populated in the middle of October.

Her Aunt Beatrice was in Bath and Sir Anthony's brother and his wife had gone to Italy for the winter months. One did not like to impose upon mere friends, though doubtless there were several who would have considered Dinah's presence among them no imposition at all.

"She can go to Malvern," Sir Anthony had said. "There will be no problem at all. Gloria will be delighted to have her." Gloria Neville, Lady Asquith, was Sir Anthony's sister.

That was when Mama had said, "No, not *there*, dearest." And when pressed by Sir Anthony, she had flushed and looked uneasily at Dinah, who was also waiting for her answer, and said evasively. "Oh, well, it is large and cold and rather cheerless and . . ." She had looked appealingly at her husband.

"And haunted," he had said, grinning at her. "You believed all those stories, did you not, my love? Mrs. Knole should have been an actress instead of a housekeeper. She would have been a sensation on the stage. You believed everything she told you. But tell me— did you ever actually encounter a ghost or anything resembling a ghost during the two weeks we spent at Malvern? Any wisp of white disappearing around a dark corner? Anything that went bump in the night?"

"It pleases you to make fun of me," Mama had said, on her dignity. "I *felt* it, Anthony."

He had grinned again, set an arm about her shoulders, and hugged her to him. Mama, quiet, delicate, dreamy, had always insisted that some people were more sensitive to the spirit world than others and that she was one of those people.

Dinah was another. People identify their world through the five senses, she had always maintained.

But what if there were a sixth sense or a seventh or eighth that it had pleased a Supreme Being not to gift us with? How could we know for sure that there was not a great deal more to be experienced if only we had the sensual equipment? Perhaps the spirit world was only a touch away—except that *touch* was the wrong word to use because it was one of the five senses that could not locate the world beyond.

Dinah had often sensed her father's nearness long after his death when she was eight. And her grandmother's.

"Dinah," Sir Anthony had asked, his arm still about Mama's shoulders, the grin still on his face, "would it frighten you to go to Malvern until the children are spot-free and roaring with health again? Would you be afraid of being gobbled up by ghosts?"

"No," Dinah had said. And she had spoken the truth. She accepted the existence of a world beyond this natural one. She was not afraid of it as her mother was.

And so as the carriage completed its turn about the bend in the driveway and Malvern came into full view, she gazed at the house with curiosity and some excitement, but with no dread at all. It was an old house, built in the fifteenth century close to the coast in Hampshire, though several owners since then had made changes or additions in the styles then current. So there was an arched gateway set in a square tower, clearly leading through to a courtyard. And there were numerous other towers and battlements and shaped gables and pinnacles. Certainly the house did not present a neat or classical facade or skyline. But it was fascinating.

"It looks a right gloomy place to me, mum," Dinah's maid, Judy, said, peering out of the window with a frown.

"It looks wonderful," Dinah said. And she looked forward to meeting Lady Asquith, whom she had met and liked on a couple of occasions. Lord Asquith had died a few years before. Dinah had never met the new baron, Lady Asquith's son. She did not know if he was in residence or not.

Edgar Neville, Lord Asquith, was taking tea with his mother. But he had finished both eating and drinking and was standing at one of the long mullioned windows of the drawing room, staring out onto a gray and gloomy late afternoon.

"If Uncle Anthony had to send the child here," he said, "I do think he should have been more definite about the day. If I just knew for sure when to expect her, I could send some good stout men to accompany her the last ten miles or so. I could even go myself. But it would have been far better if you had just made some excuse, Mama."

"Impossible," Lady Asquith said. "Anthony's request was most urgent. Besides, I will enjoy the female company. I am quite sure your worries must be groundless, Edgar. Surely there is no real danger to an ordinary traveler." Her cup clinked against the saucer as she set it down. "And I am equally sure she will be mortally offended if you refer to her as a child, Edgar. Girls of her age are usually sensitive about such matters."

He turned to look at her in the late afternoon gloom. The lamps and candles had not yet been lit. "For goodness sake, Mama," he said, "how old can she be? Seven? Eight?"

"More like eighteen or nineteen," his mother said with a laugh. "You were not really listening when I read Anthony's letter to you, were you, Edgar? Did you imagine that it was Angela who was coming? But she is in quarantine with John while poor Clinton is all over spots."

"He said the eldest daughter," Lord Asquith said, looking at her blankly.

"The eldest daughter is Dinah," his mother said. "Dinah Ridding. His stepdaughter, dear. He always speaks of her as if she were his real daughter. He and Winifred are absurdly fond of each other, you will recall. Dinah must be nineteen. She made her come-out not this past spring but last year. It is a young lady we are expecting, Edgar, not a child."

"Damnation!" he said. "Pardon me, Mama. I pictured a child who would be spending her days in the nursery and the schoolroom. This changes everything." He frowned.

"I will take her under my wing," his mother assured him. "You need not concern yourself about her, Edgar. Though," she added with a sigh, "it is high time you concerned yourself with some young lady, dear. I am beginning to feel a hankering for some grandchildren of my own. And you will be thirty before we know it."

Lord Asquith frowned again. "In two and a half years' time," he said. But he was saved from having to comment on the rest of what his mother had said. Sounds from outside caused him to turn sharply back to the window. "This must be her," he said, watching a strange carriage being drawn into the courtyard by four horses. "And none too soon. It will be dark within the hour. We had better not say anything to her,

Mama. Though she must be discouraged from going about alone. Damn, but I wish she were the child I was expecting.''

Lady Asquith got to her feet and left the room in order to greet her visitor in the great hall. Her son stayed in the drawing room, hoping that his uncle's stepdaughter would not turn out to be a bouncing and inquisitive young lady.

He was reassured immediately when she came into the room with his mother a few minutes later. She was slightly below medium height and slender. At first glance she looked little more than the child he had been expecting, but she possessed appealing feminine curves he saw when his eyes moved over her. Her face, framed by wispy light brown curls beneath her bonnet, was rather too thin for classical beauty, but it was saved from plainness, saved even from ordinary prettiness, by large, dreamy, long-lashed eyes, which appeared in the half-light to be a smoky gray. And she had a sweet rosebud of a mouth. A very kissable mouth.

She was not his first cousin, he thought suddenly. She was no blood relation at all. And she was just the sort of female who normally appealed to him. And just the sort he had been hoping fervently for the past ten minutes that she would be. She looked sweet and shy and timid. The sort who would cling to his mother and would always be where one expected her to be. The sort he would not have to worry about. He breathed a sigh of relief.

"Edgar," his mother said, "this is Dinah Ridding. My son Edgar, dear. You have not met before, even though my brother has been married to your mother for almost nine years.''

The girl looked at him and smiled a little hesitantly,

very sweetly. "Mama always avoids coming to Malvern," she said, "though perhaps I should not say so, should I? She is afraid of the ghosts."

Ah, yes, the ghosts, Lord Asquith thought, making the girl a bow. The ghosts and a timid little wide-eyed slip of a thing. They might make a handy combination during the next few days. Though it would be a shame to frighten such a sweet little innocent. Her mouth looked ten times more kissable when it smiled.

"We have quite a variety of them, Miss Ridding," he said. "But they will not bother anyone who knows what places to avoid and what noises to ignore."

Her eyes widened.

"Gracious, Edgar," his mother said, and she set a protective arm about the girl's shoulders, "you will be frightening poor Dinah away almost before she has set foot in the house. Have a seat close to the fire, my dear, and take no notice of any silly talk about ghosts. I have never encountered one in thirty years of living here. Fresh tea and cakes should be here soon. I daresay you are hungry."

"Thank you," the girl said. "But I knew the house was haunted as soon as I set eyes on it."

Lord Asquith smiled. Partly with genuine amusement—she was such a timid little thing. Partly with relief—she was obviously going to be only too eager to stay in places where she was supposed to be. And partly with an unaccustomed tenderness of feeling. He had not had a great deal of time for women in the past few years. But if he had, or if he had time now, she would be just the type he would be drawn to.

"I am sorry I am late," Dinah said a little breathlessly as she arrived in the breakfast room the following morning, and Lady Asquith looked up at her in some surprise while Lord Asquith got to his feet and came around the table to draw back a chair for her. "I got lost."

"But my dear Dinah," Lady Asquith said, "I had no idea you would be up so early. I had every intention of coming to fetch you to breakfast later or at the least of sending Mrs. Knole for you."

Dinah seated herself. "I know you told me yesterday that one needs a ball of string to find one's way about this house," she said. "But I thought I could remember the way down. I was wrong."

"Perhaps it would be as well if you did not move about the house at all when you are alone," Lord Asquith said. "I know that my mother will be pleased to take you about, and when I am not busy I will be happy to do so. Or there is always Mrs. Knole."

Dinah looked up at him and smiled a little uncertainly. He had lost none of his good looks or masculine appeal in the light of morning, she saw. He was the type of man she had dreamed of meeting since before she left the schoolroom, the type she had not met in two Seasons in London, though there had been several gentlemen she had liked and even a few she had been fond of. But none had that special something to make her glow with awareness and happiness and even perhaps love. By the advanced age of nineteen and with the experience of two Seasons behind her, she might have grown more practical or more cynical and concluded that there was no such man living in the real world and no such relationship. But there was. She had only to look at her mother and Sir Anthony to know that dreams could come true. And so she had accepted none of the three marriage offers she had received, even though she had felt liking and respect for two of those gentlemen and a great fondness in addition for the third.

Lord Asquith was her dream, or could be if she had a chance to get to know him. And it was not just something she saw through her eyes, though he was excessively handsome. It was something she had felt as soon as she met him the day before. He was tall and rather thin, though she recalled the latter word as soon as she had thought it. He was not thin. He was—slender. No, that was an effeminate word. He was lean. Splendidly and very attractively so. His face was somewhat austere with its hawkish nose and rather thin lips and keen dark eyes that seemed to look right through one's own eyes into one's soul. Disconcerting eyes. And dark hair, one lock of which fell frequently over his forehead.

Her dream man, about whom she had actually dreamed the night before, she remembered now as the butler stepped forward to set food on her plate. A man who was treating her rather like a child, advising her not to go about unless there was someone with her to hold her hand. The master of the house in which she had been forced to take refuge because her younger brothers and sister had the measles or would have soon and she was too young to be left in the London house alone. It was a little humiliating.

"Thank you," she said to the butler. And then she leaned forward to speak to her host and hostess. "I must have taken a wrong turning. I found myself in a maze of narrow and winding corridors. I felt as if there were someone around each corner, but there never was, though I called out twice, feeling remarkably foolish." Actually she had felt prickles up and down her spine as well. She had thought she would never find her way out. There had not been a happy feel about those corridors.

"You must have stumbled upon the white tower," Lord Asquith said. "It houses our most disturbed ghosts. Mrs. Knole should tell you the story. She does it very well. Apparently many centuries ago there was a sword fight to the death in those corridors. One of my ancestors ran his point through the heart of his wife's lover while she looked on. She pined away and died and now wanders the corridors endlessly searching for her beloved."

"Edgar!" Lady Asquith said, exasperated. "You do almost as well as Mrs. Knole. Take no notice, Dinah dear. Those old stories are just so much nonsense. Did you sleep well? I would hate to think of your nights being sleepless."

"Most of the servants will not go into the white tower even to clean or to take a shortcut," Lord Asquith said. "And who the jokester was who called it *white* I do not know. The avenged husband, perhaps. You would be very wise not to go there again, Miss Ridding. I should hate to find you there in a vaporish heap one day."

"You said yesterday that there was a wide variety of ghosts here," Dinah said, fixing her eyes on the handsome dark ones of her host. "Are there more? Will you tell me about them?"

"I would strongly advise against it," Lady Asquith said briskly. "I shall show you about the house after breakfast, Dinah. Really it is a pleasant place, you know. It is unfortunate that you are seeing it at quite the gloomiest time of the year. The glory of autumn is past and the brightness of winter not yet here. Rather a dead time of year.''

''Very suitable for All Saints' Day,'' Lord Asquith said. ''And even better for All Hallows' Eve—tomorrow night. I shall be free after luncheon, Miss Ridding. I shall give you a tour of the ghosts' haunts, if you wish. Our ghosts do not wander all about the house, you see. Each has a favorite room or part of a room. Mrs. Knole would doubtless do the honors better than I, but I would not deny myself the pleasure.''

Dinah willed herself not to flush with pleasure. His whole manner was faintly amused, she told herself, and not flattering at all. He did not believe in ghosts. He was laughing at her.

''Thank you,'' she said. ''I would like that.''

''After luncheon, then,'' he said, and he got to his feet, inclined his head to the two ladies, and excused himself.

''He is amused,'' Lady Asquith said. ''He always likes to try to convince guests that the house really is haunted. But it is all nonsense, Dinah, and I will not have you frightened. Let me make it perfectly clear now, my dear, in case Edgar neglects to tell you so later, that there is not one whisper of one story of a living person being harmed by the supposed ghosts.''

''I am not afraid of the supernatural,'' Dinah said gravely. ''Only interested in it, ma'am.''

Lady Asquith tutted. ''Well,'' she said, ''I do not mind telling you that for the first year I was here as a bride I lived in a state of quiet terror. I would hardly let go my hold of my husband's sleeve the whole time.'' She chuckled. ''It was in fact a rather romantic first year of marriage. But after that I learned more sense—about the mythical haunting, that is. Now, if you are finished, my dear, I shall show you some of the house.''

Dinah spent a wonderful hour after that following Lady Asquith about the most splendid apartments of the house. There was a great deal more to be seen, she knew, but it would have taken hours to see everything. The oak-paneled dining room with its ornate wooden screen at one end, a relic of medieval days, looked far less gloomy in the light of day. And the massive squared wooden stairway looked quite splendid—it had taken her a great deal of time earlier in the morning to find it. She loved the rooms she was shown with their variety of architectural styles and furnishings, all somehow and strangely blending into a harmonious whole.

She had never been inside a haunted house before, even though England was reputed to be full of them. She had sensed the spirit world, but she had never before stepped inside it. But Lord Asquith had been right, she thought. There was a presence in the library, or at least at one end of it, a peaceful and not at all threatening presence, though it was not a natural one. And there was a feeling in the gold bedchamber with its heavy silver-spangled gold bed-hangings. Not an unpleasant feeling, though not as peaceful a one as in the library. There was a suggestion of brightness in the large portrait gallery at the top of the house, though its many bay windows let in only the light of a gloomy day, which was trying its best to turn into a rainy day.

''This has always been a happy room,'' she said to Lady Asquith, gazing along the length of the gallery.

''It is a cold room,'' her hostess said, ''and not much used any longer except for viewing the paintings. In previous generations, when people were hardier and less devoted to their creature comforts, I believe it was a playground for the children, especially on rainy days, and a lovers' walk for the young people.''

"Yes." Dinah smiled. "That must be it. There is a happy feeling here."

"And a distinctly chilly feeling," Lady Asquith said, drawing her shawl more closely about her shoulders. "Let me introduce you to some of my husband's ancestors. You will notice a family likeness, I believe. It is really rather amusing."

One long wall of the gallery was covered with paintings of Nevilles, who could trace their line back to the fifteenth century and even earlier. And Lady Asquith was right, Dinah discovered, as she gazed at each portrait in turn. Lord Asquith had inherited his height and physique, his dark coloring and his aquiline nose, from several of his ancestors. One portrait in particular looked so like him that it quite caught at her breath. The man was dressed rather severely in a long black cloak over black top boots, a whip in one gloved hand, his other resting on the saddle of a magnificent black horse. He was bareheaded. His dark hair was cut short and he was clean shaven, though the painting was in the style of the seventeenth century and one might have expected long curls and a pointed beard. He stared unsmilingly out of the canvas from intense dark eyes.

"Oh," Dinah said to Lady Asquith, who had turned to one of the windows at the sound of rain pattering against it, "this man is very like Lord Asquith."

Lady Asquith turned back again. "Ah, yes," she said. "The dark rider. His portrait was discovered only about fifty years ago, I believe, and restored to the gallery. He was not a popular young man with his family, having decided to fight on the side of Parliament during the Civil War instead of holding firm for the king. He was banished—from Malvern, that is. I suppose he did very well for himself under the rule of Oliver Cromwell.''

He was unutterably beautiful. And so very like Lord Asquith. Dinah wondered what had happened to him when King Charles II acceded to the throne. Did he find himself in deep trouble? Or did he adjust his ways and convictions? Did he never come home? Probably not if his portrait was hidden away and came to light only fifty years ago.

"In saving you from catching the measles," Lady Asquith said, shivering, "I shall be giving you a severe chill instead, Dinah. Anthony and your mama would never forgive me. Let us go down and order some hot tea, shall we, my dear? And you shall tell me about your successes during the Season. I am sure they must have been many.''

"I like London," Dinah said, turning to walk back along the gallery to the door. "But I have always preferred the country.''

"We will go to the library first," Lord Asquith told her after luncheon, "to visit our monk.''

"A monk?" Dinah said, looking up at him with her large eyes—they were still smoke-gray in the daylight, he had noticed at breakfast.

He took her hand through his arm. It was a small and delicately formed hand, one he would have liked to cover with his own if there had been an excuse to do so. She was quite exquisite—sweet and shy without being awkward and tongue-tied. And beautiful without being in any way pretty. He found himself looking forward to the hour ahead. It would be a welcome relief from the almost unbearable tensions of the past several days and would distract his mind from the dangers of the days ahead.

He would like, he thought—and the thought surprised him since he had had little to do with women lately—to make love to her. Not just to kiss that very attractive mouth but to have her with him on a bed. He would like to put himself inside her—a thought that surprised him even more. He was not in the habit of entertaining lecherous thoughts.

"He came to Malvern at some time during the Dark Ages," he said, opening the door of the library and taking the opportunity to set his hand in the shapely hollow of her back as she preceded him into the library, "to copy some manuscripts. And he never left. Perhaps his monastery forgot about him. Or perhaps the particular Neville who was master here at the time prided himself on having a resident holy man and kept finding him more manuscripts. Or perhaps he liked the place well and dawdled over his tasks. However it was, he is reputed to have died here peacefully in his sleep when he was little short of his eightieth birthday."

"And he haunts this room?" Dinah asked, strolling across the library to the very part where the monk was supposed to appear from time to time.

"Part of it," he said. "The old library, before it was extended to its present size. Even after death, it seems, our monk likes being here too well to settle permanently in heaven."

"So he is a kindly ghost," she said, smiling and closing her eyes briefly, as if trying to imagine the monk. "He was happy here."

Lord Asquith smiled at her. He had rather expected

that she would be clinging to his arm, but she appeared to be unafraid. It would not do. He must do better with his description of the next ghost. Despite his conscience and his inclination, which did not want to frighten her. And despite his mother's admonition.

"You must not frighten the poor girl, Edgar," she had told him before luncheon. "I will not have it though I know that the prospect amuses you. She is quite a sweetheart and a guest here besides."

"Mama," he had said, "the best possible thing for her will be to be frightened out of her wits. For her own safety she must not wander. I almost swallowed my fork this morning when she announced that she had been exploring in the white tower."

"She frightened herself," his mother had said. "She will not go back there. And all this business, which you know I disapprove of, Edgar, need not touch her at all. I cannot see the wisdom of frightening her further. It is not fair."

"I wish," he had said, "that Uncle Anthony's children had chosen some other time to catch the measles."

He wished it again now. He wished he had the leisure in which to explore his powerful attraction to Miss Dinah Ridding. And he wished he did not have to frighten her.

"There is an unhappy, frustrated spinster in the chapel," he said. "She is at her best—or her worst, perhaps I should say—and her most visible in gloomy weather and at this particular time of the year, I believe. Shall we pay her a call?"

They visited the spinster. And the child in the gallery, who apparently ran from one end to the other spinning his hoop and shouting with delight. The poor mite had died very young of typhoid. And the old lady in the gold bedchamber, who sometimes, witnesses had sworn, set the rocking chair to swaying as she sat in it embroidering sheets for her grandchildren's wedding beds.

Dinah did not appear to be terrified. She even walked up to the rocking chair and set her hand on the back of it.

"I daresay," she said, "that she was lonely in her old age and gained happiness and some sense of purpose from working at her embroidery."

He smiled rather tenderly at her as she looked down at the chair. Her nerves were considerably stronger than he had guessed. Or else she believed so little in ghosts that the past hour had been a pleasant story time for her.

"Don't ever go into the white tower again," he said, his voice very serious.

She looked up at him.

"There is very definitely an evil presence there," he said. "One that might do harm to someone who had the misfortune to be there at the wrong time. You must promise me not to set foot there again."

He was standing in the doorway. She came toward him and stopped a little way away. She smiled.

"But no one has been harmed yet?" she said. "I don't believe it would happen. Those passions were of another time and belong now in another dimension. They cannot hurt the living."

Damn! She really was not afraid.

She set her head to one side. "Why are you worried about me?" she asked.

He felt almost as if she could see through his eyes to the truth. He smiled and reached out to touch her cheeks with the fingertips of both hands. "All Hallows' Eve is approaching," he said. "The time when all souls are reputed to return to their earthly homes. An old house like Malvern might get decidedly crowded on that night. I don't want you in a place where they might cut up nasty for old times' sake. Promise me?"

She smiled slowly. "But you do not believe in ghosts," she said. "Do you? You have been trying to frighten me, but your eyes are too expressive. They have been laughing."

"I can see," he observed, "that I should have turned Mrs. Knole loose on you. She would soon have you shivering in your slippers."

"I have never even met the famous Mrs. Knole," Dinah said.

"You cannot say you have lived until you have done so," he said. "I shall see that it happens soon, Dinah. May I call you Dinah? You are, after all, a step-cousin, if there is such a relationship."

She smiled at him again.

"You must call me Edgar," he said. "A good medieval name, you will note. I am named for a thousand ancestors."

"I like it," she said. "Edgar."

He lowered his hands hastily when he realized that for no reason whatsoever he had been about to lean forward and kiss her smiling mouth. He offered his arm.

"Tea in the drawing room?" he said. "My mother will be relieved to see that you have not been spirited away by ghosts. Besides, it will be warmer down there."

"Yes," she said. "And thank you for introducing me to all your ghosts."

"Oh, not all, by any means," he said, drawing her hand within his arm again. "These are only the indoor ones. I shall leave Mrs. Knole to tell you about the outdoor ones."

"Oh," she said, looking up at him brightly, "are there some?"

Mrs. Knole would be sent to conduct her down to breakfast the following morning, Dinah had been told. It was quite unnecessary to send an escort since she had now memorized the route from her room to the grand staircase and was unlikely to get lost again. But she was looking forward to meeting the famous housekeeper.

Dinah stood absently brushing her curls before retiring to bed. She thought of the children and wondered if they all had the measles yet and were feeling very sick. She thought of Lady Asquith, who had made her feel so welcome at Malvern. Dinah had been very much afraid she would be imposing on a lady who was not really any relation of hers. And she thought of Lord Asquith—Edgar. The brush paused against her head. He was wonderful. She had always believed in love at first sight and now she knew that it really did happen. Even if, alas, it was sometimes one-sided. Edgar, she feared, saw her as a younger relative— step-cousin he had called her—to be treated with courtesy and even friendliness but also with some amusement. He had definitely been trying to scare her with the ghosts.

She sighed. For one moment in the gold bedchamber she had thought he was going to kiss her. He had not, of course. He had turned away and suggested going down for tea. But Dinah had been disappointed. She had been kissed three times, by three different gentlemen, and not one of those kisses had been in any way unpleasant. But there had very definitely been something missing from them.

Edgar had not told her about the ghost in her room, she thought, setting down her brush. There was certainly one there, though the feeling was very faint. Perhaps it was just that her little turret room was quite close to the white tower, she had thought at first. Perhaps the very strong presence there had spilled over. But no, it was not that. This was no frightening ghost. Only a rather sad one. And the feeling was very faint.

Dinah climbed into the high four-poster bed and blew out the single candle on the table beside her. She would ask Mrs. Knole about it in the morning, she decided. And about the outdoor ghosts too. Edgar had said there were some. She had not felt them herself because she had not been outside since her arrival. The rain had stopped, she realized when she listened closely for the sound of it against the window.

Dinah woke up at some time during the night. She was not aware that anything had woken her—there was no remembered sound. And yet, she thought, she had not floated to the surface of sleep as she sometimes did in the night only to realize that it was not morning yet and that she could allow herself to float back off again. She had come suddenly and totally awake. Her eyes had opened.

Whatever it was, she thought, it was outside the house and not in. She lay very still and listened.

Nothing.

The bed was warm and cozy. She was sleepy. But

she was also curious, and curiosity was never to be denied for long, she knew from experience. She lifted away the bedclothes, swung her legs over the side of the bed, and crossed the room to the window. She drew back one side of the heavy curtains.

He was directly below her room. A man wearing a long, dark cloak and hat. He was standing very still and looking away to one side—in the direction of the sea. And then he looked up intently at the white tower and held his gaze there for a long while.

It was impossible to see who he was, though she guessed that it was Lord Asquith. What was he doing? she wondered. And what time was it? Had he heard a noise and was investigating? Or was he merely unable to sleep and was out walking? But he was not walking. He was standing still.

Whatever he was doing, she decided, it was none of her business. And at any moment he was going to shift his gaze to her window and see her spying on him. She let the curtain fall over the window again and returned to the bed. She lay down and covered herself gratefully with the blankets. The room was chilly.

But she knew as soon as she closed her eyes that she was not going to sleep. Her brain was racing and her heart thumping with something very like excitement. And she knew, though she lay there determinedly for several minutes, that she was going to get up again and peep out of the window once more. Would he still be there? Surely he would have gone by now and she could return to bed satisfied.

Finally she could resist the urge no longer. A moment later she was at the window and drawing back the curtain a little more cautiously than she had the first time. And peering downward.

He was still there. Or rather, he was there *again,* she thought with a frown. This time he was astride a magnificent black horse, which was pawing the ground as if eager to be off and galloping. And he had dispensed with his hat. Now he was unmistakably Lord Asquith. And he was looking directly up at her.

Dinah clung to the curtain, mortified. He could not have failed to see her, though there was no light behind her. She was wearing a white nightgown. She raised one hand in acknowledgment of his presence, though she did not wave it. And she wondered if she should immediately drop the curtain back into place. He looked quite gorgeously beautiful, she thought despite her embarrassment. Gloriously romantic.

And then he raised his arms to her, beckoning with both.

She leaned closer to the window. ''Me?'' she said, laying one hand against her bosom and forming the word with her lips, though no sound escaped her. And then she felt remarkably foolish. Who else could he mean?

He continued to beckon. But what could be wrong? For what could he possibly need her that necessitated his coming beneath her window and beckoning her? Had someone been hurt? Or was he merely trying to arrange a clandestine meeting with her? She drew back a little at the thought. But she could not resist leaning forward for one more look down. He was still beckoning with both arms, though his horse was more impatient now, and it looked as if he should have both hands on the reins.

What should she do? But it was a foolish question, Dinah admitted as soon as she had formed it in her mind. She would never sleep. She would worry and wonder. She must go down. Of course she must. She hesitated after hurrying through to her dressing room, but she decided against the delay of dressing. She pulled on her half boots and drew a warm gray cloak about her shoulders.

She knew the way downstairs, she told herself as she let herself out of her room and looked about her somewhat fearfully. Even in the dark. It was not really dark anyway. Her eyes were accustomed to it and she could see quite clearly. She did not know if she would be able to get out through the front doors. Perhaps they would be too heavily bolted for her strength. But probably not. As she found the staircase without any real difficulty, her mind was occupied with working out how she was to get from the front doors to the foot of her tower. But she thought it was not far if she turned right outside the courtyard and if there were no unknown obstacles in the way.

The front doors were not bolted at all. But of course. Edgar must have gone out this way. Neither was the courtyard gate locked. And there was no obstacle outside more serious than a large flower bed that had to be skirted. The white tower rose large and massive in the darkness, and Dinah shivered despite herself as she circled around it and came to the narrower, more elegant tower that held her room.

She looked up at her window. Yes, it was unmistakably hers. She was in the right place. But there was no one standing beneath it except her. She was too late. Whatever he had wanted her for must have been urgent, and she had made no signal to assure him that she was coming. When the curtain had dropped back into place, he must have assumed that she was ignoring his plea. He had gone away. Dinah stood on the wet grass between the white tower and hers and felt a great disappointment.

He would think that she had not cared. And she had missed some sort of adventure. She would die of curiosity between now and morning, when he would explain what he had wanted and when she would be able to explain that she had come only to find him gone.

She sighed and turned to look around her. Should she walk about in the hope of coming upon him? But she did not know the grounds of Malvern and could easily get lost. Besides, she noticed when the first disappointment was fading, the house looked very large and very dark and very ominous. She had not given a thought to fear until this point, but now her heart was beginning to beat uncomfortably. And suddenly the thought that there were outside ghosts at Malvern as well as indoor ones gave her a twinge of uneasiness. And the next night was All Hallows' Eve—the night for ghosts and the spirits of the dead.

No, she would return to the house, she decided, and to her bed. And she shuddered at the conviction that a hand was going to tap her on the back at any moment. She glanced nervously over her shoulder. And almost jumped with fright when a dark figure came striding out of the deeper darkness from the direction of the sea. He was on foot and covered from shoulders to booted feet by a dark cloak. He wore a hat.

He stopped walking abruptly and stared at her.

"What are you doing?" he asked after a moment's silence. His voice was low and ominously tense.

Dinah licked her lips and looked behind him. "Where is your horse?" she asked.

"My horse?" he said, taking the remaining steps that separated them and gazing at her with eyes that seemed disconcertingly dark—and angry. "Where is my horse? In the stable where it belongs. I asked you what you were doing."

"What did you want?" she asked. "Was there some trouble?"

His eyes sharpened on her but lost none of their anger.

"You saw me?" he said. And he glanced up to her window and took her by the wrist to draw her away, around the base of the white tower toward the courtyard arch. But he glanced up at the white tower too, she noticed. "Foolish girl. You should be in your bed, not wandering about outside where you might come to all kinds of harm."

"But I thought you needed me," she said even as she realized that she had been mistaken. It could not have been her window that he had been looking at. It must have been someone else's. He had been beckoning to someone else.

He drew her to a halt and turned her. He was still furious, she could see. And his rather austere face, which she had seen as beautiful during the day, now looked forbidding and even frightening. She would not want to cross his will, she thought. And yet she seemed unwittingly to have done just that.

"Listen to me," he said, his voice cold. "You are a guest in this house. Has no one ever explained to you that it is ill-mannered to wander about someone else's house and property unescorted and uninvited?"

He might as well have slapped her face, she thought. He could not have stung her more. His hands were on her upper arms. She rather thought his fingers might leave bruises there. She swallowed. There was no answer to such a question.

"This is a rough part of the coastline," he said. "There are smugglers here, not to mention other assorted villains. Do you want to be murdered? Or ravished?"

He waited for her answer.

"No," she said in a voice that was little more than a whisper. "I'm sorry, Edgar. I thought you needed me."

He gazed at her, and some of the tension went out of his face. "Dinah," he said, "you are my guest here. You are under my protection. It is my duty to look to your safety. Forgive me that burst of temper. I came outside to get some air. I often do when I cannot sleep at night. I paused below the white tower to decide which direction to take. I am sorry I disturbed your sleep and gave you the wrong impression. Let me take you back to your room."

He locked the gate and bolted the front doors behind them and gave her his arm. They walked upstairs and through the maze of corridors in silence, Dinah feeling more mortified with every step she took.

"Where did you ride?" she asked as they approached her room.

"I did not ride," he said. "I walked toward the cliffs. The sea air is better than a lullaby, you know."

"Thank you," she said when they came to a stop outside her room and he set a hand on the doorknob.

He reached out his free hand and with the forefinger lifted back one side of her cloak. Her eyes lowered to his chin when she knew he had seen her nightgown. He let the cloak fall back into place again.

"Foolish Dinah," he said. "Were you not afraid?"

"Only when I was outside and you were no longer there," she said. "Nervous more than afraid."

"You must not leave your room at night again," he said, "or wander during the daytime. Promise me?"

She lifted her eyes to his again. "I am sorry, Edgar," she said. "Truly. Don't scold me. There is no need. And I am not a child."

He smiled slightly and looked more like the daytime Edgar again despite the darkness. He set one finger beneath her chin. "Believe it or not," he said, "I had noticed that." And he lowered his head and kissed her very lightly on the lips, lingering there for a few moments before lifting his head.

She swallowed again.

"Foolish Dinah," he said, and he opened the door and gestured for her to step inside. "You have been in all sorts of danger since you left this room. Good night."

"Good night," she said, turning to look at him as he closed the door, leaving her alone inside her room.

She touched her lips. He had kissed her quite differently from those other three gentlemen. All of them had set their arms about her and drawn her against them. Edgar had touched her only beneath the chin and on the lips. And yet she had felt those other kisses only on her lips. She had felt Edgar's on her lips and in her toes and in every cell of her body between those two extremities.

A gentle, cousinly kiss for a rather troublesome young step-cousin, she thought in some disgust, kicking off her half boots and unbuttoning her cloak to let it drop in a heap on the floor before diving rather inelegantly into the promised warmth of her bed.

She wondered what he had done with his hat when he had ridden briefly out of the stables.

* * *

Dinah dismissed Judy when Mrs. Knole arrived to accompany her downstairs to breakfast the following morning. She smiled.

"I have not met you before, Mrs. Knole," she said, "but I have heard a great deal about you. From both Lord and Lady Asquith and my mother."

"Have you, madam?" the housekeeper said, looking quite unsurprised and quite unimpressed. She was a tall woman and wore a plain black dress that accentuated her thinness and her erect bearing. She wore her dark, silvering hair in a severe bun at the back of her head. Her nose was long and sharp, her eyes half sunk into her head. She looked rather like a cadaver, Dinah decided.

"Apparently," Dinah said, "you are the authority on the ghosts of Malvern."

"I find them interesting, madam," Mrs. Knole said, "and real. To most people they are an amusement, a curiosity." Her look bent on Dinah was faintly reproving.

"Tell me about the ghost who inhabits this room," Dinah said.

"Alas, there is no ghost in this room," Mrs. Knole said. "At least, there has not been for a long time. I have been assigning the room to guests for ten years or more and have never had a complaint."

"Oh," Dinah said, disappointed. "I thought there was. A rather sad ghost. But perhaps I am wrong. The feeling is very faint."

Mrs. Knole looked at her more sharply. "A sad ghost?" she said. "She was, madam, being unable to make up her mind to seize happiness for herself. Do you have the feeling, then? And is she still here? I must confess to having lost the sense of her many years ago.''

Dinah bit her lip and then smiled. ''There are indeed not many of us, are there?'' she said. ''And everyone else thinks us mildly insane. But I have always been able to sense the world of spirits just beyond our own, though I have never actually been inside a haunted house before. It is wonderful. I wondered yesterday when I first went into the library why the monk stays at one side of it. But then Lord Asquith explained that the rest of the library is a more recent addition.''

Mrs. Knole thawed visibly. ''Aye, madam,'' she said, ''this is a house I have never wanted to leave.''

''Tell me about the sad lady,'' Dinah said.

''She was the ward of one of the masters here,'' Mrs. Knole said. ''In the time of the great trouble, madam. In love with Charles Neville, the baron's son, she was, and he with her, but he went away to fight on the wrong side—or wrong according to his father, anyway.''

''The dark rider,'' Dinah said, her eyes widening as she remembered the portrait in the gallery.

''He came for her secretly, madam,'' Mrs. Knole said, ''or so it is said. Several times. He rode up beneath her window, calling to her, begging her to go away with him. Away across the sea where they could be safe and happy together.''

''But she never went?'' Dinah asked.

Mrs. Knole shrugged. ''She is never mentioned in records of the house later in the century,'' she said. ''She seems to have disappeared—whether to another home and a husband or whether to join her lover, no one knows. I rather think she did not go with him.''

Dinah's heart was thumping suddenly. "The dark rider," she said. "Is he one of the outside ghosts?"

"Aye, madam," Mrs. Knole said. "He does not appear often. But the fact that he appears at all makes me think that he never succeeded. Why would he keep coming back else?"

Dinah was wide-eyed. "And why is she still here?" she said. "Her presence is faint, as if she is about to give up the struggle, but she is still here. And she is still sad."

"Perhaps she needs someone to give her the courage to leave," the housekeeper said. "Perhaps even at this late date she can span time and go with him. Who knows? She did not disturb your sleep, madam? I can have you moved to a different room if you wish."

Dinah shook her head. "No," she said. "Oh, no, please don't do that, Mrs. Knole. Have you ever seen the dark rider?"

"Once, madam," Mrs. Knole said. "It was on this day many years ago. Galloping toward the cliffs, he was, his dark cloak billowing out behind him. But the gardener and his wife, whom I was with at the time, laughed at me and swore it was a swirl of black dust. It was a stormy night."

"Oh," Dinah said. "And he was bareheaded, Mrs. Knole?"

"That he was," the housekeeper said. "Though I daresay his hat might have been blown away on such a night anyway. Her ladyship will be thinking that I have got lost with you this morning, madam."

"Then we must go down," Dinah said, preceding her guide out of the room. "Though I know my way downstairs very well now. When you have time, Mrs.

Knole, will you tell me about the other outside ghosts?''

Her heart was thumping with excitement. And perhaps with something else too. Terror? No, it was not quite that. But more than just excitement certainly.

She had seen two men the night before. She had seen Edgar, cloaked and wearing a hat and on foot. And she had seen the dark rider, cloaked and bareheaded and astride his black stallion. It was his sad and timid lady love to whom he had been beckoning, not her.

''But the sun is shining at last, Edgar,'' Lady Asquith protested to her son at the breakfast table. ''And she was cooped up inside here all day yesterday after a rather lengthy journey the day before. A drive into the village and a browse around the shops seems just the thing for today.''

''Mama,'' Lord Asquith said, trying to keep the exasperation from his voice, ''you know it is dangerous to venture beyond the limits of our own grounds. And not even quite safe within our own walls, perhaps. You cannot have forgotten about Prewett.''

''It would be difficult to forget a gardener who met with such a tragic accident only a week ago, Edgar,'' she said tartly. ''But it was an accident. It is foolish to become oversuspicious.''

''But there are strangers wandering about,'' he said. ''One of them was even foolish enough to ask at the inn about tides and moons. No, you must keep her here, Mama.''

''For four more days?'' his mother said. ''Be reasonable, Edgar. We cannot keep her incarcerated here all that time.''

"I went to talk with my men last night," Lord Asquith said. "Everything has been brought forward to tonight. The tide will not be as favorable or the light, especially if the sky remains clear. But we will be just walking into an ambush if we wait until the appointed night. Fournier agrees too. Sitting around doing nothing is trying his nerves to the limit. He was quite agitated when Dinah almost came upon him yesterday morning. By tomorrow, Mama, we will be able to begin to relax."

"Until the next time," Lady Asquith said with a sigh. "I wish—"

But Dinah's entrance at that moment, followed by the butler, put an end to her words. She smiled affectionately at the girl while her son rose to seat her.

"What a beautiful day it is," Dinah said when the morning greetings had been made. "I think I will go walking outside." She looked at Lord Asquith a little self-consciously. "If no one has any objection, that is."

"I have certain household tasks that must be performed today, Dinah," Lady Asquith said, "or I would have been delighted to take you into the village. It is a very pretty little fishing community. Perhaps tomorrow."

"Don't worry about entertaining me," Dinah said with a smile. "I shall be quite happy to explore close to the house and perhaps as far as the cliffs. They are close by and on Malvern land? I have not seen the sea for a long time."

Her face was glowing with youthful energy, Lord Asquith thought. Her remarkable eyes were wide with anticipated pleasure. She was not after all a timid little thing, he had discovered rather to his regret. He still

found it hard to believe that she had had the courage—
and the foolhardiness—to leave the house the night before merely because she had seen him standing below
her window and had thought he needed her. In reality
it was the white tower he had been standing below. He
was making very sure that no suggestion of light was
showing from Fournier's window, though he had just
left him and knew that at least one candle would still
be burning.

He had been wrong about Dinah, it seemed. Except
about one thing. His gaze strayed to her lips, which
were curved into a smile. They were quite as kissable
as he had thought they would be. More so. He had
removed his own from them the night before with the
greatest reluctance.

"Perhaps you would care to see the stables," he
suggested. "You asked me yesterday about my horse.
Do you have one of your own?"

"Oh, yes," she said eagerly—he wondered if she
knew the power of her eyes and guessed not. Women
who knew themselves to have fine eyes invariably
drooped their lashes over them in conscious invitation.
Dinah's eyes were wide and dreamy and eager all at
the same time—and quite irresistible. "In the country
but not in town. I love riding. Will we ride this morning too?"

He had not intended to. Although he did not imagine that the house was ringed with marksmen ready to
pick off anyone who was foolish enough to set foot
outside the courtyard, he nevertheless was convinced
that there were prowlers. And he did not subscribe to
the theory that Prewett's death had been accidental.

But she looked very eager. And he was as eager to
have an excuse to spend an hour with her. "I think

that might be arranged," he said, smiling back at her. "But just a short ride. I have business to attend to, unfortunately. Perhaps later in the week I can take you walking along the beach."

But this time it was his mother who was anxious. "Edgar," she said after breakfast when Dinah had gone upstairs to change into her riding habit, "is it wise, dear? Oh, I wish you had not become involved in this life, proud as I am of you."

"We will not ride far," he assured her. "And I will keep to the wide open places. You may rest assured too that I will have a pistol with me, Mama."

"And that is supposed to reassure me?" she said, looking at him in some horror.

And yet when he was outside with Dinah and walking toward the stables, it seemed foolish to think of danger. The sun was shining from a blue sky, across which fluffy white clouds were scudding. There was a fresh breeze blowing off the sea. She looked quite charming in her sage-green velvet riding habit, he thought, the brown feather of the jaunty hat curling about one ear and sometimes, in the stronger gusts of wind, brushing across her mouth so that she had to blow it away.

She was a good horsewoman, as he had expected her to be. He had paid her the compliment of mounting her on a frisky, though not wild, mare. She had a sure seat and an easy, upright posture, and her hands were sensitive on the reins. He rode beside her on Jet, his black stallion, enjoying the sight of her while at the same time keeping a careful watch on their surroundings. But they had soon ridden beyond the limits of the cultivated gardens onto the wilder and more open stretches of land above the cliffs, and he breathed more easily.

"Oh," she said when they had ridden as close to the edge of the cliff as he dared take her, "I think it must be very wonderful to live close to the sea. Look at the sun sparkling on it. And the lovely salty air." She breathed it in deeply.

"There are paths down to the beach," he said. "One very steep one here and one less steep off to our left. I'll take you down one day—if you like the feel of sand in your shoes and clothes and sand in your mouth and hair, that is." He smiled at her.

"I think the joy of it would compensate for the discomfort," she said.

Perhaps after tonight, he thought, looking at her rosy cheeks and at the pleasing arch of her back as she sat her horse, he would be able to permit himself some relaxation at last. Perhaps he could allow himself to enjoy her visit more. Perhaps he could flirt with her a little. Or even allow something rather more serious than flirtation to develop if she was willing and if his cousins did not recover too quickly from their illness.

The thought surprised him. He had not given much consideration to beginning a serious relationship with a woman. Certainly he had never met the woman who would provoke such an intention. Until now.

But such thoughts on this particular day were dangerous. He realized that when his wandering attention was caught by a glimpse of movement at the corner of his eye and he looked up sharply in time to see someone duck down out of sight at the head of the less steep of the two paths down to the beach. The local men or women would not have avoided being seen even though they would, strictly speaking, have been on Malvern land. They would more probably have hailed him and waved.

"We had better return to the house," he said to Dinah, turning his horse unhurriedly so as not to alarm her and moving between her and the prowler on the path. He only hoped that the watchers were not permanently on duty—he had seen no sign of anyone last night, though he had looked carefully—and that his own men would do a good job that day of carelessly making common knowledge the fact that everything was to happen in four nights' time, as originally planned.

"We were to attend a masquerade ball tonight for All Hallows' Eve," Dinah said. "Sir Anthony and my mother and I, that is, in London. And doubtless there would have been dimmed candles and ghost stories and other foolishness to frighten everyone. I am not sorry to be missing it."

"You do not frighten easily, Dinah, do you?" he said, half with admiration and half with regret.

"But people always seem to believe that ghosts are out to harm the living," she said, "when usually they are living still in their own time and quite unaware of us and the nineteenth century."

"A very sensible attitude to take," he said, amused, and yet looking keenly ahead to the line of trees that separated the clifftop from the cultivated gardens. "But when you live in a haunted house like Malvern, Dinah, you would need a strong constitution indeed to poke your nose beyond your bedsheets on this night of all nights. Sometimes the living can be snatched up quite unwittingly into the land of the dead. If you got in the path of the sword fight in the white tower, for example, you might find that though the fighters were spirits and unaware of your presence, the swords were very real. Or perhaps in following a ghost you would run into an obstacle that was not there in his time or fall down a steep staircase that has been built since he lived.''

She was looking back at him, intently, lips parted. ''You do it very well,'' she said. ''There are hands about to claw at my back.''

''Better that,'' he said, ''than sword points through your heart. Be thankful at least that we are more than two miles from the graveyard. The village children, I hear, sleep three to four to a bed on this particular night of the year.''

He was rather disappointed when she smiled. ''I think,'' she said, ''that you will not be happy unless I am blubbering with terror tonight. I think you are very proud of your home and its history, Edgar, and like to see your guests do it proper homage. I do, believe me. I have never been so fascinated in my life.''

They were back in the stables and he slid thankfully from Jet's back and lifted her to the cobbles of the yard. No, she was not easily scared. He grinned down at her. But it did not matter. He must not worry that she would leave her room that night as she had the night before. The night before she had seen him and misunderstood. But she had looked mortified when he had first lashed out at her in his anger and then scolded her. And he knew she had been embarrassed as he conducted her upstairs and back to her room in silence. She would not make the same mistake again tonight.

''You have discovered my secret,'' he said. ''And since you are my guest, Dinah, and a well-behaved young lady, you will at least flatter your host by pretending to cower beneath the blankets tonight and by appearing at breakfast tomorrow looking suitably pale.''

''Done,'' she said, slipping her hand through his arm for the walk back to the house. ''And I shall be fearfully glad that October is safely past for another year.''

''And so shall I,'' he said fervently.

Dinah enjoyed the morning ride and had to admit afterward that for the hour of its duration all her attention, all her senses, were focused upon her riding companion. It was not surprising, of course. He was exceedingly handsome and he was amusing, especially when he tried to frighten her with ghosts he clearly did not believe in. But there was something more than a physical awareness and an emotional pleasure in his company. There was . . . Oh, it was just that she was in love with him, whatever that term meant. It was not a feeling that could be analyzed in words.

And it was not something one could be reasonable about, either. She might tell herself with the greatest good sense that she had met him only two days before and had spent very little of the intervening time in his company. She could tell herself that she really did not know him well at all. But good sense did not have anything to say to anything. She was in love with him and she was enjoying the feeling, since she would not allow herself to dwell upon the tragedy of the fact that as soon as the children were well she would be leaving him, perhaps never to see him again.

Her mind was focused upon him for that hour. But for the rest of the day she could not stop herself from thinking of something else. Or *someone* else rather.

The dark rider. The man who looked so much like Edgar that she had thought he was he the night before. Perhaps it was the likeness that made her think so much of the rider. And she was quite convinced that it was the dark rider who had beckoned to her the night before—or rather to the sad lady who still lingered in her bedchamber. Even though Edgar had a black stallion quite as powerful and full of energy as the one that had appeared last night, she was convinced that she had seen one of the Malvern ghosts.

Foolish, foolish ward of that former master of Malvern, she thought. If she herself had a chance to ride off into the happily-ever-after with such a very beautiful and romantic figure of a man, she would seize it in a moment.

Would he come again that night? she wondered as she sat in a salon during the afternoon listening to the conversation between Lady Asquith and the vicar's wife, who was paying a call. Or rather not listening. Her mind kept wandering and she kept having to recall it. The vicar's wife would think her very ill-mannered.

Perhaps he would come. It was, after all, All Hallows' Eve, the night of all nights when he might be expected to come. She knew she would stay up and watch for him. Though, of course, she thought regretfully, she would be able only to witness unrequited longing. Tonight she would know that it was not Edgar below her window but the dark rider. There would be no point in going down to him. Not that she would have the courage to do so again anyway. If Edgar had been furious the night before to find her out-of-doors, there was no knowing what his mood would be if he were to catch her at it again.

But she could scarcely wait for the night to come.

There was a strange, inexplicable longing in her to see him again. Perhaps it was the fact that he had been faithful to his true love for almost two centuries, returning again and again to reach out his arms to her in a mute plea to her to join her life to his. How wonderful it would be to be the object of such intense and lasting love. And perhaps it was his uncanny resemblance to Edgar and the fact that he appeared to be looking up at *her,* to be reaching out his arms to *her.*

Ah, the romance of it, Dinah thought. Sometimes real life seemed very dull in contrast. Instead of yearning for her and reaching out arms for her, all Edgar could do was tease her and try to terrify her. He obviously did not have a romantic bone in his body.

And so there was Edgar as he was and Edgar as he might have been—the dark rider.

It was in many ways a dull day, though Dinah was too deep in thought to feel great boredom. Apart from the morning ride and the afternoon visit, there was the stroll about the courtyard with Lady Asquith, who claimed to feel too fatigued from her morning work to walk farther. And hours of embroidery and conversation indoors. And the chance to play the pianoforte in the music room for almost an hour.

She scarcely saw Lord Asquith except at meal times. Even after dinner he disappeared, reappearing only to disturb the quiet coziness of the evening by frowning and then smiling brightly as if he had just realized that he should and looking rather as if his nerve endings were poking through his skin. He jumped quite visibly when a footman came into the drawing room with the tea tray and bumped it rather noisily against the door, and then he barked at the poor man, who turned as red in the face as a strawberry.

"Well, Dinah," Lord Asquith said when the tea tray was removed again later, "it is time for bed. May I escort you to your room?"

It was a cheering prospect. Five whole minutes alone with him. But as they ascended the stairs in silence after saying good night to Lady Asquith, she felt embarrassment at the memory of having to be taken back to her room the night before. And his mind was clearly preoccupied with something else.

"I think, Edgar," she said, "you are afraid that all the ghosts will come out tonight."

"Am I?" he said, rewarding her with his first real smile of the evening. "And you too? Would you like to have your maid sleep in your room?"

"There is a very heavy woolen blanket on my bed," she said. "I think that it will provide sufficient protection if I pull it up about my head."

He smiled again and took both her hands in his as they stopped outside her door. "Sleep well, then," he said. "And don't be afraid. There are not really any such things as ghosts, you know."

"You have changed tactics," she said. "You think that if you tell me in that very serious tone that there are no ghosts I will start to wonder if perhaps you are trying to save me from a well-founded fear. And consequently my heart will thump with terror all night long."

He laughed and lowered his head. "Dinah," he said, "you are such a delight. Let me kiss you."

"You did not ask my permission last night," she said, her heart beginning really to thump, though not with terror.

"That was not a kiss," he said, releasing her hands

and setting his own at her waist. "That was a mere meeting of lips."

"There is a difference?" she asked.

"There is a difference." He drew her lightly against him and touched his mouth to hers, his lips slightly parted.

The first part of her to react was her knees. They felt decidedly wobbly, so that she had to lean into him and spread her hands against the reassuring solidity of his chest. And then it was her temperature. It soared so that she might have wondered whether she had somehow contracted the measles after all if she had been able to think that clearly.

"Witch!" he said, raising his head after a wonderfully lengthy embrace. "This is an appropriate night for our first proper kiss, Dinah."

"Our first?" she said and then could have bitten out her tongue. It was as if she were angling for the promise of more.

"Our first," he said, laying one forefinger along the length of her nose, "but not our last if I have anything to say in the matter. Good night, Dinah."

And he opened her door and gestured as he had the night before for her to enter. And as he had done the night before, he closed the door behind her so that she was left staring vaguely and stupidly at the wooden panels, wondering how many kisses there would be between the first and the last and hoping there would be too many to count.

Or perhaps he was teasing her again, toying with her.

She turned around to face the room and addressed the sad lady with some severity. "You had *that?*" she said, gesturing behind her to the closed door and what had just taken place beyond it. "And yet for almost two centuries you have been too faint-hearted to go after more? When he loves you so deeply and so constantly? You are foolish indeed. And now you are fading away, almost decided that you will be done with him and with happiness for good and all. Well, all I can say is that you will have created your own hell when that happens. There will be no blaming the devil or a harsh Judgment Day. Only yourself. If you want happiness, you must seize it. Now! Perhaps in another few years or decades it will be forever too late."

The sad lady did not reply, and Dinah was left frowning fiercely at emptiness.

She awoke feeling so sad that there was pain. She had been crying, she realized, reaching up a hand and touching the wetness of her cheeks. She had been dreaming. Edgar had been sitting on the side of her bed and leaning over her, brushing back the hair from her face with a warm and gentle hand. And then he had kissed her as lightly and as lingeringly as he had done when he escorted her to her room—and with parted lips again so that it had seemed a marvelously intimate kiss despite its lightness.

There had been more, too. He had undone the buttons of her nightgown and slid his hand inside, along the flesh below her shoulder just above her breast. Even in her dream she had not dared imagine his hand moving lower, though she realized now that both breasts were peaked and almost painful to the touch.

She felt infinitely sad. Two more hot tears spilled over and ran diagonally down her cheeks as she lay with closed eyes trying to recapture the dream. But it had been a wonderful dream, if somewhat lascivious.

Why had it made her so sad? Was there part of it that she could not remember? Had he said something? His mouth and his hand had been tender. Surely he could not have said anything to contradict what they had told her.

But no, of course, she thought, and she opened her eyes. The terrible sadness did not come from the dream or from inside herself. It came from the room. It was all about her, a drenching sadness and longing that had penetrated even her sleep and her pleasant dream.

If the sad lady was fading away, she had made a full reappearance for All Hallows' Eve. Dinah could feel all the agony of her indecision and longing, of her timidity that she could not make up her mind to convert into boldness. And if the agony was so intense, Dinah thought, then the lady must be being enticed again. The dark rider must be there outside.

The thought made her realize fully that she had been sleeping when she had intended to wait up for him. Her heart beating with excitement, almost as if it were she he was coming for instead of the sad lady, she swung her legs over the side of the bed and darted to the window. And yet she did not have to pull aside the curtains. They were half opened already. But they had been closed when she came to bed, Dinah thought, stopping short of the window. She knew because she had had to pull one aside to gaze out into the darkness and had been very careful afterward to lap one over the other so that no chink of light would show between them in the morning.

Her heart beat a little faster and she stepped forward to occupy the narrow space that would give her a view out. She looked down, almost afraid that he would not be there and that she would have to admit that her imagination had become overactive.

His horse was as impatient and as full of energy as it had been the night before. And he was showing as much skilled horsemanship as he had then, controlling it with his knees while his head was tilted back to look up at the window and his arms reached up and beckoned. The sadness, the longing, the indecision, the fear, the love, were intensified a hundredfold as Dinah gazed back down at him.

But the window was nailed shut and the door of her chamber was locked from the outside. Did he not realize that? Probably not. It had not been so when he was still at home. But in the last few months it had been so, ever since Lord Asquith, her guardian, had intercepted a letter to her from Charles—his beloved son and therefore the more hated for his defection to the other side of battle lines she neither understood nor cared about.

He stretched his arms out to her and spread his fingers. There was intense hunger in his upturned face.

But soon—very soon now—there would be dreadful wrath in the house, even worse than there had been in the weeks before Charles left and in the days following his hasty departure. For soon all would be known. And yet would she avoid that wrath even if she could now? For going with Charles would mean hard times, perhaps a long sea voyage if he was determined, as he had said in another letter that he was, to escape his father's wrath and his own unhappiness to a new world. She could not face those hardships. Not now.

She spread a hand just below her waist and rested it against her rounding form. *Charles! Oh, Charles. Our child. Our future. Our happiness.* She rested her forehead against the glass and gazed down into his much-loved face. And she knew with a sharp pain, almost as if he had shouted out to tell her so, that this was the last time he would come. If she did not go with him tonight, that would be the end. There would be no other chance.

And she knew that the locked door was an excuse for her cowardice. For Martha would have come to open it if she had pleaded well enough. Martha had always loved her. Martha had been more like the mother she had never known than a mere servant. She could have gone to him if she had been really determined to do so.

Forgive me, Charles, she begged him with her eyes. *Forgive me, my love. Don't leave. Come back again. Please come back. Perhaps tomorrow I will find the courage. Or the next day. Charles, don't leave. Forgive me.*

Charles Neville turned his hands palm in again and beckoned to her.

Dinah stepped back from the window and drew a slow and ragged breath. "Fool," she whispered. "Oh, foolish girl. Your child might be lost just as easily here, you know, even with the care of doctors and midwives. Either to death or to the care of a grandfather who will despise you and keep you from your child. And he might live if you go with your dark rider. He loves you and will care for you to the best of his ability. Go to him."

But the sad lady was too intent on her own misery to pay Dinah any heed.

"You are right about one thing," Dinah said. "I felt it with you there. This is the last time he will come. But he has come and has kept coming for almost two centuries, you foolish girl. What further proof of his devotion could you have? Would you wish him to keep coming for *five* centuries?''

The sad lady said nothing, and forgetting for the moment in her feeling of urgency that the space before the parted curtains was occupied, Dinah stepped forward again to see if the dark rider was still there.

His hands were holding the reins. His head was bowed down so that his chin was resting on his chest. His shoulders were slumped in defeat. But he raised his head again slowly and he raised his arms once more in a gesture of supplication and longing. He did not beckon.

Charles! Don't go away. Don't leave me. Oh, dear God, how can I live if you go away? Please, Charles, please. I am going to have your child.

Dinah pulled herself back again. But the panic in her was as strong as it was in the sad lady.

''Go!'' she commanded. ''Don't you see? In a moment he will be gone, and he will never return. You will be sorry for all eternity.''

But there was no response to her plea. She ran without thought into her dressing room and dragged on her half boots and drew her cloak about her with hasty hands. She paused only after she had the door of the bedchamber open and was halfway across the threshold.

''Look!'' she told the invisible lady at the window. ''It is unlocked. I will even leave it open for you. I shall try to delay him. Oh, do come. This is your last chance for happiness. Your last chance in all eternity.''

And she raced along winding corridors and down the grand staircase and through the great hall and out through the front doors, which were again unbolted, through the courtyard and around the flower bed and about the base of the white tower.

But he was gone. There was no one there at all on the grass beneath the window of her bedchamber. Dinah stood very still, her heart leaden. She had missed her chance. The poor sad lady had missed her chance. She closed her eyes briefly and felt too full of leaden despair even to cry. Then she raised her head and looked up at her window.

She was dressed in a white nightgown rather like Dinah's except that there was a deep frill about the neck. Her hair was blond, almost as pale as the gown, closely curled about her head and down over her shoulders. Her face was narrow and pale and sweet. It would probably be beautiful if animated. She was gazing downward a little to Dinah's left, a world of agony in her face. Her lips were moving.

"Oh," Dinah whispered, "are you still here? Can I not see you down here just as I could not see your lady when I was up there?" She was about to step forward to the spot where his horse had been standing, but she was afraid of the passions she might find herself caught up in. She stood where she was.

"Wait for her," she said, still in a whisper. "Please wait. She will come. She is having your child and everyone will know about it soon. Please wait a while longer."

But what if he had already gone? she wondered. What if he had already galloped off toward the cliffs and was preparing to set off for the New World without his lady and their child? And what if she should come down after all just to find that after almost two centuries she had missed him by five minutes?

Dinah looked up to the window again. The dark rider's lady was looking urgent now, and she was holding up a staying hand, which she pressed against the glass before turning quickly and disappearing.

"She is coming," Dinah whispered. "Please wait. She is coming."

But what if he was gone already? She must stop him, she thought, that mindless urgency on her again. She must go after him and bring him back somehow. Perhaps he was here and she could not see him. Perhaps he had seen what she had just seen and would wait for his lady to come down to him. Or perhaps he had gone, having given up finally after almost two hundred years.

She picked up the hem of her cloak and nightgown and began to run in the direction she and Edgar had taken with their horses the previous morning. It was not even very dark, she half noticed as she ran. There was light from the stars and the sliver of an old moon.

The clifftop was deserted. Dinah could see that from some distance away and slowed her pace to a walk. There was no sign of either horse or rider. So either she was far too late or else he was still back at Malvern waiting for his lady. She hoped the latter. Oh, she hoped it. But she kept walking. She wanted to assure herself that he was not out of sight on the cliff path or else out on the water on a boat already.

There was no one on the path. It was dark and deserted. But when she lifted her head and looked out to the water, she could see the ship, lying dark and still and silent not far from the shore, its masts reaching toward the stars, and a smaller boat being rowed toward the shore by two oarsmen.

Oh, dear God, she thought. Dear Lord. They were coming for him already. In a few minutes' time they would be rowing him back to the ship and he would be gone. And yet his lady was coming. Dinah was quite sure that that was what her gesture at the window and her sudden disappearance had meant.

She was about to hurl herself down the path in a desperate bid to stop him in time when she realized that the direction the little boat was taking would not bring it to the beach below. It was rowing off to her left. He must, then, be on his way down the less steep path. That was why she had not seen his horse. He could not have taken his horse down this path. It was too steep.

Dinah turned blindly and dashed across the clifftop toward the path that Edgar had indicated the previous morning. And stopped dead at the top of it.

There were two men on the path, neither one of them the dark rider. They were both crouched down behind rocks and coarse grass, and both staring so intently downward that they were unaware of her presence above them. If they were ghosts, of course, they would remain unaware. But she knew they were not ghosts.

Smugglers? Were they waiting for the boat to arrive at the beach so that they could go down to unload the forbidden cargo? Dinah felt terror at the thought, and her first instinct was to turn and run back the way she had come, back to the safety of Malvern. The dark rider was forgotten for the moment and she was fully aware of the peril of her situation. Edgar, she thought, would be furious with her if he ever knew.

But there was something strange about the two men. If they were awaiting the arrival of the boat, why were

they not down on the beach so that they might help
unload whatever was in it as quickly as possible? Why
were they holding back? One of the men, she could
see, had a long gun lying on the path beside him.

There was still the urge to run. But there was also
curiosity and the strange feeling that somehow she was
needed. By whom she did not know. She moved over
to the face of the cliff on the inside of the path and
began to edge her way downward, keeping her back
against the cliff and knowing that even if the men
looked back they would very probably not see her
against the dark and rough wall of rock.

She did not have to go down very far. After turning
an almost imperceptible bend she could at last see
down onto the beach itself. And she could see more
men down there. She counted them. Two standing
close together at the water's edge, both dressed in long
black cloaks, and three standing a little behind them,
their eyes searching the beach and the cliff path. But
they would not be able to see either her or the two men
crouched behind rocks.

One of the cloaked men was Edgar. She knew it as
surely as if she were close enough to see his features.
He was part of a smuggling gang and he was about to
be caught red-handed by the coastal patrol. The little
boat was almost at the beach. She hated him in that
moment. And felt a knee-weakening need to save him.
But it was too late to save him. She tried to remember
what happened to convicted smugglers. Years in jail?
Transportation? Hanging? She swallowed awkwardly
and fought the sudden urge to cough.

And then her eyes widened in horror and her hands
clawed at the rock on either side of her. The man with
the gun was picking it up and lifting it to his shoulder

and taking careful aim at the figures below. At one figure. At Edgar.

Dinah could no longer think of clever and impossible ways to save him. She stepped out into the path and cupped her hands about her mouth and shrieked.

"E-D-G-A-R!"

She saw, as if it all happened in slow motion, Edgar and the others wheel about and crouch down at the same time. She heard the deafening roar of a gun firing. She saw the boat arrive at the beach and one of the oarsmen leap out. And she saw Edgar push the other cloaked figure toward the boat and heard him yell something before racing up the beach toward the path. It must have all happened in seconds, for almost before his full name passed her lips she was being seized in an iron grasp and a hand was clamping over her mouth—too late.

"Goddamn it, I missed him!" the man with the gun hissed—in French. Dinah scarcely realized that she had translated the words in her head. "Damned wench!" And he rose to his feet, gun in hand, and began to run down the path. The man who held Dinah followed him, urging her ahead of him with his knee.

"Out of my road!" the gunman roared as the two parties drew together on the path, and Dinah moaned in terror against the hand over her mouth as he raised his gun to his shoulder again. But she was almost glad of the hand a moment later as Edgar's arm appeared from beneath his cloak holding a pistol and there was a loud crack and the gunman pitched forward on his face. The hand over her mouth stopped her from screeching. The arm clamped about her waist prevented her from falling in a heap to the path.

The sight of the little boat pulling away from shore

seemed almost an irrelevance. And yet, one part of her mind told her, a customs officer was dead and no smuggled goods had been landed.

"Careful, *monsieur,*" Dinah's captor said. "I have this wench before my body. And will perhaps slice her pretty throat if you do not immediately hail that boat and recall it to shore."

Her mouth was suddenly freed and a moment later the hand returned to hold the blade of a knife against her throat. She pressed her head back against his shoulder.

She met Edgar's eyes for what seemed an endless moment. They were totally inscrutable. He lowered the pistol to his side.

"Now, *monsieur!*" her captor snapped, and the knife pressed inward a little. Dinah breathed shallowly so that she would not move.

Edgar muttered something to the man immediately behind him, and only then did Dinah notice through the redness of terror that the man also had a gun, trained directly on her. And then Edgar turned, cupped his hands about his mouth, and yelled, stepping well forward as he did so.

"Fournier," he shouted, "keep going! All well here!"

But the last words were drowned out in the roaring of the gun and Dinah slumped forward, unaware for many moments that someone had caught her before she reached the ground and held her tightly enough almost to accomplish what the bullet had not done. She nearly suffocated.

"He is dead," she heard a voice say through the buzzing in her ears. He spoke in a quite unemotional and matter-of-fact way, much as he might speak if he were a hunter and had shot down a bird. "We will take care of these two, sir, shall we? I don't believe there can be any others or they would be here by now."

"No," another voice said, the voice of the man who held her. Edgar's voice. "This was just the regular guard. They were not expecting us for four more nights. Yes, bury them, Trevor. And then get home as fast as you can, the three of you."

Dinah did not want to open her eyes. She did not want to have to deal with any of the events of the past several minutes or with the new knowledge they had brought her. She did not want to think about the two poor members of the coastal patrol who had lost their lives this night in the pursuit of duty. One of them by a bullet from Edgar's gun. If she had the choice, she would choose never to open her eyes or think again.

Edgar slid an arm beneath her knees and stood up with her. She lay limply in his arms, her head against his shoulder. She wanted to wake up in her own bed and find that it had all been a nightmare. Please, dear God, let me wake up in my own bed, she prayed silently. But the dream—or the reality—continued. She knew that he was carrying her down the path toward the beach and then along the beach. His boots made no sound, and she knew they were on sand.

She was limp in his arms. She must have fainted. He did not know quite where he was going with her except that he felt he had to be beneath the safe shelter of the cliffs. He was unaware of the small boat approaching the ship and of the ship preparing to hoist sail for France. He felt no exultation at the success of the night's work and no horror at the ugliness of it. Not yet. He was not even thinking of those things yet.

He could only see in his mind's eye Dinah held captive against that ruffian's body, his knife arching her neck back and almost nicking the skin. Dinah frightened and helpless yet unhysterical. And the man would have killed her too without a thought. Lord Asquith felt an unpleasant churning in his stomach when he thought of the quick decision he had made to have Trevor shoot the man, though there was little enough to aim at without having to go through Dinah. His decision to trust Trevor's marksmanship might have ended her life. His stomach churned again.

They were close to the cliffs, out of sight of the path. Safe. Though safe from what he did not know. The night's business was over. He went down carefully on one knee, cradling her in his arms, keeping them about her as he set her down, resting her against his inner thigh. Her cloak fell partly open to reveal her nightgown. It reminded him again of how helpless she had been.

"Dinah," he murmured, and he withdrew his arm from beneath her knees and stroked back the hair from her face with light fingertips.

She opened her eyes. It seemed that she had not fainted after all.

"Foolish Dinah," he murmured, the words more a caress than a reproof. "Foolish, brave, impossible girl. You might have been killed."

"They were going to shoot you," she said. "One of them had the gun to his shoulder already. He was going to kill you." She raised one hand and touched her fingers to his lips. Her hand was shaking slightly.

"But they didn't," he said. And he took her hand in his, lifted it, and kissed her palm.

"Edgar." Her voice was trembling too.

He lowered his head and touched his lips to hers. Warm, sweet, and trembling. "You are safe now," he said against them. "And so am I, love. We are both safe."

The truth of his words hit him with dizzying force and he could feel the sand beneath him and hear the wash of waves against the beach and smell the salt of the sea. He felt very, very alive. He parted his lips and touched his tongue to her lips and was equally aware of her warmth and aliveness.

"Edgar." Her arm came up about his neck and she turned in to him and left her lips parted beneath his so that his tongue could circle the warm moistness inside and finally, when she moaned, enter her mouth slowly, tentatively, deeply.

He wanted her as he had not wanted a woman in several years. He had been too busy for women, his life too fraught with danger. He had sublimated the energies he had once used on women into the life he had been leading more recently. But he wanted Dinah with all the desire that had been kept in check for too long. He wanted her now.

"Sweet love," he murmured against her ear, and he murmured countless endearments against her eyes, her temples, her throat, her mouth, as his one hand sought out the inviting warmth beneath her cloak and roamed over the firm young breasts and found the buttons extending from her throat to her waist. He undid them one by one and slid his hand inside, over her smooth firm shoulder, down to the silky skin below and on down to the soft swelling of her breast. He cupped his palm beneath it and touched his thumb to her nipple, feeling it harden with answering desire.

God, he wanted her. His need pulsed through him.

He wanted to be inside her. Inside her he wanted to release all the tensions and all the self-discipline that had become a way of life with him. He wanted to give all of himself to her and become vulnerable again, human again in her arms.

He withdrew his hand from her breast and reached down to draw up the hem of her nightgown. He felt the slim smoothness of her ankle. And kept his hand there, stroking it lightly over the lower part of her leg. He wanted her more than he had ever wanted a woman—even the most beautiful and the most skillful of the courtesans he had once possessed. The physical desire for her body was hammering through him. But there was something else too. Something that was at war with his desire. There was tenderness and affection and—something else. She was not just a woman to cater to his desires. She was Dinah.

And then he listened to what she was saying, to what she had been saying for a little while, he realized.

"No," she was saying, her voice small and bewildered. "Please, no." She would not actively stop him. He could tell that. And she wanted him as he wanted her. Her body told him that. But the part of Dinah that was beyond the desire wanted him to stop, was begging him to stop, and would be shamed and sorry if he did not.

He kissed her warmly on the mouth. "All right, my love," he whispered to her. "It's all right." And he continued to kiss her until the roaring of his own blood in his ears had reduced to a mere thumping and she had relaxed in his arms. He lifted his head and looked down into her eyes. God. Oh, God, she was precious to him.

She gazed back at him before wriggling out of his

arms and getting to her feet and setting herself to rights, her back to him. Then she stood silently, looking out to sea. He stood up behind her and set his hands gently on her shoulders.

But she whirled on him, her eyes blazing, and struck his hands away. Then she raised the side of one fist and pounded it once against his chest. "You are a smuggler," she said, disgust and contempt loud in her voice. "And a murderer. Don't touch me!"

He was taken aback. Shaken. "Neither, Dinah," he said, taking a step toward her. But she took two back.

"I suppose it is a ghost ship," she said, pointing dramatically into the distance. "I suppose that was a ghost boat that pulled in to shore. You are a smuggler. A base, thieving smuggler."

"No," he said.

"And a murderer," she said. "I saw you shoot the one customs officer. You gave the order for the shooting of the other. Your lackeys are burying them even now where their families will never find them to mourn them. You are a murderer. You deserve to hang."

"If I had not shot him," he said, "then he would have shot me, Dinah. And if I had not told Trevor to shoot the other, he would have killed you. Self-defense both times. Not murder."

"Murderer!" Her voice was shaking.

"And customs officers, Dinah?" he said. "Customs officers speaking French? And preparing to shoot a man in the back? And willing to slice the throat of an innocent young woman in order to bring smuggled cargo back to shore?"

He saw the uncertainty in her face. Clearly she had not had time to consider those matters.

"They were thugs," he said. "Hired killers. In all

fairness, I suppose they would call themselves patriots.''

She searched his eyes and said nothing. She looked small and slender in the moonlight. And utterly vulnerable. He saw her again as he had seen her a matter of only minutes before, clamped against the body of a desperate and murderous ruffian, his knife against her throat. The image took itself one step farther and he saw the blood welling from her throat and soaking down over the knife and the hand and her cloak. He might at this moment be carrying her bloody and lifeless body back to Malvern to explain to his mother. To explain to her mother and stepfather. To explain to his own conscience.

''And you.'' His voice was very quiet, but he could feel his hands close into tight fists at his sides. ''What the devil are you doing out of your room and out of the house and down here almost getting yourself killed? I want an explanation, and it had better be a good one.'' He could hear the coldness and the suppressed fury in his voice.

''I saved your life,'' she said.

''You damned little fool,'' he said. ''And almost lost your own in the process. But that does not answer my question.'' She did not step back when he took a step forward this time. He took her by the shoulders and shook her none too gently. ''I should beat you until you are too sore to sit down.''

''You are not my father,'' she said, clinging to his elbows. ''Or my husband. I do not have to explain myself to you. I saw the ship and the boat and came to the top of the path and saw those two men. And when I went down a little way, I saw you and the other men on the beach. And then one of the two was going to shoot you.'' Her voice shook. ''He was going to kill you.''

''You did not see the ship from your room,'' he said in exasperation. But his fury had ebbed as quickly as it had come and he saw it for what it was—horror at what he had almost caused to happen to her.

''Edgar,'' she said, ''who were those men if not customs officers? And do you make yourself very rich by smuggling? Please say no.''

''No,'' he said. ''I am not a smuggler, Dinah.''

''What, then?'' she said.

He kept his hands on her shoulders and drew in a deep breath before letting it out slowly. ''I think I had better tell you the truth,'' he said. ''It cannot do a great deal of harm now, I suppose. I had already made it known that this was my last assignment, and even if I had not decided to end it, circumstances would now force me to do so. Obviously my cover has been shattered and I can be of no further use. Not in my present capacity anyway.''

She looked at him mutely. She was biting her lower lip.

''For a few years,'' he said, ''I was an active agent for our government, spending most of my time in France gathering what information I could.''

''A spy,'' she said.

''I suppose you could call it that,'' he said. ''More recently the convenient situation of Malvern has enabled me to offer safe landing and safe departure to other agents. Safe until this time, that is. Something went horribly wrong and Fournier fled to Malvern, the fool, more than a week early and trailing a whole army of thugs behind him. He has papers and information that must be safely delivered in France. After that I suppose he will have to disappear. His name and face must be too well known for him to be of much use to anyone for a while."

He watched her swallow. "You have been harboring a spy at Malvern?" she said. "Where?"

"In the white tower," he said. "You almost came upon him there when you got lost, Dinah. It must have been his presence you felt. Fortunately you thought it was ghosts."

"You tried to scare me with them to keep me out of the way," Dinah said.

"To keep you safe," he said. "One of my men, who was employed as a gardener at Malvern, was killed the day after Fournier's arrival."

"Oh," she said, her mouth forming the word, though there was not much sound.

"I made arrangements for Fournier to leave tonight," he said, "instead of in four nights' time when the tides would be more favorable and the moon in its least damaging phase. There would have been too large a reception committee waiting for us then. Tonight, thank God, there were only two."

"So," she said, "it was probably not you he was going to kill."

"Doubtless his first shot was intended for Fournier," he said.

She looked down at her hands, which she held palm up between them. "I think shock is wearing off and reality intruding," she said, her voice very steady. "Hold me, Edgar. Will you, please?"

"Come here," he said, wrapping his arms tightly about her and bringing her full length against him. She turned her head to lay it against his shoulder. And then she began to tremble in convulsive jerks and he knew that if he let her go she would crumple to the sand. He rocked her against him and laid his cheek against the top of her head.

She felt warm and comforted and safe. And everything was all right. He was not after all a smuggler but an agent acting for England against the power of Napoleon Bonaparte. And he was not a murderer either. He was a killer, certainly, and those two men were probably not the only two he had killed. But he was part of the war effort and killing was acceptable in war if it was absolutely necessary. The deaths of those two men had been necessary. She shivered as her trembling came under control.

But she could not help remembering that he might have been dead now if she had not come when she had. And that she might be dead if he had not acted so decisively. She could still feel the cold terror of the blade at her throat. And she knew that her dreams would be haunted for a long time to come by the events of this night.

But she was warm and safe now. Safe in the arms of a man she had known for only two and a half days, on a deserted beach in the middle of the night one mile from home and her bed. In the arms of a man who had been kissing her just a few minutes before in a deep and intimate and suggestive manner and whose hand had been inside her nightgown touching her more intimately than she had allowed him to touch her in her dream—centuries ago when she had been asleep in her bed. The man whose hand had been coming underneath the hem of her gown to discover her nakedness and who had stopped only when she had repeatedly begged him to do so and when she had already been giving up hope that he would heed her words.

Safe!

She raised her head and looked into his face. "Edgar," she said.

But he surprised her by smiling—no, *grinning* was a more appropriate word, and she did not continue. "I think you have been compromised quite sufficiently that you will have to accept my marriage offer. Wouldn't you agree, Dinah?" he asked.

"Of course not," she said, her eyes widening. "How absurd!"

"Alone with me on the beach after midnight," he said, echoing her thoughts of a moment before, "in nothing more than your nightgown and a cloak. I think you are going to have to marry me, Dinah."

"Silly," she said. "No one need know unless you tell them. Besides, we have known each other for less than three days. It would be foolish to marry on such short acquaintance."

"I just might decide to tell the world," he said, "and force your hand. And I might have agreed with the rest of what you said three days ago. Two and a half days is not at all long enough to fall in love and to know that one has found the treasure of one's life, is it?"

"No," she said, and then she looked more deeply into his eyes. "What a lovely idea. I am not, am I?"

"The treasure of my life?" he said. "I think you are, Dinah. In fact, I am certain you are. Absurd, am I not? Do you like me well enough to let me pay court to you? I shall invite my aunt and uncle and young cousins here for Christmas, shall I? And come to London for the Season? And perhaps spend part of the summer with your family? And perhaps make my offer at the end of the summer. Will that be long enough, Dinah? Or will you need longer? I know you are very young.''

"I am nineteen," she said with some indignation. "You cannot be that sure that you will want to. Can you?"

He bent his head and kissed her softly on the lips. "As sure as that I am standing here compromising you dreadfully," he said.

"Well, then," she said, "you must be as foolish as I. A fine couple we will make."

He drew back his head and looked into her eyes. "Translate for me," he said.

"I love you," she said, and laughed rather breathlessly. "It is ridiculous and impossible after two and a half days. But it is so."

"Perhaps," he said, "I will make my offer during the Christmas holiday. Shall I? To your mother, Dinah? Is it to her you would wish me to speak?"

"Yes," she said. "And to Sir Anthony, if you please. He has been as good as a real father to me. At Christmastime, Edgar? That soon?"

"Or when I escort you home after the measles have finally run their course," he said. "Shall we wait and see if we still think ourselves foolish when that time comes? I had better get you back home, love. If you are missed, you know, we will be an old married couple long before Christmas."

She laughed shakily again and did not protest when he wrapped one arm about her waist, kissed her once on the lips, and began to walk with her back along the beach toward the cliff path. She rested her head against his shoulder and gave her attention to foolish and wonderful nonsense talk. Until they were at the top of the path and on the clifftop again, that was.

Ahead of them, not too far off, a huge black stallion was pawing the ground while a dark-haired, bareheaded man in a long black cloak swung down to the ground and lifted down after him with infinite care and tenderness a blond, curly-haired lady, whose light-colored cloak swung open to reveal a white nightgown beneath. He kissed her swiftly before turning to slap the horse smartly on the rump and set it galloping alone back toward Malvern. Then he set his arm protectively about the girl's shoulders and hurried her toward the path that Dinah and Lord Asquith had just vacated.

"Oh." Dinah stood stock still and stared.

"What is it, love?" Lord Asquith asked, tightening his arm about her waist.

Dinah smiled radiantly. "She came down," she said. "At last she found the courage and the means. And she was not too late. He was there waiting for her after all."

Lord Asquith kissed her ear. "Now what are you raving on about?" he asked, laughter in his voice.

She looked up at him quickly and then gestured to the couple, who had almost come up with them. "The sad lady," she said, "and the dark rider. There."

He looked right at them. "Dinah," he said, and his voice was even more amused, "are you seeing ghosts? Don't worry, darling. I'll protect you." And he chuckled and tried to kiss her mouth. But she twisted her head away and watched the dark rider and his lady pass them. He swung his lady up into his arms and proceeded down the path with her.

"You don't see them?" Dinah said. "They are *there*, Edgar, as plain as day."

"The dark rider?" he said. "You mean my shady Roundhead ancestor, Dinah? And the lady he haunts Malvern to rescue?"

"Yes," she said. "He did finally persuade her to leave, you see. I am so glad, Edgar. So very glad. She was with child, you see, and would have been facing terrible scandal and heartache had she stayed. Now at least they have a chance for happiness. Oh, they are going to be happy. I know they are."

He turned her toward him and framed her face with his hands. He was no longer laughing. "Dinah," he said. "Not only do you believe it, but it is so, is it not? Mrs. Knole has always said that there are some people—very few, she says—who are so close to the spirit world that sometimes they can see it. I have never believed her. But it is true, isn't it?" He frowned.

"Yes," she said. "She was so sad, Edgar. She was in my room. And locked in there, though she knew a servant who could be persuaded to set her free. But she was a timid soul, poor lady. And so very deeply in love."

"And you persuaded her to leave?" His eyes were searching hers.

"Perhaps in a way," she said. "Although she actually left almost two hundred years ago, Edgar. I ran to the cliffs to stop him. I thought he had given up and gone without her just when she was finally making up her mind to leave. But he waited long enough. Perhaps he would never have left without her."

"That is what you were doing out here?" he asked.

She nodded. "I am sorry, Edgar," she said. "I know it was against your express wishes, but I forgot them when I felt her sadness and longing and when I knew she was increasing. And when I thought he was going to leave. I ran down to stop him.''

''And last night?''

''I saw him,'' she said, ''but I thought he was you, Edgar. When he beckoned, I went down. He looks just exactly like you. I knew she must not let him go.''

''Because he looked like me?'' he said.

''Perhaps.'' She smiled.

He kissed her then, keeping his hands at her cheeks for a little while before wrapping them right about her and hugging her close.

''So I am your dark rider,'' he said after a while.

''No,'' she said, ''you are Edgar. The dark rider has a lady and he is almost two hundred years old. A little too old for me.''

''So,'' he said, ''you will make do with second best.''

She shook her head. ''I do not envy her,'' she said. ''I only feel happy for her. For I know how it feels to love, and now I know why she longed to be in her lover's arms. I don't love him, though he is a wonderfully romantic figure. I love my flesh-and-blood Edgar.''

He smiled at her and kissed her again.

''I hope the boat was there waiting for them,'' she said, and she felt suddenly anxiety. ''I hope they got away safely. Do you think they did, Edgar?''

''Maybe we had better look down and you can tell me,'' he said.

The scene from the edge of the cliff was the same as the one she had seen less than an hour before. The ship was in deep water beyond the bay, the small boat approaching the shore rowed by two oarsmen.

"Can you not see them?" she asked.

"The moonlight is lovely on the water," he said. "Not at all sinister, as it should be on All Hallows' Eve."

The boat disappeared onto the beach and reappeared again a few minutes later with its two passengers. The dark rider held his lady on his lap with her arms wrapped about his neck. He slipped his hand beneath her cloak, and Dinah knew that he was touching the swelling that was the child he had just been told about.

"Oh," she said, and the images blurred before her vision. "They are safe, Edgar. They are on their way. I think they will have a happy life. After so long they deserve it. They will be happy, will they not?"

He turned her toward him and kissed her once more. "They were happy, my love," he said. "Just as we will be. If the power of love can bring happiness, then they must have lived a long and prosperous and happy life together. And so will we. I love you, sweetheart."

She wrapped her arms about his neck and smiled at him. And set her head against his shoulder and breathed in the warm masculine smell of him. "Take me back to Malvern, then, Edgar," she said. "Take me home."

The dark rider and his lady, on their way to a new life and to happiness, were temporarily forgotten.

Black Magic

by
Anita Mills

The Cornish Coast: October, 1860

IT WAS A BARREN PLACE, this high, rocky cliff that towered above the wild, crashing sea. Thick, heavy clouds reflected off the water, making it seem as though sky and ocean were one vast, turbulent expanse of gray. The woman walked alone, her arms crossed against the wet salt wind, her face as desolate as the day.

As much as she mourned Ned, as much as she still longed for his embrace, reason told her that she had to think of their daughters. But reason could not ease the ache, the void in her heart. Not when the only love she'd ever known lay buried somewhere on Indian soil, the victim of a bloody, senseless rebellion. It had been almost two years since they'd told her how he'd died, and still she could not forget, nor could she forgive his father for what had happened.

It was not the same for Callie and Katie, she reflected sadly, for with the resilience of children, they seemed willing to let Ned become an ever more distant memory. But it had been different for them, she supposed, for they'd scarce had the chance to know him. In '54, he'd gone off to the Crimea to make his father proud, leaving her with the two girls, the eldest of whom was then but four. And two years later, he'd been dispatched to India, where Sir Richard felt he could rise faster. And with less danger, he'd told her. The bitter irony was that he'd fallen.

She knew both girls longed for Seaton Hill, for the house filled with servants, for the horses, for the companionship of cousins and friends, even for their stern, cold grandfather. But she could not go back to Ned's father's house. Not yet. Not until the bitterness passed. Not until she could forgive Sir Richard. Maybe never.

If only . . . that was the trouble, the world was filled with if onlys. If only Ned had been stronger, more willing to stand up to his father's ambitions . . . if only he'd chosen to stay home with her and their daughters . . . Sometimes the anger within her nearly overshadowed her grief, and she blamed him for leaving her behind to contend with the interfering old man.

She looked down at her mother's damp letter and reread the blurred lines.

The General's man was here today again, acting as bold as you please, saying I was to tell you that if you are unwilling to bring the girls back, Sir Richard is inclined to have you declared unfit to keep them. I did not tell him where you are, but I know not how long I can deny all knowledge, dearest. It is but a matter of time ere he discovers you, I fear. Perhaps if you could but make your peace . . .

The words faded. *Peace? How could Mama even think it?*

"Mama! Mama!"

"Callie, *will* you wait up?"

Sarah Seaton turned from the sea to her breathless

daughters. The younger, eight-year-old Calista, stumbled over the rocks, her black hair tangling over her eyes, her arms cradling something. Katherine, two years the elder, pushed past her to tattle.

"It's a filthy cat, Mama!" she gasped. "A carriage hit it, and Callie will not let the man put it out of its misery!"

"He's going to *kill* it! And it isn't old! Mama, he's going to use a rock!"

Sarah's gaze dropped to the black kitten that huddled against her hoyden daughter's soiled smock, and she sighed. The frightened animal was dripping blood.

"Callie, whatever—? Dearest—"

The younger girl swallowed hard, then lifted her large blue eyes to her mother's. "It's hurt, Mama."

"So I see."

"The driver told his man to get rid of it," Katie explained. "He told him to take it away and bury it, and then he went on. But Callie snatched it before it was done."

"Please, Mama—I'd keep him. I'll take care of him, I swear it!" Callie begged. Looking back, she caught sight of the fellow lumbering across the rocks toward them, and this time, when she turned again to her mother, there was an even greater urgency in her voice. "Please, Mama—please." The black cat ducked his head deeper under the child's arm. "See—he *knows*, Mama! He doesn't want to die."

When he saw Sarah, the man removed his cap respectfully before he approached her. Stopping a few feet back, he mumbled apologetically, "I got ter do it, ma'am—Mr. Simpson said I was ter."

Never having had much fondness for cats, Sarah was inclined to give it over, but as tears spilled onto Callie's cheeks, she hesitated. "Let me see it," she said finally, reaching for the cat.

As her fingers brushed against the animal's back, it hissed and spit, and when she touched it, it dug its claws into Callie's arm. The child bit her lip and held on. As nearly as Sarah could see, at least one hind leg was badly broken, and possibly the animal's hip was broken also.

"Callie, it is best to let him have it," she said gently. "You don't want it to suffer, you know."

"No!"

"Callie—"

"He's going to kill it, Mama!"

The big man, unable to perceive that Sarah agreed with him, insisted doggedly, "Gave me a penny fer it, he did. I got ter."

"I know. Callie—"

"No!"

"You heard Mama—it's going to die," Katie insisted. "Besides, you don't want it. Black cats are for witches," she declared with a superior air. "They cast spells on the creatures."

"I won't let him die! I won't!" Clutching the cat more tightly, the little girl turned and ran, startling the man, who stared after her. "I got ter—"

"Calista! Callie!" Sarah called after her. It was useless—no doubt the child truly believed she could save the cat.

"You want me to catch her, Mama?"

Sarah drew in her breath. She didn't want either daughter to witness death. It was painful enough to live with the knowledge of it without seeing it. Finally, she shook her head.

"No. No doubt she will take the creature to Mrs.

Foote, who will tell her the same as we have." Putting an arm around her elder daughter, she drew the girl close to her, then looked up at the fellow. "If you will wait a few minutes, then come to the cottage, I shall see you get the cat. But I'd not have you do anything where the girls can witness it. Do you understand that?"

"Yes, ma'am." He squinted into the rolling clouds. "How'm I ter know when ter come?"

"You could count to two hundred," Katie suggested.

"Can't."

"Oh. Well, maybe—"

"Never mind, Katherine. He can sit here until you ring Mrs. Foote's bell. Is that all right with you, sir?"

"Uh-huh," he agreed, nodding.

Sarah gathered her black fringed shawl closer about her shoulders and started back to the cottage she'd recently leased with the hope that Sir Richard would not find them. "You must not vex her over this, you know," she said finally. Then, before the child could protest, she added more severely, "I should wonder if both of you do not take a chill."

"It's only a cat," the girl muttered, unmollified.

"Katie—"

"But I don't know what she wants it for, anyway, Mama. Auntie Foote said to let him have it also. She told her it was going to die and not to bother you with it."

"I take it this happened near the cottage?"

The little girl squirmed, then confessed, "Not precisely, Mama. It was on the village road." Perceiving that her mother frowned, she hastened to add, "But we weren't going anywhere—we were just going to watch the road, as there is not much else to do.'' She shuddered visibly. ''I told Callie it was too bloody to touch, but she wouldn't listen. You know how she is.''

''Yes, but she has a kindness we must not entirely discourage.'' Even as Sarah said it, she could not help thinking that there was possibly too much of Sir Richard in Katie, too little of the Winston side of the family. ''Come on,'' she murmured, settling her shoulders. ''This is not like to be pleasant.''

''She'll get over it,'' Katie promised. ''And I'd much rather have a dog than a half-dead cat.''

''I'm afraid we don't have much room for either, dearest. Besides, I don't think Auntie Foote would approve.''

The child sighed. ''I cannot think why that would make any difference, Mama. It isn't as though she does not depend on you, after all.''

''There you are wrong, Katie—I'm afraid I quite depend on her.''

But the child was not convinced. ''I thought we lived on your portion. Auntie Foote says so. She says that is why we don't live at Seaton Hill anymore. That you don't want Grandpapa's money.''

''Money is not quite everything, Katie. With Mrs. Foote and Tom, we are able to be independent.''

He was nearly too tired to face the day. Mrs. Springs had labored a day and a night to bring forth her child, and in the end, he'd had to dose her heavily with laudanum and take the babe. The birth had been far too hard, but it did no good to tell Will Springs he was wearing out his young wife. Next year it would be the same tale—another child born too close to the last. At nineteen, the girl already looked ten years older. By twenty-nine, she'd be lucky to have her teeth.

He leaned back in his chair and closed his eyes, his mind oblivious to the sound of his housekeeper humming tunelessly as she bustled about him, making order of his existence. It was always the same with every difficult delivery—he felt drained and yet relieved every time both mother and child survived. His thoughts turned to Anne and the small blue babe that had perished with her; then he forcefully pushed them from his mind, wishing that birthings did not bring back the painful memory of his greatest failure. It did not seem right that the horror of the end had nearly erased the two years of happiness that had preceded it.

Somehow he managed to doze off, only to be rudely awakened by the frantic pounding at the door. He groaned inwardly, hoping that Mrs. Clark would turn whoever it was away, hoping it was nothing more than someone come to get a remedy for something easy like a queasy stomach. Something Mrs. Clark could take care of. He closed his eyes again, but he could not help hearing part of the exchange just outside his book room.

"Whatever—what is *that?* Here now," the woman protested, her voice rising imperiously. "Ye cannot bring that filthy creature inside! Dr. Davies is not in, I tell ye!"

He could scarce make out what was going on, but he could hear a child crying, blubbering breathlessly something about someone trying to kill someone. Reluctantly, he opened his sore eyes and rubbed at the stubble on his cheek and chin before heaving himself from his chair. It did not sound like anything that a bromide or a cough syrup could mend.

"Go on wi'ye! I'll not have blood on the carpet, d'ye hear me?"

He managed to stumble to the door. "Mrs. Clark, we do not turn patients away," he mumbled sleepily.

"Well, we don't treat *them* neither!" she shot back, unrepentant. " 'Tis a cat, sir!"

Blinking his surprise, he shook his head in an effort to clear the cobwebs from his brain, then looked down at the very pretty child who stood determinedly in his hall. He didn't recognize her, but there was an enormous appeal in wide blue, tear-filled eyes. Her lower lip trembled as she stared up at him. She swallowed hard, then looked down at the bloody ball of fur in her arms.

"He was going to kill it, sir—and—and Mama said I was to let him do it—but—but I couldn't, sir—I—I just *couldn't!*" Once the words started they tumbled out, punctuated by gasps.

"I'm afraid I do not—" He stopped.

Her small, blood-stained arms tightened about the animal, prompting a feeble yowl of protest as the bloody fur shifted. The little girl stroked it soothingly, then looked up stubbornly. "I brought him to the doctor, sir," she insisted, striving to regain her composure. "The sign says you are a doctor." The blue eyes seemed to accuse him.

For a moment, he considered denying it, then sighed. "Yes. I'm afraid I am. But—"

The small chin quivered again as the child perceived he meant to deny her. Very carefully she unfolded her arms and held the half-limp animal out to him. "Please, sir," she begged, "if you would but look at him.'' This time the tears spilled over. Her voice dropped to a near-whisper. "He's so dreadfully hurt that—that—well, surely you must see he has need of you—surely—"

"Ye heard Dr. Davies," Mrs. Clark declared before adding more kindly, "Can't ye see the man's tired beyond bearing? Been up all night bringing a babe into the world!"

But he was staring into the little girl's face, seeing himself as he had been once, a boy willing to try to right the ills of the world. But that was when he'd believed he could struggle with death and win. Before Anne. His gaze dropped to the dangling black leg and he saw a fragment of blood-smeared bone protruding above a nasty break. If there was nothing worse, if it did not die from the shock . . . He sucked in his breath, then exhaled heavily.

"Mrs. Clark, clear the table."

At first the woman did not think she'd heard him correctly. "Well, I never—not on my table! Dr. Davies, 'tis a dirty, nasty creature!"

"And fill a basin with water, if you please," he continued, unperturbed.

"Oh—thank you, sir!" Callie drew the cat closer and crooned softly to it. "You are going to get well . . . you are going to get well—I know it."

"I'm afraid I cannot offer you a miracle, child," he told her. "It may not survive the surgery." He reached for the animal, lifting it gently from her arms. "Come on, you little ape," he murmured, carrying it toward the back of the house.

"It's not an ape," Callie protested, trailing after him.

" 'Tis heathen, it is—putting a cat on a table where

folks eat,'' Mrs. Clark muttered. Nevertheless, she began to wipe the already spotless top with a cloth. When she finished, she pursed her lips and surveyed Callie. ''Ye don't look familiar, else I'd send to yer mama to come for ye. Ye ought not to watch, ye know.''

''I am Miss Calista Seaton,'' Callie answered, ignoring the other. She made a wry face as she said it, then explained, ''There are always Calistas in the family, but I really think Katie ought to have been it, for she is the eldest.''

''An unusual name,'' Davies murmured, laying the cat on the clean table.

''Everyone calls me Callie—except Grandpapa, who is so very formal, you see.''

''Humph! Ye're far too young to be about alone,'' Mrs. Clark said dampeningly. ''Yer parents ought to watch ye.''

''There's just Mama and Katie and Auntie Foote— and Tom, of course, although he merely sleeps in the loft and fixes things for us.''

''And the *formal* grandpapa,'' he reminded her.

''Oh, he does not—'' Callie stopped, catching herself before she betrayed anything more.

''Seaton.'' The woman's brow furrowed. ''Seaton. Where have I heard—?''

''We live up on the hill.''

''Oh—in the Bromleys' cottage?'' Mrs. Clark's curiosity piqued, she was suddenly quite interested, for the mysterious woman there was the subject of much village gossip. In the month or so since the cottage had been occupied, there had been but glimpses of the reclusive creature walking above the sea. Rumors had it that she was possibly a castoff mistress come to hide her shame on the barren Cornish coast, or that she kept apart because she had some other terrible secret, but in truth no one knew much about her. And the boy who ran her errands had proven an unsatisfactory source of information, for he was either half-witted or cleverly hiding something.

"She is Mrs. Seaton, then?" the woman asked slyly.

"Well, I suppose—" Once again, Callie caught herself.

"The basin, Mrs. Clark," Davies cut in impatiently, well aware of his housekeeper's prying ways. He glanced at the child. "You can come back later to see how your kitten fares."

"If you do not mind it, I should like to watch," Callie protested. "Tom says I am pluck to the bone, sir."

"And too pert by half, no doubt," the woman sniffed, miffed that he'd intervened before she could learn more. She poured water into the basin. "Will ye be wanting anything else, sir?" she asked Davies.

"We'll have to wash the blood away, so I expect you will need to hold it." His eyes again met Callie's. "Are you quite certain you won't bring up your breakfast? I'll not have time to tend you also."

"I won't," she promised solemnly. She dug into the pocket of her stained smock and drew out a coin. "I was saving this for Auntie Foote's birthday, but if you can fix him, I'd pay you."

"All I can do is try, child." He peered at the mangled leg and considered his options. "Mrs. Clark, we'll need something to hold this straight. Hopefully, if gangrene does not set in, it will heal, though I expect it to be stiff." Turning the animal over, he examined the break. "I don't know."

"A useless leg—'tis kinder to let the creature expire, for how he is to catch mice, I am sure I don't know," the woman murmured. But as she peered over his shoulder, she added, "Poor little thing."

"How old do you think he is?" Callie asked him.

"Lacking experience in cats, I cannot say with any degree of accuracy." He began washing the injured leg despite the animal's protests. "Mrs. Clark, wrap his front legs in a towel, will you?" Then, as the water seemed to shrink the black fur, he answered Callie. "Less than six months, I'd guess. What's its name?"

"I don't know."

The animal was struggling frantically now, prompting Mrs. Clark to literally tie the towel over its head and the entire front half of its body. Still the towel jerked about while the kitten within mewed hysterically. Callie's knuckles were white against the polished tabletop as she leaned her head down next to the thrashing cat and whispered soothingly over and over, "Good kitty . . . good kitty . . ."

"A bit of whiskey, Mrs. Clark—and a little sugar. As for you, Miss Calista, you'd best stand back. I've no wish to see you lose an eye."

He stopped trying to work on the frightened cat until he forced a half a dropperful of sugared whiskey down its throat. Then he stroked its back, feeling all the while for telltale lumps. When the kitten calmed down, he carefully rewrapped its front half and began setting the bone, finally closing the wound and splinting the leg. All the while, the child's wide blue eyes followed his every movement. Tom, whoever he was, had been right—she *was* pluck to the bone. When he straightened up, he felt oddly satisfied.

Callie eyed the leg, which stuck straight out in back

of the kitten, dubiously. "Will it always look like that?"

"I hope not. But he probably will not walk entirely right. And, unless infection sets in, he ought to live."

She pushed the coin across the table toward him. "Thank you, sir."

"You'd best save that for your aunt's birthday," he answered, handing it back.

"Well, she is not my aunt precisely, but—" She stopped, then shook her head. "Mama said we are never to beat out the tradesmen. Though what she is to say about this, I don't exactly know. Auntie Foote cannot abide creatures in the house, you see."

"Would it help if I kept your cat for awhile?" he found himself offering.

The little girl's hand reached to stroke the matted fur on the animal's head. "No, sir. He needs me." Once again, she raised her eyes to look at him. "I shall like being needed, you know."

He didn't know why he'd insisted on walking her home, and as he trudged the steep hill beside her, he was acutely aware of how tired he was, how much the raw chill of the air seemed to penetrate his bones. He belonged in bed, lest some new sickness should summon him out again this night. To make matters worse, he could smell the rain in the air.

But he had come, he supposed wearily, because his sense of propriety required it, because he was not so modern as to think a female child ought to be about unattended. That, or perhaps he feared that her family would not let her keep the animal after all his work to save its leg. Yet he knew that it would be days before Mrs. Clark spoke to him if he carried it back home with him. And a good housekeeper was hard to keep in this wild, isolated place.

Beside him, the child was silent. Finally he asked, "What do you mean to name it?"

Her arms tightened briefly around the awkward bundle in her arms, but as the cat protested, she relaxed her hold. "I shall have to think a bit, sir." She looked up. "Katie says it is a witch's cat, you know."

"Katie must have an imagination."

"I don't think so. She's my sister." She looked down at the cat, wishing for once that Katie could be right, for the notion intrigued her. Darting a quick glance up at Dr. Davies, she asked, "Do you believe in magic, sir?"

"If you are asking if I believe in witches, the answer is no, I'm afraid." Then, perceiving that perhaps he had disappointed her, he added, "But I do believe in miracles. What was it that the poet Cowper said? 'God works in mysterious way, his wonders to perform.' I'm inclined to agree with that, for I have seen too many cases where my patients ought to have died, and yet they have survived despite me."

For a moment, an intense sadness moved over her face like a shadow. "Papa took a cannon shell in his middle, and there was not enough left of him to bring home to bury."

"Your mother ought not to have told you that."

"She didn't. I was listening when the officers came."

"They ought not to have told her that either." As he looked down on her tangled black hair, he felt an overwhelming sympathy for the child beside him. "I'm sorry."

She nodded solemnly. "Auntie Foote says it has affected Mama's mind, and we must not vex her."

"Perhaps she is mistaken."

"I don't think so. Mama is forever walking alone—and she never smiles anymore."

"Your mama needs time to ease her grief," he offered gently.

"It has been a long time, sir."

He had no answer for that, for she was too young to understand that some things never entirely healed. He resisted the impulse to smooth her hair, to hold her close and comfort her, telling himself that he had no wish to get involved, that he had enough pain of his own. Instead, he jammed his hands in his pockets and fell silent.

"Well, we are here." She stopped, glancing up at him hesitantly. "She may not let me keep him, you know."

"Your mama?"

"Yes." She regarded the cat wistfully. "And I so would like to have him—I—I *would,* sir."

He didn't know why he did it, but he found himself asking, "Would it help if we were to beard them together?"

"I don't know," she answered truthfully. "But I daresay it cannot make anything worse." She hung back as he reached for the iron knocker. "You see, they do not know where I have been." Swallowing visibly, she added in a smaller voice, "I—I told you—I was supposed to give him over to be killed, but I could not, sir—I *could* not."

"Of course you could not." He banged the knocker loudly, then forced a smile. "Perhaps we can persuade this Auntie Foote and your mother. An animal who has survived what we have done to him deserves to live, don't you think?''

She stroked the soft fur lovingly. ''He was brave, wasn't he?''

He did not get to answer. The door opened, and he faced a woman well beyond middle age. ''Mrs. Foote?'' he hazarded.

''I am Emma Foote,'' she acknowledged before her gaze dropped to the child who stood almost behind him. ''Callie! Where have you been? Your poor mama has been half out of her mind with worry. Why, we sent Tom into the village to look for you!''

''I'm afraid she was at my house.'' As the woman's eyes surveyed him suspiciously, he hastened to explain, ''I am Dr. Davies—Spencer Davies.''

''A doctor! She isn't—?''

He felt Callie's hand touch his, and he squeezed it. ''Not at all.''

''Callie? Oh, Callie!'' A younger woman pushed past Mrs. Foote. ''You have given us such a fright! Where on earth—? Callie, you had no right to worry us so!'' Then, aware of the stranger's scrutiny, she stepped back, flushing. ''What you must think me, sir—I have not even thanked you for bringing her home, have I?'' She hesitated, then thrust out her hand. ''I am Sarah Seaton—Callie's mother.''

''Mrs. Seaton,'' he acknowledged gravely.

His grip was firm and warm, the sort that reassured one. Nonetheless, she pulled her hand away quickly. No man had so much as held it since Ned had gone away. Certainly not Sir Richard, not even in shared grief.

''She's still got that nasty old cat, Mama,'' another

child said behind her. Then: "What's that thing on its leg?"

"Dr. Davies fixed him. He says he will but walk with a limp," Callie responded quickly. "He will be nearly as good as ever."

"Really?" For a moment, the other child was intrigued. "You took him to the doctor?"

"Uh-huh." Callie stroked the cat's fur tenderly. "See—he loves me."

"Er—may I come in?" Spencer Davies inquired politely.

"Oh, of course." Sarah moved out of his way. "How unmannerly you must think me, sir."

"Not at all. Your concern for Callie is quite understandable." He knew he ought to leave, to go home to bed, and yet he felt a sort of obligation to the little girl and the cat she wanted so desperately to keep. As he stepped inside, the welcoming warmth of the fire in an ancient stone fireplace seemed to draw him. Behind him, Emma Foote threw the latch, closing the damp, nearly raw wind out.

"And this is my other daughter, Katherine," he heard Sarah Seaton say.

The girl made a brief curtsy, then turned to her mother. "You aren't going to let her have it, are you?"

Callie rubbed the small, furry head again. "Please, Mama, please! He's going to live—he is!"

"We'll speak of it later, dearest," Sarah murmured. "I'm quite sure Dr. Davies has no wish to hear us brangle over a cat."

Afraid that meant her answer was going to be a resounding no, Callie tried to postpone it. "Could Dr. Davies stay to tea, Mama?"

Sarah looked briefly at Mrs. Foote, then nodded.

"If you do not mind tea and buttered bread, you are most welcome, sir." As if to explain the meanness of the offering, she added, "We live rather simply here."

There was no mistaking the mute appeal in Calista Seaton's eyes. "Actually, I have a fondness for buttered bread," he found himself saying. "My own tastes are rather simple also, I'm afraid."

"Then it is settled!" Callie crowed, casting a smug glance at her sister. With the air of a grand lady entertaining a gentleman of distinction, she led him to a rocking chair drawn close before the fire, tossing over her shoulder, "Katie, do fetch the footrest, for you must surely see Dr. Davies is quite done up."

As he leaned back, the elder child dutifully slid the worn ottoman in front of him. His eyes took in the blackened teakettle that rested on a ledge inside the fireplace, sending a stream of steam into the air. Sarah Seaton was right—it was an exceedingly simple place, one furnished plainly, without so much as a single piece pretending to ostentation. Aside from the lack of clutter associated with the Bromleys' lively brood, it appeared much as it must have for a century or more.

"We have leased the furniture also," Callie hastened to explain. "It is not at all to Mama's taste."

"Callie—"

"Well, you said—"

"Never mind what I said," Sarah declared dampeningly.

He turned his attention to the women. The older one wore a clean blue gown of indiscriminate style, over which hung a white apron, the sort that one would expect to see on a menial rather than a relative. But she moved about with a degree of authority that indicated if she did not entirely rule the roost, she certainly could be expected to express her opinion without fear of being turned off.

The younger one—she was beyond the blush of youth, perhaps a year or two past thirty—was in obvious mourning. Everything about her bespoke it, from the black cotton dress that buttoned from her neck to her waist to the way she held her hands. Her eyes were as blue as Callie's, but they were not nearly so bright, so filled with life. And her hair, usually a woman's greatest vanity, was pulled back severely and knotted plainly at the nape of her neck. She had been a pretty woman once. Well, he conceded judiciously, she still was, for not even sadness could change the fine, even profile of her face, nor the elegance of her carriage.

Sarah Seaton was clearly a woman whose loss had altered her circumstances greatly, sending her and her children into that genteel poverty far too often associated with widowhood. He looked at Callie's mother and felt a genuine sympathy for her. It had been hard enough when he'd lost Anne. But whether he'd wanted it or not, he'd been left with the means of his livelihood. Apparently Sarah Seaton had not been nearly so fortunate. And it was a pity.

"Tell me, Dr. Davies—are you always in the habit of staring?" she asked coolly.

"What? Oh. Your pardon, Mrs. Seaton." He paused to pass a weary hand over his face, then smiled sheepishly. "I have scarce slept," he murmured apologetically. "It seems that most babes either come in the night—or after it."

Emma Foote carried the tea tray over to the small table and poured three cups. Sitting down, she gestured to him to take one. "You seem a trifle young to be a doctor, sir," she told him, "but then I seem to be reaching an age when everyone looks rather young to me.''

"I am seven and thirty. And if you would hold a lantern above my head, you would see I am possessed of more than my share of gray hairs.''

"Seven and thirty,'' she repeated, shaking her head as though she did not quite believe him. "And of course there is a Mrs. Davies? Perhaps she may be persuaded to call, for we are so very isolated here. And I am sure dear Mrs. Seaton would enjoy her acquaintance—wouldn't you, Sarah?''

"Well, I—''

"My wife died some years back, I'm afraid.'' Even as he said it, he felt a stab of pain. He looked to Sarah. "Callie tells me you are a widow, Mrs. Seaton.''

"Yes.'' Her fingers shook as she lifted the cup. "Though sometimes I think I shall never get used to the notion.''

"He was a very brave young man,'' Emma Foote murmured.

He saw the distress in the younger woman's face, and he sought to rescue her by changing the subject abruptly. "If you've no wish for the cat, I suppose I could take it. My housekeeper is not particularly fond of animals, but she will not be unkind to it.''

"No!'' Callie wailed from her place beside the fire.

"Well, I—''

"Please, Mama—*please!* He won't be the least trouble, I promise you—word of a Seaton!''

"Callie, it is unbecoming to beg,'' Sarah said firmly. But as she looked into the welling eyes, she felt a stab of guilt. In her own grief and anger, she'd robbed her daughters of much. She drew in her breath, then exhaled slowly ere she nodded. "If he recovers, no doubt he will prove to be a mouser."

"Then I want a dog!" Katie protested.

"One animal is more than enough," Mrs. Foote declared firmly. She turned to Sarah. "Surely you do not mean to keep it inside?"

"Yes," she answered simply. "He cannot survive out."

"How's he to—? Mama, I don't want to clean up after him," Katie said.

"I shall see he is civilized," Callie promised.

"Yes, well, see that you do," Emma Foote murmured. "Oh, dear, I have quite forgotten the bread and butter, haven't I? I shall be back in a trice."

Still cradling her new-won cat in her arms, Callie followed Mrs. Foote into the small kitchen area. "He's nice—Dr. Davies, I mean—isn't he, Auntie?" she murmured, trying to soothe her.

For a moment, the old woman's bird-bright eyes darted to where the doctor sat conversing politely with Sarah. "I think we ought to open the peach preserves," she answered obtusely. Then, leaning lower, she whispered, "He's a handsome enough man that if I were thirty years younger, I should discover an ailment. I only wish—" She caught herself and shook her head. "No, it would not serve."

"What?"

"Nothing. Besides, it would take a miracle."

Before Callie could press her further, Mrs. Foote hastily arranged slices of bread in a circle around a large round platter. In the center, she put the butter and a small dish of the precious peach preserves. "There," she declared. "Fit for the queen herself."

"Queen Victoria? She eats bread and butter?"

"And jam, like the rest of us. What's good is good, no matter what you've got," the old woman declared triumphantly. "And there's none as have got better peach preserves than mine."

They sat, chairs drawn before the fire, and gorged on her exquisite preserves, slathering it over the rich Cornish butter on fresh bread, not minding that it was not clotted cream and scones. When admonished not to eat with the cat on her lap, Callie reluctantly pushed it off and went to wash her hands. It followed a few awkward steps after her, then discovering that effort too great, crawled to rest against Dr. Davies' foot.

He sat there, feeling a measure of contentment as he listened to the fire pop and crackle warmly, in contrast to the wind that howled outside. He ought to go, but he was loath to rise, to face that raw, wet wind yet. He was so tired he had to blink to stay awake, he had to blink to focus on the Foote woman as she rattled on about smugglers and all other manner of nonsense.

And all the while, Sarah Seaton sat there, pleasant yet oddly distant, as though if her composure slipped she would shatter. He'd seen women like that before, women afraid to live again, women who let grief suck the life from them. And he wanted to shake her, to tell her to let go of the past while she was still young enough to live the future. And then he caught himself before his fancy roamed too far. Who was he to shake anyone for sharing his own faults? Maybe she could no more let go of her memories than he. Besides, he couldn't think rationally anymore . . . not at all . . .

"Mama, I think Dr. Davies has gone to sleep," Katie decided.

"Don't be silly," Callie retorted, only to be drawn

up short. He did look as though he slept. As Auntie Foote's eyebrow rose in disapproval, Callie hastened to defend him. "Well, if he has, no doubt it is because he was awake all night. It cannot be easy to be a doctor."

"No. No, of course not," Sarah murmured. Rising, she picked up her fringed shawl and started to place it over him. His head lay back awkwardly against the top of the rocker, and for a moment she stared down into his face. Asleep, he looked quite youthful, despite the sprinkling of gray in his wind-rumpled, soft brown hair. She felt a surge of tenderness for a man who would take the time to bring Callie home when he was so obviously exhausted. "Poor dear. Katie, fetch a pillow, will you?"

She lay the shawl over his shoulders and started to tuck it around him, then hesitated awkwardly. He was as solid as Ned had been, and somehow it did not seem right that she should be touching him. And yet there was a vulnerability in his face that was missing when he was awake, a vulnerability that seemed to reach out to her. She was being silly, she decided. It was but her own loneliness hoaxing her.

Katie handed her the flat feather pillow, and this time Sarah resolutely thrust it between his head and the wooden chairback. When she looked up, Emma Foote was smiling almost slyly at her. "Well," Sarah snapped with asperity, "you would not wish him a stiff neck, would you?"

"No, of course not, dear. I was but wondering what we should feed him for dinner."

"No doubt he will waken before then."

But the first spray of cold rain hit the windows, sounding like several pebbles thrown by a child. Then came the wind, blowing in from above the crashing sea. The howling mingled with the slap of waves against the rocks below and the sudden, hard-pelting rain that rattled the panes. Despite the high glass chimney, the change in the air caused the lamp to flicker.

"Even if he does wake, you cannot mean to send him out in this."

"He can have my mutton stew, for I am sick of it," Callie offered.

"Mine also," Katie chimed in.

"Scarce a meal fit for company," Emma Foote protested. "If I'd have known, I'd—"

"Well, you could not have known," Sarah declared impatiently. "And he may not wish to stay."

Callie retrieved her reluctant cat from the doctor's foot and carried him to the hearth seat. Settling him on her lap, she began stroking the thick black fur. Bending low, she whispered, "He wants to stay, doesn't he?" into the cat's twitching ear. And to her, it seemed as though the animal nodded.

"What are you going to name the creature?" Katie asked, dropping down beside her. "Blackie? Smoke? Soot?" she suggested.

"Magic," Callie answered without thinking. And as she said it, the cat began to purr. "Magic," she repeated, warming to the idea. "He likes it."

Spencer Davies woke slowly, aware first of the awful crick in his neck, then of the whispers around him, and finally of the savory smell of food cooking. He'd been dreaming, but he couldn't remember about what. He opened his eyes and blinked, trying to assimilate his surroundings. When he saw Sarah Seaton, consciousness flooded back. He sat up sheepishly.

"Must've dozed off," he mumbled apologetically. "Your pardon."

"We did not mind at all," she reassured him. "Though I'm afraid all we have to offer tonight is mutton stew."

"Oh, I could not impose. Indeed, I—" His words were cut short by a flash of lightning, followed by a crash of thunder that seemed to shake the room. "Must've slept harder than I thought," he admitted. "Comfortable chair."

"It was Papa's," Callie informed him. "It is the only piece Mama brought from—"

"Callie!" Sarah reproved sharply.

"Sorry, Mama."

"Ah, the mysterious woman who has set the village tongues to wagging," he teased.

For a moment, Sarah was taken aback. Then she shrugged. "Oh. Yes, I suppose it must seem so," was all she said.

He would have liked to pursue the matter, to discover whence she came, but it was as though she'd closed the door on him. Instead he rose, straightened his rumpled coat, and walked to peer out the window. It was already dark, and he could see nothing beyond the sheet of water that poured down the pane.

"Not a fit night to be out, is it?"

"No, but perhaps it will subside before supper is done," Sarah murmured.

"I ought to be going home. Mrs. Clark—"

"Oh, do stay, sir!" Callie pleaded. "I have already said you can have my portion."

"I'd do no such thing, my dear."

"Oh, I shan't mind it," she assured him blithely. "I cannot abide it."

"Not a very good thing to say," he chided.

"Well, I ate my share of it yesterday," she declared, unabashed. "When Auntie Foote makes mutton stew, she always makes too much, and we must save it in the cold cellar."

"I thought you liked it," the old woman said, obviously injured.

"Actually, Mrs. Foote's stew is quite good, sir," Sarah told him.

In the end, he decided to stay, telling himself that only a fool would attempt the rocky path down the steep hill in a raging storm at night. Though he supposed Mrs. Clark would be scandalized if he did not get himself home soon.

The food was good albeit simple fare, and despite their avowed dislike of it, both little girls partook of it also. During the meal he observed all of them, noting that their manners definitely betrayed breeding far above their current existence, and once again his curiosity was piqued. Why would a woman of obvious high station choose to live in near poverty in such an isolated place? Did she have something to hide beyond her grief? Or were her circumstances so limited that it was all she could afford? Surely, if the latter were the case, she could apply to live on some relative's sleeve.

As the plates were removed, he studied her covertly, wondering what had made a woman so young decide to wither in her widow's weeds, when there must have been a dozen suitors willing to assume responsibility for her and her children. She was still trim enough, and if she would but forgo that ridiculous hairstyle, if she would but attempt to make herself more attractive, there was no question she could improve her situation. It was a waste, an utter waste, he found himself deciding. And if she would not think of herself, she ought to think of those children.

"I'm afraid you are staring again," she chided him.

"Hmm? Oh." He shrugged casually, then leaned back in his chair before he admitted idly, "I was wondering why a woman like yourself has not rewed."

Callie rubbed Magic, wishing her mother would not give him a sharp set-down for his impertinence. Instead, Sarah stared into her teacup for a long moment before meeting his eyes. "One could ask the same of you, couldn't one, Dr. Davies?" she countered finally.

"In my case, I—"

Auntie Foote leaned closer to hear him, but she was destined for disappointment. Whatever he meant to say was drowned out in the loud pounding and urgent shouts at the door. "Good heavens!" she gasped, frightened. "You do not suppose it is smugglers?"

"Auntie sees smugglers at every turn," Katie explained, disgusted.

Apparently Tom did also, for the boy came down from his own meal in the loft to answer the door. At first, it was difficult to make heads or tails of the excited, nearly hysterical conversation, but the words "Dr. Davies" stood out.

Squaring his shoulders resolutely, Spencer went to the door. "I am Davies," he declared above the din.

"Oh, thankee, God!" the fellow cried. "Missus Clark said ye might be here. Ye got to come, sor—it's real bad like—real bad!" He began to blubber, and had to stop to wipe his streaming eyes. At first, Spencer thought it was the rain, but then he knew better, for the man went on, "Storm caught 'em out, sor! My boy was with 'em! And—and—"

Spencer turned around quickly, barking at Sarah, "Have you any brandy? Or any spirits at all?"

She shook her head. "Only tea."

"Ain't got time fer tea!" the fellow fairly howled. "Boat's down—pieces is a-washing up on the rocks. My boy's down there—and—and they ain't all dead!" Behind him, lightning flashed again and again, and the rain blew through the door.

"Damn! I don't have my bag," Spencer muttered. "I'll be right there as soon as I get it."

"Tom can fetch your bag," Sarah offered quickly. She turned to find her cloak. "Bar the door, Emma," she ordered.

"Where the devil—?"

"Perhaps I can be of help." Sarah's eyes met Spencer's. "My husband was in the military, sir, and I have seen grievous injuries before."

"It won't be pretty," he warned her.

"Sarah, you cannot!" Mrs. Foote protested. " 'Tis not at all the thing for a gentlewoman . . ."

But her words were lost in the howl of the wind as Sarah ducked outside. At first, the wet blast nearly tore the cloak from her back, but she managed to close the frogs and pull it closer about her. Tom ran after her to thrust one of two parafin lanterns into her hand, then continued on down the hill ahead of her. Spencer Davies took the lantern, holding it high to light the rocky path.

Emma Foote watched nervously until both yellow balls of light faded from sight, then closed the door and barred it. Rain soaked her apron, her gown, and the floor beneath her feet. When she turned back to the girls, it was difficult to tell what disgusted her the most.

"Well, do not be standing there gaping," she said crossly. "Just because your mama's a foolish creature silly enough to go off into a night like this . . ." Her voice trailed off, and she shook her head. "How she's to show to advantage when she's half-drowned, I'm sure I do not know," she added obtusely as she sought her mop. "More like to catch her death, I'd say."

But for all her rough tongue, the old woman was an easy touch, and once the floor was mopped and the room set to rights, she let Callie and Katie stay up for a while to keep her company. Outside, the storm showed no signs of abating, and frequent flashes of lightning illuminated the otherwise dim room. Finally, when the smoke from the old cruzie lamp became too thick, she blew it out, and the three of them sat before the fire as the rest of the room was plunged into darkness.

"We could tell witches' tales," Katie suggested. " 'Tis the right sort of night."

"Witches' tales!" the old woman snorted. "I should think not. You are better advised to study your Scripture like a God-fearing Christian."

"Do you believe in witches, Auntie?" Callie asked curiously.

"I don't believe in 'em, and I don't not believe in 'em," Mrs. Foote declared. "I just don't talk about such things." She shuddered visibly. "An awful night. An awful night," she repeated. Then, turning her attention to them, she decided rather abruptly, "Off to bed, both of you. No sense in everybody worrying, is there?"

Callie carried the cat with her into the small room she shared with her sister. As Katie undressed and pulled her nightgown over her head, her voice was muffled. "If you think I am about to sleep with that creature, you can think again, Calista Seaton."

"He won't take up any room," Callie promised.

They were in complete darkness, and it wasn't until Katie slid beside her into bed that she felt the cat. Afraid her sister would tell, the younger girl offered, "I'll let you hold him a little while."

"Thank you, no," Katie snapped peevishly. "I don't—"

"Do you think he could be a witch's cat?"

"If he wasn't, you'd have been birched for scaring Mama like that. And Auntie Foote and Mama would *never* have let you have him." Katie yawned. "But whoever heard of naming a creature Magic?"

"I think it suits him." For a moment, Callie was quiet, then she could stand it no longer. "And I think he is magic, you know." Her voice dropped to a whisper. "I wished Dr. Davies would come home with me. And I wished he would stay to tea. And I wished he would stay to dine with us."

"You were afraid Mama meant to birch you."

"It doesn't matter. He stayed."

"I suppose the storm had nothing to do with it?" Katie countered sarcastically.

Callie rubbed the cat's ears affectionately and listened to it purr. "Maybe he caused the storm, Kate."

This time, Katie sighed her disgust. "Go to sleep."

Broken only by the rain and the rumbling thunder, a silence of sorts enveloped the small room. Callie sank into the featherbed and closed her arms over her cat. "You know," she said softly, "I think I shall marry a doctor when I grow up."

"Don't be silly," Katie murmured drowsily. "Seatons make grand marriages. Now—*will* you go to sleep, or must I call to Auntie?''

But for a long time after the older girl slept, Callie lay awake stroking her cat, wishing fervently that she could make her mother happy.

The rain was cold, the rocks slick, as they edged their way down the steep, zigzagging path to the roiling surf below. Beneath them lanterns bobbed, and there mingled shouts and anguished cries as each new body was discovered broken upon the rugged, rocky beach. Only once did anyone call out, ''This un's alive! Over here!''

Throwing propriety to the howling wind, Sarah grasped Spencer Davies' arm tightly and held on, slipping and sliding her way down. Her teeth chattered, and her hair dripped water into her eyes, telling her she looked a fright, but she didn't care.

''You ought to have boots for this,'' he told her.

She shook her head. ''I could not feel the rocks through the soles, and I should fall. This way at least I know where they are.''

He wished he'd not allowed her to come, for by the sound of it, the sight below would probably turn her stomach. ''Mrs. Foote was right—you'll catch your death in this.''

''I am never ill, sir—never.''

They were nearly down. Only one last rock jutted out over the water, then cut steeply into a cavelike crevice eroded by centuries of tides. It was the shortest way. He stopped, held up the lantern, and looked at her.

''Can you jump, do you think?''

"Better than you, no doubt, for I have skirts to break my fall."

"I'll attempt to catch you," he promised.

He tried to set the lantern down, but the wind blew it, sending it tumbling into the rough seas. Muttering a curse under his breath, Spencer allowed himself to slide the length of the rock into the narrow crevice. Almost immediately he felt a tug at his sleeve.

"One's alive—mebbe two!" someone shouted over the wind.

"Be right there!" he shouted back. Looking upward, he held out his arms to catch Sarah Seaton. She came down in a swoosh as her wet skirts billowed, then enveloped the both of them like a heavy sack. His hands slid over her ribs before he could grasp her waist. Her corset stays felt like bands of steel beneath her wet gown. But he'd give her one thing—she was as pluck to the bone as her daughter. "Are you all right?" he asked quickly.

"Yes," she answered simply.

She pushed her soggy, tangled hair back from her face and tried to see. A villager held out his lantern, and she gasped. At her feet lay a man scarce past his boyhood. There was no need to ask—his head lolled back, and his vacant eyes stared. His arm hung as though it had nearly been pulled from the socket.

"Drowned. Poor devil," the villager muttered.

"How many?" she heard Spencer Davies ask.

"Four drowned, two was beat to death on the rocks, and the Hicks boy managed to crawl to land. Johnny Burton's in a bad way—chest crushed, by the looks of it. They were fishing and couldn't make it in before the storm hit."

"Billy Stowe's missing," someone added. "No sign of 'im."

As though to give the lie to the other man's words, several bottles of unstamped whiskey lay broken upon the narrow beach, and the remnants of crates bobbed atop the wild, white waves. Spencer fought his own rising anger. It did no good to preach, not now, not when smuggling was a way of life. Instead, he turned his attention to the pitiful survivors.

One look told him that Johnny Burton could not be saved. He shook his head, again repressing his anger. "As soon as your fellow fetches my bag, I'd have you give him laudanum," he told Sarah.

"How much?"

"Enough to ease him—twenty drops or so."

She didn't need to ask anything more. Pity overwhelmed her when she looked at the man. He knew. As Spencer Davies moved on to examine the other survivor, she knelt beside Johnny Burton and took his hand, while someone held a lantern above her. Johnny struggled to sit, then fell back coughing as the pink foam welled from his mouth. Not knowing what else to do, Sarah raised his head to her lap and held him, stroking his wet hair but avoiding his bruised temple.

"It was the rocks," the man above her said.

It seemed an eternity before Tom came crawling down with Davies' medicine bag. Finally, after the doctor rummaged through it, Tom brought her the laudanum. There was nothing to put it in, no water to cut the taste of it, but she knew it did not matter. Unstoppering the bottle with her teeth, she quite literally poured half the contents into Johnny Burton's mouth. He choked and sputtered, spraying the bloody foam onto her cloak, and then he managed to swallow.

She sat there in the rocky mud cradling him until the fear gradually faded from his glazing eyes, and all the while she continued to stroke his hair, knowing that there was nothing more she could do. He seemed to ease for a time, then stiffened, reaching upward, before he fell back limply into her arms. He was gone.

She felt the hysteria rising within her until she could stand it no longer. Easing him from her lap, she rose to lean against a cold rock. Tears came, followed by racking sobs. The man who'd held the lantern for her reached out awkwardly to comfort her, then dropped his hand.

The old pain washed over her as fresh now as if she'd just been told. Had Ned died like that? In a stranger's arms? Or had there been any to hold him at all?

The Hicks boy was luckier. He'd survived with naught but numerous cuts and bruises. Spencer finished closing the worst of his wounds and stood to call for the laudanum. He didn't see Sarah Seaton. Someone thrust the bottle into his hand and he guessed at enough to ease Robert Hicks' pain before the boy was carried up.

"The woman's in a bad way, sir. Took it hard when Burton passed on."

The woman? He must've meant Sarah Seaton. "Where?" was all Spencer asked.

"Crying her eyes out over there."

The surge of energy was gone, replaced by a fatigue greater than any he'd ever known. He felt as if he carried the weight of ten on his shoulders, that he walked on limbs of stone as he slogged his way through the mud to her.

"Mrs. Seaton?" He touched her shaking shoulder

gently, but she did not respond. For a moment, he felt utterly helpless to comfort her. "Sarah," he tried again, turning her around. "There was nothing you could have done, my dear."

He couldn't tell whether she shook from sobbing or from the cold, but her whole body trembled. Without thinking, he drew her against him, holding her. As his arms closed around her, she shuddered, then went utterly to pieces, crying hysterically into his coat. Against his chest she babbled almost incoherently something about "my poor Ned," and "I should have been there—I should!" He was at a loss to follow her.

"Sarah . . . Sarah . . ." he murmured soothingly, smoothing her wet, tangled hair against her back. Pins came out in his hand. "There was naught you could do . . . there was naught you could do."

"I could have been there! But he would not let me go!"

"Shhhhh. Who would not let you go?"

"Sir Richard. He—he said Ned did n-not n-need me!"

Others were gathering around, curious at the sight of him holding the strange woman. Reluctantly, he set her back and brushed at the wet streaks on her face. "Come on—we've got to get you inside and dry, Mrs. Seaton, before you are taken ill yourself." His hand dropped down to clasp hers; then he turned to the silent villagers. "I shall take Mrs. Seaton home. You can take the Hicks boy to my house and explain to Mrs. Clark that I shall be there directly." He looked to where Johnny Burton lay and sighed heavily. "Someone had best carry up the bodies. I shall execute the necessary papers tomorrow."

The climb up was even more arduous than the journey down, but between him and the boy Tom, they managed to push and pull Sarah Seaton over the slippery rocks. Once into the main cartway, she fell in beside them silently, and scarce a word was spoken before they reached the cottage door. But it didn't matter—he was too tired for the niceties of speech, anyway.

She was composed now, though her face was white and drawn in the yellow lantern light, and her eyes were haunted still. He wished again he'd not allowed her to go with him. It had been a man's work, not something for a gentlewoman to witness.

She stopped outside her door, but she did not look at him. "I'm sorry," she mumbled, then fled inside, leaving him to wonder what she meant.

"For what? You were magnificent, Mrs. Seaton," he called after her.

There was no answer, and he wasn't even sure she'd heard him. Tom hesitated before blurting out, "Things ain't easy fer her, ye know." Then he too was gone.

His body aching, Spencer Davies walked slowly down the steep hill into the village. He felt defeated. It was all so senseless. Seven men and boys dead over a few cases of whiskey. Over an obstinate refusal to pay taxes on them. Resolutely, he forced his thoughts away from death and tried to think of the living.

He could still feel the stays of Sarah Seaton's corset beneath her wet gown, and he could still feel her body against his. And the loneliness nearly overwhelmed him. It had been so long, so very long since the last time he'd held a woman. So very long since he'd known the joy of loving one.

The sun streamed through his bedchamber window, making it seem as though the storm had been only a bad dream. But as he sat on the edge of his bed he looked down, seeing the cuts and scratches on his hands, mute testimony to the desperate digging they'd done amongst the rocks. These were the hands that had sewn the Hicks boy up. These were the hands that had not even tried to save Johnny Burton. As he sat there, the memory of the whole night's events flooded over him again, and he recalled Sarah Seaton.

Rising with a groan, he poured water into the washbowl. It was cold, too cold to shave with. He opened the door and bawled, "Mrs. Clark—hot water, if you will! And a strong cup of coffee also."

It did not take her long to come up. Obviously, she'd been waiting for him to rise, waiting to hear of the wreck. She set a steaming pitcher inside his door.

"The coffee is ready when ye are come down." When he did not answer her, she added, "There's patients already awaiting fer ye. Mrs. Wilson's boy's got the cough, and the Seaton child's back with the cat." She sniffed. "Next thing ye know, they'll be a-bringing ye horses. Ye'll have ter make it plain ye don't mean ter make it a practice, I'd say."

"Well, I suppose I could treat the scours," he teased her, grinning.

"Oh, be done with ye!"

She retreated, leaving him to his toilet. He stripped out of his nightshirt and stood before his cheval mirror, thinking he was neither so young nor so handsome as the boy who'd once thought he could save the world from pestilence. At seven and thirty, there was a line or two here and there, not to mention a bit of telltale gray in his hair. That it was to be expected was not in truth much consolation until it was weighed against the alternative.

He washed quickly, promising himself a soaking bath ere the day was done, then changed the water for shaving. He worked the brush over the soap, making a lather, then began to cover the stubble on his face. It wasn't a pretty face, but then neither was it the sort that made anyone cringe, he decided judiciously, wondering what Mrs. Seaton had thought of it.

Sarah Seaton. He could close his eyes and feel those corset stays still. It was a pity—she was a pretty woman, far too much so to wither alone. And once again he wondered how she came to be in this wild corner of Cornwall, where life was isolated and hard, where many were too poor to pay for his services, where bills ran "until the next catch"—or until the next illegal cargo landed.

It was, he decided, that she was impoverished and possibly unwilling to hang on a richer relation's sleeve. Briefly he wondered if Mrs. Clark had cooked the goose that Will Springs had given him the day before. If not, he just might send it home with Miss Calista Seaton. Or he might take it himself.

When he came down, he discovered the child with the cough and quickly dealt with that problem—the juice of a lemon, four tablespoons of rum, and a bit of honey in a bottle of water. And orders to prop the boy up at night. And of course the usual request that if he ran a fever, his mother was to bring him back for a powder. He didn't want to prescribe salicylic acid salts unless necessary. People were too inclined to look for quick cures and abuse them.

Calista Seaton waited patiently in his front saloon, seated in his favorite wing chair, her feet dangling more than half a foot above the floor. On her lap, the black kitten played with the tassels that closed her cloak. Her black stockings had a hole in them, but she made no effort to hide it.

"Well, he does not appear to have taken a turn for the worse," Spencer observed, smiling down at her.

"No," she declared proudly. "In fact, he gets around rather well, sir, and Auntie has decided he's quite civilized—when he is not under her feet."

"I see."

She squirmed in the chair and twisted her head to look up at him with those lovely wide blue eyes. "You must wonder why I am here."

"It had occurred to me to inquire," he admitted. "But as I have not yet breakfasted, perhaps you would care to join me?"

"We had porridge." She wrinkled her nose as she said it, indicating quite clearly that it was not a particular favorite.

"A coddled egg, perhaps? Or toast and jam?" he coaxed.

"Well—"

"And perhaps a bowl of milk for—"

"Magic," she reminded him.

"For Magic." He turned to his housekeeper, who hovered curiously behind him. "Mrs. Clark, we shall require a bowl of milk for Magic—and something for Miss Seaton also."

"Toast and jam," Callie said quickly.

"And hot chocolate, I expect."

It was not until the child was settled across from him at the table, her napkin tucked over her clean smock, that he asked casually, "If it is not Magic in need of my attention, I assume there must be something else.''

She nodded. "Mama."

The memory of Sarah Seaton as she'd clung to him, sobbing and shaking, came vividly to mind. "Your mama's ill, then?''

She shifted in her seat and looked down at the cat on the polished floor. "Well, she does not *appear* ill," she conceded. "But something is quite wrong with her. They do not know I am here," she admitted truthfully. "But I had to come, sir.''

"Oh?" He passed the toast rack to her. "Perhaps you had best tell me about it.''

"You don't mind?''

"No.''

"I knew I liked you when you saved Magic," she declared. "I knew that you would be the sort of person to care when Mama does not wish to get out of bed.''

"Perhaps she is but tired," he offered. "She did not pass a pleasant night.''

The black kitten dragged its splinted leg over to his foot, then climbed with determination into his lap, where it found the sausage on his plate more to its liking than milk. Holding Magic away from his food, Spencer waited for Callie to tell him more.

"If it were only that, sir!" She stopped to take a goodly bite of her toast, then chewed it. Swallowing, she managed to go on. "When Papa—when Papa first died, she stayed abed for days, and Grandpapa said she'd lost her mind.''

He nodded. "Many people grieve alone, I'm afraid.''

"Well, that is how she looks this morning—the very same way—and—and I'm afraid." She fixed her eyes on her plate. "You may think it silly, but I know she is sadder again."

"I don't think it silly at all."

She sucked in her breath, then let it out quickly. "Then would you come to see her, sir?"

"I can scarce go where I am not called, Callie, particularly not if your mama means to remain in bed."

"You could say you came to look at Magic, couldn't you? I could go home, and you could come to see him."

By nature he was not a meddler, but it was difficult to resist the appeal in those blue eyes. And he had to admit that Sarah Seaton had occupied much of his thought since the previous night. He could still smell the rain in her wet hair. When he looked down, the black kitten had a paw in his plate and was making a valiant effort to capture his half-eaten sausage. He pushed it gently off his lap, although not before its claws made a trail down his leg; then he tossed the meat after it.

"Civilized, eh? Go on, you little heathen, eat it, though I am fairly certain that Mrs. Clark will disapprove of both of us." Reaching for the pot, he warmed his coffee, then remarked, "I suppose I could do that."

"Would you? I *knew* when I saw you that you were the best of gentlemen, sir!" She jumped up and scooped Magic into her arms. "I will go home and make certain she combs her hair before you come." With that obtuse statement, she was off, leaving the crust of her toast still on her plate.

Mrs. Clark stood in the doorway, shaking her head. "That child is too forward by half, if ye was ter ask me. 'Tis plain to see there is no father in the house."

"Her father was a soldier, I'm told. I believe he died either in the Crimea or in India."

"She's old enough to be off ter school."

"There's an older one also." He rose and stretched. "I suspect they are suffering hardship since he died, and there is no money for anything."

"The poor thing," she murmured sympathetically. "An awful thing to lose her papa."

"Yes. You haven't put the goose in the pot yet, have you?"

"Wrung its neck this very morning—all plucked and ready fer it."

"Well, I have decided I favor the cold pork from yesterday."

She cast him a knowing look. "Would ye be telling me as you're giving away a fat goose?"

"Yes."

Regret crossed her face, then she sighed. " 'Tis a good person ye are, Spencer Davies—better'n me. Meself, I'd just give 'em a piece of it."

"There are four of them, Mrs. Clark—two women and two children. And we can spare the goose."

"Aye. God grant that they appreciate ye fer it."

He felt a fool, trudging up the hill with a goose wrapped in paper, carrying his bag, ostensibly for the purpose of examining a cat. But foolish or not, he also felt almost young again. Gone was the ache, the fatigue of his work, replaced by an anticipation at the thought of seeing Sarah Seaton again.

Mrs. Foote opened the door and seemed quite surprised to see him. Behind her, Katie Seaton looked up from what appeared to be her lessons, while her sister continued working as though she'd not noted him. But she managed a quick peek out of the corner of her eye. The child was a baggage, no doubt about it.

"Yes?" Mrs. Foote prompted.

He felt utterly callow, as unaccomplished as a youth about to embark on his first flirtation. "I was in the neighborhood," he began, knowing how implausible that must sound, given that there was nothing else on the hill, "and I thought perhaps I ought to look in on Callie's cat."

"It's getting about—one could say too well, in fact," the old woman declared. "But you may see for yourself." She stood back to let him enter.

"And I brought something for Mrs. Seaton."

"Oh? I'm afraid she is a trifle indisposed this morning." Nonetheless, she took the package and peered at it curiously.

"It's just a goose—but a fat one," he hastened to add. "My housekeeper was but saying earlier that we can scarce eat all I am paid, and well—well, anyway, it is already dressed and ready for the pot," he finished rather lamely.

"How very kind of you, sir."

Katie rose and peered at the unwrapped bird. "Can we have it roasted, Auntie? I am ever so tired of stew."

"I have never claimed to be a cook," Mrs. Foote sniffed. "Indeed, but I—"

"I know—you were Mama's nurse."

Callie continued to sit, her book perched on one knee, her cat on the other. Without looking up, she said, "Auntie, I think all you do is salt it and put it into the oven."

"Exactly," her sister agreed. "It cannot be nearly so difficult as a stew, I'd think."

"Well, I am sure we shall manage. Thank you, sir."

He walked to where Callie sat, her head down, her hand stroking the thick black fur. "And how is Magic today?"

"Better, sir." Her eyes darted to the closed door, then back to him. "But perhaps as you are here, you could see to Mama."

"Nothing's wrong with Mama," Katie protested. "She is just—" She stopped and sighed. "Well, you know."

"She cried half the night. You heard her, and don't say you did not."

"She's sad, that's all."

"She's always sad," Callie shot back.

He looked at Mrs. Foote, and the old woman appeared truly distressed. "Surely you must understand, Dr. Davies, but that man's death brought back unpleasant memories, and her health has not been the best since—" Her eyes met his briefly, then she averted her head. "You must not think I blame you, sir, for she would go."

"Perhaps if I looked in on her, I—"

"Would you, sir?" Katie asked eagerly. "Maybe she is but in need of a tonic—or an elixir—or something."

"Something," Callie agreed. "She needs to forget Papa, for he is not coming back."

"Callie!"

"Well, I can scarce remember him, but I cannot think he would wish for her to be sad. Mama always says that if you love someone, you want the best for them, after all." Callie's hand continued to stroke the black cat. "I would wish for her to be happy again."

"It takes time, Callie," Mrs. Foote reminded her. "You must not expect too much of her."

"He was never at home, Auntie, so how can she—?"

" 'Tis enough, Calista," the old woman interrupted sharply. "I'd not hear you criticize your mama or your papa."

"I wasn't, but . . ."

Mrs. Foote's birdlike eyes darted to his face again. "Do you think perhaps a tonic would help, sir?"

"Perhaps," he agreed noncomittally.

She nodded, then walked to open a door. "Mrs. Seaton—Sarah—?" she began tentatively. "Dr. Davies is come to see how you are."

"I am not receiving," the woman in the bed mumbled.

Mrs. Foote shrugged expressively and shook her head. But he moved past her into the bedchamber and pulled a chair close to the bed. "Leave us, and shut the door," he ordered. Turning his attention to Sarah, he said, "I was under the impression you were ill, Mrs. Seaton."

Her eyes were red, her head a disarrayed mass of black silk against the pillow. She clutched the coverlet to her chin.

"I am never ill, sir."

"But you are not feeling at all the thing, are you?" he murmured soothingly.

"No, but it isn't your fault. It isn't anyone's fault but mine."

"Blue-deviled, eh?"

"Yes."

She did in truth look awful. He reached to touch her forehead to reassure himself that she was not feverish, but her brow was cool. His hand lingered to brush the hair back lightly.

"There's nothing you can do," she said dully. "There isn't anything anyone can do."

The resignation in her voice made him angry. She was too young to curl up like a dying leaf on a vine. She still had too many years to live. And if he could go on without Anne, she could survive also.

"Get up," he said curtly.

"I beg your pardon?"

"Get up," he repeated.

"You have no right—"

"Mrs. Seaton, what I am going to say, I'd say beyond the ears of your children. Now—do you get up, or do I dress you?"

"I have not the least intention—" Before she knew he meant to do it, he'd snatched the coverlet from the bed. "Really, sir, but—but—" she spluttered, her own anger rising. "You have no right to come here—you have no right to interfere!" But even as she sat up, he yanked the sheet from her hands, then stood towering over her. She crossed her arms over her breasts and leaned forward to hide from him. "Get out," she managed to say evenly. "Get out."

"Mrs. Seaton, you are in need of strong medicine," he declared. "Now, do you get up and dress yourself, or must I do it?" he repeated.

"This, sir, is indecent!"

"You are not possessed of anything I have not seen, I assure you, Mrs. Seaton," he answered calmly, reaching for the neck of her nightgown. As he undid the first button, he met her eyes soberly. "Well?"

"I think you are mad, sir." Both her hands caught at his. His fingers loosed the second button as his eyes seemed to bore into hers. His eyes were light brown like his hair. And his hands were strong. She looked away.

"I'm on the third button, Mrs. Seaton," he reminded her.

"You cannot ravish me in my own house, sir!"

"On the contrary. It is my intent to dress you."

"I can dress myself," she muttered.

He released the neck of her nightgown and straightened. "I thought you might prove to be a reasonable woman. I'll give you five minutes to make yourself presentable and come out."

"You cannot—"

"Do you want me to come back and finish the task?" he countered.

"No, of course not!" she snapped crossly. "I want you to leave me alone!"

"That, Mrs. Seaton, is a lie."

Before she could think of a suitable rejoinder, he was gone, leaving her sitting there, her hands on the buttons at her neck. She was so angry her fingers shook. How dare some country bonesetter touch her like that—as if she were some sort of common trollop! She was Sarah Elizabeth Winston Seaton, daughter of a baron, daughter-in-law to General Sir Richard Seaton! She swung her legs over the side of the bed and reached for her petticoat and pantalettes. If Ned were alive, he'd have run Spencer Davies through for his importunity! He'd have— She dropped her head into her hands as the hot tears stung her eyes. Ned was gone forever.

Katie regarded him anxiously when he came out. "Did you give her a tonic?"

"Not yet."

"Is she as mad as fire?" Callie wanted to know.

"Something like it."

The little girl sighed. "She's always either mad or sad."

"Callie! I'm sure Dr. Davies—"

"Well, she is. Even Katie says so."

"Did not."

Mrs. Foote bore a look of long-suffering. "If you are going to brangle, I would you did it outside. I seem to have a surfeit of nerves myself this morning." She looked down to where Magic was dragging his splinted leg toward Spencer Davies. "And I pray you will take that creature with you, Calista. I am sure he needs to be out to—" Her face reddened. "Well, I am sure he does."

Callie scooped up the kitten and held it close, whispering so low that her words were indiscernible to the others, "They don't know you are magic, but I do."

"What?" Mrs. Foote demanded suspiciously.

"Nothing, Auntie."

The door to the bedchamber opened, and Sarah Seaton emerged in another black cotton dress. She'd washed her face and combed her hair back into the ugly roll on her neck. But her chin was held high, and her blue eyes were defiant.

"Dear Sarah—only look! Dr. Davies has brought us a goose this morning!" Mrs. Foote tittered nervously.

"Whatever for?"

"Why, to eat, of course," the old woman answered.

But Sarah wasn't looking at her. "Now that I am up, I trust you mean to go," she told Spencer.

Her voice was husky, probably from crying, but he found it appealing. "I thought you might prefer a walk in the sun," he said, ignoring the gibe.

"No."

"I cannot think you would wish anyone else to hear what I mean to say to you."

"I have had enough lectures of Sir Richard!" she retorted angrily.

"The air might do you good, dear," Mrs. Foote offered timidly. "But do take a cloak, or the black merino jacket."

"Half an hour," he coaxed. "Then you can tell me to mind my own business."

"I scarce need half an hour for that," she muttered.

"Sometimes there is more solace to be had in speech than in laudanum, Mrs. Seaton."

"I don't—" She stopped. It had taken six drops of laudanum in the night before she had slept.

"We were thinking that perhaps you are in need of a tonic, Sarah," the old woman told her.

There was not a tonic on earth that could cure what ailed her, and Sarah knew it. But they were both watching her, and she was too proud to cry in front of them.

"There's naught you can say in half an hour that will change anything, sir."

"I might surprise you."

"And then you will leave me in peace?"

"Then you may wish me at Jericho."

"All right." Even as she said it, she surprised herself. She'd meant to come out and send him on his way, but there was something in his eyes that stopped her, something that bespoke a genuine concern for her. However, that did not mean she was any more willing to be bullied by him than by Sir Richard. "If I am not back within the half-hour, Mrs. Foote, you have my leave to summon the constable," she muttered grudgingly.

Outside, the two girls sat on the step, teasing Callie's kitten with a string, watching him try to bat at it without putting weight on the splinted leg. When the door opened behind them, Callie jumped up and picked up the little cat, giving Spencer and her mother room to pass.

"Where are you going?" Katie asked curiously.

"Walking," Spencer answered.

"Can I come?"

But Callie caught at her sleeve and pinched her arm. "Auntie has things for us to do."

"I cannot think what."

"Well, she does," the younger girl asserted definitely.

"I shan't be long, anyway," Sarah promised them.

Katie waited only until they were beyond hearing before she rounded on her sister. "You just didn't want to go, did you? Well, I did, and—" She stopped. "What are you doing?" she demanded crossly. "Are you kissing that thing?"

"Hush—I'm trying to cast a spell."

"You don't even know any magic words," the older girl said scornfully.

"Maybe he will be like Aladdin's lamp, and I will merely have to wish."

"Oh, for—" But Callie continued rubbing her cheek against the animal's soft fur, whispering to it. "What sort of spell?"

"You'll see."

"I won't believe it unless you tell me now," Katie challenged. "How else am I to know if it works?"

"You won't tell?"

"Word of a Seaton—cross my heart."

"If you tell, it might not work." Callie leaned closer

to whisper into Katie's ear, "I want Mama to marry Dr. Davies."

"*What?*" the older girl fairly shrieked. "Of all the— the nonsensical notions, Calista Seaton, this one must surely take the biscuit! Mama would never—besides, she does not even know him!"

"I said it was a spell," Callie insisted defensively.

"Well, it won't happen. Never ever ever."

"We'll see. Magic knows he can do it—don't you, Magic?" she murmured to the kitten.

Neither said a word as they walked up the steep path. He let her lead the way, while he tried to compose his thoughts before he spoke. He knew she thought he did not understand, but the trouble was that he understood all too well, and yet he was not at all certain he could reach beneath that shell of grief without reliving his own pain.

She stopped on the barren cliff and stared silently into the churning water below. The sound of the surf crashing over half-submerged rocks mingled with the cries of gulls and the wind that whipped at her cloak. For a time he stood silently beside her, looking downward.

"I find it strange you should like this place," he said finally.

"It is empty."

"There are those who count it haunted, you know. There are those who say the gulls cry for the souls lost down there." When she said nothing, he went on, "The Cornish are a rough lot and not above a bit of privateering—in the most macabre way, in fact. That big piece of rock down there—'tis called the Devil's Stone. In times past, they hung lanterns up here to draw ships in, and when they broke up below, they swarmed down to profit on the destruction.''

She shuddered. "Not a very delicate tale, is it?''

"I'm not a very delicate man, I'm afraid. I've seen nearly everything in my time.''

She half turned to look up at him. The sun glinted off the strands of silver in his brown hair. "No. No, you are not.''

She was perhaps the loveliest woman he'd seen since Anne. Despite the straggling tendrils of black hair that escaped the awful bun, despite the eyes reddened by crying, or the fact that she had the sniffles, he felt his pulse race when he looked at her, something that had not happened in a very long time. And he was at a loss to explain it.

He took out his handkerchief and handed it to her. "Blow your nose, will you?''

It bore the masculine scent of the Hungary water he'd used, and as she put it to her nose, she was nearly overwhelmed by the acute loneliness she felt. She blew noisily, then wadded the cloth, wondering if he expected it back in that condition. Instead, she tucked it in the pocket of her cloak.

"Thank you.''

"I have seen a lot of death and dying,'' he went on matter-of-factly. "And I've seen what it does to the living—the denial, the anger, and finally the inevitable acceptance of what cannot be changed.''

"Please, I don't want to talk about it.''

"Do you think you are the only one who has ever grieved, Mrs. Seaton?'' he asked, his voice going harsh. "Do you think you are the first widow in the world?''

"No, of course not,'' she snapped.

"You cannot progress beyond the anger, can you? Do you know what this does to your children? You would rob them of a mother, Mrs. Seaton."

"You have no right to interfere, Dr. Davies, none at all!"

"Spencer—the name is Spencer—Spence to my friends."

" 'Tis none of your affair!"

"What bothers you the most—that he left you alone by dying?"

"No! He had to go—Sir Richard made him." But even as she said it, she knew it was not so. "I could not make him stay!" she cried.

"And that hurt you, didn't it?"

"Of course it hurt. And—and then he did not come home." She fumbled in her pocket for his handkerchief and blew her nose again. "He did not come home," she repeated brokenly. "He left me behind for his father to bully." Hot tears scalded her eyes. "You cannot possibly understand!" She turned and would have stumbled back down the path, but he caught her. "Let me go!" But his hands gripped her elbows, holding her. "Let me go!"

"I know," he said softly, turning her around. "Believe me when I say I know."

"You cannot! It is not the same for a man! You could go on—you did not have to live in someone else's house!"

He shook her then, and for a moment, she stared. "You want to live, Sarah—you want to live! Do you hear me? You've got to. For Callie. For Katie. Look at you—you've made yourself the living dead. And it is insane—do you hear me? Insane! I'm telling you you do not have the right to weep and wither forever. Live,

Sarah—live!'' Her eyes were huge, frightened almost, and he could not bear it. ''God, Sarah—Sarah—''

His arms closed about her and his mouth sought hers. Her eyes fluttered, then shut tightly as she felt the strength of his body against hers. For a moment, she allowed herself to savor the feel of a man's embrace, of a man's breath caressing her face, of a man's lips promising nearly forgotten passion, and she sagged against him, clinging to him as though he were life itself.

His hands slid under her cloak and moved over her back, holding her, feeling the warmth of her flesh beneath her gown, and the odd thought crossed his mind that she wasn't wearing her corset this time. ''You are still flesh and blood, Sarah,'' he whispered against her lips. ''You are still young enough to love again.''

Her mind told her it was too soon, her body that it had been too long. With an effort, she pushed him away and stood panting as though she'd run. ''How dare you, sir? How dare you?'' she demanded, summoning up all the anger she could muster. ''I may be a widow, but I am decent!''

He'd been unprepared for the effect she had on him. ''I'm sorry,'' he said simply. ''I should not have done that.''

Somehow his words disappointed her. Her chin came up. ''No, you should not,'' she managed more calmly.

''It was my intent to ask you to think of your daughters.''

''If I did not think of them, I would not be here.'' She pulled her cloak about her as though she chilled. ''Good day, sir.''

He stood rooted to the rocky ground, torn between

what he'd intended and what he'd wanted to do. She was perhaps fifty paces ahead of him before he decided to go after her.

"Look," he said apologetically, "I am not at all in the habit of molesting females."

"I assure you I did not think anything of it."

They fell silent, and it wasn't until they'd nearly descended the steep path that she spoke again. "Was your wife pretty?"

"Yes." He took a deep breath and looked away. "She had hair like spun gold and a smile as warm as the summer sun. She was the light and joy of my life. And then she died in childbed, and I could not save her."

She felt a stab of sympathy for him. "What happened to her? I—I'm sorry—it is rude of me to pry."

"No ruder than I have been." When he raised his eyes again, they were bleak. "It would have been our first child."

"I am sorry."

"No. The sorrow is mine. I was a doctor—I should have known something was wrong. But I waited too long—I told her the first always came hard."

Without thinking, she laid her hand on his arm. "You don't have to tell me, Spencer—truly you don't."

"I have to tell somebody, I suppose. God knows I cannot live with it. The babe came breech. I tried to turn it, to no avail. She bled and bled—and I—and I could not stop it, Sarah! She died." His shoulders shook briefly, then he seemed to gain control. "The babe did not survive." His mouth flattened and he exhaled heavily. "It was a girl, and she would have been Callie's age now. Perhaps that is why I like your little daughter." When he looked at her again, his eyes were wet. "You do not have the market on anger and sorrow, Sarah Seaton. God knows none has more regrets than I."

Her mouth twisted, and she nodded, unable to speak as the tears scalded her eyes.

"Mama! Mama!" Katie ran up, then stopped to catch her breath. "There is a letter from Grandpapa in the post!"

Sarah went pale, then recovered. "I shall be right in." Forcing a smile, she extended her hand to Spencer. "Good day, sir. And thank you for the goose. It was quite kind of you."

"Auntie is roasting it," Katie told him.

He had no excuse to linger further. Somehow disappointed, he retrieved his bag and started the rest of the way down the hill to home. When he turned back briefly, he could see that Sarah had already gone into the cottage. Squaring his shoulders, he told himself that he'd pushed too far for both of them, that all he had managed to do was expose the rawness, the hurt, that had never healed in his own soul.

Callie watched him until he was out of sight, then turned to her sister. "It did not go very well, did it?"

"Well, you can forget your silly spells, Calista Seaton," Katie whispered smugly. "He made her cry."

Sarah lay awake far into the night, listening at first to the distant rumble of thunder, then to the steady rain upon the roof. At first, she'd been unable to sleep for the bitter anger that Spencer Davies had reawakened within her. Then, as the night wore on, she had to admit the truth of much of what he'd said. It was the anger, and then the guilt, that grieved her more than the memories.

The memories themselves were pitifully few, thanks to Sir Richard. Wed at nineteen, she'd scarce had two years with Ned before he was first called away, and even those years had been spent under his father's thumb. There had been hurt and recrimination even then, hurt that he could leave her and Katie when there had been no real need beyond Sir Richard's ambition. Oh, he'd come home on leave from time to time—long enough to get Callie. Callie. His father had won that one also, for it had been he who'd insisted she be named Calista. Ned had gone, and the birth had been difficult. She'd never forget, nor forgive Sir Richard. When she'd awakened from the chloroform, he'd already named the child she'd wanted to call Elizabeth.

From the beginning, there had been the aching loneliness, the struggle to accept that she could not win over his father, the anger that Ned could leave her again and again. And the final anger that he'd gotten himself killed to please Sir Richard. He'd done everything to please his father.

As the rain pelted the windows, she tossed and turned, unable to reason it out anymore, wondering if Ned had ever truly loved her, or if their marriage was also the result of his father's ambition. And she began to wonder if his gentleness, his consideration as a lover, concealed a lack of any real passion. Certainly he'd never kissed her as Spencer Davies had—and Spencer Davies was nearly a stranger.

Did she cling to her widow's weeds out of guilt? Or was it that she could not face the truth—that Ned had loved Sir Richard more than his wife? She simply didn't know anymore.

"Mama?"

She rolled over as a flash of lightning illuminated the child in the doorway. It was Katie.

"Are you awake, Mama?" she asked tentatively.

"Yes."

The bare feet hurried across the floor and the little girl scrambled quickly into bed beside her. Sarah held her, smoothing her hair back from her temples.

"I couldn't sleep, Mama."

"Neither could I."

"Callie has her cat, but I've got nobody," the child murmured, burrowing against her.

It was as though Spencer Davies' words echoed in her ears. *Do you know what this does to your children? You would rob them of a mother . . . You would rob them of a mother . . . You would rob them of a mother . . .*

"You'll always have me," she promised gently.

"But you are always sad."

A new wave of guilt washed over her, and her arms tightened about Katie's shoulders. "I know, but I am hoping to change that, dearest. After all, I have you and Callie to love, don't I?"

"Yes." The child stirred slightly and twisted her neck to look at Sarah in the darkness. "Mama, are we going back to Grandpapa?"

Sarah was uncertain how to answer that, for she did not doubt that Katie missed all the grand things Sir Richard provided. Finally, she sighed. "I don't know."

"Well, I like Seaton Hill," the child conceded judiciously, "but it seems Grandpapa is forever making you do things you do not want." Her eyes were luminous in the dark. "I think he makes you unhappy."

Out of the mouths of babes . . . Sarah had no answer for that.

"Mama?"

"What?"

"Do you like Dr. Davies?"

And she wasn't ready to answer that one—not yet. "Why?" she countered.

"Callie thinks you do."

"Do you?"

"Well, I don't dislike him," Katie admitted. "And he seems to like you." She waited, and when Sarah said nothing, she pressed it. "Don't you think he likes you?"

The memory of Spencer Davies' kiss flooded Sarah's consciousness for a moment, and she was glad the child could not see her clearly. "Yes," she answered simply.

"Auntie Foote thinks him handsome."

"Katie—"

"Callie has hopes of him, you know."

"Oh? Well, I am not at all sure Dr. Davies thinks quite like that, so I wouldn't depend too much on what Callie hopes."

"No, I suppose not."

"Surely you do not think that I ought to set my cap for him," Sarah ventured cautiously.

"Not if you don't want to." The child pulled away and sat up in the bed. "I'm not frightened anymore, Mama." Swinging her feet over to the side, she rose and padded toward the door. Turning back there, she blurted out, "I think you ought to find someone who would not be forever leaving us."

"Maybe someday I will."

Puzzled, Sarah lay back and stared at the ceiling. What had Katie intended—to give her permission to throw her hat over the windmill for another husband?

And once again, the image of Spencer Davies came to mind. It was a ridiculous notion, one that did not bear thinking about. And yet as she closed her eyes she could feel his lips on hers, the strength of his arms encircling her.

"Well?" Callie demanded as Katie slipped back into bed. "Oooh, your feet are cold—get them off me."

Ignoring her, the older girl planted the offending feet firmly against her sister's warm backside. "Well, what?"

"Did you ask her?"

Katie sighed. "I tried."

"And?"

"I think she might like him."

"It would be a good thing, you know. She wouldn't have to go back to Grandpapa."

"I suppose." Katie reached over Callie's shoulder for Magic. "You said I could hold him if I asked."

He felt taut, tense beyond bearing, and his irritability drew sighs of resignation from Mrs. Clark. Still, he managed to go about his work, treating everything from Mrs. Williams' ague to the ribs Tim Rider got broken in a drunken brawl. He'd heard nothing from any of the Seatons, not since that day he'd made such a cake of himself on the hill.

Finally, after a protracted debate with himself, he'd made up his mind to call there again. If he had to, he'd say he'd come to check the cat's splint. And he'd take some of the buns Mrs. Clark had baked. And perhaps a trinket or two for Katie and Callie. God knew they did not appear to be possessed of much.

Once decided, he bathed and dressed with all the care of a suitor, taking the time to splash a little extra

Hungary water on his face. When he came downstairs, Mrs. Clark could scarce contain herself.

"Only fancy, Dr. Davies," she began, "but yer Mrs. Seaton—"

"She isn't my Mrs. Seaton," he interrupted brusquely.

"Well, then 'tis a pity," she shot back, unabashed. "I had it of Mrs. Burton that she called to pay her condolences over Johnny, ye know," she went on slyly.

"Oh?"

"And here ye was a-wasting a good goose on her," she murmured, shaking her head. "And her a-giving Mrs. Burton twenty quid ter help her with the burying. Ye've found yerself a rich widow, Dr. Davies."

"You must be mistaken."

"Had it of Mrs. Burton, who pried it out of the oldest girl. Yer Mrs. Seaton ain't poor atall—quite the contrary, if ye was ter have the truth o' it." Knowing that she had his full attention now, she nodded. "Rich. Was wed to General Seaton's son, the child said."

He had to sit down. General Seaton. General Sir Richard Seaton—old Bluff 'Em and Drub 'Em? Surely not. But even as he denied it, he did not truly doubt it. Seaton. Why had he been so obtuse as not to make the connection?

"Though what she's doing here, I am sure I don't know," Mrs. Clark sniffed. "Ye'd think with all that money she'd a-gone to Brighton."

He had to go—Sir Richard made him . . . He left me behind for his father to bully . . . If I did not think of them, I would not be here . . . Sarah Seaton had come to Cornwall to hide. But the child had said her grandfather had written. And there was no mistaking that it was unwelcome news to Sarah.

If he'd felt foolish before, he felt doubly so now.

How she must have laughed up her sleeve at the goose. And no wonder she repulsed him on the hill. She probably thought him not up to her weight at all.

"Was ye going out, then?"

"Eh? Oh, no. No, not at all," he murmured, chagrined.

She eyed him skeptically. "Then we are having guests, and ye fergot ter tell me?"

"No."

"Humph! Seems ter me 'tis a waste to wear that fer Mrs. Chambers' colicky baby. But then ye know what ye are about, I'll be bound."

Instead of paying a call on Sarah Seaton, Spencer stayed home to see the baby and to close a nasty cut over a boy's eye. For his efforts, he got two grimy pence and the promise of five pounds of salted pork "before the winter comes."

He was about to close his small office and retreat to his book room when he heard her in his hall. For a moment, he stood stock-still, straining to hear what she was saying to his housekeeper. Then he threw open the door.

She looked up apologetically. "I realize it is quite late, sir, but Callie seems to have come down with a sore throat."

He stared. Gone were the black dress and the bun. She wore a blue jacket trimmed in black braid over a matching wide, full skirt. The color made her eyes as blue as Callie's. And perched jauntily atop her curled hair was a small, rounded hat. The gauzy veil seemed to float above her brow. She was even prettier than he'd imagined she could be.

"A sore throat, eh?" he asked, turning his attention to the child at her side.

"Yes, sir."

Callie still clutched her kitten. Sarah shook her head. "She goes everywhere with that cat, I'm afraid. And no doubt if she would not be forever outside without a wrap, she'd not have the complaint."

"Well, let's have a look," he murmured. "Come on inside."

It was a room lined with shelves, some with thick, musty books, others with an impressive assortment of tins and bottles lined neatly along them. Against one wall were his desk and consulting chairs, and across the room was his examining table.

"You did not bring Magic in here," Callie observed, admiring the office. "Why didn't you tend to him in your office?"

"Somehow I rather thought I should eat Magic's hair rather than have it show up in someone's wound. Foreign bodies tend to fester, you see."

"Oh. Well, it's a nice office. Don't you think so, Mama?"

"Yes."

He lifted the little girl onto the table and drew out his depressor. "Open your mouth and stick out your tongue as far as you can," he told her.

"Ahhhhhhh."

He did not believe he'd ever seen a healthier pair of tonsils anywhere. And there was not the least irritation, not even one small patch of red in the whole throat. He looked up to her mother, but Sarah was hovering anxiously at his shoulder, unaware that Callie was shamming it.

"Is it serious, do you think?" Sarah asked.

"Nothing that a bit of hot water, honey, and lemon juice will not cure," he assured her. "But if it gets worse, I might recommend a purge,'' he added meaningfully.

"I expect it will get better," Callie insisted quickly.
"She did not seem to feel very warm, but she said she could not swallow.''

Callie squirmed and looked down at the cat, saying nothing.

"Well, I don't think any harm will come to her from it.''

"I'm relieved.'' Sarah hesitated, then blurted out, "Sir Richard comes next week to see where we live, and I'd not have him say I have neglected her.''

"Well, he cannot complain of her health.''

She loosened the strings on her black silk purse, opening it. Drawing out a small coin purse, she inquired politely, "What do I owe you, sir?''

"Nothing.''

"Don't be absurd. I can afford it, I assure you.''

It was the worst thing she could have said. "Callie, why don't you show Mrs. Clark how Magic has prospered?'' he suggested. "She might even discover a saucer of milk.''

The child jumped down eagerly, then recollected herself. One of her hands crept to her throat. "How long before I am well?''

"Probably tomorrow.''

He waited until she was gone, then closed the door after her, and turned to face Sarah Seaton. "Why did you let me bring you the goose?'' he asked almost angrily. "Why didn't you tell me you were the rich Mrs. Seaton?''

She seemed taken aback for a moment, then moved to stare at one of the neatly arranged shelves. "I fail to see what difference that makes. And we did enjoy the goose.''

He wanted to shout that she'd made a fool of him, but instead, he accused her, saying, ''You let me think you were poor.''

''I fail to see—''

''It makes every difference, Mrs. Seaton.'' His mouth twisted wryly. ''You see, I was beginning to fancy myself some sort of Galahad.''

''I thought Galahad was the young knight who went in search of the Holy Grail.''

''Lancelot, then.''

Her eyebrows rose. ''Didn't he cuckold King Arthur with Guinevere?''

''Obviously you are better read on the Arthurian legends than I,'' he snapped.

''I think I should rather compare you to Gawain,'' she said softly. ''Or perhaps Gareth. Good day, Dr. Davies.'' As she left, she placed a guinea on his desk.

He did not accompany her out. For a long moment, he listened as they left, then he picked up the guinea and threw it against the wall. But the irony of it all wasn't lost to him. For the first time since Anne's death, he'd fancied another woman—and that woman was beyond his touch.

Ten different people must have told him when Sir Richard Seaton arrived, and nearly every one of them had been in utter awe of the elegant, black-lacquered equippage and the bang-up foursome pulling it. The old general himself had waved stiffly to the small crowd as he passed through the village on his way up the hill.

''A right starchy old gent,'' Mrs. Clark described

him. "Got side-whiskers to his chin. But the horses was spectacular."

And as each new patient came in throughout the day, Spencer had to listen to reports of every apparent glimpse of the old Tartar. He worked steadily that day, trying to keep Sarah Seaton from his mind, but it was a losing battle. Perhaps a hundred times or more he found himself wondering how the general's visit was going, if the old man was bullying her.

But he was busy, as busy as he'd ever been, with a steady stream of complaints ranging from indigestion to an infected tooth to a broken bone—and nearly everything in between. By midafternoon, his tiny anteroom was still jammed with people from as far away as Bude. He ought to have been gratified by the extent of his reputation, but instead he was preoccupied, wondering about Sarah Seaton and her father-in-law.

At half-past three, while he was examining old Mrs. Paxton for another of her imaginary megrims, the door burst open. It was Callie Seaton, and her hair was in its usual wild disorder, her stockings twisted and rent by brambles. She was breathless from running. And tears streaked her small face.

"Dr. Davies! Dr. Davies!" She stopped for breath and choked back tears. "He's going to take us away! There has been an awful row!"

Mrs. Paxton, whose mouth had been drawn into a thin line of disapproval, was suddenly acutely interested. "Aren't you one of the Seaton girls?" she asked.

"Yes, ma'am. But—" She turned to Spencer. "Please, sir—can you not do something? He won't let me take Magic!"

He was already removing the smock he wore over

his coat. Going to the door, he called for Mrs. Clark, and when that lady appeared, he ordered tersely, "Measure out two doses of salicylic acid powder for Mrs. Paxton, will you? And tell the others I'll be back later. No," he amended, "if it is but a remedy on the shelf, take care of it. Come, Callie."

"But what is it, Doctor—what do I have?" Mrs. Paxton demanded peevishly.

"Dyspepsia," he told her over his shoulder.

"But it isn't my stomach."

"Of the nerves."

"Dyspepsia of the nerves? How dreadful! Did you hear him, Mrs. Clark? 'Tis no wonder I am miserable!"

He stopped only to advise those in the outer room that he had been called to an emergency, that he did not know when he'd be back. Then he followed Callie.

She fairly ran ahead of him all the way up the hill, and he was hard-pressed to keep up. Finally, just a few yards short of the cottage, she stopped and waited. "You won't let Grandpapa do this to Mama, will you?" she asked anxiously. "He says no female alone is fit to raise us, but Mama is—she is!" As she spoke, the black kitten roused from its resting place on the porch and came to rub up against his leg. The splint was still intact. Callie bent to pick Magic up, then rubbed her cheek against the small black head. "He made me put him outside, for he cannot abide small creatures!" she recalled indignantly.

The carriage that had drawn so much comment was pulled up nearly to the door, and everything about it from the shiny lacquer to the brass trim bespoke wealth. Nonetheless, Spencer squared his shoulders and shook his head. "No, Callie, I won't let him do this to your mama," he promised her grimly.

Before he could knock, she opened the door, shouting, "Mama, Dr. Davies is come!"

The old man in the chair turned his head, frowning. "I thought I said you could not bring that cat into the house, Calista."

Sarah's eyes were red, her color heightened. "As it is my house, she may do as she pleases," she said coldly.

"Yes, well, when she is at Seaton Hill, she will not—"

Spencer moved to stand before him. "You seem to be under a somewhat mistaken impression, sir." As the old man's eyes raked over him, he gambled. "I'm afraid I cannot allow you to take the girls."

"Here, sirrah, what's this?" the general demanded, rising. "Who the devil are you?"

His eyes on Sarah, Spencer responded baldly, "Mrs. Seaton and I are to be married, sir. Did you not apprise him of that, my dear?"

"Married!" Sir Richard turned to Sarah. "You cannot be serious."

For a moment she was nonplussed, then she managed to recover. Flashing Spencer a look of gratitude he would remember all of his life, she nodded. "I was but waiting for you to tell him," she said softly.

He crossed the few paces to her and put a reassuring arm about her shoulders. Facing the old man, he repeated, "I cannot allow you to take the girls, sir. You see, I fear the house would be far too empty without them."

"Who the devil are you?" Sir Richard demanded again.

Katie spoke up. "He's Dr. Davies. He's a famous doctor."

"A country bonesetter!" the old man scoffed. His eyes sought Sarah's. "I can give them everything—everything. What can he do for them?"

Spencer looked from Katie to Callie, then smiled. "I am not without funds, sir—and I can give them love."

"Love! Love does not pay the bills, sirrah."

"There is my portion," Sarah reminded him.

There was an awkward silence. Then the general addressed Katie. "Would you not rather live at Seaton Hill, Katherine?"

Callie held her breath, but Katie did not disappoint her. "I should like to visit you, Grandpapa," she answered sincerely, "but I would very much rather live with Mama."

"Calista?"

"I want to live with Mama and Dr. Davies," Callie responded promptly. Then, evidently realizing how she must sound, she added more kindly, "But I should not mind visiting you—providing I may bring Magic, of course."

"I see," he said heavily.

It was as though the starch and bluster had left him, and for once he appeared to be what he was rather than what she'd always feared. His shoulders slumped slightly in defeat. Then he regained his dignity.

"Very well." He looked at Sarah. "I hope you know what you are about, madam. I suppose I must wish you well if I am to maintain any influence over my flesh and blood," he admitted grudgingly.

"Thank you, sir." For the first time since she'd

known him, Sarah felt sorry for him. "I shall see that the girls come to visit you."

He nodded. "I suppose that is about as well as I can do, isn't it?"

"Yes."

He turned to Spencer. "And you, sirrah—if you are unable to send them to a good school, you apply to me—d'you hear?"

"Yes, but I expect we shall manage."

"Aye." The old man forced a smile. "Aye, I expect you will. For all that I have disputed with her, she is a good woman. My son had no complaint of her."

A liveried coachman stuck his head in the door and cleared his throat. "How long is the horses to stand, sir?"

"I'm coming." Sir Richard bent slightly to embrace Katie. "You be a good girl now."

"Yes, sir."

Then he enveloped Callie in his arms. "Aye, and you can bring this miscreant, I suppose. But until then, you be good to your mama and your sister."

"Yes, sir."

It was not until the carriage wheels could be heard bouncing over the narrow, rocky path that passed for a road that Sarah dared to believe he'd gone. She looked up at Spencer. "Thank you, sir—thank you." Then, acutely aware that he'd not removed his arm from her shoulders, she stepped away. "I have never encouraged falsehoods, but—"

"Er—perhaps you would walk with me?" he cut in quickly. "I expect the sun is already setting over the water."

For the first time since Sir Richard had arrived, Mrs.

Foote dared to speak up. "Do go on, dear—when you are returned, the girls and I shall have made dinner."

"Stew?" Katie asked, disgusted.

"Would you not prefer pasties?" Mrs. Foote asked.

"Oh, yes!"

Sarah felt awkward now. "How cold is it?"

"Not cold at all, if you wear your wrap," he assured her.

Callie waited only until they were out the door before turning to her sister and crowing, "I told you Magic could do it—I told you!"

Katie looked at the innocent ball of fur with new interest. "Do you suppose if I wished on him it would come true?"

"What would you wish for?"

"A pink dress for the wedding."

"I expect he could do it."

"It isn't Christian to put any store in such things," Mrs. Foote declared sternly. Nonetheless, she unbent enough to stroke the kitten between its ears. "Pretty kitty, pretty kitty," she crooned.

The sky was pink and orange as Sarah walked silently beside Spencer, wondering what she ought to say. She was not green enough to believe that he was head over heels for her, that he'd acted from any but the kindest of motives. And yet she was loath to tell him she understood and certainly did not expect him to marry her.

Smoke and the sea air mingled, giving a headiness to the breeze that caught tendrils of her hair, loosening them. When they reached the top, the sun was a brilliant ball of orange halved by the sea horizon. She stood there, seeing not the usual barrenness, but rather the intense beauty of the place.

"It is lovely, isn't it?" she said finally.

"Yes." He paused. "I hope you do not mean to cry off, Sarah. And before you say anything, I'd tell you that I do not mean to spend a single penny of your money. You can put it into trust for the girls, if you wish."

"We scarce know each other, Spencer."

"Neither of us is in the first blush of youth, my dear." He reached to turn her around to face him. "We do not have to look for the grand passion, you know. I expect that is past us, but we can be comfortable. And I know I shall love the girls like my own. I already know I love you, Sarah."

She could not meet his eyes. "I don't think I ever had a grand passion, Spencer. I think it was an illusion, something I wanted to believe, rather than the truth."

His arms went around her, holding her close, and he bent his head deliberately to hers, seeking her lips tentatively, then with an urgency that belied his words. And she returned his kiss until she was utterly breathless. When at last he released her, she had to hold his arms to steady herself. He searched her face.

"Well?"

"It's madness—but yes." Her almost shy smile lit her eyes. "It *is* madness, isn't it? To be in love already, I mean?"

He drew her against him again and kissed her thoroughly. And when his mouth moved from her lips to her ear, he whispered, "Not madness, love—magic."

The Ghost of
Castle Ravenswych

by

Charlotte Louise Dolan

October 1808

ALL HALLOWS' EVE, a night when specters and wraiths and ghosts walked the land—when anyone foolish enough to stray from the safety of his cottage might expect to encounter bogles and banshees and phantoms. A night when decent folk prudently locked their doors and stoked their fires and tried not to listen too closely to the sounds of darkness.

Rowena Linley stood at the window of her great-uncle's library and looked boldly out into the night. In the distance, the sky glowed red from the bonfire the villagers had lit to scare the demons away. Nearer at hand, the soft light from the full moon struck the iron deer standing eternal vigilance in front of Castle Ravenswych and made it seem as if they, too, had come alive for this one night.

Beyond them, a narrow pathway wound its way down the hill, at the bottom of which, out of sight from the castle, a copse of trees hovered around the Drowning Pool, their branches stretched protectively above it.

Spring-fed, the small, almost perfectly round pool

was so deep that not even the brightest sunlight could illuminate its dark waters, and the villagers avoided it all year, not just the night before All Saints' Day. Perhaps because it appeared bottomless, there were vague rumors whispered around the countryside about tormented souls who had sought an end to earthly sorrows in its cool waters, and who had—at least in the official opinion of the church—earned for themselves eternal damnation rather than a surcease of sorrows.

Uncle Timothy had never been one to listen to fanciful myths, nor had he believed in such things as ghosts. And as delightful as Rowena found it to curl up in bed with a book of truly horrifying tales of the supernatural, she had likewise never understood how grown men and women could be well and truly frightened by childish stories of headless apparitions, or how they could in their own minds transform the screech of one branch rubbing against another into the eerie cry of a suffering spirit.

Behind her Rowena heard someone open the door, and her temper rose. The only ghoul she herself had ever encountered was right here in the castle, but despite his efforts to intimidate her, he did not have the power to frighten her in the slightest.

Not bothering to turn around, she said, "Do not sit in my uncle's chair."

"Uncle Timothy is dead and buried," Mr. Nevil Hewley replied with forced joviality. "So the chair now belongs to his heir, the new Lord Cheyne, who, I am sure, will not object to my using it since he is presently with Moore, fighting the French in Spain."

"And Uncle Timothy was not your uncle," Rowena said, wishing for the hundredth time that there were some way she could rid herself of her unwelcome

guest. Only two weeks ago they had buried her great-
uncle, and a week later Mr. Hewley had arrived from
London bearing with him a document signed by her
uncle, appointing the aforesaid Mr. Hewley as guardian of the person of one Miss Rowena Linley, who,
lacking at present only a day of being twenty, was
quite capable of taking care of herself.

"But Lord Cheyne himself gave me express permission many years ago to call him uncle," Mr. Hewley
said smugly.

"Only because he did not know you very well,"
Rowena retorted. In her opinion, the only serious mistake Uncle Timothy had ever made was trusting this
slimy creature standing behind her, whose clothes bespoke a gentleman, but whose actions were those of
the most repulsive bounder. An obsequious coxcomb,
he was determined to wed above his station.

Several years before Rowena was born, Uncle Timothy's only son David had died childless. After a suitable mourning period, his widow had married a
wealthy tradesman in London, and in due course had
produced a son. Lacking any direct descendants, Uncle Timothy had made the mistake of considering his
daughter-in-law's son, Nevil Hewley, as if he were in
truth related by blood, writing to him regularly albeit
infrequently, and following his career with interest.

Unfortunately, after one brief introduction when
Nevil had been a babe in arms, Uncle Timothy had
never again laid eyes on the obnoxious Mr. Hewley,
and the good opinion he had gained from the very
respectful letters the younger man had written was
completely erroneous.

"In due time you will learn to show me more respect," Rowena's unwelcome guest interrupted her

thoughts, "and speaking of time, I am afraid the hour has come to end your maidenly coyness and set a date for our wedding. I have a special license with me, so we need not wait for banns to be called."

Rowena could hear the smirk in his voice, and she rolled her eyes at this evidence of his undaunted egotism. Despite her efforts to deflate his pretensions, he persisted in thinking himself irresistible to all females. Apparently the young ladies in London were not as particular as they were here in Northumberland.

"Play a different tune," she said, tired of his dogged efforts to cajole her into marrying him. "There is nothing you can do to force me to marry you." At first she had been gentle with her rejection of his suit, not wanting to cause unnecessary pain. But when that had not worked, she had resorted to plain speaking, and had finally been driven to outright rudeness. None of it had had the slightest effect on the conceited Mr. Hewley.

What would it take to make the man leave her alone? To make him once and for all abandon his ambitions to acquire a well-born wife? To make him slink back into whatever hole he had crawled out of?

"I am afraid you underestimate me, my sweet," he said, and to her surprise, she heard the sound of the door being locked. "I have sent my valet to Newcastle on an errand from which he will not return until tomorrow, and your servants have already retired to their own quarters. They will not be able to hear your cries."

Turning around, she saw that her unwelcome visitor had appropriated her uncle's burgundy velvet dressing gown and leather slippers for his own use. Mr. Hewley was not as large a man as her late uncle, so he looked ridiculous rather than suave, but his expression was a self-satisfied smirk.

He held up the key for her to see, and when she did not react, he shoved it into the pocket of the robe and began to stalk her, his arms stretched out as if he expected her to try to dash past him and throw herself dramatically against the locked door.

"Oh, do be serious," she said, walking over and sitting down in her own wing-backed chair, which was a smaller version of her uncle's. "This little farce you are acting out will never play in London—indeed, it would be booed off the boards even here in the provinces."

Since she was not acting out the role he had planned for her, he was obliged to tag along after her, and obviously disgruntled, he sat down in her uncle's chair and said petulantly, "I am quite serious, as you will learn before this night is over. And by morning, when your servants discover us here, you will be quite amenable to becoming my wife. No, I rather think you will be begging for me to make an honest woman out of you."

He began to shift uncomfortably, and Rowena made no effort to hide her smile. As much as he wanted to prove himself her master by defying her even in such minor matters, he had never yet managed to sit for more than a few minutes in Uncle Timothy's chair.

"The Brignalls do not gossip," Rowena said. "Nor are they deceived by your pretense of being a gentleman. No matter what elaborate scene you arrange for them to see, they will never say anything to anyone that would damage my reputation. In fact, they will more than likely swear an oath on a stack of Bibles that you were never alone with me for one minute."

Lurching to his feet as if forcibly ejected from the chair, Mr. Hewley scowled down at it, and his leg twitched as if he were going to kick the offending piece of furniture. But then he apparently recalled himself to the business at hand. He tugged on the sash of his robe, smoothed his hair with the palms of his hands, straightened his lapels, and said, "You still do not catch my meaning. By the time the first light of day streaks the sky, I shall have had my way with you."

Knowing it would aggravate him, she picked up the heavy glass decanter from the little table beside her chair and poured herself a healthy portion of brandy, which was not, in Mr. Hewley's opinion, a suitable beverage for a lady. Nor was it at all to her taste, Rowena admitted to herself after taking a sip, but then irritating Mr. Hewley must always be her primary aim.

"So you intend to assault me, after which I shall be so overcome by your manly prowess that I will agree to marry you? My dear sir, you belong in Bedlam."

"It will not be assault," he said, again tightening his sash. "I am quite capable of seducing the most reluctant virgin until she is panting in my arms, as you will find out to your own delight, my dear Rowena."

"I am afraid you misunderstood the terms of the guardianship papers," she said, unobtrusively setting down her glass and grasping instead the neck of the decanter. "Because my uncle was misguided enough to name you guardian of my person does not mean that you may molest me with impunity."

"A man has whatever rights he is strong enough to seize," Mr. Hewley said, lunging at her. It was a bit awkward for him, since she was sitting down and the wings of the chair were in his way, but by bending his knees, he managed to get close enough to slobber all over her neck. The strain of maintaining such a contorted pose was apparently too much, and without any further by-your-leave, he grabbed her roughly around the waist and attempted to hoist her out of her chair.

Reaching the end of her patience, Rowena swung the decanter and smashed it against the side of his head.

With a moan he collapsed, much of his weight coming down heavily on her lap, but she set down the decanter, which had not broken, and by using both hands she was able to shove him the rest of the way off onto the floor.

Rising to her feet, she rolled him over on his back, removed the key from his pocket, picked up her shawl, and marched resolutely toward the door. Behind her she could hear him already beginning to stir. Apparently she had not hit him hard enough. Not that she had wanted to kill him. That would have meant a messy inquest, with private family matters made public.

But on the other hand, she thought, turning the key in the lock and pulling open the door, it was long past time to rid herself of this nuisance permanently. She had no intention of spending the next twelve months until her twenty-first birthday fighting off the amorous advances of her guardian.

Feeling as if his head had been split open, Nevil pushed himself to his feet and stood swaying slightly while his brain caught up with recent events. The open door told its own story, and he cursed under his breath when he saw it. Under no circumstances could he allow Miss Linley to escape the trap he had set for her, for it was clear to him that she would never allow him a second chance.

He staggered for the first few steps; then his legs and brain began to respond with increasing strength. By the time he reached the hallway it was empty, and the heavy front door stood wide open. Surely she would not have gone out on such a treacherous night?

And if she had done something that foolhardy? It did not bear thinking about—with her black hair and wearing a black dress, she would vanish effortlessly into the darkness.

Hurrying across the worn flagstones, he peered out into the night and saw the shadowy figure of a woman running toward the pathway, her white shawl clearly visible in the moonlight, fluttering like wings, as if beckoning him to follow.

With a cry of triumph, he was after her, feeling the thrill of the chase—feeling the blood heating up in his veins at the thought of what he would do to her when he caught up with her.

The path was crooked, which gave her an advantage since she was more familiar with its twists and turns than he was, but on the other hand, her gown was not made for running in. As desperate as she was to escape, she nevertheless could not prevent him from gaining on her.

Halfway down the hill and only a few steps behind her, he saw her pale, frightened face turned back toward him, which only made him laugh with triumph. "You are mine!" he cried, reaching out to grab her dress.

But just as his fingertips grazed the silky cloth, the sash on his robe came undone, the garment flew open, the night air chilled his passion, and before he could recover from the shock, one slipper flew off. Unable to check his headlong descent, he measured his length on the ground with such force that his breath was knocked out of him.

For the second time in the space of a few short minutes he was too stunned to move, and he could hear the running footsteps of his prey becoming fainter and fainter.

Suddenly there was a terrified scream, cut off by a loud splash, and then . . . dead silence. Not a sound. With growing horror he pushed himself up, located his slipper, which was lying beside the path a few yards uphill, donned it, retied the sash of his robe, and then moved cautiously down the hill to investigate.

The path ended at a small, round pool, in the center of which floated a white shawl. Ripples still agitated the surface of the pool, as if a heavy object had just been cast into the water . . . or as if a young girl, intent upon escaping her pursuer, had not been able to check her steps in time . . . as if she had fallen screaming into the pool.

Mr. Hewley wiped the sweat from his forehead with his sleeve. He must fetch help—find someone to jump in and pull her out. He would do it himself, except that water had always terrified him, which meant he would have to rouse the servants. On trembling legs he turned away from the hideous sight of that ghostly white shawl floating there, taunting him. . . .

Feeling a growing nervousness, he looked around at the still woods, whose shadows could conceal any number of secret watchers—human or otherwise.

An owl hooted, and a little animal scuffled in the leaves beside the path, and Nevil hurried faster, unable to keep from looking back over his shoulder, needing repeated reassurance that no one was behind him—that bony, inhuman fingers were not stretching out to catch him and pull him back into that dark, menacing water.

By the time he reached the welcoming light streaming out through the open doorway of the castle, he had reconsidered the wisdom of waking the servants. Dressed as he was in his lordship's robe and slippers, what possible explanation could he offer them? No, before he interrupted their sleep he would need to change into something more suitable.

He tugged the big door shut behind him and leaned against it, feeling relief that he had regained the safety of the castle.

But was he safe? If he told the Brignalls that Miss Linley had run out into the night, might they not accuse him of some impropriety? Might they not bring charges of murder against him? Besides, the girl was quite clearly past saving. She had doubtless drowned before he had even managed to reach the water's edge.

And despite what the Brignalls were bound to say, it had not really been his fault. After all, if she had only agreed to marry him the way any properly brought-up young lady would have done when ordered to by her legally appointed guardian, then none of this would have happened. Better to let the servants discover for themselves that she had drowned.

But would they? Would the shawl still be there as mute evidence by morning?

Unfortunately, if it was not still visible, the hue and cry might go on for weeks, and he would be forced to take part in an extended search for his missing ward. He would have to pretend to look for her even knowing precisely where she was.

No, this must be ended at once—tonight.

Thinking quickly and with such cunning that he

amazed himself, he tugged the door open again, went back into the library, retrieved several objects, carried them out and laid them along the path, then returned to the library, jerked on the bellpull vigorously, and darted out into the hall and hid himself behind a suit of armor.

A good ten minutes later Brignall's gruff voice sounded a few yards away from Mr. Hewley. "What's this door doing open. I bolted it myself."

"There's no one in the library. Who do you suppose rang for us?" his wife replied, making Nevil want to shriek impatiently at the two of them.

"What's that on the path?" Brignall said abruptly, and Nevil's hopes for the success of his spur-of-the-moment plan grew stronger.

Without hesitation, the old woman hurried out into the night, and Nevil heard her say, "Why, saints preserve us, 'tis that book of poetry Miss Rowena was reading. And there—there is his lordship's decanter, and 'tis drained dry! Oh, something terrible has happened, I feel it in my bones."

"Nonsense," her husband said, peering out uneasily from the relative safety of the doorway. "Miss Rowena would never have gone outside on such a night."

"Well, you may cringe inside the walls of the castle like a craven coward, but I am going to see if I can find Miss Rowena," Mrs. Brignall called back to him.

Muttering to himself, the old man went out to join his wife. Nevil could hear their voices growing fainter and fainter, and he could only pray they went all the way to the pool.

He had done all he could. Emerging from his hiding place, he hastened up to his room and bolted the door behind him. Without even bothering to take off his clothes, he dived into his bed and pulled the blankets over his head.

But no matter how he tried to cover his ears, it seemed to him as if he could still hear voices calling, "Rowena . . . Rowena . . . where are you, Rowena?"

The next morning, Mr. Hewley was suitably shocked to discover what had happened to his hostess, but as he pointed out to the Brignalls, no good ever came of going outside on All Hallows' Eve.

His expressions of concern were met with hostility and suspicion, and he wanted nothing more than to depart from this accursed castle and return to his own house in London. But first his testimony was needed at the inquest. He could not, of course, testify to anything other than the victim's state of mind: "Yes, of course she was grieving for her uncle, but I would not say she was despondent."

After due deliberation, the verdict of death by misadventure was brought in, and the villagers were all suitably relieved that their beloved Miss Rowena had not deliberately killed herself. Suicides were not allowed to be buried in consecrated ground, after all— but then, since the Drowning Pool never gave up its victims, that was rather a moot question, in Nevil's opinion.

Still, as soon as he was free to leave, he had his valet pack his trunk and summon the hired carriage from the village. As quickly as common decency allowed, he set off for London, vowing to himself that nothing would ever make him return to Northumberland.

* * *

"Good riddance is what I say," Brignall muttered as soon as Hewley's carriage was out of sight. "I misdoubt I have ever met such a hypocrite in my life."

"And as for you, young lady," his wife said, turning to the girl who stood hiding in the shadows, "that was a rash and foolish thing you did that night. If you had paused to think things through, you would have realized that your actions were only causing you more complications, rather than settling your problems."

"Keep in mind that it is not easy to think things through properly when a lecherous cad is chasing you with evil intent," Rowena pointed out. "Is he truly gone?" she asked, wishing she could see his departing back for herself.

"Yes, he's gone, and from the look of relief on his face, he'll not come sniffing around here again, trying to assault any of our young ladies," Brignall said. "But you should have come to me rather than faking your own death. I'd have sorted out that miserable cur fast enough."

"I'm sure you would have," Rowena said, tucking her arm through his and laying her head on his shoulder. "But he had the law on his side, you know, and he really could have dragged me off to London, where nobody knows me, and where no one would have taken my word against his, so it is better this way."

Mrs. Brignall shook her head. "Has it occurred to you yet that you will not be able to leave this castle for a full twelve months? If you even set one foot outside, someone from the village or some poacher may see you, and then all of this play-acting will be for naught."

That had *not* occurred to Rowena, and she uttered an unladylike oath when she fully realized the situation she had thrust herself into with her rash actions. Not to enjoy the sunshine in the garden, not to walk to the village for tea and gossip, not to ride *vente à terre* across the countryside . . .

"Botheration, that wretched man is ruining my life even in his absence. I should have thrown him into the water instead of that large rock."

"Now then, it will not be that bad," Mrs. Brignall said, putting her arm comfortingly around Rowena's waist. "You will still have your books and your music, and they should keep you tolerably entertained."

September 1809

Jolting along over a road that seemed to be composed entirely of ruts and boulders, Marcus, Lord Cheyne, was tired—tired of soldiering, tired of lying in a hospital being poked and prodded by doctors, tired of jouncing the length of England in a hired carriage with very worn springs.

Ultimately he would make a complete recovery, the surgeons who had sewed him back together had reassured him. The pain would eventually ease, they had pledged when he struggled to walk again. He would sooner or later regain his strength, they had promised every time they bled him. Given sufficient time the fevers would become milder and someday cease altogether, they had vowed every time the ague struck, leaving him too weak to lift his head off his pillow.

But none of them held out any hope that he would soon be able to join Wellesley in Spain. And the old men in the War Office were not known for their understanding in such matters. Now that you are the fourth Earl of Cheyne, they had explained while offering him a desk job in London, it would be most unfortunate if you were to be killed in battle.

Marcus was not the least interested in spending his days reading battle reports and tallying lists of provisions purchased, but he had been too tired to argue his case properly. It had taken less effort to resign his commission and hire a carriage to take him to Northumberland, where Castle Ravenswych awaited him.

Only once, when he was about seven or eight and his father was briefly stationed in Edinburgh, had he ever visited the castle. He did not really remember his predecessor, the third earl, other than as a large, gruff man who had seemed impossibly old even then. That was now over twenty years in the past, and the old gentleman had died nearly a year ago, only a few months short of his eightieth birthday.

Centuries old, the castle stood on the spot where an earlier earthen fortification had guarded the border against marauding Scotsmen. It was the pride of the Cheynes that the castle had never fallen by force of arms or by treachery, and the sons born inside its walls had always been quick to pick up their swords and march into battle in defense of king and country.

Distracted by his thoughts, Marcus only became aware that the carriage had stopped when the driver opened the door and let down the steps. Peering out, Marcus saw the remembered bleak stone walls of Castle Ravenswych.

As always, the long hours of immobility had stiffened his muscles and joints, and he had to accept the impassive help of the hired coachman. "Shall I ring the bell, m'lord?" the man inquired.

His great-uncle's solicitor had said something about

a pair of caretakers, but waiting for them to admit him was to risk collapsing where he stood, which would be a novel but not much desired way to take possession of his estate.

"No, I have a key," Marcus said, producing an oversized, ridiculously ornate brass key from his pocket. Shrugging off his would-be helper's hand, he walked unaided the few yards from the carriage to the castle.

The coachman hurried to unlock the door, which swung open on well-oiled hinges. Entering his new home, Marcus was glad to see that inside the castle some concessions had been made to comfort.

Without conscious decision, he crossed to the door on the left, which was slightly ajar. Pushing it open, he entered a smallish chamber snugly furnished as a sitting room.

Bookshelves lined one of the walls, and faded tapestries depicting various battle scenes brought color to the other three walls. Oriental rugs softened the ancient stone floor, and two comfortable wing-backed chairs were positioned in front of the fireplace.

Marcus had an overwhelming feeling of déjà vu before he realized he was in the same room where he had sat for so many hours listening to his great-uncle's tales of the glories and heroism of the Cheyne family.

A decanter of brandy stood on the table between the chairs, and a fire was burning cheerfully in the fireplace. Evidently the old couple taking care of the place were also taking advantage of his long absence to make themselves comfortable.

With the last of his energy, he crossed to the larger of the two chairs and sank down in it wearily, too tired even to keep his eyes open.

"Shall I see if I can locate any servants, m'lord?" the coachman asked as solicitously as the most devoted nurse.

Marcus knew he should pay off the man and send him on his way, but he was too tired. Already he was having trouble staying awake. "Yes, yes," he said. "And see if they can prepare some food for both of us."

But the chair was not as comfortable as it looked, and after a few minutes of shifting his position, he got up and moved to the other chair, which although a bit small for his large frame, was still comfortable enough that he soon lost the struggle to stay awake.

The stones were cold behind her back, the dust from the tapestry was tickling her nose, and Rowena was justifiably angry at the man who had put her in such a ridiculous position. Who he was, she could not fathom, unless—

He did have a key to the front door, and the coachman had called him "m'lord." With a sinking heart, she realized that the intruder was undoubtedly the new Lord Cheyne, and as much as she might wish it, the Brignalls could not throw him out on his ear.

A slight snore interrupted her thoughts, and she ventured to peer around the edge of the hanging. Lord Cheyne appeared to be sleeping. If she was quick enough, she might be able to make her escape before his coachman returned.

Tiptoeing over to him, she inspected the new owner of Castle Ravenswych. He did not look at all a gentleman—his jaw was too strong, his nose too aquiline, his brows too fiercely straight.

In addition, he was lean to the point of gauntness,

and his chin was covered with stubble, as if he had not bothered to shave in a week.

His appearance would have frightened her, except that his dark chocolate hair curled the merest bit at his neck . . . and his eyelashes were much too luxurious . . . and his mouth bespoke a passionate rather than a harsh nature.

You will have the ladies in London swooning at your feet, Cousin, if you go there for the Season, Rowena thought to herself. And prudent fathers in Northumberland will be locking up their daughters when you are around.

She started to turn away, but something else about his appearance bothered her. Studying him more carefully, she finally realized his skin was too pale for a soldier, who could expect to spend a good part of his life out-of-doors.

Had he also been shut up inside for months just as she had been? But no, that was highly unlikely.

While she stared at him, memorizing his features, he stirred in his sleep, and she hurried to make good her escape before his servant returned with the Brignalls in tow.

Only later did it occur to her to wonder what color his eyes were.

Sir William Cheyne it was who followed King Richard to the Holy Land, Uncle Timothy's deep voice echoed in Marcus's ear. There Sir William battled bravely against the infidels, but unfortunately he died of a fever on the journey home.

It was Edgar, the first Baron Cheyne, who brought treasures back from the New World for good Queen Bess, but you'll find no Spanish goblets or Toledo blades in this castle. Edgar invested his share of the spoils in more ships, and during his lifetime he raided the Spanish galleons with such impunity that the price upon his head was ten thousand gold doubloons.

And do you remember John, the first Viscount Cheyne? Have I told you how he lost a leg fighting against the Roundheads? His grandson, Maximillian, was my grandfather, and he gained us the earldom by helping defeat the rebellious Highland clans in the uprising of '15.

Those were glorious days, nephew, glorious days, and it is your duty to follow in their footsteps. We Cheynes have always been in the thick of the battle, never cowering at the rear. Remember that, boy . . . remember that . . .

The sound of someone clearing his throat pulled Marcus out of his sleep, and he opened his eyes to see three faces peering intently at him. His coachman looked worried, and the old man hulking behind him was fierce enough to frighten little children into behaving.

The ancient crone peering around the other side of the coachman would have had to stretch to reach five feet tall, and she was so old, her skin was like brittle parchment. At first glance, she looked like a proper witch, with scraggly gray hair sticking out from under her mobcap, but her expression could only be described as motherly.

With an inward sigh, Marcus admitted to himself that he would have preferred it if she had been scowling. He was quite tired of well-meaning people hovering over him, treating him as if he were a small child, all of them positively brimming over with good intentions.

"This is Lord Cheyne," the coachman said. "And these here are the Brignalls, m'lord. They say as how there are no other servants living in the castle, just a pair of women from the village that comes up twice a week to help clean."

Before Marcus could open his mouth, the old woman bobbed a curtsy and began to fuss over him like a broody hen with only one chick. "Can't you see how exhausted his lordship is? Brignall, you look lively now and build a fire in his lordship's room. Such a sorry welcome as you're getting, m'lord, but if you'd sent us word you were coming, we'd have made better preparations." She rattled on, apologizing, scolding, explaining, until Marcus's head began to ache.

"If I might have something to eat," he murmured when she momentarily paused to take a breath. "And something for the coachman, too."

"Now, then," she said, her hands flying up to her cheeks, "my wits have surely gone begging. You just sit here and don't move, and quicker than a cat's wink I'll fetch you something tasty."

"If you don't mind, m'lord," the coachman said nervously as soon as the housekeeper was out of sight, "I'll just carry in your things and then be on my way."

"You don't wish to sup with me?" Marcus said with a smile.

"No offense and all," the coachman said, his eyes shifting uneasily around the room, "but this place is enough to make anyone feel twitchy. And as for that housekeeper, why, I couldn't swallow a morsel of food fixed by an old witch like that."

Considering the repellent tisanes, the foul-tasting decoctions, and the nasty potions he had been forced to swallow in the hospital, Marcus rather thought that even a witch's brew would taste good in comparison.

But he gave the coachman permission to leave as soon as he had unloaded his vehicle.

"If you wants my advice, m'lord, you'll come along with me and leave this accursed place."

"But I don't want your advice," Marcus said, opening his eyes and giving the coachman a look black enough to send the poor man scurrying out of the room to attend to his duties.

"You've got to get rid of him, and the sooner the better," Rowena said, popping a slice of the apple she had just peeled into her mouth. "Not forever, of course, just until my birthday. On All Saints' Day my guardian will no longer have any legal power over me, and that interloper up there can have the castle with my best wishes."

"Don't talk nonsense, my girl," Mrs. Brignall said, sliding a pan of custard into the oven. "Whether you like it or not, he's Lord Cheyne of Castle Ravenswych, and it's past time he took his rightful position here."

"Bah, he's no better than Mr. Hewley—so worn down by dissipation he's forced to go on a repairing lease before he returns to a life of gaiety and frivolity in London."

"Now, that's enough of that kind of talk, young lady," Mrs. Brignall said, waving a floury rolling pin in Rowena's face. "I'll agree that Mr. Hewley is a thoroughly worthless sort, but Lord Cheyne has been a soldier for years."

"Soldiers, bah! I have met enough of them in Newcastle to know that they are the worst carousers of all, so do not expect me to make allowances for him on that account.'' Besides which, Rowena added to herself, I can tell by looking at my Lord Cheyne that he is a long way from being a saint.

''Then you will show him the respect he deserves because he is the head of the family,'' Mrs. Brignall said firmly. ''Why, he is your second cousin, which makes him the closest relative you have left on the face of this earth. And you would do well to remember that like it or not, you are the one who has no legal right to be living here in the castle, so I would advise you to mind your manners, or you will answer to me.''

Her cheeks burning from the reproof, Rowena picked up another apple and began to peel it. ''My great-uncle would have left Castle Ravenswych to me if it had not been entailed. He told me so before he died.''

''And if you would finish peeling those apples, I could get this pie in the oven,'' Mrs. Brignall said sharply, then betrayed her emotions by wiping her eyes with the corner of her apron. ''I remember what a dear little boy he was, so sweet and kind, like a little angel. And to see him so burnt to the socket, it fair makes me want to weep.''

Rising to her feet, Rowena hugged the older woman, who had gruffly mothered her ever since the day she had appeared on the doorstep, a newly orphaned and very frightened seven-year-old.

''I have no doubt but that you will soon fatten him up with your good cooking, Mrs. Brignall,'' she said reassuringly. ''For there's no one in all of Northumberland who can match you in the kitchen.''

''You'll not get me to deny that,'' Mrs. Brignall conceded. ''Now you finish this pie for me, there's a good girl, while I take up a tray with a few little things on it to hold his lordship until I can fix him a proper meal.''

Never had Marcus eaten such delicious food, which would have won acclaim in London, Paris, or even Vienna. He took a bite of a fluffy scone positively slathered with pale yellow butter and golden jam, and at the first taste, memories swirled through his tired brain. He smiled with pleasure, and the old woman spoke up with satisfaction quite clear in her voice.

''You never could get enough of my orange marmalade.''

Although he still did not remember her, the memory of the little boy he had once played with became clearer. ''That month I spent here as a child—who was the lad I played with?''

''That would be my grandson, Will. He's grown a deal since then. He's a blacksmith now in Newcastle, and he's going to make me a great-grandmother any day now. He asks after you now and again.''

Standing over him while he ate, the old woman began to relate to him the news of various and assorted tenants and neighbors, none of whom he knew from Adam. Fortunately, now that she was over the excitement of his arrival, her voice was quieter, and he found it vaguely soothing.

Without even noticing what he was doing, he managed to eat everything on the tray. Replete with good food, he leaned back in his chair, only to have Mrs. Brignall announce that she would now make him his dinner.

* * *

Rowena paced back and forth in her room—six steps to the door, turn, then three steps to the wardrobe, then five steps to the window, six to the door—

After only four days of confinement in her room, she was ready to scream with frustration. She could not fetch a book from the library, because Lord Cheyne preferred to sit there—in *her* chair, no less. She could not play the pianoforte in the music room lest he hear her. She was even forbidden to help in the kitchen, for fear he would drop in to chat with Mrs. Brignall and find her there.

It was grossly unfair that he was enjoying all the comforts of the castle while she was trapped in this one room.

Thanks to Mrs. Brignall clucking over him and stuffing her nourishing food into his mouth every time he opened it, his lordship was making a recovery that was nothing short of miraculous, although the housekeeper insisted he was still suffering from a lowness of spirits, which worried her no end.

But that was patently ridiculous. Why should he feel depressed? He had the run of the castle, whereas she, after a three-day grace period during which Lord Cheyne had kept to *his* room, was now a prisoner in *her* room.

And all because his lordship could never be counted on to stay in one place long enough for her to escape from these too-familiar walls, which every day seemed to close in on her more.

Stopping by the window, she looked down at where Lord Cheyne had been enjoying the sunshine she was forced to forego. The chair he had been occupying was now empty, which meant he could be anywhere.

No, she corrected, hearing voices in the hallway, he

was not anywhere, he was right outside her room. Tiptoeing over to the door, she pressed her ear against the panel and listened intently.

"And what is in this room, Mrs. Brignall?" he asked, his deep voice unmistakable. Without waiting for a reply, he rattled the door handle, and Rowena could only be thankful that this time she had remembered to lock the door, something she too often forgot to do.

"I don't rightly know, m'lord, and that's a fact," Mrs. Brignall lied. "The key's been lost for as far back as I can remember, and the late earl never saw any point in having a new one made."

"Well, I am not my great-uncle," Lord Cheyne said firmly, "And I do not like the idea of locked doors in my castle with no keys that fit. I shall send Brignall for the locksmith without delay."

Rowena dug her nails into her palms to keep from pounding on the door in frustration. Really, the new earl was impossible. Cousin or no cousin, now that he was well enough to travel, she had to figure out some way to get rid of him.

Abruptly realizing that the voices in the corridor had ceased, she left her listening post and threw herself down on the bed.

What would it take to drive Lord Cheyne away—not permanently, of course, but just for another three weeks—just until her birthday, when she could miraculously come back to life and take control of her inheritance and go wherever she wanted to go and do whatever she wanted to do.

Her mouth turned up at the corners when it struck her what an enviable position she was actually in. Being dead, could she not come back as a ghost? How brave would his lordship be if confronted by a tormented specter from beyond the grave?

What would a ghost who had drowned look like? Wet? Covered with slimy weeds?

She screwed up her face in disgust, some of her first enthusiasm for the project waning, then bethought herself of the bilious green shawl the vicar's wife had knitted for her several years ago. Unraveled, it would make very realistic slimy weeds.

She could even drape some in her hair—

A pounding at the door interrupted her thoughts, and a moment later she heard Mrs. Brignall frantically calling her name. Hurrying to the door, Rowena let the housekeeper in. She had never seen the older woman so distraught.

"We must hurry, Miss Rowena, we've not a moment to waste." Mrs. Brignall grabbed an armload of clothes from the wardrobe and headed back out the door. "Despite my efforts to persuade him it is pointless, his lordship insisted upon sending Brignall into the village for the locksmith. The best I could do was to persuade his lordship to go along on the expedition. I've given Brignall orders to delay things as much as possible, but we've got to have you moved out of this room before they return."

Loading her arms with books, Rowena hurried after the housekeeper. "Where are you going to put me that his lordship won't find me?" she asked. "He has a deplorable habit of snooping around in all the corners of the castle."

"I've already given him a thorough tour of the rooms in the east wing, which is far enough from his bedroom that he's not likely to notice me bringing trays up to your room."

"What this castle needs is a few secret rooms and hidden passageways," Rowena said crossly. "Then I could wander at will and spy on that wretched man."

Working together, they soon cleared the room of all signs of occupation, and then, at the last moment, Rowena remembered to lock the door again. Retreating to her new room, she surveyed the mess wearily. The only advantages that she could see was that the room was slightly larger, and she had a different view, neither of which would be enough to keep the boredom away for more than a day or two.

Ignoring the clothes which needed to be hung up and the books which needed to be properly arranged, she dug out the green shawl and began to unravel it.

For a room that had been locked up for years, everything was surprisingly free of dust, Marcus observed once the locksmith had opened the door and then departed.

Not only that, but a scent of lavender lingered in the air, so faint he could not be entirely sure he was not imagining it.

"There, m'lord, 'tis like I said. There's nothing in this room worth fetching the locksmith for," Mrs. Brignall said, folding her arms across her chest and looking at him with an I-told-you-so expression on her face.

"Just so, Mrs. Brignall," he said with a smile. "You and my uncle were right, and I was wrong."

"Well, now, if you're done with your exploring for today, I'll just go and fix you a bite to eat to hold you until dinner is ready. You must be famished after your excursion into town."

Maybe she did put something magical into the food

she was always shoving under his nose, Marcus thought, because despite the unaccustomed exertion, he felt stronger now than he had since he'd been wounded. Apparently the cooler northern air was likewise efficacious, because this was the longest he'd gone between bouts of fever since he'd been wounded.

The only thing that still bothered him, he realized, walking over to the window and looking out, was the feeling that there was something in the castle he needed to find. Usually he was not given to having such fancies, but even now the castle seemed to be waiting expectantly, as if the very walls held secrets it was his duty to discover.

A few days later, Marcus paused at the kitchen door and heard Mrs. Brignall say, "We can't leave his lordship alone, and that's that."

"Well, you can stay if you're that worried about him, but I'm not about to miss the christening of my first great-grandson," Brignall retorted.

"How can you even think of such things? Why, we'd be gone a good three days at the very least, what with traveling there and back," Mrs. Brignall said with just as much determination as her husband. "And his lordship's not well enough to be left alone for an hour, much less three days. No, I refuse to consider it.'

The dispute might well have escalated into physical violence had not Marcus stepped into the room and told them both that his lordship could manage on his own for a full week if necessary. "After all, I have been a soldier for many years, and soldiers early on develop great skill in fending for themselves. Not that any particular effort will be involved, considering how well stocked you keep your larder, Mrs. Brignall.''

The housekeeper was not easily convinced, but with Brignall's help, Marcus finally persuaded her that no baby should be christened without both its great-grandparents in attendance.

"Now I have brought up enough food to last you for three days, but if there is anything I have forgotten, it would probably be best if you fetched it during the night," Mrs. Brignall repeated for what was surely the hundredth time. "Lord Cheyne is usually in his room by ten, but to be safe, you'd better wait—"

"Until midnight. I will be careful, Mrs. Brignall, I promise. Now be sure you give that baby a kiss for me." Putting her arm around the housekeeper's shoulder, Rowena began easing her in the direction of the door.

She would be careful, of course. Such a golden opportunity was not likely to come her way again. If she worked very hard, her costume would be completed before the sun set, and then this very night the haunting of Castle Ravenswych would begin—and Mrs. Brignall would not be around to stop the ghost from walking.

As soon as the Brignalls were out of sight, Marcus strode out of the house and set off down the path, deliberately ignoring his housekeeper's repeated admonitions not to exert himself in the slightest while she was gone.

He had listened for too long to the people who told him he must not push himself—he had been playing the role of invalid for too many weeks. Now he craved not only exercise but also escape from the stone walls of Castle Ravenswych.

At the bottom of the hill the path entered a grove of trees and then came to an abrupt end at the edge of a small pool. Almost perfectly round, the dark water was as smooth as a looking glass, not a single ripple marring its surface.

Standing there alone, staring down into its depths, Marcus realized how empty his life had become. He had nothing to live for, no one to care about.

Now that his great-uncle was gone, he had no family left, and so many of his comrades had given their lives in Spain, he couldn't bear to remember those days. What was worse, even while he stood there, more English officers and men were suffering, starving, fighting, and dying on those dusty plains.

So low were his spirits that the pool of water tempted him to an extraordinary degree. Its enticing stillness beckoned him; its seductive depths assured him an end to his loneliness.

Peace, it promised him—no more dreams—no more despair—no more suffering . . .

Shaken, Marcus stepped back from the edge of the water. As hard as it was to get through each day, he could not accept such a solution. Without a backward glance he turned away from the alluring pool and retraced his steps, climbing slowly back up the hill to the castle.

The answer lay not in giving up, but in going on. As soon as he could persuade the War Office that he was fully recovered, he could rejoin his regiment in Spain. Even if he died in battle, at least his death would not be pointless.

He entered the castle by the kitchen door and quickly filled a leather pouch with enough food and water for a day. Setting out a second time, he chose the path that led out across the moors.

Before the sun was directly overhead, he reached the end of his endurance, but he knew from experience that sitting down was a mistake. He had learned in Spain to push himself beyond the limit, to maintain a steady rhythm, to set one foot in front of the other no matter how impossible that might seem. Eventually he would get his second wind.

But this time his body did not cooperate—this time he could not stop his legs from buckling, and he was frequently forced to sit on the ground and rest, and each time it took longer before he was able to stand up again.

He ate the cheese and bread, but the food gave him no energy. By the time he gave up and began to retrace his steps, he was beginning to have doubts that he would be able to reach the castle.

With the setting of the sun came a chill wind, and for a brief moment he was afraid that he would die a needless death after all. But then a flash of lightning lit up the sky, and he could see the castle silhouetted only a short distance away from him.

Finding it to be so close gave him renewed determination to reach the safety and warmth that it offered, and despite an overwhelming desire to lie down where he was, he forced himself to go on, lifting one foot and then the other, the way he had learned on the retreat to Coruña.

By the time he reached the door to the kitchen he was soaked to the skin.

The clock in the hall below chimed twelve times as Rowena crept along the corridor toward Lord Cheyne's room. If only it was mid-summer instead of early autumn. Why had it never occurred to her that this was the wrong time of the year to be wandering through a drafty castle wearing a gown that was soaking wet?

Fortunately, this first haunting could be brief—she had only to give Lord Cheyne the merest glimpse of the ghost.

She had debated with herself as to whether or not she should carry a candle, and in the end she had decided that her costume would have no effect whatsoever if Lord Cheyne could not see it properly. Moreover, she could "vanish" quickly and easily by the simple expedient of blowing out her candle.

Reaching her intended victim's room, she peered through the keyhole, but the room was too dark for her to see anything. Cautiously, her heart pounding in her chest, she opened the door. The light of her single candle showed her that the bed was occupied, and it was her good fortune that Lord Cheyne slept with the hangings tied back.

Suppressing a smile, she pulled several strands of "weeds" over her face, and then, taking a deep breath, she began to groan quite artistically.

Lord Cheyne did not stir. Apparently he was a sound sleeper.

Taking another breath, she began to wail, making her voice rasp eerily up the scale and down again, then letting the cry die away with a gurgle.

The sleeping man stirred restlessly, and she was about to try an even louder wail when he gave a low moan.

Shivers went up and down her spine, and she almost fled the room, so deeply did the sound affect her. But Uncle Timothy had not raised her to be a coward, so she tiptoed bravely forward, raising her candle so that she could see better.

"Dear God," she whispered when the light struck his face. Reaching out, she tentatively laid her hand on his forehead.

He was burning with fever—hotter even than Mrs. Taylor had been before she died of pneumonia. Rowena wished desperately that the Brignalls would magically reappear, but of course they did not. There was no one to help Lord Cheyne except herself, and like a complete idiot, she was dripping wet and covered with green yarn.

Feeling as if even a second's unnecessary delay might cost him his life, she sped back through the twisting corridors to her own room, where she stripped off her wet garments and pulled on her plainest and most practical gown.

Then, grabbing some clean cloths and the pitcher of water she had used to soak her costume, she hurried back through the shadowy passageways to her patient.

With trembling hands she dipped one of the cloths in the pitcher and wrung it out. "Please, you must not die," she crooned, wiping his face.

Pulling the covers down, she discovered his chest was bare, which should have shocked her, but which did not. What did stun her was the number of scars on his body—some small, some large, some silver with age and others still an angry red.

How much pain he must have suffered—perhaps was still suffering. And in her ignorance she had scoffed at him, had belittled what it meant to be a soldier. Thinking only of her own selfish wants, she had even begrudged him the comfort of his home.

Tears filled her eyes as she touched the marks of

battle. Then, without conscious thought, she bent over him and pressed her lips to each of the scars, as if by doing so she could erase the pain he had suffered.

He lay so still that only the terrible heat from his body persuaded her that he was yet living.

"I shall not let you die," she said fiercely, picking up her cloth again and beginning to sponge off his muscled torso. "You are a Cheyne, and a Cheyne never gives up. You must live—you must!"

Was he getting any cooler? If anything, he seemed hotter, and she began to despair that her efforts would be inadequate.

The pass above him was filled with snow, but Marcus was being consumed by fire. If he could only climb a little higher, the snow would cool him, would stop the burning. . . .

Then he could feel a woman's hands touching him, putting out the flames—I will help you, she said—you are not alone—together we can go on. . . .

The first soft rays of sunlight crept into the room, bringing with them a most welcome sight. The drops of water beading Lord Cheyne's forehead were sweat, not just moisture from her cloth. His fever had broken—he was going to live!

With a prayer of thanksgiving, Rowena smoothed the covers over him. Discretion demanded that she leave him now, before he woke up, but she could not bring herself to act prudently. Instead she enfolded one of his large hands in both of her own, and held it pressed to her cheek.

"You are beautiful, my lord," she said, admitting to herself that she was becoming quite intrigued by

the new master of Castle Ravenswych. "I think I would
be a fool to allow any fancy London ladies to see you,
for they would all of them lose their hearts to you, and
that would be needlessly cruel, do you not think? For
I must tell you truly that I have quite changed my mind
about scaring you away from the castle. I am determined instead to devise a way to keep you here with
me."

She smoothed back a lock of hair that had fallen
across his forehead, then bent and kissed him lightly.
"Do you realize, my lord, that I have no idea what
color eyes you have? You must admit that is a defi-
ciency that really should be remedied as soon as possible. Will you not open your eyes and look at me?"

All too soon the shivering started—at first a barely
perceptible tremor in his fingers, which in her ignorance she thought meant that he was waking up at last.
But rapidly the shivers became more pronounced, his
teeth began to chatter, and soon his whole body was
shaking uncontrollably.

Hurrying to the carved walnut chest in the corner of
the room she dragged out an eiderdown quilt, but when
she went to lay it over him, she discovered to her horror that all the bedclothes were soaking wet.

Oh, if only Mrs. Brignall were here!

As much as she hated leaving him alone, Rowena
had no choice but to abandon her patient long enough
to fetch dry sheets and blankets from the linen closet.

Dear God, don't let him die! I cannot bear to lose
him!

*Get up, get up, someone was calling to him, but
Marcus lay in the snow, unable to push himself to his
feet.*

His comrade was tugging at him, rolling him over, trying to drag him along with the retreating army.

No, it wasn't a fellow officer—it was the woman again, and she was crying—hot tears that seared his soul.

As much as he wanted to do as she bid, he could not make his arms and legs respond . . . could not drag himself upright to march another mile and then another and another. . . .

It was too far to the coast where the boats waited, and the snow was so cold. . . .

It was not the neatest job of making a bed that Rowena had ever done, but then it was vastly more difficult to get sheets properly arranged when there was a very large man sprawled in the bed. Not that it made any great difference whether the sheets were smooth. Lord Cheyne was in no condition to mind a few wrinkles.

All that actually mattered was getting him warm again, and to her dismay, his body was still racked with convulsive shivers. What more could she do to warm him up?

A fire in the fireplace? A quick glance showed her the coal scuttle was empty. She would have to go all the way to the cellars—but no, she could not leave him alone that long.

She knew the men who joked about needing a woman to warm their bed were speaking of a different kind of need, but surely it would help if she shared the heat of her body with him?

Before she could have second thoughts she slid under the covers and pulled him into her arms. With his head pillowed on her shoulder, she lay there for hours, praying desperately that he would live. If he died . . .

But no, she could not think about that. He had to live.

The sun was beating down on her unmercifully, parching her lips, scorching her unprotected skin—

Rowena awoke with a start, confused at first and then horrified to find that the man whose bed she was sharing was again burning with fever, even hotter than the last time. Or perhaps she only thought so because she was so close she could feel the heat from his body the full length of her own.

But that was unimportant. However high his fever was, she had to bring down his temperature as quickly as possible.

She began at once, her previous experience enabling her to fall into a steady rhythm, all her movements automatic. Dip the cloth in the pitcher, wring it out, then wipe it gently over Lord Cheyne's muscular arms, over his scarred chest, over his handsome face . . . dip and wring . . .

This time her efforts did not seem to be having the required effect. . . .

Come with us, we will show you the way, the voices called to him. Looking toward the light, he could see Lieutenant Crowley, who had fallen at Vimeiro, and Captain Thomas, who had died at Coruña, and Ensign Wallingford, who lay in a shallow grave outside Sahagun.

Laughing and smiling, they beckoned him, and he started to move toward them.

But someone was holding him back, refusing to let him go. . . .

Lord Cheyne's eyes were open, and Rowena could see they were so dark as to be nearly black, but Lord Cheyne did not seem to see her.

She shook him gently, trying in vain to rouse him from his stupor. Then, to her horror, his features became peaceful—his face took on the same serenity of expression her uncle's had worn just before he took his last breath.

"No, no!" she cried out, clutching his face with both hands. "Don't give up now! I shall not let you die! Stay with me!"

Her heart was breaking at the thought of losing him. "No, no, don't go," she moaned, cradling his head against her bosom. "Please, please, you must live. I need you."

Hot tears flowed unchecked from her eyes and fell onto his burning face—if only there were some way to bring his fever down, but she had tried everything.

In desperation, she pressed her lips to his, willing him to live—

If at that moment she could have given her life for his, she would not have hesitated.

"You must not leave me—I need you—I won't let you die—you must stay with me," she crooned over and over again, rocking back and forth in her grief.

How long she held him, she did not know—a minute or an hour or ten hours, she could not have said how long it was before his breathing became less ragged, before his eyes looked into hers instead of into eternity . . .

Before the shivering started again.

* * *

The fever returned twice more, but each time with diminishing intensity. The chills were also less severe, which meant there was no longer a good reason for Rowena to warm his body with her own.

But she did.

After two nights and two days of tending him, she needed the rest, or at least that was the way she justified climbing back into bed with him. But in her heart she knew that was not the reason she lay beside him for hours, holding him close in her arms, pressing secret kisses on his face.

She could not leave him.

It was almost as if she had in truth traded her soul for his life.

She could not think about the future—about what would happen when the Brignalls returned, about what this man would say when he finally woke up.

But for the moment she was content. Nothing seemed real to her but this man in her arms.

She could never leave him.

Mrs. Brignall had other ideas, of course. "You get out of that bed this instant, young lady, or I'll take a strap to your behind," she hissed. It was a favorite threat of hers, but one she had never actually put into practice.

Still, Rowena knew she had to obey. Once reality intruded, dreams faded away, no matter how desperately one tried to hold onto them.

Being careful not to disturb the man beside her, she slipped out of the bed, then tiptoed into the corridor. Mrs. Brignall was right behind her, not waiting for an explanation.

"With all the things I have been worrying about the whole time I was gone," she said indignantly as soon as the door was closed, "I never dreamed his lordship would seduce you! But what is done is done. You shall have to be married at once, of course, for I'll have no one snickering behind their hands about any seven-month baby."

"Hush up, Mrs. Brignall," Rowena said impatiently. "Lord Cheyne has been too sick even to know I was in his bed, so let us have no more talk of seduction and marriage. He has been most desperately ill, with high fevers followed by chills. Last night he almost died, but I think the worst is now over."

With no more talk of impropriety, Mrs. Brignall quizzed Rowena about the nature of the illness, then announced that she would take over the nursing of the invalid.

"I am not too tired to help." Rowena protested.

But Mrs. Brignall would not listen. "Brignall can help me, for it isn't right that an unmarried lady like yourself should be tending to a gentleman's personal needs, even if he is her second cousin. Suppose he was to wake up and find you alone with him? I doubt he'd listen to any excuses you might try to make. No, his honor would demand that he lead you to the altar, and then you would find yourself well and truly trapped, young lady."

To be married to Lord Cheyne—to be with him forever—it would be heaven.

Unless, of course, he despised her for tricking him into a marriage not of his own choosing.

Hiding her pain from the housekeeper, Rowena finally agreed that no, it would not do for Lord Cheyne to see her when he awoke.

* * *

At first Marcus could not remember where he was. The air smelled too cool and crisp for him to be back in Spain, and his bed was steady, which meant he was on land rather than on board ship. And judging by the softness of his bed he was no longer in the hospital, where the furnishings had been Spartan indeed.

Forcing his eyes open, he saw the figure of a woman seated beside him in the shadows, and the events of the last few weeks came back to him in a rush—the journey to Castle Ravenswych, his apparent good health, then the all-too-familiar attack of the ague.

He remembered also the woman who had doubtless saved his life—a young woman she had been, with long, silky black hair and gentian-blue eyes brimming over with tears. Her hands had been soothing, her voice gentle, and only her stubborn determination had kept him on this side of the River Styx.

"Who are you?" he said, and his voice felt rusty with disuse. "And how long have I been sick?"

"I'm Mrs. Brignall, of course, and you've been sick three nights and two days," an old voice answered, and then the seated woman rose from her chair and approached near enough for him to recognize his housekeeper. "It's lucky for you I could not rest easy in my mind thinking about you here alone. I made Brignall bring me back early."

"No, no," he said, rolling his head weakly back and forth on the pillow. "It cannot have been you who nursed me—she was young and beautiful and smelled of lavender."

The housekeeper gave a snort of disbelief. "There's no accounting for the strange visions that the fever brings, but as much as it pains me to admit it, it's been nigh on fifty years since I was either young or beautiful.''

"It cannot have been you," Marcus still protested weakly. "Unless you shared my bed. Unless you kissed me."

His words clearly amazed the housekeeper. "What a shocking accusation to make! And me old enough to be your grandmother!"

Abruptly he felt too tired to continue the argument—it was obvious that he had little chance of persuading her to alter her opinion about what had transpired when he had been feverish. And if he was honest with himself, he had to admit it could have been the fever deceiving him with false visions.

Wearily he shut his eyes, and the memories flooded back—the dulcet voice that had whispered in his ear, the gentle hands that had brought him soothing coolness, the soft lips that had caressed him. The fierce determination to keep him alive.

No, despite Mrs. Brignall's assertions that the young woman was a figment of his imagination, the beautiful black-haired woman must have been real. But who could she have been?

There was no one else in the castle; he had searched it from the cellars to the top of the tower, and had found no sign of any other human being, other than the Brignalls. Which raised another question. If the young woman was real, then why was Mrs. Brignall lying about her having been there? His uncle had trusted the Brignalls completely—it was unlikely that they were engaged in any illicit activities.

But suppose the young woman was more than a figment of his imagination . . . and yet not completely real?

He could almost believe the castle was haunted. Since the day of his arrival, he had frequently had the impulse to look over his shoulder. So strong was the feeling that someone was watching him that each time he had done so, he had been a little surprised to discover he was alone.

"Tell me, Mrs. Brignall, is there a ghost in this castle?" he asked finally, unable to find any other explanation for the young woman who had called him back from the grave.

"If you ask around in the village, you'll hear fanciful tales told by those who've never set one foot inside these walls," she said scornfully, "but I've lived here all my life, and I've never seen nor heard anything the least bit odd."

He hoped she was right. He did not want his black-haired beauty to be a ghost, Marcus realized as he drifted off to sleep. He wanted a flesh-and-blood woman in his arms again—soft, sweetly scented flesh, and hot-blooded kisses to heat his own blood to a boil . . .

He found her again in his dreams, but no matter how he pursued her, she stayed always out of reach; no matter how desperately he tried to catch hold of her, she eluded him effortlessly.

The clock in the hallway below chimed twelve, and Rowena shivered in the darkness outside Lord Cheyne's bedroom. It would not do, of course, for her to creep inside even for a few precious moments, but, oh, she was sorely tempted.

She had not seen him for too long. Even an hour away from him was unbearable, and three days without even a glimpse of him was cruel punishment indeed.

Although he had awakened the morning after Mrs. Brignall had returned, he was still not strong enough to leave his bed. Reports from Mrs. Brignall that he was recovering nicely were not enough. Rowena wanted to see him with her own eyes.

Frustrated beyond measure, she leaned against the door, pressing herself against the unyielding wood. Knowing he was so close and yet beyond her reach was torture.

Ever since she had left him she had suffered from an emptiness that could not be filled by food, no matter how temptingly prepared by Mrs. Brignall, for hers was not a hunger of the body.

Her heart ached with the need to see Lord Cheyne again, to touch him, to hold him.

No, she admitted finally, she could not be satisfied any longer with holding his unconscious body. She wanted him to be awake—to look at her and know she was there. She wanted him to wrap his arms around her, to kiss her back. She wanted one more time to experience that feeling of her soul reaching out to his— of their spirits coming together and blending, merging, becoming one.

Mrs. Brignall did not understand—or rather, Mrs. Brignall understood too much, and she had made it quite clear that she would not allow Rowena to do anything scandalous. "A ghost he thinks you are, and a ghost you will have to remain, at least until after your birthday. And even then, it would be best if folks were never to find out you've been staying here un-chaperoned with Lord Cheyne, even if he is your sec-ond cousin," she had said in a voice that had brooked no argument.

Could Lord Cheyne fall in love with a ghost? And

if he did, would he be angry when he discovered it was all a trick? When he found out she had been hiding in his castle for a full year?

Angry? He would doubtless be furious—not because he would begrudge her a roof over her head and food to eat, but because of the deceit involved.

Despairing, Rowena abandoned her futile post by his door and wandered through the castle, upstairs and down, wishing there were someone who understood—someone she could talk to.

"Uncle Timothy," she murmured, "I wish you were here again, just for a while. Maybe you could help me."

In her mind she could see his face crease with a broad smile, could hear him say gruffly, "Well, child, whenever my pain became too much to bear, you were always able to comfort me with your music."

Marcus was not sure what woke him. The rain beating against the windowpanes? A distant rumble of thunder?

Or was it the faint scent of lavender that seemed to whisper his name?

Too wide awake to sleep, he threw back the covers, swung his legs over the side of the bed, and then was forced to wait until his head stopped whirling.

What he wanted was a hot toddy, but it was not fair to wake up either of the Brignalls at this hour. After so many nights of sitting up with him, they had earned their rest. If he went slowly and rested frequently along the way, he could make it to the kitchen and back, and Mrs. Brignall would never find out he had made an illicit midnight excursion.

Pulling on his breeches and taking but a single candle with him, he set off through the corridors, steadying himself with his free hand against the wall, and cursing the weakness in his legs and the dizziness in his head.

He did not realize at first that he was lost—well, not actually very lost, since he was still inside his own castle. Yet somehow he had taken a wrong turn, and now he was not precisely certain where he was in relation to the kitchen, or in respect to his bedroom.

So much for taking the risk of disobeying Mrs. Brignall. She was bound to scold him unmercifully if she discovered him wandering around.

Coming to a place where the corridors branched, one going to the right and the other continuing straight ahead for a short distance and then veering off to the left, he considered which way he should logically go. Reviewing in his mind the general layout of the castle, he realized that the kitchen was more than likely to the right.

What was not as obvious was why he chose to take the left-branching corridor, which was clearly leading him farther away from the kitchen. He was about to turn and retrace his steps, when his attention was caught by the faint sound of music from somewhere ahead.

Hearing it, he could not have turned back if a platoon of French grenadiers had been blocking his way. With each step he took, the music became clearer and more haunting, and soon he was close enough to tell that someone was playing expertly on a pianoforte. To his way of thinking, the notes being drawn out of that prosaic instrument were so heavenly, one could easily have imagined the musician was no mortal being but an angel, playing on a celestial harp.

At last he reached his goal. Standing in the doorway of a room that should have been empty, he lifted his candle, straining to see, wishing he had brought a pair of candelabra with a dozen candles in each.

Just for a moment he caught a glimpse of a black-haired woman bent over the keys, and then an errant draft danced over his shoulder and capriciously blew out his candle.

Out of the darkness still came the rippling melody, blending with the rain outside, catching at him, pulling him forward.

"I have been searching for you," he said softly, stepping into the room. "Who are you? Why did you leave me?"

The music swirled around him, the tempo increasing, but instead of answers, all it brought him were more questions.

"My name is Cheyne," he said, "and this is my castle—my room—my pianoforte."

The music changed, became mocking, as if the woman were laughing at him for thinking he was master here—for thinking he had any control over her—for thinking he could stop her from going wherever she desired to go, from doing whatever she wished to do.

Wanting to get close enough to touch her, he took another step, then paused, finding it increasingly difficult to walk forward blindly. With the rational part of his mind, he knew the stones beneath his feet were solid, yet still he could not entirely rid himself of the feeling that if he took even one more step he would plunge into a deep abyss.

"Will you not talk to me?" he asked. "I want to be your friend."

Again only the music answered him, becoming so

filled with melancholy, expressing such painful longing, it seemed as if the woman were weeping, as if her tears were welling up out of her soul.

"You held me and comforted me when I was suffering," he said. "Will you not let me hold you now?"

The music became angry—no, the violence it was expressing was not anger, but passion. She was making it quite plain that she did not wish to be comforted—she wanted to be loved. The sheer intensity of her desire made his blood heat up and roused in him an answering passion.

"I need you, too," he said, but his words were sucked into the maelstrom of sound, becoming part of the music. "You belong in my arms, in my bed. I want to see your face again, caress your breasts, feel your heart beating against mine."

The music became wilder, almost out of control.

"I want to lose myself in you," he cried out, determined that she should hear him, that she should acknowledge his presence. "I want to join our bodies and our souls for all eternity."

His entire being caught up in the intensity of the sound, he took anther step forward, and it was worse than he had feared. The stone floor remained solid under his feet, but the music stopped so abruptly, he staggered and almost fell.

Gradually he became aware that the silence around him was now cold and empty, and though he listened intently, all he could hear was the echo of the last crashing chord.

"Don't leave me," he begged in despair, but he knew it was already too late. A flash of lightning lit up the room, showing him quite clearly that he was alone.

Chilled to the bone, overwhelmed by his loss, he knew he had to find her, had to discover where she had gone. Retracing his steps, he groped along the wall until he found the doorway. Then he blundered along the corridor, cursing his lack of light and refusing to admit what any sensible person would know immediately, namely that he had no chance of finding his mysterious lady love.

All too soon his physical weakness forced him to abandon the attempt entirely, and it took the last of his energy to push the memories of the strange encounter out of his mind enough that he could sleep.

Rowena was still shaking by the time she reached the safety of her own room and turned the key in the lock.

Lord Cheyne had attracted her even when he had been feverish and unconscious. Awake and standing only a few feet away from her, he had been overwhelming.

His words had made her feel things she had never felt before—his simple questions had awakened parts of her she had never even known existed.

The need he had aroused inside her had been so strong, so overwhelming, she had panicked and run away.

And now?

Now she was too drained of energy to stand up, but too agitated to lie down.

Now she could not seem to make up her mind whether to laugh or to cry.

Even while she was berating herself for being too much a coward to speak openly to Lord Cheyne, she was relieved that she had managed to escape from him.

Her fascination with Lord Cheyne was doubtless going to drive her stark, raving mad—or perhaps she was already crazy?

Moving to the window, she pushed aside the heavy draperies and looked out. The rain had stopped, but dark clouds still scudded across the sky. The silvery light from the full moon was not sufficient to illuminate her heart and show her what she must do.

What *did* she want?

If she wanted Lord Cheyne, why was she now shivering here alone in her room? Why was she not back in his arms—back in his warm bed?

And if she wanted to be free of him, why did she not leave the castle entirely? Find someplace else to hide for the last two weeks until her birthday? Someplace where there would be no chance of encountering him—where the sound of his voice would not be heard at odd times of the day or night?

Leave him? She could never leave him. She was bound to him by an unbreakable bond—a bond that was stronger than marriage vows.

But could she stay with him?

Oh, dear. It was all Lord Cheyne's fault that her thoughts were so muddled. Obviously he was the one responsible for her addled brain. That devilish man had clearly bewitched her until she could not think properly.

She covered her mouth with both hands to hold back her laughter; then, abruptly, tears were streaming down her face.

Whatever was she going to do?

"And just what do you think you are doing?"

Caught in his nightshirt with his breeches in his

hands, Marcus looked around to see Mrs. Brignall scowling at him, her hands on her hips.

"It should be obvious that I have decided to get up today," he answered mildly.

"Don't be ridiculous. You're not at all fit to be out of bed, so climb right back under the covers this instant," she ordered in a voice that a master sergeant would have envied.

"I am really quite determined to have my own way," he said with a smile. "So either you may help me get dressed or you may send Brignall up to do the honors."

She blustered for a few more minutes, but when he made it clear that with or without help he was determined to abandon his sickbed, she left him, muttering imprecations on the foolishness of all men.

Brignall, when he appeared a short time later, was not only willing to aid and abet Marcus in disobeying Mrs. Brignall's direct orders, but he was also a good source of information.

"A pianoforte, m'lord? Why, in the music room, of course, m'lord." Brignall's tone of voice was patient, as if he were humoring a small child.

"And where might the music room be?" Marcus asked a trifle sharply.

Brignall was quite willing to give detailed directions, but after the third or fourth turning, Marcus called a halt to the recital. "If you have no objections, Brignall, I think it might be best if you were to show me the way."

"Aye, m'lord, doubtless you're right. 'Tis remarkably easy for a stranger to miss a turning and go hopelessly astray."

With great effort Marcus resisted the impulse to

point out that as owner of the castle, he could hardly be classified as a stranger.

It was even harder to be patient with the weakness of his own body. Luckily the music room, which the night before had seemed so far from his bedroom, turned out to be only a short distance away.

"Here we are, m'lord," Brignall said, opening the door and standing aside for Marcus to enter.

The room was dark and filled with pale shapes crouching in the shadows like sleeping ghosts.

"If I had known you were musically inclined, I'd have readied this room for you, m'lord," Brignall said, moving to the window and opening the draperies.

Sunlight spilled into the room, chasing away the gloom and transforming the ghosts into nothing more alarming than sheet-shrouded furniture.

To his surprise, Marcus realized he had seen this room briefly when Mrs. Brignall was giving him a tour of the castle, but at the time he had not paid it any particular attention.

"Here is the piano you were asking about," Brignall said, grabbing one of the sheets and pulling it away.

Marcus crossed the few feet to the gleaming rosewood instrument and tentatively touched the ivory and ebony keys, but his uneducated fingers could not produce the enchanting music he had listened to the night before.

Glancing around, he could see no sign that anyone had been in the room for months. "Is this the only piano in the castle?" he asked.

"There was never a need for two," Brignall replied, and again his condescending tone was mildly irritating to Marcus. "Miss Rowena was the only one who ever played. His lordship had this instrument sent up from London just for her.''

''Miss Rowena?'' Marcus asked, his heart speeding up. Could it be that he was actually going to discover the identity of the nocturnal musician?

Brignall waved his hand toward the fireplace, and looking where he was pointing, Marcus saw a small portrait hanging above the mantel. Eagerly he moved forward, then reached up and took the painting down. ''Who is she?''

''Well, his lordship had one brother—that'd be your grandfather, m'lord—and one sister, who was Miss Rowena's grandmother. So by my reckoning, that'd make her your second cousin.''

Staring down at the picture in his hands, Marcus felt dizzy with relief. It was she—the hauntingly beautiful young woman who had saved his life and then enchanted him with her music. Her eyes, her smile—everything about her face was as familiar to him as his own. Even the painted image of her was so compelling that every fiber of his being cried out that she belonged to him and he belonged to her.

How had he been so lucky? What had he done that the gods had blessed him so? Rowena—an angel's name, and an angel's face. The two of them belonged together, and now that he had found her at last, nothing and no one would ever separate them again.

''Where is Miss Rowena? I wish to meet her at once.'' The need to hold her once again in his arms was too strong to be denied—even a second's delay was too painful to be endured. But Brignall did not immediately answer, and when Marcus turned to look at him, the old man was red-faced with embarrassment.

"Come, come, Brignall, I know she must be staying here in the castle, or at least nearby. I heard her playing the piano in this room only last night."

"I am afraid, m'lord, that—that she is dead."

Marcus was stunned. Dead? How could she be dead? No, he would not—could not—accept that. She had to be alive. She had to be!

"Maybe you had best sit down, m'lord," Brignall said solicitously, uncovering a comfortable-looking chair. "You're looking as pale as this sheet."

Slowly Marcus sank down onto the proffered chair. But Rowena could not be dead. She had saved his life. When he was dying, she had pulled him back into the world of the living . . . or had she?

The question tormented him. Had she called him back from the grave . . . or had she *sent* him back?

If she had already crossed over to the other side, that would mean only her spirit was left here in the castle—that she was now a ghost, without real form or substance.

That thought was too impossible to accept, too painful to contemplate.

"Tell me what happened," he said hoarsely. "How did she die—and when?"

"She drowned last year about this time—on All Hallows' Eve." The old man's voice was filled with ancient rage. "Death by misadventure, they said at the inquest, but I say it was all his fault. If they'd asked me, I could have told them how he was persecuting her, how he was trying night and day to force her to marry him—"

"Who? Tell me who you are talking about."

"Why, her guardian, of course. That flashy London coxcomb, Mr. Nevil Hewley. Determined to marry above his station, he was. Testified under oath that he went to bed early that evening, but I wouldn't believe a word that miserable worm said, no, not even if he were to swear on a stack of Bibles.''

Marcus had never seen the normally taciturn old man display so much emotion.

'' 'Tis my suspicion,'' Brignall continued, pacing back and forth, his fists clenched as if ready to punch the deceitful Mr. Hewley in the face, ''that he tried to force his attentions on the poor girl. Why else would she have fled the castle on such a night, when all manner of spirits walk abroad? The trouble is, m'lord, no one else was awake to witness Hewley's foul deeds, so no one will ever be able to prove he was lying.''

Marcus, who had survived numerous campaigns only because he always kept his head in the thick of battle, was now filled with such murderous rage he could scarcely see the portrait he held in his hands.

Then his vision cleared, and he knew what he had to do—he knew why the tormented soul of this innocent girl had come to him in the guise of a ghost.

''I shall avenge your death, fair Rowena,'' he whispered in a voice too low for Brignall to hear. ''I swear on the graves of my comrades that the man who persecuted you shall not escape his just punishment.''

Then, in a louder voice, Marcus said, ''Tell me more about this Mr. Hewley. How did my uncle come to appoint him guardian of my cousin?''

''I cannot believe you told his lordship that Mr. Hewley was no better than a murderer,'' Mrs. Brignall said, slamming a plate of food down in front of her husband. ''Especially when you know good and well that no one even died.''

Rowena could not hold back a chuckle, which unfortunately only made her the next target for Mrs. Brignall's wrath.

"And as for you, young lady, I'd like a proper explanation of what you were doing in the music room in the middle of the night."

"I was playing the piano," Rowena said in her meekest voice. "I was having trouble sleeping, what with the storm. Really, Mrs. Brignall, there was no reason for me to anticipate that Lord Cheyne would be so *foolish* as to leave his sickbed in the middle of the night after you had given him orders to rest for another week."

Thrusting a plate of food at Rowena, Mrs. Brignall began to animadvert on the irresponsibility of certain grown men who obviously were so accustomed to risking life and limb on the battlefield that they would not even listen to the very best advice.

Brignall winked at Rowena, and she smiled back at him while Mrs. Brignall continued to fuss.

"Sometimes I think I am the only person in this castle who has a particle of common sense, and I vow, if things continue in this manner much longer, I shall also be driven to do something singularly foolish, and then how will you all manage, I ask you?"

The old woman was truly upset, Rowena realized. Standing up, she gave Mrs. Brignall a hug. "Now, I will agree that we have not always shown good judgment, and we are sorry for that, but you must admit that no harm has been done."

Mrs. Brignall snorted, clearly not appeased by Rowena's attempt to mollify her. "So it's sorry that you are? Then why are you not taking your meal on a tray in your room? Are you secretly hoping that Lord

Cheyne will discover you sitting here as bold as brass in the kitchen?''

Before Rowena could deny having any such thought in her head, Brignall spoke up. ''Now cease your fretting, old woman, and let us eat our food in peace. His lordship is safely napping in his own bed, so there is no danger except in your foolish head. You have always been too inclined to see disaster where none exists.''

No sooner were the words out of his mouth than footsteps were heard on the stairs, and Rowena barely had time to duck under the table before Lord Cheyne entered the kitchen.

Without preamble he announced, ''Brignall, I wish you to ride into the village immediately and post this letter off to London.''

A moment later Rowena heard Mrs. Brignall ask, ''To Mr. Nevil Hewley? Oh, m'lord, you shouldn't do anything rash just because Brignall spilled his budget.''

''I have thought it all out quite clearly, Mrs. Brignall,'' Lord Cheyne's deep voice replied, ''and I am determined to conduct my own investigation into the events of last year. To that end, I have cordially invited Mr. Hewley to come here and discuss various papers my uncle left behind. Once he is here, he shall not leave until I am satisfied that I have learned the truth about Miss Rowena's death.''

In the dead silence that followed his speech, Rowena's heart was pounding so loudly in her ears that she feared Lord Cheyne must hear and discover her hiding like a little child under the table.

But after what seemed like an eternity, she could hear his footsteps receding and the sound of a door closing.

"Well, now we are truly in the suds," Mrs. Brignall said.

Crawling out from under the table, Rowena was inclined to agree with her. "At least if Mr. Hewley discovers I am still alive, he will not be able to drag me off to London—not while Lord Cheyne is here to protect me."

"That is little enough to be thankful for," Mrs. Brignall said with a sniff. "His lordship may certainly be counted on to protect you from your wicked guardian, but who is going to protect you from his lordship? He will not be overly pleased to discover how you have deceived him."

After admitting to the housekeeper that she had been right about the dangers of wandering around the castle, Rowena hurried back to her own room. Even with the door locked securely behind her, however, she could not feel completely safe.

Would Lord Cheyne be angry when he found out she had been living in his castle? Remembering the things he had said to her in the darkness of the music room, she rather thought he would be delighted to discover she was not a ghost.

On the other hand, just thinking about the things he wanted to do to her sent frissons of fear up her spine . . . while at the same time her toes curled up in anticipation of the delights to be found in Lord Cheyne's arms.

The few days until her birthday now seemed an eternity. How could she hide in her room until All Saints' Day? How could she bear not seeing Lord Cheyne for so many days—not hearing his voice, not feeling his lips touch hers?

The prudent thing to do was to wait patiently in her

room until she was twenty-one, at which time she would be free to do whatever she pleased.

Unfortunately, her longing to be near Lord Cheyne was so strong that such circumspection was totally beyond her capabilities, which meant her only other alternative was to be extremely careful when she spied on him.

Again she decried the lack of secret passages, but then she consoled herself with the knowledge that the castle did offer an infinite number of nooks and crannies where she could conceal herself. Moreover, the walls of the castle were hung with dozens of tapestries for her to hide behind, and the corridors were so crooked that there would always be a bend she could duck around if she inadvertently allowed him to spot her.

And she had a set of keys for every door in the castle.

His beloved Rowena had come back to him. Marcus caught her in his arms, felt her lips brush against his—

No, no, she was fading away, dissolving into cold mist even while he tried to hold her fast—

Marcus awoke with a start, his heart pounding. It was still dark in his room, and his bed was empty. As always when he woke up from this dream, he could detect the tantalizing scent of lavender.

Knowing if he lay in bed he would only toss and turn for hours, he threw back the covers and got up. Walking bare-chested over to the window, he stared out into the night. The full moon was setting, but it still gave sufficient light to illuminate the landscape below.

Not that he needed light to see beyond the path leading down the hill to the perfectly round pool where his love had drowned—its image was burned forever on his memory.

He cursed its still waters, swore a thousand oaths at the fate that had kept him away from the castle until too late.

But even while railing against the circumstances that had taken Rowena away from him, he knew in his heart that he had no power to alter the reality of his situation.

He had fallen in love with a beautiful ghost, and nothing he might do could bring her back to life. The satisfaction he would receive from avenging her death was small consolation indeed.

Especially since he was not at all sure he wanted to rid Castle Ravenswych of its ghost. His soul was in torment also—why should the fair Rowena's spirit find peace when there could be no peace for him?

But such selfish and ignoble thoughts were not worthy of him, and he knew that when Hewley arrived from London—which should be any day now—he would somehow force the man to confess his guilt.

And then he would devise a suitable punishment for the villain, who should have protected Rowena, but who had instead apparently hounded her to her death.

Seeing Lord Cheyne was not enough, Rowena acknowledged. Hiding in the shadows beside his chiffonier, she fought against the almost irresistible temptation to cross the few steps to where he stood silhouetted in front of the window.

She longed to caress his bare chest—yearned to kiss his lips again—needed to press herself against him.

Hardest to resist was the desire to take him by the

hand and lead him back to his bed, which she already knew was large enough for two. With every fiber of her being, she wanted to pull the covers up over both of them, wanted to feel the heat from his body warming hers, wanted to join her soul with his.

In less than forty-eight hours she would be one-and-twenty and could reveal her presence to Lord Cheyne.

So short a time until she would discover if he could forgive her for her deceit, or whether he would banish her forever from the castle.

Would she ever be this close to him again? So close only a few steps would take her into his arms?

But in truth, at this moment he was as far away from her as if he were on the moon, whose light was not sufficient for her to see the expression on his face.

Was he happy or unhappy? More important, was he thinking about her, or were his thoughts more prosaic? She had to bite her tongue to keep from asking him.

As soon as his visitor was ushered into the library by a disapproving Brignall, Marcus knew his task was not going to be easy.

In outward appearance Nevil Hewley was the quintessential London gentleman. From the top of his pomaded locks to the tips of his polished Hessians, he was dressed to perfection in a way that Marcus could never hope to emulate, even were he to hire himself a London valet and pay thousands of guineas to the best London tailors and haberdashers.

Moreover, Hewley's handshake was cordial, his manner affable, his expression sincere. No one meeting him could doubt that he was an honorable man.

No one would distrust him—except, of course, an officer like Marcus, who had vast experience interrogating captured French soldiers. He was an expert at reading the signs that proclaimed more loudly than words that a man was lying.

In this case he could see quite clearly that Hewley was ill at ease, nervous, and hiding some guilty secret.

Proving that Hewley was directly or indirectly responsible for Rowena's death would be another matter altogether.

"Won't you be seated?" Marcus asked, indicating the larger of the two wing-backed chairs.

Hewley started toward the proffered seat, but then he paused, and after a short hesitation he moved a small ribband-back chair closer to the fire and settled himself upon it.

It was clear that Hewley had been in this room before, because he had obviously discovered for himself how uncomfortable the late earl's favorite chair was.

"You said you have some documents among your uncle's papers that concern me," Hewley said without preamble. "Could you tell me what they pertain to?" The flame of greed burned quite clearly in his eyes.

"Tomorrow will be time enough for such things," Marcus said, playing the role of congenial host. "You are doubtless fatigued from your long journey. Would you care for a little reviving brandy?" He raised the heavy glass decanter, and to his surprise his guest grew pale at the sight of it.

"No, thank you," Hewley said, rising to his feet. "As you have surmised, I am quite tired, and I believe it would be best if I retired early this evening."

"You make a habit of retiring early, do you not?" Marcus asked.

Hewley looked puzzled. "Why no, not as a general

rule, my lord. I wonder where you got that impression.''

''You testified at the inquest that you had retired to your room hours before Miss Rowena drowned.''

Hewley stiffened, then made a conscious effort to relax. ''Ah, yes, that unfortunate incident.''

Incident? Marcus thought. You can dismiss a lovely young woman's unnecessary death as an unfortunate incident? A gentleman Hewley might appear to be, but in truth he had the soul of a Philistine.

''I deeply regret that I allowed such a situation to develop. Rest assured,'' he said, ''that if I had had any idea my ward was in such a state of melancholy, I would have secured the very best medical treatment available for her.''

''So you think she deliberately killed herself?'' Marcus asked, feeling a strong urge to close his fingers around Hewley's neck and choke the truth out of him.

''Of course. Given the circumstances, there was really no other conclusion possible. To be sure, the verdict was death by misadventure, but I am quite sure it was only feelings of loyalty for our family which caused the magistrate to ignore the evidence that indicated suicide.''

''Our family?'' Marcus asked coldly. ''I was unaware that you were in any way related to me or to my cousin.''

The telltale signs of nervousness were becoming easier to read in Hewley's countenance. ''Well, as to that, although I admittedly have no actual blood relationship with the Cheynes, still Uncle Timothy—that is to say, the late earl—always treated me as if I were his nephew, so I have been accustomed to thinking myself a part of the family.''

When Marcus did not immediately respond, Hewley gave a weak titter, then visibly pulled himself together. "I would not presume, of course, to lay any claims against the estate, nor would I expect you to acknowledge such a tenuous connection when you go about in society. I am quite satisfied to know that your great-uncle felt such affection and trust for me that he appointed me guardian of his grand-niece, and I do not need any public recognition of that fact."

Marcus stared at Hewley until the other man's forehead glistened with sweat. Curse the lying little worm! Was there no way to force him to tell the truth?

It was unfortunate that Castle Ravenswych did not come equipped with dungeons filled with instruments of torture. A firing squad would also be handy, Marcus thought with regret.

"So you were fast asleep when Miss Rowena left the castle?" he inquired abruptly.

"I could not swear to that," Hewley replied smoothly, rapidly regaining the composure he had lost. "No one is quite sure when she went out, so it is impossible for me to say if I was already asleep or if I was still awake. All I can swear to is that when I retired for the night, she was reading in the library. Then in the morning I was informed that she had drowned at some undetermined hour."

Although his speech was conciliatory, there was a look of challenge in Hewley's eyes, and Marcus realized he had lost the advantage when he had made his questioning too obvious. It was clear that Hewley knew what he was trying to do, and therefore he would be doubly on his guard lest a slip of the tongue betray him.

* * *

She should have made a peephole in the tapestry, Rowena decided, so that she could watch the interrogation taking place right under her nose, so to speak.

Not that she needed to see her guardian's face to know that he was lying. It was also obvious from his tone of voice that Lord Cheyne had reached that same conclusion.

Unfortunately, as laudable as it was for Lord Cheyne to try to discover the truth, it was clearly an impossible task he had set for himself. Hewley was prepared to lie about the events of a year ago until he was blue in his face.

Unless . . .

A plan sprang full-blown into Rowena's mind. All she needed was to secure Brignall's cooperation, and twenty-four hours from now, on All Hallows' Eve, Hewley's bravado would crumble.

"The thing to do, m'lord," the old man said earnestly while helping Marcus on with his jacket, "is force that mealy-mouthed Hewley to go out with you this evening—at eleven of the clock if you can arrange it. Even London society folk know that tonight is the night when ghosts and spirits and haunts are free to walk abroad. And Mr. Hewley being such a coward, you have but to drag him down that path where Miss Rowena fled in terror a year ago and force him to look at the Drowning Pool in the moonlight, and you'll easily scare him into confessing his guilt."

Would it work? Marcus wondered. Perhaps if Hewley was superstitious enough—or perhaps if his lies did not rest easy on his conscience. "Eleven o'clock?"

" 'Tis the hour when we discovered Miss Rowena

was missing,'' Brignall said, holding out a perfectly ironed neckcloth.

"Hewley claims he was already in his room by then,'' Marcus pointed out, taking the cravat and winding it around his neck.

"Bah, he is like a cur trying to persuade its master that a fox has raided the chicken house when there are feathers all around its mouth.'' The look the old man gave him said more clearly than words that if Marcus was taken in by Hewley's lies, then he was seven times a fool.

"Do you wish to accompany us on this expedition?'' Marcus asked, wondering why Brignall looked as if he were still concealing something.

"Now then, you won't be needing no witnesses to what you'll be doing, and Mrs. Brignall will suspicion something if I'm not lying beside her in bed.''

With shock mingled with amusement, Marcus realized the true motives behind the old man's suggestion. Brignall was hoping that in the morning people would discover that Nevil Hewley had come to the same end as had Miss Rowena a year earlier.

"I am not going to push him into the pool, you know,'' Marcus said mildly, checking his appearance in the cheval glass. "No matter how fitting such a punishment would be.''

The old man was quick to deny any such notions, but Marcus could not tell if the indignation was real or feigned. On the other hand, since it was easily apparent that the old man would have no qualms at all about holding Hewley's head underwater, it would indeed be a good idea for Marcus and Hewley to go alone into the woods that evening.

Leaving his room and going in search of his guest,

Marcus began to plan just how he would persuade—coerce?—Hewley into taking part in the evening's entertainment.

One thing Rowena knew for certain: There was no way she was going to go out into the crisp October night wearing a dress that was dripping wet. There was no point, after all, in pretending to be a ghost only to end up actually dying of a chill.

Surveying herself in her cheval glass, she also began to wonder at the efficacy of her ghost costume. The only light, after all, would be the moon, which was not as full as it had been a year ago.

On the eve before All Saints' Day last year, wearing this same black dress, she had vanished from Hewley's sight by the simple expediency of standing very still next to a tree and turning away from him so that he could not see her pale hands and face. If she wanted to scare him on this night, she had better wear something more noticeable.

Besides which, she admitted as she rummaged through her wardrobe, the black dress covered with green yarn was not a garment that flattered her at all . . . and this evening Lord Cheyne would discover she was not a ghost. Did she want him to see her looking absolutely ridiculous?

No, she did not, she decided, pulling from the wardrobe a beautiful silvery gown which she had made shortly before her great-uncle's last illness.

Holding it up in front of her, she could see it would suit both her purposes: It would be easy to see in the moonlight, and more important, it was very flattering and set off her black hair to perfection. Surely Lord

Cheyne would find himself attracted to her if she was wearing such a lovely dress . . . would he not?

Stepping out of her black dress, Rowena pulled on the silvery one instead. If he would only give her a chance to explain why she had deceived him, she was certain she could persuade him to be reasonable.

Actually, she was not certain at all. To be sure, any reasonable person would understand and sympathize with her, but everyone knew men were not always swayed by sense and logic.

If his self-esteem was threatened, if his masculine pride was wounded, might he not act out of anger and do something rash? Such as banish her forever from Castle Ravenswych?

On the other hand, she thought with a smile, she did not have to go meekly away just because he commanded her to. She could simply refuse to comply with his wishes, and there would be nothing he could do to force her to leave—except pick her up bodily and remove her.

Her smile became wider. If he picked her up, she would wrap her arms around his neck and kiss him again, and she was willing to wager he would not be able to put her down unless it was in his bed.

Humming cheerfully, she picked up her black cloak and draped it over her shoulders, then pulled the hood up over her head. Wearing it, all she had to do was crouch down, and she would easily be mistaken for a bush or a large rock, allowing her to make a dramatic appearance at the proper time.

Really, this promised to be a most exciting evening—and if she was clever, it would be even more exciting for her *after* she frightened off the obnoxious Mr. Hewley.

* * *

Marcus stood at the window of the library, staring out into the night. The moon was waning, and clouds raced across the sky as if pursued by demons. Even so, there was sufficient light to see the path that led down to the Drowning Pool. Behind him, he could hear his London visitor fidgeting impatiently in his chair.

"It is clear to me, my lord, that you have gotten me here under false pretenses," Mr. Hewley said with determination.

"How so?" Marcus asked, turning around to face his guest.

"I have asked repeatedly to see the documents pertaining to me that your uncle *supposedly* left, but this entire day you have managed to avoid producing any such papers. Therefore, I am forced to conclude that no such documents exist."

"I admire your powers of deduction," Marcus said, not trying to hide his amusement, which only angered the other man even more.

"It may seem like a clever joke to you, my lord, but I find nothing funny about being dragged away from my business in London to travel for two days, only to discover when I get here that it is nothing but a hum. And now I am facing another two days of being jounced about in a coach before I am back in London. Really, it is inexcusable behavior on your part." Standing up, he glared at Marcus. "So now if you will excuse me, my lord, I shall instruct my valet to begin packing my things so that I may leave in the morning."

"But I will not," Marcus said, keeping his voice carefully bland.

"Will not what, my lord?"

"Will not excuse you. We still have things that must be settled before I allow you to leave."

Hewley began to bluster, but his words carried no real conviction. "Really, my lord, you are becoming impertinent. *Allow* me? I am not one of your minions, that I must await your permission before I act. I intend to set out tomorrow morning early for London, and nothing you can do will prevent me."

"Actually, there are any number of things I could do," Marcus said. "I could, for example, lock you and your valet up in the dungeon in the cellar—or would you prefer to be locked up in the tower, where the view is better? Alternatively, I could chain you to your bedposts."

His hands shaking, Hewley forced a tremulous smile. "Really, my lord, I find you most amusing. But I am feeling a trifle fatigued, so with or without your leave, I shall now retire to my room."

"Just as you did a year ago? Was that before or after you caused a young girl to drown herself?"

Fear and guilt obvious in every line of his body, Hewley began to edge toward the door, but Marcus casually moved to cut him off. "What happened last year on All Hallows' Eve, Hewley? According to the Brignalls, you had been harassing Miss Rowena ever since Uncle Timothy's funeral."

"Indeed not. To be sure, I did extend a formal proposal of marriage, but I never tried to force her to accept," Hewley said, his eyes shifting back and forth rather nervously, as if he were seeking a way to escape the trap he now found himself in.

"*Force?* What an odd word to use. So you did not

try to *force* your attentions on Miss Rowena. Methinks the gentleman doth protest too much.''

Visibly pulling himself together, Hewley said indignantly, ''You may play around with words all you wish, my lord, but you will find no one who can rightly accuse me of improper behavior. There was a formal inquest, as you very well know, and Miss Rowena's death was ruled an accident.''

''Perhaps no one accused you of—how did you phrase it?—improper behavior because no one went looking in the right place. Perhaps no one thought to ask Miss Rowena?''

Hewley laughed. ''Now I see what it is. You are clearly deranged, my lord. How can someone ask Miss Rowena anything when she is dead?''

''Did you not know? Her ghost still walks these halls. Her soul is too tormented to find peace in the grave.''

''Do not be absurd. There are no ghosts, only silly people with vivid imaginations.''

''Does this mean you do not believe in demons and banshees and bogles either?''

''Of course not. Despite what you apparently think, I am not a gullible yokel from the provinces.''

''Then surely, being a sophisticated London gentleman who is too modern to believe in ancient superstitions, you can have no objections to strolling down to the Drowning Pool with me to visit the scene of the, uh, accident as you called it?''

''First thing in the morning,'' Hewley said, trying to brush past Marcus.

''Tonight,'' Marcus said, catching hold of his guest's arm. He looked down into the other man's eyes, wordlessly daring him to attempt to break free, but Hewley capitulated immediately.

"Whenever you wish," he said, curling his lip with contempt. "I believe the experts are in agreement that it is wise to humor deranged people."

His show of bravado was not very convincing because the sweat on his forehead betrayed him.

Keeping a firm grip on Hewley's arm, Marcus led the way outside. "I believe the moon was full last year, and the sky was clear, was it not, my dear sir?"

"I could not say," Hewley said flatly, his voice betraying no emotion. "As I have told you repeatedly, I did not go out that evening."

They reached the path, and Marcus could detect a holding back on Hewley's part—a reluctance to proceed down the hill. "Have you ever seen the Drowning Pool?"

"Once—during daylight, of course," Hewley was quick to reply. "The day after the unfortunate accident."

"I shall have the truth out of you one way or another," Marcus said mildly when they reached the halfway point.

"I have told you nothing but the truth," Hewley replied. "Over and over I have told you, and sooner or later you will have to accept it."

"Perhaps."

The pool was even more alluring in the moonlight than it had been when Marcus had seen it in broad daylight, as if it were in truth enchanted.

"Well, we are here, my lord, but I do not see any ghosts."

As if his words had conjured up the spirit, a silvery

apparition rose from the ground and pointed an accusing finger at Hewley.

"You sent me to my grave," the ghost wailed in an unearthly voice. "In my uncle's study, you tried to assault me."

Whimpering in terror, Hewley tried to pry Marcus's fingers away from his arm, but Marcus only tightened his grip.

"You chased me down the hill," the lovely spirit accused mournfully, "laughing at my terror."

"I meant you no harm," Hewley said, his voice rising hysterically. "There was no reason to run away—it was not my fault!"

"You forced me to choose death before dishonor, and now I have come to demand your soul in payment," the ghost said, taking a step forward.

With a terrified shriek, Hewley managed to jerk his arm free and Marcus could hear him blundering his way back up the hill.

There was no point in chasing him, Marcus realized. As appealing as it was to envision tossing Hewley into the pond, such action might mean losing his only opportunity to converse further with the ghost, who until now had only spoken to him in his dreams.

But what did one say to a ghost? How could he explain that even if they had to wait through all the long years until he was an old man and could join her in the grave, they would still be together for all eternity?

The spirit took a step away from him, and he cried out frantically, "Rowena—don't go! Don't leave me with nothing."

Instead of vanishing, the ghost bent and picked up something dark from the ground. "I am not leaving," she said matter-of-factly. "But it is a trifle chilly out this evening, and I see no reason to stand here shivering."

Could a ghost feel the cold? How odd. . . .

Without pausing to consider the possible consequences of his actions, Marcus took two steps forward and grasped the ghost's arm.

To his astonishment, he found himself holding onto a real live woman. There was nothing the least bit ethereal about her.

For a brief moment, it almost seemed as if his intense longing for Rowena had brought her back from the grave. "What the devil is going on here?"

Without making any effort to free herself, the previously silent "ghost" became remarkably talkative. "I know it was a silly thing to have done," she said, "but really, that man was impossible. I simply could not face an entire year of fighting off his unwelcome advances, and he refused to listen to reason."

"I am not interested in hearing explanations," Marcus said.

"You are not?" she asked, her voice no longer matter-of-fact.

"Definitely not." With trembling hands, he pulled her into his arms. The scent of lavender washed over him, weakening his knees, and her curves fit against him as if she had been created especially for that purpose.

Surely he had died and gone to heaven, because such ecstasy was not of this world. Nothing he had experienced in life could equal the satisfaction of holding her in his embrace.

Then, with a delightful laugh, she wrapped her arms

around his neck and kissed him, but instead of her kisses satisfying his desire, he found himself wanting more—needing more.

They had been apart a lifetime, and now they had to be together.

"Rowena," he whispered between frantic kisses. "My love," he said, running his hands over her curves, pulling her even closer to him. His spirit was already one with hers, and now his body cried out to join with hers also.

His hunger for her became so great he started to lower her to the ground, impatient to cover her body with his own.

Just in time he realized what he was about to do. "No!" he cried out hoarsely.

Rowena became still in his arms, looking up at him in the moonlight, her pale face betraying no emotion. Then suddenly she wrenched herself free and began to dash up the hill.

With an anguished cry, he ran after her, but so swift was she that he would not have caught her had not her cloak become entangled in a bramble bush.

With scarcely a pause, she undid the ties and ran on, leaving the garment behind, but the delay was sufficient to allow him to catch her just as she reached the top of the hill.

His momentum carried them both to the ground, and she lay panting beside him.

"Don't ever leave me—promise you will never leave me again," he managed to gasp out. Then, holding her head with both hands, he kissed her.

She made no effort to move out of his embrace, but her face was wet with her tears, and she said not a word.

Feeling as if he were damned for all eternity, he rolled over onto his back, taking her with him. "Rowena, promise me you will never leave me," he repeated. "I cannot live without you. We belong together." Words were inadequate to explain, and he had just lost the chance to show her by his touch—by his kisses—how much he loved her.

Her tears were soaking through his shirt, burning his flesh, causing unbearable agony in his soul. Nothing he had suffered as a soldier was equal to this pain.

"You said no," she whispered, and her voice was filled with an anguish equal to his own.

"I can explain," he began, but she shook her head.

"You said no explanations," she said angrily, "and now *you* wish to explain?"

Her past had not mattered to him—even his own past had no longer mattered. Once she was in his arms, he had needed no explanations . . . but unfortunately he had not recognized her need to explain.

Stroking her hair gently with one hand, he said quietly and calmly, "I'm sorry. Tell me now. I want to know what happened, why you pretended to be dead."

She told him everything that Hewley had done a year earlier, and everything she had done, and he suffered the months of her loneliness with her.

"And so you see, until my birthday I was still legally under his control." She paused, then went on. "I would have asked for your help, but I was not sure what you would do when you discovered my deception. I was not sure you would *listen*," she said.

He laughed and kissed her lightly. "And now are you willing to *listen* to my explanation too, instead of running away?" She moved against his chest, and he took it to mean an assent. "The 'no' was intended for me, not for you. When you kissed me, I wanted nothing more than to throw you to the ground and love you, but that would have meant I was no better than Hewley."

She explored his face, caressing his cheeks and his chin and his lips gently with her fingers, her touch as delicate as a butterfly's wings. Then, with a smile in her voice, she said, "But there is a vast difference between the two of you. You see, I want very much for you to love me—right here, right now." She shifted her weight on top of him, and he felt his blood heat up even more.

"No!" he said, sitting up with her still held fast on his lap. "Do not ever think that I do not love you, because you have my heart and my soul, and I would die if you ever left me. I love you, Rowena, and I want you to be my wife. Will you marry me?" Even knowing what her answer must be, he felt as if his very life hung in the balance.

Her cheek pressed against him, she whispered, "Of course I shall marry you, Marcus," and her breath warmed his ear even while her words warmed his heart. "And I promise I shall never run away from you again. To leave you would be to die, for I have loved you throughout all time and eternity. I was not truly alive before I met you, and having found you, I know I shall never truly die, because our love is too strong ever to end."

"You are so perfect—I want everything to be perfect for you."

"There is nothing easier," she said with a light laugh. "Your bed is much warmer and softer than the ground, and a perfect place for making love.'' She scrambled off his lap and stood up, then held out her hand to him.

Taking it, he stood up, and just the touch of her fingers on his own was enough to make his resolution weaken. Somehow he found the fortitude to say, "I want us to be married before we sleep together."

"I am afraid it is too late for propriety. We have already spent too many hours together in your bed."

At her words, his dreams of her shifted and rearranged themselves, and he realized they were in truth memories—beautiful memories of holding her in his arms, of feeling her warmth beside him, of feeling her lips caress him.

Leaning against him, she said, "If I had not already tasted your lips—if I had not already felt your naked flesh against mine—perhaps then I would be content to wait. But having sampled such delights, I cannot wait another day, nor even another hour. Indeed, it would be most selfish of you to expect me to do so."

Reaching up, she pulled his head down as if she were going to kiss him again, but instead she nipped him on the neck with her teeth, making him give a startled yelp. "Just a reminder, my love, that I have been known to employ drastic measures when someone attempts to coerce me into doing something I do not wish to do."

Laughing, he picked her up in his arms and swung her around. "I can tell I am going to be living under the cat's paw."

"More than likely," she said, linking her arms around his neck. "But I shall see that you enjoy every minute of it."

* * *

The moonlight coming in through the window bathed them in its cool light, but nothing could quench the fires that Marcus was igniting with every kiss, every touch of his hands.

She had never known . . . never dreamed . . .

She tried to draw back within herself, to retreat, to hide—

He followed, his mouth easily destroying the barriers she tried to erect.

"Marcus," she cried out in desperation, but her voice was only a weak whisper. "You will destroy me."

"I will love you," he replied, his own voice taut with emotion.

"It is too much. I cannot endure it." She was not sure if she said the words or only thought them.

His hands and mouth moved lower, and she could no longer speak, she could no longer think, she could no longer escape.

"Marcus, Marcus, I need . . ." She did not know what she needed.

"My love," he whispered. "You are so beautiful, my love." Then he bent his head and found her nipple and took it into his mouth, caressing it with his tongue, tugging on it gently, and in an agony of need she clutched at him, trying to pull him closer.

Suddenly he was inside her.

She could not move—she could not speak—she could only lie there trying to breathe, waiting. She did not know what she was waiting for until he began to move, to withdraw . . .

"No—no—"

She tried to say, don't leave me, but before she could utter the words, he surged back into her, coming in even farther this time, filling her more completely.

Withdrawing, then returning, and with each thrust she felt the tension build.

"Come with me," he cried out, and she tried.

Her body knew what to do better than she did, and her hips began to match his rhythm. Then the driving need took control of her mind—of her soul, and nothing mattered except following where Marcus was taking her.

She wanted more.

She could not bear any more. If he did not stop, she would surely die. If he stopped—

She shattered into a million pieces, and each piece was a spark falling through the night.

Gradually she became aware that his weight was heavy on her, and the night air was cool.

Someone should pull the covers over them . . . someone who was big and strong and not too weak to move his littlest toe the way she was . . .

"Are you all right? Did I hurt you too much?" he asked.

"I feel . . . I feel as if someone has taken me apart and put me back together again. I am sure that I shall not be able to move a muscle for at least a sennight."

His large chest shook with laughter. "Then I suppose you shall just have to lie still and let me do all the work."

To her amazement, she could feel him growing larger inside of her, filling her and at the same time creating a hunger in her.

Then he began to move, slowly this time . . . so slowly it was pure agony, exquisite torture, unbearable delight.

Given sufficient encouragement—and Marcus was apparently a master at that—she discovered that she did still have a little energy left after all.

Epilogue

THE HOUR WAS LATE, the guests had all gone home, and the study was quiet at last. Sitting there on Marcus's lap in front of a crackling fire, Rowena was so comfortable she saw no need to move.

Although the celebration afterward had lasted for hours, with toast after toast drunk in honor of the Lord of Castle Ravenswych and his new Lady, the wedding itself had been quick—a matter of driving to Newcastle for a license, and then exchanging their vows in the parish church.

To be sure, it had taken a week of loving before either of them had been willing to leave his bed, which was now definitely their bed, but none of their guests had known that interesting little detail.

Drowsily, Rowena watched the flickering flames dancing in front of her. Never still, the images formed and reformed themselves.

Out of the corner of her eye she noticed Uncle Timothy sitting beside her in his chair, and she felt an overwhelming contentment with life.

Uncle Timothy?

Turning her head, she stared at his chair, which was, of course, empty.

"What's wrong?" Marcus murmured sleepily, his arms tightening around her.

"I must have been dreaming," she said. "I was

looking at the fire, and out of the corner of my eye I saw—I mean I *thought* I saw—Uncle Timothy sitting in his chair.''

Feeling a twinge of regret that it had all been a fantasy, she turned her head back and stared once more at the fire.

Once again she was positive she could see Uncle Timothy out of the corner of her eye. Jerking around to see, she was disappointed anew.

''If you are going to keep fidgeting, you will have to find another place to sit,'' Marcus said, making no move to release her.

''Marcus,'' she whispered, ''it is so very odd—every time I stare at the flames, I can see Uncle Timothy out of the corner of my eye, but when I turn my head, he is not there.''

Marcus shifted position slightly, and then gave a low whistle. ''I can see him, too. Good lord, there is a ghost here in the castle after all.''

''What do you suppose he wants?'' Rowena whispered, and then the words came into her mind as if she were actually hearing them.

I want to apologize, dearest child, for having made such a terrible mistake—for having so misjudged Hewley's character. Will you forgive me?''

''Of course I forgive you, Uncle,'' she said, not feeling the least bit ridiculous talking to a ghost.

I did the best I could to rectify my error.

Vivid images filled Rowena's mind—an image of Hewley's sash coming untied while he was chasing her down the hill, an image of Marcus's candle being blown out when he discovered her in the music room, an image of a bramble bush reaching out to catch her cloak.

With a smile, she related it all to Marcus. "Did Uncle Timothy speak to you, too?" she asked.

To her surprise, Marcus looked somewhat abashed.

"Well, did he?" she said, wondering if Uncle Timothy had decided to play the role of heavy-handed chaperone. Had he, for example, berated Marcus for anticipating the wedding?

"All he said was—" Marcus paused, then continued ruefully, "that someday I shall have his permission to sit in his chair, but only after I have filled the castle with sons to carry on the tradition of the Cheynes."

Laughing, he stood up with her in his arms. "Since I have long coveted that chair, I advise you to cooperate, wife."

"So long as you are able to fulfill your husbandly duties, my love, you will find I am all amiability."

The Holybrooke Curse

by
Gayle Buck

THE EARL OF HOLYBROOKE lay dying. Downstairs, in the uninviting parlor, were gathered his remaining relations. They had all been summoned to await the conclusion of the earl's rotten life.

"His lordship was an evil man in his day, one who cared for naught but his own pleasure and amusement," said Lady Serena in her quavering voice to no one in particular.

A few of the others stirred, but Lord Watersham in particular was discomfited. He frowned and cleared his throat portentiously. "Here now, Mama. It isn't the thing to speak ill of the dying."

One of the other gentlemen, obviously a man of considerable fashion judging from the quantity of falling lace at his throat and edging his coat sleeves, smiled. "You are too nice by half, cousin. But then, you were not well acquainted with my father."

Lord Watersham answered the viscount stiffly. "Perhaps not, Taredell. However, I believe it safe to say that respect must always be reserved for those on their deathbed."

The lady attired in elegant's widow's weeds tittered. She pretended to smooth a fold in the large fichu crossing her breast. "La, you can scarcely expect

233

Taredell to feel any but the most unnatural of emotions, my lord. It has been an open secret these past eight years that he was cut out of the succession after a particularly grievous quarrel with his lordship, the earl.''

"My misfortune was always your good fortune, was it not, Aurelia?" Lord Taredell asked quite gently, swinging his foot in a leisurely fashion.

The lady stiffened in her chair. "I hope that I am not so lost to sensibility as to *gloat*, as you seem to imply, my lord! Pray recall that I, too, have sustained a bitter loss.''

"My pardon, Aurelia. I had quite forgotten your declaration of undying grief at the untimely passing of my brother these five years past." Lord Taredell contemplated the silver buckle of his shoe. "Strange, indeed. I had never thought either of you particularly content once the blissful hours of your scandalous elopement had been made public.''

Mrs. Holland clutched her bottle of smelling salts, which she was never without. Pale and beautiful, the very picture of martyrdom, she said in tragic accents, "Am I to be so maligned even at this dreadful hour? I would not have come to this house, in which I never received any but the most callous of attentions, if it was not for my children. Indeed, nothing else would have induced me to do so but my sacred duty. At least none can say that I am not a devoted mother!" With a theatrical gesture she took recourse in her smelling salts.

The young girl sitting beside Mrs. Holland, whose striking dark looks strongly favored the widow's, placed slim arms about her.

A handsome youth sprang up from the same sofa,

his fists tightly clenched. "Sir! I demand an apology for my mother," he exclaimed, his blue eyes ablaze in an earnest young face.

Lord Taredell regarded the youth for a moment. The faintest of smiles touched his lips, at sight of which the youth flushed. "You remind me vaguely of my brother, bantam. For his sake, then, the apology is yours."

The youth stood irresolute a moment, uncertain how to respond to that softly mocking voice.

A hand dropped onto his thin shoulder.

"That will be enough, Percival. The viscount was but voicing his thoughts. There is little enough in that to drive a wedge between nephew and uncle, I should think," said the gentleman attired in military togs.

Percival Holland glanced from his mother's brother across to his paternal uncle. "Very well. Apology accepted, my lord," he said stiffly.

"Good lad. Now attend to your mother." Colonel Caldar waited until the youth had returned to his former place beside Mrs. Holland before he glanced again at the viscount. The gentlemen measured one another for a long moment, much to the interest of a small lady sitting a little apart from the rest.

Miss Penelope Childe had contributed little to the conversation for the last hour, being more interested in listening to the oddly assorted members of the group. Her quiet attention had made her almost invisible, as had also her dress. She was demurely attired in a countrified fashion, her fichu modest and her pale blue gown belted with a ribbon of the same color. The beribboned lace-trimmed cap that graced her light brown hair was much simpler in style than Mrs. Holland's own fulsomely trimmed headdress.

Penelope could not be considered to be a great beauty, for there was nothing outstanding in a diminutive stature and a pleasant countenance. Her eyes were her best feature, being large and a luminous gray. However, as often as not, her gaze held such a thoughtful expression that it was apparent that her character was not one that would easily regard frivolous conversation.

Lady Serena suddenly spoke again, and her discourse drew the attention of all in the room. "His pleasures were unholy. Wicked, wicked! I do not like to think of them. There are ghosts restless in this house. I have felt their cold fingers on my face at night."

Lord Watersham dropped his heavy hand onto her ladyship's slight shoulder. "Pray do not excite yourself, Mama." He glanced apologetically about the fascinated circle. "She is not herself. Hasn't been since we arrived. It is all becoming too grave a strain, I fear."

Lady Serena's head turned so that she glared up at her son. "You are a fool, Ambrose! You have not the wit to understand these things. My brother amused himself by sacrificing others, never counting the destruction of those lives he touched. But now those long denied their rights—indeed, their very lives!—begin to cry out for recompense." She shuddered suddenly and seemed to shrink in upon herself. "It is an ill wind that begins to gather."

There was silence, stunned and embarrassed.

"For my part, I'd just as lief have the business done with," said Colonel Caldar with all the abrupt style of his military calling. The gilt of his gold buttons

gleamed dully, reflecting the meager fire as he shifted
his tall form at the mantle.

The colonel's sentiment was heartily agreed with,
though most would not have actually voiced it. But
then, of them all, Colonel Caldar would be the least
affected by the unlamented earl's demise.

Penelope, seated too far from the hearth to feel any
advantage against the chill, gathered closer her soft
wool shawl. She glanced around at the respective faces
of her companions, wondering at their thoughts. She
knew none of them well and some not at all, though
most were in some fashion obscurely related to her.

She had come to be one of this uncomfortable gathering by circumstance of her betrothal. Her father had
appealed to Lady Serena to chaperone Penelope so that
she could meet with the gentleman who had contracted
for her hand.

Lady Serena clutched at her shawl and drew it up
once more over her frail shoulders. She stared into
space, her watery blue eyes unfocused, and her lips
moved as though she were holding conversation with
an entity only she could see.

In the short space of her acquaintance with Lady
Serena, Penelope had come to pity the elderly woman.
Lady Serena was obviously much affected by the strain
of the vigil, and though Penelope had yet to hear that
her ladyship had been close to her brother, it must be
a difficult thing to await the death of her sibling.

Penelope's gaze lighted on Lord Watersham as he
bent to say something in Lady Serena's ear. Certainly,
Penelope thought, Lady Serena could not rely on Lord
Watersham for insight into her obvious suffering, for
that gentleman was too pompous of opinion and short

of understanding to offer the sort of quiet sympathy best suited to the occasion.

As for the rest, Penelope had in a few short days also formed opinions about their characters. Her eyes traveled to the handsome youth and pretty young girl seated on the settee opposite with their parent. The two younger Hollands were inoffensive and prettily behaved; not so their mother.

Mrs. Holland was fragile in appearance and wore her lengthy self-imposed bereavement like a badge of honor, but underlying the surface softness was a steely determination to protect her children's birthright. Penelope, who had already known that the viscount had been barred from the succession by the earl's wishes, had quickly learned that Percival Holland stood in direct line to inherit the title. No doubt Mrs. Holland hoped also for a substantial settlement for her daughter, Guineveve. It would not grieve the woman in the least when her father-in-law, the earl, was dead, yet Mrs. Holland had several times expressed herself distressed by the inevitability.

Penelope had nothing but contempt for Mrs. Holland's hypocrisy, but she had warmed quickly to the woman's brother, Colonel Caldar. The colonel was forthright and unpretentious in both his speech and his dress. He wore the regimentals with proud, erect carriage, obviously very certain of himself. He was on leave from the army to give his sister support during this trying time.

Penelope glanced from Colonel Caldar to Lord Taredell. There could surely be no two gentlemen so dissimilar in appearance and evident character.

The viscount sat at his ease, one knee slung over the chair arm. His elegant silk coat, accentuated by the lavish fall of lace from about his throat down over a striped waistcoat, and his cashmere breeches seemed almost foppish in contrast to Colonel Caldar's simpler attire. The hilt of a short sword, visible where his coat had fallen open, seemed incongruous.

Lord Taredell's expression, too, was different. Whereas Colonel Caldar's innate honesty was plainly writ upon his countenance, Penelope found it difficult to read the viscount's face. Lord Taredell's half-hooded eyes and the habitual twist of a smile that set his lips effectively barred any from discerning his true feelings or thoughts.

Penelope thought Lord Taredell was characterized by distant arrogance. His eyes were often mocking and cold when her glance chanced to meet them. The viscount was her second cousin once removed, and on the basis of only a few days' acquaintance she already heartily disliked him.

Lord Taredell, whatever else he might be, was also her betrothed.

The door to the parlor opened and a soberly dressed gentleman stepped over the threshold. His entrance sparked immediate interest.

"Ah, Fennell. Is there any change?" asked Lord Watersham.

Mr. Edward Fennell shook his head as he crossed the room to the small group gathered before the hearth. He said gravely, "I fear not. I have just spoken once more to the physician, whose opinion it is that, contrary to what was expected a few hours ago, his lordship will most likely linger at least the night, though he is not expected to ever regain his senses."

"A very sad business, slipping into helpless insensibility," said Lord Watersham, shaking his bewigged head.

"Quite, my lord. However, one can only be thankful for it, for his lordship does not appear to suffer greatly since the coma came upon him a few hours ago," said Mr. Fennell.

"You are more charitable than I, Edward. I would have preferred our esteemable parent to have remained in possession of his faculties," said Lord Taredell with a frown.

Penelope stared, wondering whether she had heard right. She glanced swiftly from Lord Taredell to Mr. Fennell, realizing that what she had assumed to be simple coincidence in a certain resemblence of features was actually indication of kinship between the two gentlemen.

"Oh, indeed! We can all well imagine what you wished to persuade his lordship to in his last hours," said Mrs. Holland. Her smile scarcely tempered the jealous vitriol of her words.

Mr. Fennell turned a reproving eye on Mrs. Holland. "One could hardly fault Lord Taredell for wishing to bid a proper farewell to his lordship." Mrs. Holland was suitably silenced, though her annoyance was plain in the tightening of her full lips and the flash of her eyes.

Penelope regarded Mr. Fennell with approbation. She had been shocked and disgusted by Mrs. Holland's blatant accusation and she heartily approved of the manner in which the gentleman had handled the encroaching woman.

Mr. Fennell turned his attention once more to the others. "Since there is not likely to be any change now until late this evening, if at all, I have taken the liberty of requesting dinner in two hours. I trust that is amenable to all?"

"Eminently so, Edward. As usual you have anticipated us all. At this moment, at least, I am glad that
you were appointed to look after the family's affairs,"
said Lord Taredell, sliding his leg off the chair arm.
He rose lithely to his feet, standing well over average
height.

"Quite so. It was a good thing when you became
the earl's secretary. I said so at the time," said Lord
Watersham.

"Did you, Ambrose? How felicitious of you, to be
sure, whereas I have always thought Edward deserved
better than to be used as an ill-treated servant by the
esteemed earl," said Lord Taredell.

There was an uncomfortable silence, broken at last
by Mr. Fennell himself. "Your championship has often been a mixed blessing to me, Taredell," he said
dryly.

The viscount laughed and Penelope stared, wondering at the sudden clearing of his countenance. Lord
Taredell clapped an affectionate hand to Mr. Fennell's
shoulder. "I am certain that was so. However, there
are none which can say you have not kept intact both
dignity and equilibrium through the many trials you
have been made to suffer. My hope is that you fare
better by his lordship's death than you ever did at his
hand whilest he lived."

"One can but hope for the best for us all," said
Mrs. Holland. She bestowed a condescending smile
on Mr. Fennell. "However the earl might have dealt
with you, Mr. Fennell, I am certain that he must have
made proper provision in acknowledgment of your superior services. In any event, you may rest assured of

retaining your position at Holybrooke. I am not one to turn off one so excellent as yourself.''

Mr. Fennell made an ironic bow. ''Your consideration is much appreciated, ma'am.''

Lady's Serena's quavering voice floated over the gathering. ''Escort me to my rooms, Ambrose. I am made fatigued by this talk of death and inheritance. I shall rest an hour before dressing for dinner.''

''An excellent notion, Mama,'' said Lord Watersham approvingly. He solicitously aided Lady Serena out of her chair and began with her the slow progress of her uncertain steps toward the door. Her ladyship's shawls had slipped once more from her shoulders to her elbows, and one end trailed across the carpet.

''I, too, shall seek my couch. This past hour has been most traumatic to one of my delicate sensibilities,'' Mrs. Holland declared, rising. ''Guinevere, you will attend me.''

The girl threw a beseeching glance in the direction of her brother and he rose nobly to the occasion. ''I am positive Guin is not in the least tired, Mama. I should like it if she were to keep me company, for otherwise I will be most frightfully bored.''

Mrs. Holland smiled on her son. ''Of course, my dear. I had not thought of it, but naturally, if you wish it, Guinevere must keep you suitably entertained. So go along, the pair of you. I shall be quite all right with my faithful maid to attend me this one time.''

''Thank you, Mama,'' said Guinevere breathlessly as she and her brother sped from the parlor.

Mrs. Holland sighed before she turned her considering gaze on the quiet lady opposite. ''Perhaps I might trespass on your good nature, Miss Childe? I do so dislike walking about alone in this dreary place.''

Though reluctant to be in company with the woman whom she had so quickly come to despise, Penelope nevertheless rose to her feet. "Certainly, Mrs. Holland."

"I have a matter to discuss with Miss Childe that unfortunately will not wait," Lord Taredell said.

Penelope looked around, surprised, and met Lord Taredell's eyes. His half-hooded gaze was compelling. A frisson of premonition went up her spine, but what it might foretell she did not know.

With quiet acquiescence, Penelope said, "Of course, my lord. As you will."

Mrs. Holland was obviously displeased. Mr. Fennell stepped smoothly into the breech. "It will be my honor, ma'am," he said, offering his arm to her.

"Thank you, Mr. Fennell," she said austerely.

When the door had shut upon the departing couple, Penelope turned a wary glance upon the viscount. She could not imagine what the matter was to which he had referred.

Lord Taredell had taken an informal stance at the mantle, laying an arm along it, and now he flicked a careless hand. "Pray be seated, Miss Childe. I am in no mind to scold you, as your eloquent expression seems to imply."

Penelope chose a carved and gilt armchair nearer the hearth. A slight flush had come into her face that had nothing to do with proximity to the fire. She was unused to being addressed so, and she said quietly, "I would be most astonished if you were to do so, my lord."

Lord Taredell gave his twisted smile. The firelight exaggerated its devilish character. "Pertness was not among those many excellent qualities that were extolled by your father.''

"I doubt that you have requested my presence to discuss my failings of character, my lord," said Penelope.

He regarded her with half-smiling mockery. "No, I shall leave that necessity until we have had opportunity to come to know one another better."

"Perhaps that would be for the best," Penelope agreed evenly. "I should not like to judge you prematurely, my lord."

Lord Taredell gave a bark of laughter. He eyed her appreciatively. "You are spirited, I shall grant you that. Perhaps you are also nimble-witted enough to hazard a guess why you come to find yourself so abruptly one of this dismal party."

At his words Penelope could not help but recall her last interview with her father. It had not been a happy one for either of them. "My father thought it proper that I should become acquainted with my betrothed. Lady Serena agreed to offer safe chaperonage, so despite the sad circumstances, I was sent to meet you, my lord," she said woodenly.

"You were sent at my express command, Miss Childe," said Lord Taredell, suddenly harsh of feature. "I wished you to perceive with your own eyes and ears the way things stand with me. I do not wish later to hear reproaches that you were deceived."

"If by that you are referring to your unfortunate disinheritance, it was made quite plain to me at the outset. I harbor no hidden hopes that the title will be miraculously restored to you so that I might become a countess."

Lord Taredell gave the slightest of bows. "I perceive that you are an intelligent woman. I am fortunate indeed in my choice.''

Penelope continued as though his lordship had not spoken. She said significantly, ''Just as I do not pretend that my family's fortunes will abruptly swing about without the advantages of this marriage agreement.''

There was a short silence, during which he stared consideringly down at her. He said finally, ''You play devilishly hard, Miss Childe.''

''As do you, my lord.''

''It is to be expected of one of my exalted background, however. In you, it but points up the differences in our stations. You would be considered a rough-mannered country miss in London, Miss Childe,'' said Lord Taredell.

''Perhaps, my lord, but I will not willingly lay aside my honest feelings.''

''By all means, retain whatever feelings you wish, Miss Childe. So long as you do not burden me with them, for I detest hypocrisy,'' said Lord Taredell.

Penelope said nothing, believing that silence at that point was the better part of dignity. She knew that his lordship alluded to Mrs. Holland, and though the implication angered her, her pride would not allow her to inform him that she was nothing like his sister-in-law.

Lord Taredell crossed to the side table upon which had been set decanters and glasses. As he poured two small measures of wine, he glanced around at her with the twisted sardonic smile prominent. ''Who knows? We might get along agreeably enough. I acquire a respectable bride and mother for my heirs, together with a handsome addition to the maternal estate entailed to me, whilest you—''

He had brought the wineglasses back with him and he cocked a brow as he held one out to her. ''What do you acquire, Miss Childe?''

Penelope's heart had begun to hammer uncomfortably at his mention of heirs. She knew little about the relations that passed between men and women, but it was enough to realize that it would compel an intimacy that she was not ready to assume.

She hoped that her discomfiture was not apparent in her expression. She accepted the wineglass from his hand, being careful not to come into contact with his fingers. She raised her eyes to his mocking face. ''I, my lord? I think the terms of the marriage settlements spell it out well enough. My family will no longer be encumbered by mortgages that could not be rendered.''

''You dislike me.'' It was softly said.

Penelope regarded her betrothed for a long moment, taken aback by this abrupt statement. She thought dispassionately that she might have considered the viscount to be strikingly attractive, if not for the cynicism that marred his handsome countenance and that was reflected in his hazel eyes.

''Come, Miss Childe. Acquaint me with the full measure of your honest feelings. I assure you that this once you shall have my full undivided attention.''

Despite the lively mockery in his voice, there had gathered a stillness in his eyes. For once she had no difficulty in interpreting his expression. She could not justify polite pretense where there was already such certainty. It was hardly for her to disillusion the gentleman, and so she gave him honesty where he perhaps did not expect it.

"Most cordially."

The viscount held her eyes, but her steady gaze did not waver.

"It is to be hoped that your dislike of me does not hinder you unduly in taking up your proper role, Miss Childe," he said softly.

"I shall fulfill my duties and wifely obligations, my lord. I do not promise more," said Penelope.

She hesitated, remembering what her father had explained to her with painstaking bluntness. Lord Taredell's choice had descended upon her for the express reason that her family's vast mortgaged lands marched side by side with the estate that had been entailed to him by his mother, an inheritance of which the Earl of Holybrooke could not deprive him. The viscount had bought her hand for the price of the mortgages and a generous addition to his existent estate.

Though her lot was painful to contemplate, Penelope understood the necessity of her loveless marriage. "Nor do I expect more of you, my lord."

"Then lest we lose the poignancy of the moment, let us toast the excellent understanding we have attained," said Lord Taredell. With a mocking salute, he tossed off his own measure of wine.

Penelope touched the cold edge of the glass to her lips but barely tasted the wine before setting it down. She rose to her feet. "I pray that you will allow me to be excused, my lord," she said in a formal manner.

The viscount bowed to her. "We shall meet again at dinner, Miss Childe."

Without a backward glance, Penelope went out of the parlor.

* * *

Penelope would have infinitely preferred not to have had to meet any of the houseparty again that evening. She trifled with the notion of requesting that a tray be brought up to her room, but the chill gloom of her bedroom ultimately drove her forth.

As she returned downstairs, she glanced in at each door that chanced to be open. Room after room was dark and musty, undoubtedly full of cobwebs and dirt, with nothing but the hulking shapeless masses of furniture hidden beneath dustcovers. Once or twice she detected the smell of damp rot.

The present earl had obviously not been interested in entertaining of late, nor even to be particular about simple upkeep. Penelope had heard through her maid, who had gathered all the gossip in the place, that when the housekeeper had died, the earl had not bothered to replace her.

The result was obvious. Once a proud country home, the manor house was tumbling down with not a hand to stay it. The Earl of Holybrooke was reputed to be a very wealthy man, but in Penelope's opinion his lordship had proven himself a poor steward. It occurred to her to wonder whether the earl had deliberately set about destroying all that he had to leave behind so that little of true value would be inherited by his relations. Anyone who was so lost to natural feelings as to be capable of disinheriting a son was surely capable of such callous and deliberate despoilment, thought Penelope pensively.

Even as the earl lay dying his word was law and his orders that as little as possible should be spent on the manor were honored by the last of his once-vast retinue. The presence of several guests had not made any difference to that blind adherence by the skeleton staff. Since Penelope had arrived in Lady Serena's train, she had yet to have a decently cooked meal or an adequate fire in her bedroom.

She paused before the open door of the parlor. It was one of the few rooms downstairs to possess that magical sign of habitation, a hearth fire. Yet the parlor was still pervaded by the deep gloom that seemed to characterize the house. The once-rich green damask coverings of the armchairs and the settee were worn, the brocade drapes had frayed, and the oriental carpet had become dulled by the dirt of countless years. The spare candles in delicate gilt girandoles had been lit by an unseen hand and only accentuated the long shadows of autumn that pressed close about the house.

As Penelope crossed the threshold into the room, an icy draft flitted across her face, as though some hidden door had been soundlessly eased shut. She shuddered, not altogether from the pervading damp and chill. The old Tudor manor house had from the moment she had set foot inside it worked potently upon her sensibilities. She was a practical woman, but she could not but observe that Holybrooke was truly an appropriate setting for the ghostly presence that Lady Serena had claimed to have sensed.

"Miss Childe."

Penelope nearly came out of her skin, so deep was she in her contemplation.

A warm hand caught her elbow, steadying her. She stared up at the gentleman who had seemingly materialized beside her. "Mr. Fennell!"

"My apologies for giving you a fright," he said, releasing her. As he stepped back, a quizzical smile touched his face.

Penelope felt foolish. She laughed at herself. "It is quite my own fault. I was recalling what Lady Serena said earlier and allowed my imagination to run away with me. I am not usually so nervous, but since I have come here—" She did not finish, instead making an eloquent gesture.

"It is indeed understandable. The circumstances are such that—"

Mr. Fennell paused, and a muscle ticked in his jaw. He said gravely, "Keeping vigil for the dying is never an enviable task and it always, I suspect, lends an atmosphere of unpleasant anticipation. For those who are only vaguely connected with the family, such as yourself and Colonel Caldar, it must be tedious in the extreme. Certainly you must yearn for pleasanter surroundings."

Penelope was grateful for his ready understanding. As she seated herself on the settee, she said, "I hope you do not think me unfeeling, Mr. Fennell."

He sat down also. "Not in the least, Miss Childe. I am only astonished that you have not already declared your intention of immediately returning to your own home."

The gentleman's bright, sympathetic gaze and intelligent face were all that was friendly. Penelope hesitated, feeling drawn to disclose her oddly unsettling interview with Lord Taredell and the extent of her own unhappy circumstances. But she did not, after all, for that would be a breach of confidence to the viscount.

Instead she shook her head. "Lady Serena has been kind to me. I could not repay her with desertion at this dreadful juncture. Her ladyship seems in need of support."

Mr. Fennell rose smoothly to his feet. "Ah, Lord Watersham."

Penelope was startled that he had taken her up so quickly, but then she realized that Mr. Fennell was merely observing the civilities upon Lord Watersham's entrance. After a short exchange with Mr. Fennell, his lordship turned to her and she murmured a greeting before inquiring, with a quick look toward the door, "Will Lady Serena not be joining us this evening, my lord?"

Lord Watersham regretfully shook his head. "Her ladyship is completely put about by this ghastly business. I considered that a bowl of broth in her room would be better for her nerves than to come down to make one of this grim gathering. Lady Serena agreed."

"I quite understand," said Penelope. Her voice carried more feeling than she had intended, for it did not go unnoticed.

There came a lazy laugh from the direction of the door. "I suspect that you do indeed, Miss Childe." Lord Taredell came into the parlor and greeted the trio already before him.

Penelope was discomfited when Lord Taredell, with a pleasant nod for Mr. Fennell and for Lord Watersham, chose to stand beside her shoulder. His hand rested easily upon the back of the settee, and she was acutely aware of his nearness.

A short moment later Colonel Caldar escorted in Mrs. Holland, followed by her two children.

"I perceive that we are all gathered, so let us repair to the dining room. Miss Childe, you will honor me with your company," said Lord Taredell, holding down his hand to Penelope.

With all eyes on her, Penelope had no alternative but to accept his lordship's escort. Without a word she rose, her hand in his strong clasp. He placed her fingers lightly on his elbow and led her into dinner.

Lord Watersham appropriated Mrs. Holland to himself while Percival gallantly accompanied his sister, leaving the colonel and Mr. Fennel to bring up the rear.

Dinner was a monotonous affair. The beef entrée was indifferent, the fish underdone, the vegetables overcooked. It was a wonder that the Earl of Holybrooke had not expired years previously if this was the sort of fare his lordship was served, Penelope thought, outraged that such sloth was tolerated.

Conversation was as limited in quality as the fare, except for a lively discussion between the two younger members at table, as Percival and Guineveve recalled to one another how their afternoon had been spent in exploring the old manor house.

As the covers were removed, the ladies started to rise in deference to the custom of leaving the gentlemen to their after-dinner wine. However, as Penelope stood up, the viscount's steely fingers closed about her wrist and stayed her. Startled, she looked down into Lord Taredell's gleaming eyes.

"We shall not linger long over our port, my dear lady. Perhaps you will be good enough to see that coffee is served in the parlor in a quarter hour."

Penelope's cheeks flamed at the viscount's possessive address, but she managed to reply with quiet dignity. "Of course, my lord."

She went from the dining room, pausing only long enough to give the viscount's instructions to the dour butler.

Mrs. Holland and Guineveve accompanied Penelope to the parlor. Scarcely had the door been shut and the ladies seated than Mrs. Holland said, "I vow, Miss Childe, I was never more astonished in my life than to hear Lord Taredell address you so intimately. It is my understanding that you have but just met, but yet appear to be on such very good footing with his lordship."

"It is true, ma'am, I am scarcely acquainted with Lord Taredell," said Penelope with a smile. "However, one must allow for the whimsies of one's betrothed."

"Oh, to be sure." Mrs. Holland smiled slightly. "However, I have yet to hear that his lordship is in the habit of dispensing endearments except upon ladies with whom he is very well acquainted, indeed."

"I am sure I do not know what you mean, Mrs. Holland," said Penelope stiffly.

Mrs. Holland gave a tinkling laugh. "What an innocent you must be then, Miss Childe. Why, even my Guineveve knows more of the ways of the world than you profess to."

Penelope glanced at the girl, who appeared embarrassed to be brought to notice in such a vulgar fashion. "As to that I cannot say. However, what little I have come to know of Guineveve leads me to believe that she is as sweet as nature allows."

Penelope received a startled glance followed by a grateful smile, and she returned her attention to the girl's mother. "As for Lord Taredell, I cannot judge where I do not have the knowledge to guide me."

Mrs. Holland regarded Penelope with a small superior smile. "My dear Miss Childe, surely you must suspect it already? Taredell is a devil shod in gentleman's clothes. He is a scandalous rake as well. He will make yours a burdensome life of unhappiness in bed and out of it.''

Penelope stared at Mrs. Holland. She could scarcely contain her indignation at the woman's effrontery. Very quietly she said, ''Your confidences are undoubtedly meant to be illuminating, but I think they are also quite unsolicited.''

Mrs. Holland's pale, beautiful face tightened, while Guinevere glanced away, biting her underlip in embarrassment.

''Very well, Miss Childe! I have attempted to be your friend, but you have rejected my overtures. I shall say nothing more to you, except this—pray do not think for one moment that an alliance with Taredell will advance you in any degree. My son inherits the title and I shall do everything in my power to see that it remains so!''

''Mama!'' Guinevere's interjection was agonized.

Penelope cast a glance at the girl and she pitied her. Guinevere Holland, though young in years, was sensitive to the inappropriateness of her mother's hostility. For the girl's sake, Penelope summoned up a conciliatory smile. ''Let us not come further to cuffs, Mrs. Holland. Indeed, I do not understand why we should do so at all, but undoubtedly the occasion of this visit has put us all a little on edge.''

The door opened, cutting off any rejoinder that Mrs. Holland might have made, and the gentlemen entered. Behind them, the butler followed with the coffee tray.

As before, Lord Taredell deliberately placed himself at Penelope's side. She stiffened when his fingers lightly brushed her shoulder.

''You will pour, my dear.''

Penelope inclined her head in acknowledgment, reflecting as much grace as possible over what was essentially his order.

The butler arranged the tray in front of her, but even as he stepped away, Mrs. Holland was making a gentle but pointed protest.

"Forgive me, Taredell, but as Percival's mother I must take precedence over Miss Childe."

Penelope froze, stung by mortification, her hand just touching the coffeepot.

"I think not, Aurelia. As my betrothed, it is Miss Childe's honor."

"But everyone here knows that your standing—"

Lord Taredell's steely voice cut across hers. "My standing is assumed to be all that my birth entitled me until my father is dead and the contents of his will are made public."

There was uncomfortable silence while Lord Taredell stared a challenge. His relations chose not to take up the gauntlet, instead glancing away from both him and Mrs. Holland. She saw that no one would speak for her and she subsided on the settee, high color flaming in her face.

Penelope felt the viscount's fingers tighten meaningfully upon her shoulder.

"The coffee grows cold, my dear."

Quivering inside, Penelope poured the coffee. Amiable talk started up at once. There seemed a tacit understanding among the party to pretend the unpleasantness had not occurred, even though it was conspicuous that Mrs. Holland refused to take refreshment.

A few moments later a low but heated exchange took place between Mrs. Holland and her brother. Everyone pretended not to notice, but it was difficult to do when Colonel Caldar was heard to snap, "Do not make yourself anymore the fool, Aurelia!"

Penelope was unable to hear Mrs. Holland's rejoinder, but that it was a furious one there was little doubt.

Lord Watersham had engaged Mr. Fennell and Lord Taredell in a ponderous discussion of politics, which faltered momentarily with Colonel Caldar's injunction to Mrs. Holland, but Lord Watersham determinedly picked up the thread of his former observation and plowed ahead. Lord Taredell feigned but a scarce interest in what his cousin was saying, covering a yawn politely behind his hand.

Percival had gone to sit in the window, one shoulder hunched against the talk of his elders as he stared out at the cold autumn night. He, also, had declined coffee, but in a politer manner than had his mother. He merely appeared wishful of putting himself beyond anything that was occurring in the room. He responded even to his sister's confidences in the briefest fashion.

Guineveve left her brother to his own devices and wandered over to join Penelope on the settee. She took a refill of coffee from Penelope's hands with a murmur of thanks and the casting of a shy glance.

Penelope smiled at the girl. "You and your brother favor one another a great deal."

"Oh well, of course. We are twins," said Guineveve, surprised.

"Indeed! I should have guessed, of course," said Penelope, glancing from the girl to her brother and back again. "I have observed that you are quite devoted to one another."

"Percy and I are the best of friends," said Guineveve simply.

"I envy you, then. I come of a large family, but I think my sisters and I were as often rivals as we were friends," said Penelope. "We got one another into all sorts of scrapes, but still, we did have such good times."

"That is just the way with me and Percy." Guineveve sighed a little as her eyes strayed toward her brother. "We did not wish to come with Mama to Holybrooke, but now we are rather glad that we did so. Since we have been here, we have had such fun exploring this old pile." Her eyes gleamed suddenly. "There are said to be ghosts haunting the halls, you know."

Penelope smiled. "Are there, indeed. Have you or Percival seen any such frightening characters roaming about in the course of your explorations?"

Guineveve shook her head with profound regret. "Oh, no. Lady Serena says the ghosts only appear when someone has been murdered, so I don't suppose Percy and I will be fortunate enough to witness any at all."

Penelope laughed.

After a look of wide-eyed surprise, Guineveve giggled. "Oh, that does sound so terrible, does it not?"

"Guineveve!"

The girl started badly and her cup rattled against the saucer, splashing a few drops of coffee on her skirt. Her expression changed instantly to one of apprehension. Penelope took the cup out of her hand, pitying her once again.

"What do you think you are about, miss?"

"I—I was but conversing with Miss Childe, Mama."

Mrs. Holland glanced in Penelope's direction, but her polite smile did not quite reach her eyes. "And behaved quite clumsily, I might add. You may say good night now, Guineveve. We are retiring."

The girl flushed, dropping her eyes. "Yes, Mama."

The Holland ladies made known their intention to the gentlemen. Percival, after a keen glance at his sister's downcast face, announced with a feigned yawn that he also meant to seek his bed. "So I shall myself escort my two favorite ladies," he said, offering an arm each to his mother and sister.

"Thank you, Percival. As always, you are the perfect gentleman," said Mrs. Holland.

The Hollands left the parlor.

As the last lady, Penelope could not very well remain in the parlor with the gentlemen, so after a few moments she also made her excuses.

Lord Taredell, an enigmatic expression in his eyes, lifted her hand to his lips. He did not release her hand immediately, but looked down at her with his twisted smile. "Good night, Miss Childe."

Penelope murmured something polite and escaped, glad to leave the gentlemen to themselves. As she closed the door behind her, she heard Lord Watersham's voice.

"What a surprising fellow you are, Taredell. I would not have thought it in your line at all to make up to your own betrothed, especially that little dab of a piece."

Her face burning, Penelope did not linger to hear whether the viscount made a reply, but quickly crossed the entry hall and went upstairs.

In the empty landing hall, she was startled to hear Guineveve's voice.

"Oh, Percy! She said such *things!*"

Penelope saw that a door opposite her was standing ajar, and she was about to go her way when she heard her own name.

"I know she did, Guin. She doesn't care for the Childe above half, does she?"

Penelope heard the soft sound of muffled sobs, then again Percival's gruff young voice. "Chin up, Guin. It is not much longer. When I gain my inheritance I shall do something for you."

"I don't know that I can bear it, Percy. Sometimes—sometimes I wish that I could die."

"You wouldn't see the ghosts then, would you? I tell you what, I shall get myself beheaded or some such thing and then you'll have your ghosts. That would cheer you, wouldn't it?"

There was a gurgle of laughter. "Percy, you idiot."

Suddenly ashamed that she had tarried to listen, Penelope quickly hurried on and turned the corner into her own hall. As she entered her bedroom, she thought how fortunate she had been to have the love of her parents, and how very much she liked Percival Holland.

Penelope bolted upright in her bed. Her pulses pounded as the echo of the scream died away.

Awake but with sleep still clinging to her, she heard voices raised in question and doors opening. Then she knew that it had not been some awful figment of a dream. She parted the heavy brocaded velvet bed draperies and scrambled out of the warmth of the bed.

The cold night air struck her instantly through her

chemise and the icy floor chilled the soles of her feet. Shivering, Penelope thrust her feet into slippers as she snatched up her dressing gown. She flung on the heavy garment as she fumbled her way in the dark to her bedroom door.

When she managed to get the door open, she looked out upon a scene incongruous for the late hour. Candle flames flickered over the watching painted faces of the portraits hung on the high walls. Several people unknown to her scurried to and fro while others simply stood about as though idling.

Recognizing of a sudden Lady Serena, Penelope stepped out and accosted her. "My lady! I heard the most terrible sound. What has happened?"

Lady Serena seemed to look straight through her. "The vile dastard is dead at last, thank God! I am not sorry for it, no! He deserved to die a dog's death."

As Penelope shrank back in dismay, Lady Serena's eyes focused upon her at last. Quite calmly she said, "I hated him, my dear. I hated him with a passion."

Her ladyship's maid hurried up and whispered urgently to her employer. Penelope caught the word "laudanum." Lady Serena flapped her hand as though she were brushing at an annoying fly. "Yes, yes. Very well." Without another glance or word to Penelope, Lady Serena allowed the maid to lead her back down the hall toward her rooms.

Penelope watched them only a moment before she turned her head toward the other end of the hall. Flickering light spilled out of the open door of the earl's bedroom. Without giving thought to the wisdom of what she was doing, Penelope hurried toward it.

On the threshold she hesitated, struck in that instant by the impropriety of her action in entering the earl's rooms. But then her eyes became riveted on the cause of the upset.

The body of the earl hung from the massive bed-frame. The gilt cord that normally tied back the draperies had been twisted and knotted to a far grimmer use.

Lord Taredell stood on the bed, slashing with a sword at the heavy cord. Standing below, Mr. Fennell and the butler steadied the body and waited to catch it when it should fall free.

Penelope exclaimed in horror.

The viscount's head turned and he stared at her. His eyes blazed with an emotion that Penelope dared not name.

The room swayed suddenly before her eyes. She grasped for the side of the door jamb.

Lord Taredell's voice came savagely to her ringing ears. "Edward!"

Mr. Fennell spun about. He took in the situation at a glance and quickly bounded across the room. "Miss Childe!" Ungently he grasped her by the upper arms and turned her, but not swiftly enough.

Penelope had a fleeting impression of the frayed cord at last parting, the body slumping suddenly into the butler's waiting arms, and Lord Taredell throwing down the sword as he leaped from the bed to the floor to aid with the easing of the burden.

Then Mr. Fennell had swept her out into the now-darkened corridor. Dazedly Penelope wondered where the others she had seen had gotten to.

"Miss Childe, you should not have seen that."

Penelope wrapped her arms about herself, shivering uncontrollably. Heedless of Mr. Fennell's censorous tone, she stared up into his face. ''The earl—it was the earl, was it not?''

''Yes.''

It was said flatly. There was a peculiar wildness about Mr. Fennell's eyes that, coupled with the unkempt state of his hair and dress, unnerved Penelope. He was quite unlike the correct and sober gentleman she had felt drawn to confide in earlier that evening.

''You are shaking with cold, Miss Childe. I will return you to your room.''

Penelope took a step backward, irrationally fearful. ''No.''

From behind, fingers clamped hard about her elbow. Penelope gasped, then sobbed a breath when she looked up into the hard face of Lord Taredell.

''I shall see to her now, Edward. Do you see to the other.''

Without waiting for Mr. Fennell's acknowledgment, Lord Taredell propelled Penelope through another open door. He kicked the door shut, tossed aside the bare sword in his free hand so that it clattered against the wall, and pulled Penelope along with him across the room.

Penelope on the instant realized not only that she was in the viscount's own bedroom but that he was headed in the direction of a huge velvet-draped four-posted bed. She began to struggle wildly against her captor. ''No!''

''What the devil?''

Lord Taredell pinned her arms against her sides, staring down at her a bare second before he shook her. ''I shall not have hysterics from you, ma'am!''

''Unhand me!''

He saw the direction of her wild glance. A certain

grim amusement entered his eyes. "You little fool. I have just cut down my father's murdered corpse. I assure you, ravishment is the farthest thing from my thoughts."

Penelope stared up into his face. His contempt for her was plain. Certainly there was nothing of lust in his hard eyes. Mortification flooded her face. She swallowed. "I—I was not thinking clearly."

Lord Taredell released her. Stepping around her, he lifted a decanter from the side table set against the wall. He poured a generous glass and returned with it. "Drink this."

Penelope shook her head quickly. She had folded her arms again around herself and unconsciously her hands traveled up and down as she sought to warm herself. She could not erase from her mind the hideous thing she had seen. "The earl—"

Lord Taredell caught her by the nape of the neck with one large hand. His voice was icy as he set the glass to her mouth. "Drink it willingly or I shall force it down your lovely throat."

Penelope felt the inherent strength of the fingers about her neck and, meeting his darkened eyes, she saw the implacability of his intention. Reluctantly she opened her lips and swallowed the bitter spirits.

She choked on the burning stuff and began coughing violently, alternatingly dragging in heaving breaths. All the while she was aware of the viscount's hand supporting her.

Finally, the tears still streaming from her eyes, she managed to regain control of herself. She glared up at him, saying hoarsely, "Was it truly necessary to poison me, my lord?"

Lord Taredell laughed, an exercise that lightened

the expression in his eyes and lent his handsome face surprising charm. "It was an extreme measure," he agreed, setting down the wineglass. "However, I believe fully justified under the circumstances. You are no longer paler than your chemise."

With a swift downward glance, Penelope realized that her dressing gown had fallen open so that her nightdress was plainly visible. Worse, the ribbons that laced it at the bosom had come undone. She flushed, and with as much dignity as possible drew her dressing gown together. "By your leave, my lord, I shall return to my own room."

"Not quite yet." Lord Taredell noticed the instant stiffening of her carriage, and easily guessing the leap of her thoughts, he smiled mockingly. "Whatever you might have heard to the contrary, I am not in the habit of ravishing unwilling ladies. You . . . *are* unwilling, Miss Childe?"

Penelope felt her heart begin to pound. "This is not a proper conversation."

The viscount's twisted smile became more pronounced. "Under different circumstances, it would be most proper. You may go, Miss Childe, but I must first ask you what, if anything, you might have heard or observed this evening that struck you as odd."

Instantly Penelope was thrust back to those hideous moments. "That—that dreadful scream. I still shudder, recalling it."

Lord Taredell's dark brows knitted. "Scream, Miss Childe?"

"Yes. That is what wakened me, of course—that and all the doors opening. I opened my own door and I saw everyone milling about and—and I followed the light to the earl's rooms." Penelope made a disconcerting discovery in the oddness that entered into his expression. "My lord—did you not hear . . . ?"

Lord Taredell slowly shook his head. His stern mouth was tight. "I did not hear anyone scream, Miss Childe. Nor, as far as I am aware, did anyone else."

"But . . . I did hear it. It was unearthly. It must have wakened everyone in the house."

"Perhaps you only dreamed it, Miss Childe."

Penelope could hear the measured ticking of a clock somewhere close by as she stared up into the impassive face that masked his thoughts. After several seconds she said stiffly, "I assure you that I am not a fanciful woman, my lord."

"Are you not, Miss Childe?"

Penelope saw the flick of his gaze in the direction of the bed. She flushed. "You have sufficiently insulted me, my lord." She whirled around to the bedroom door.

Before she had completely fumbled it open, the viscount reached past her to flatten a palm against the panels of the door. His weight effectively stopped it from opening. The firelight glinted in his eyes as he caught her startled gaze. "It would be best if you do not repeat to anyone else what you thought you heard, Miss Childe. My father is dead—murdered. Under the circumstances such talk could only arouse unnecessary speculation."

Penelope was acutely aware of how near he stood to her. The silk brocade banyan he had tossed on accented the breadth of his shoulders and the power inherent in his athletic build. She felt short of breath, as though his very physical presence threatened dominance of her own character. Undoubtedly that was precisely the effect he strove for, she thought, but the realization did not entirely dispel her unease. She stammered, "Of course, my lord. You may rely upon my discretion."

Lord Taredell held her eyes a moment longer, but he was apparently satisfied with what he saw. He withdrew his hand from the panel and opened the door. "I shall escort you to your room, Miss Childe."

"That will not be necessary, my lord," she said. But even as she made a polite refusal, the viscount placed her arm through his and stepped down the hall with her.

It was but a short distance to her room, though Penelope felt the way to be infinitely longer. Lord Taredell paused before the door that she had left ajar. He cast a keen glance about the shadowed bedroom. "Except that the fire has died, everything appears in order."

Penelope realized with astonishment that he was actually taking the precaution of looking for a lurking intruder. Before, she had heard but not really fully taken in what the viscount had said regarding the Earl of Holybrooke's death. She stared with frightened eyes around the bedroom, but she saw, with a sense of relief, that there was no place that could provide adequate concealment for a murderer.

A manservant hastened up to them. "My lord! Mr. Fennell begs that you join him. The magistrate and the physician have been sent for and are expected shortly."

Lord Taredell nodded his understanding.

Penelope saw the new grimness that suddenly bracketed his mouth. She realized the significance of the message and she pitied him for the ordeal he had yet to endure. Hesitantly she touched his sleeve. "There will be questions, of course. I am sincerely sorry for it, my lord."

The viscount unexpectedly caught up her hand and carried it to his lips for the briefest of salutes.

"Good night, my dear lady."

It was so softly spoken that Penelope thought she must surely have mistaken his words. Lord Taredell had already turned on his heel and was swiftly striding away, so that she had not the opportunity to judge anything from his expression.

Penelope went inside her bedroom and slowly closed the door. As an afterthought, she locked it.

For the remainder of the night, Penelope slept badly, alternately waking to lie tense in anticipation of hearing again the awful scream or to stare up into the black shadows of the bed canopy as she wondered what Lord Taredell was going through. In the end, she finally fell into a deep slumber at nearly dawn and so did not wake until much too late for breakfast. The maid brought her a cup of chocolate, after which Penelope requested that a hipbath be filled.

It was therefore time for luncheon before Penelope emerged from her bedroom and went downstairs. Entering the dining room, she found that she was one of the last to appear.

"Ah, Miss Childe, there you are. I was just saying I thought you must have lost your way this morning because you never came down for breakfast. I was about to send a servant up to guide you," said Lord Watersham.

"I appreciate the kindness of your thought, Lord Watersham."

Percival and Guineveve both greeted her with re-

serve, though not, Penelope believed, with unfriend-
liness. However, Mrs. Holland spared her only the
barest of nods.

Colonel Caldar stood up to hold a chair for her.
Penelope slipped into the seat with a smile and a murmur of thanks.

She declined the footman's offer to serve her plate,
requesting instead only tea and a bowl of barley soup.
She turned then to Lord Watersham and Mrs. Holland. "I am most sorry for your loss." Both froze in
their mundane pursuit of sustenance to stare at her.

"What did you say, Miss Childe?" Mrs. Holland
asked sharply.

Penelope looked from one to the other in growing
horror as she realized that they did not already know
about the earl's death. "I *am* sorry. I thought you
knew."

"The earl—he's dead?" exclaimed Mrs. Holland.

"Nonsense! Taredell or Fennell would have told us
before this," said Lord Watersham. His expression
changed. "Come to think of it, where are they? Odd,
I have not seen either of them this morning."

"Very odd, indeed! I must see Taredell at once,"
said Mrs. Holland, throwing down her napkin and rising precipitiously from the table.

On the heels of her exclamation, the door to the
dining room opened and the viscount's familiar mocking voice said, "Behold me, Aurelia."

He was instantly cannonaded by questions.

"Is it true, Taredell?"

"Has his lordship been carried off at last, then?"

"When is the sollicitor arriving? I want the will to
be read at once."

Without replying to his relations, Lord Taredell

slanted a glance in Penelope's direction. "Your sense of discretion is amazing, ma'am."

"I—I had thought everyone must surely have been informed," said Penelope.

"A natural assumption, Miss Childe," said Lord Watersham indignantly. "So we should have been. I am insulted, 'pon my word!"

"Peace, cousin, I pray you. I have been up all the night with the business, as has Edward. Surely a man can be allowed to address his first mouthful of the day before he is torn apart by his relations?"

"As to that, well, of course," said Lord Watersham, somewhat abashed. "I suppose that I can wait a few moments longer."

Lord Taredell made an ironic bow to his lordship as he signaled the footman to prepare him a plate from the several dishes on the side table.

"I shall not be so accommodating, however. I wish to know why Miss Childe is so far in your confidence, Taredell. She is the least of us all and yet she knows more than anyone," said Mrs. Holland.

"Exercise a modicum of restraint, Aurelia. At least let the man have his meat," said Colonel Caldar. "In any event, his lordship knows his own business best."

"You may think so, but in this instance I do not!"

Penelope created a diversion. "Coffee, my lord?"

Lord Taredell met her eyes. The faintest of smiles touched his lips. "Thank you, Miss Childe; black, please."

"My lord, I must demand—"

The door opened again, interrupting whatever Mrs. Holland meant to say. Mr. Fennell entered. His expression was tired as he said, "The magistrate has just this moment left, my lord."

"Magistrate! Whatever was that fellow here for? Surely there was no question of how the earl died," said Lord Watersham, frowning heavily as he looked from one to the other.

"None whatsoever, cousin. It is an indisputable fact. The earl was murdered," said Lord Taredell harshly.

His statement struck those who had not been aware of the truth with varying degrees of effect.

Colonel Caldar swore pithily and fluently.

Mrs. Holland stared a moment. Then, with an odd little smile, she turned her eyes in the direction of her son. "Percival."

Percival looked horrified and stunned, as did his sister.

Lord Watersham's countenance had acquired a peculiarly unhealthy cast. He cleared his throat. "How, Taredell?"

"He was hanged from his bedframe."

Lord Watersham shook his head as though attempting, but failing, to take in the news. "Perhaps . . . suicide? His lordship was known to be in great pain, was he not?"

"It was the physician's opinion that my father had neither the strength nor the presence of mind to accomplish such an act on his own," said Lord Taredell.

"But that means . . . Good God!"

Lord Taredell's smile was more twisted than usual in response to the colonel's horrified exclamation. "You are quite right, sir. One amongst us is capable of murder."

Instant expressions of denial and revulsion sprang from most lips.

Penelope herself uttered rejection of the hideous assertion, yet as instantly she realized that it was undoubtedly true. Someone in the household had hated the earl enough that he or she would not allow his lordship a natural death. She recalled Lady Serena's declaration of hatred for the earl, and then her eyes went to Mrs. Holland, who had stated just as vigorously that she would do anything to ensure her son's claim on the title. Perhaps Mrs. Holland had feared the possibility of the Earl of Holybrooke returning to consciousness and repenting of his callous denial of his original heir, Lord Taredell.

Penelope stared at Percival Holland, who indisputably had the most to gain from the earl's death. Something of her thoughts must have showed on her face. As Percival's eyes rose to meet hers, he flushed, then turned deathly pale.

He sprang to his feet, knocking his chair over backward. "I did not do it, I swear!" His desperate young voice broke the tableau.

"You stupid young chub!" exclaimed Colonel Caldar.

"Of course you did not, Percy!" Guineveve leaped up to stand beside her brother and put an arm around him protectively.

"That will be for others to decide," said Mr. Fennell very quietly.

"How *dare* you, Mr. Fennell!" Mrs. Holland's voice throbbed with fury. There was nothing of the frail beauty now in her flashing eyes or outraged posture. "What of yourself, sir? The earl was your father, as well as Taredell's. No, I will not be silent, brother! It is no secret; it is well known to us all. Perhaps, Mr. Fennell, you hoped to discredit my Percival with this foul deed and so gain something that you would not otherwise receive!"

"We are all of us suspect, one way or another."

Lord Taredell's steely tone cut across the rapidly accelerating accusations. The tumult was checked as all eyes riveted upon him. Deliberately, he set down his coffee. "I could be said to have the darkest motive of all, for there was little of affection between me and my father. As Edward said, there will be conclusions drawn and a decision come to by the investigating authority. In the meantime, we are all requested to remain at Holybrooke."

"I shall need to apprise my superiors, my lord," warned Colonel Caldar.

"Of course, Colonel. That is understood. I shall trust you to put the matter as discreetly as possible," said Lord Taredell.

Colonel Caldar stared at the viscount and gave an abrupt nod of understanding.

"I must go tell Mama," said Lord Watersham. He was obviously extremely shaken. "The news will be most unsettling for her, I fear. I do not anticipate bearing this intelligence, I can tell you."

"Lady Serena is already aware of her brother's death, my lord," said Penelope gently. "Her ladyship spoke about it to me last night when I was roused from my own bed and went to discover what had happened."

"What is this? What do you mean—roused from your bed, Miss Childe?" asked Lord Watersham sharply.

Penelope heard with astonishment the suspicion in his voice.

Lord Taredell smoothly interjected. "My father's valet discovered his lordship and immediately came to waken me. The man was not as quiet about the business as one could have wished. Undoubtedly, since you are situated in the other hall, your own rest remained undisturbed.''

Lord Watersham nodded, suddenly deflated. "I shall go up to see my mother," he said heavily, and left the dining room.

"I, too, shall make my excuses. I would like to change into more seemly attire," said Mr. Fennell.

For the first time Penelope noticed that Mr. Fennell wore the same coat and breeches as he had the evening before. No doubt, in the haste of the moment, he had thrown on those things closest to hand when he had left his bed.

"Of course, Edward." Lord Taredell rose out of his chair to clasp the man's shoulder. "Thank you for all you have done this night."

Mr. Fennell's smile twisted in a fashion very like the viscount's own. "It has been a devilish night, Taredell."

"Go to bed. I shall have you called when the solicitor arrives," said Lord Taredell.

Mr. Fennell made a gesture of protest. "But you, my lord?"

"You forget, Edward. I am used to gaming the night away and the next day as well," said Lord Taredell.

Mr. Fennell laughed, nodded, and went out.

Lord Taredell turned back in time to observe his betrothed's face turn paper-white. As he watched, her hand crept to her throat. "Miss Childe?"

Penelope looked up at him, her eyes haunted. "I thought I heard—" At his altering expression, her scattered wits swiftly reasserted themselves. With a swift glance about at the others, who were all regarding her with mild curiosity, she managed a small laugh.

"It was nothing, my lord. My nerves are sadly wanting, I fear."

"I quite understand, Miss Childe. It is extremely unnerving to learn that one's host has been murdered," said Lord Taredell with irony.

Mrs. Holland came from around the table. "Taredell, you will send for me also when the solicitor arrives. I shall lie down until then, for I am quite overcome by this tragic communication and the unwarranted and scandalous suspicions cast upon my dearest boy."

"Of course, Aurelia." There was enough mockery lacing the gravity of Lord Taredell's voice to arouse a renewed flash of anger in his sister-in-law's eyes. She swept out of the dining room with her head held high.

Percival and Guineveve exchanged a speaking glance. Then in one accord they hurried out. As the door swung shut, Percival was heard to call, "I shall race you to the gallery!"

Colonel Caldar shook his head. He glanced at the viscount. "Pray call upon me if there should prove a need to do so," he said quietly.

Lord Taredell nodded and the colonel exited also.

Penelope freshened her tea from the still-warm pot. She was surprised when she saw Lord Taredell put down his fork. Throughout the tense proceedings he had continued with his meal in the calmest manner.

But now the viscount laid his head to rest against the back of his chair and with a long sigh closed his eyes. He appeared incredibly tired and his formidable presence had lessened to the degree of vulnerability.

She felt a wave of compassion for him. It must surely be a terrible burden to have to deal with the violent death of one's parent, no matter how estranged one was from that parent, and to know that a member of one's own family had been responsible.

He seemed to have dropped into a light doze.

Penelope did not wish to disturb him by any noise she might make in finishing her light luncheon, so she carefully set down her cup and quietly rose from the table, intending to leave the viscount to whatever moments of peace he would have before the servants reappeared to clear the covers.

She had taken scarcely two steps from the table when he spoke. "No, stay."

Penelope turned. "My lord?"

He sighed again and opened his eyes. "Miss Childe, must I repeat myself to you? I had thought I was very clear."

"Of course not." Penelope returned to her chair, to sit with stiff posture and with her hands folded. "What is it you wished, my lord?"

Lord Taredell reached over the corner of the table to take one of her hands. He turned it over and drew his thumb across her palm. "You have had bad reports of me already, I am certain," he said with the faintest of smiles.

Penelope did not pretend to misunderstand him. All too vivid was her memory of making an absolute idiot of herself in his bedroom the night before. "Yes, my lord. Mrs. Holland was so obliging as to inform me." She willed herself to ignore the caressing action of his thumb.

"Just so. You will undoubtedly hear worse of me before the question of my father's death is resolved."

"It is shocking. Everyone must feel the horror of it," said Penelope.

"Not everyone, my dear." His voice was suddenly

cold. His long fingers tightened about her hand. "You heard it again, did you not?"

Penelope swallowed, startled by the intensity of his voice. The strange expression in his eyes made her heart hammer. She tried to pull away her hand. "You are hurting me, my lord. Pray let me go."

"Answer me, damn you. You heard it again in this very room, did you not?"

Penelope shrank back from the inexplicable black fury in his eyes. "Yes, I heard it. That—that dreadful, horrible scream. But no one else did so. I thought surely I must be imagining it this time."

Lord Taredell slowly released her hand, only to lift his own hand and draw it over his face in an infinitely weary gesture. "You did not imagine it, Miss Childe, not this time nor the first. You have been privileged, if you will, to hear the curse that has haunted our ancestors for centuries."

Penelope stared at him, quite bereft of words.

At her shocked expression, Lord Taredell gave a bark of unamused laughter. "We are neither of us mad, my dear. You have heard it and I believe quite implicitly that you have done so."

"But that is sheer nonsense. I do not believe it," said Penelope. Her entire being revolted at the thought that there could exist a physical manifestation of the supernatural. Yet she felt a chilling shiver crawl up her spine.

Lord Taredell shrugged, as though the matter were of no more importance. "As you will, Miss Childe. However, you cannot fail to understand now why I enjoined your silence upon the matter."

"Quite! Everyone would have thought I was mad."

Lord Taredell actually laughed, and his entire face

lightened in an amazing fashion. For an instant, Penelope had a glimpse of what his character might have been like in other circumstances.

He stood up and held out his hand to her. "The servants are undoubtedly waiting to clear the covers." Obediantly, Penelope placed her hand in his and allowed him to draw her to her feet.

Instead of ushering her immediately out of the dining room, Lord Taredell frowned down at her in a considering way. "We will not speak of this again, except that I want your word of honor that you will instantly inform me if you hear it again."

Penelope regarded him somberly, attempting to read more than his hooded gaze would reveal to her. "Is it so important that I do so, my lord?" she asked quietly.

"More than you now know, my lady," he said grimly.

A manservant stepped into the dining room. "My lord, the solicitor has arrived and is waiting in the study."

"Very good. I shall be with the gentleman directly."

Lord Taredell turned back to Penelope and raised her hand to his lips. Then, with a flicker of his twisted smile, he showed her out of the dining room. In the wide hall he separated from her.

Penelope watched the viscount striding swiftly away down the hall. She turned to mount the narrow stairs, her brows knit by a frown. It had been already a singularly unsettling morning. Not the least disturbing had been Lord Taredell's abrupt change of behavior toward her.

His bid for her complicity and his almost solicitous tone had left her very confused. She had thought there to be between them nothing but rude antagonism. However, that was hardly true now, though she could not have explained what had changed. Nor could she explain why her heart was still pounding from the effect of his last lingering glance.

As Penelope reached the upper landing, she was hailed by Guineveve.

"Miss Childe, have you seen Percy?"

Penelope smiled at the girl. "Why, no. I have just come from the dining room. I thought you had gone off to explore again."

"Yes, so we did for a while. Then Percy began hiding from me, daring me to find him. And so I have, every time, until now."

Penelope laughed. "I am certain he cannot have gone far, then. It is too damp and cold for him to have gone out-of-doors, of course, so he must be close by. In fact, I would not be in the least surprised if he were not listening to us this very moment."

Guineveve looked swiftly up and down the hall at the various doors. "That would be just like him, indeed."

"Guineveve? Drat the girl, where has she gotten to? Guineveve!"

The girl sighed. "That is Mama. I shall have to go to her. Whenever she is restless she wants me to read to her. I have no notion why, for it does not soothe her in the least. She says she is made irritated by the quality of my voice." The animation had gone completely out of her countenance, and her manner as she fiddled with the laces of her bodice was far from happy.

"There is something to be said for it, however. If Percival is not within earshot, as we suspect, then he will not know that you are no longer searching for him.''

Guineveve's deep blue eyes brightened. ''Oh, how very entertaining. He will stay in his hiding place simply forever, wondering how I came to be so stupid not to discover him. Won't Percy feel the fool when he finally comes out to find me.''

Penelope smiled as the girl went off humming. She was glad that her little suggestion had worked to such good effect, for she had seen that Guineveve's position with Mrs. Holland hardly rivaled that enjoyed by her twin brother.

Penelope turned into the second hall and went on to her room. She had scarcely stepped foot across the threshold before Lady Serena's maid was knocking at her door with the request that she visit with her ladyship at her earliest convenience.

Penelope went at once and found the lady in her sitting room. Lady Serena greeted her warmly and urged her to sit down. Penelope did so with an expression of thanks.

Lady Serena signaled the maid to leave them. She turned to Penelope. ''You must wonder why I have summoned you, Miss Childe. I shall tell you without being unduly roundabout. When I wakened this morning I recalled that I had seen you in the hall last night, and that you had said you had heard a terrible sound. Then I knew that I must speak with you, for you had been touched by the curse.''

Penelope shuddered. ''Pray do not phrase it just so. It rather unnerves me.''

''Quite. That same disconcertion is what I have anticipated ever since we arrived, for I, too, am peculiarly sensitive. I had hoped never to hear it again,'' said Lady Serena. "Odd, that you should be so attuned when you have but the vaguest blood connection to the family."

Penelope stared at the elderly lady. "But then—last night, did you hear the scream as well, my lady?"

Lady Serena nodded. "Oh, yes. It is the second time in my life that I have done so, though I do not recall observing the ghosts in the hall before. I had thought that part of the old tale to be an exaggeration."

"What do you mean? What ghosts?" Penelope suspected she already knew as a fresh chill crawled up her spine.

"Surely you noticed? Besides myself, you and my maid, all the others did not really exist."

"I—I cannot accept that."

Lady Serena reached out to touch Penelope's hand. "Think, my dear. What sort of attire had they?"

Penelope had a sudden sharp recollection of the turmoil in the hall. Those others who had hurried before her, and who Lady Serena now said did not exist, had worn lace ruffs and garters such as had not been seen for nearly three hundred years.

"It is not possible!"

Penelope was truly shaken. She dared not believe in the material existence of the supernatural. It was so much more comfortable to think of it as an intangible, something spoken about on a Sunday morn in chapel.

Despite Penelope's denial, Lady Serena apparently gathered that she was convinced. Her ladyship smiled a little. "Miss Childe, have you heard or seen anything else? This morning, perhaps?"

Penelope stared at her companion in morbid fascination. "You know that I have, for you have done so yourself."

"Yes." Lady Serena looked away, appearing suddenly very frail. "I fear where death will strike, my dear. I was glad when my brother died. He was an evil man and should by rights have been murdered years before this. But I do not wish death upon anyone else."

"What do you mean?" Penelope asked sharply as fear contracted her heart. "Surely you do not believe—"

"The harbinger we have heard, you and I, is only heard when there is murder to be done," said Lady Serena. "It is our family's curse, but our blessing as well, that it be so. We are in a fashion forewarned, you see." Lady Serena's eyes abruptly acquired an unfocused appearance and her lips moved without sound issuing forth.

Penelope took urgent hold of her ladyship's hands. "My lady! Do you know who it will be, my lady? Can you tell me that? Lady Serena! Please, if you know, you must tell me!" Her voice unconsciously rose as she pleaded with the unresponsive woman. Lady Serena's maid returned.

"Her ladyship must rest now, miss."

"Of course. I shall go." Penelope rose, reluctant but aware that she had no other choice in the matter. Lady Serena had effectively placed herself beyond anyone's reach. Penelope allowed the maid to usher her to the door.

As she started through it, she was startled to hear her name called. She turned quickly. "Lady Serena!"

Lady Serena turned her head. Penelope was dismayed to see tears coursing down her withered cheeks.

"My son is a fool," she said falteringly, "but I love him for all of that."

"Miss, if you please."

Penelope did not linger any longer. She had only one desire now and that was to find Lord Taredell at once. She had to talk with the viscount. He was the only one who could forewarn Lord Watersham of the danger in which he stood and be believed.

Penelope swiftly retraced her steps. If she was fortunate, Lord Taredell would be found to be still closeted with the solicitor. Otherwise she would have to waste precious moments in looking for him.

Rushing out upon the landing, Penelope nearly collided with Mr. Fennell. The gentleman steadied her. "Miss Childe!"

"Forgive me! But I must find Lord Taredell at once," said Penelope breathlessly, attempting to brush past the gentleman.

However, Mr. Fennell did not immediately release her arm. His keen gaze raked her face. "You are upset, Miss Childe. Perhaps I may be of some service to you?"

Short of jerking herself free, Penelope could not escape without risking further offense to him. "Only help me to find Lord Taredell," she begged.

A frown creased his brow and he said slowly, "His lordship is in the study. I have just been informed that the solicitor is waiting upon us all."

"Thank God!" Penelope loosed herself from his slackened fingers and started down the stairs, her skirts lifted high so that she would not trip as she ran.

"Miss Childe!"

She did not check her pace at Mr. Fennell's call, but nevertheless he caught up with her at the bottom step.

Once more he took hold of her elbow. "Miss Childe, your manner alarms me. Pray, whatever the matter is I think that I should be told."

Penelope's one thought was to impress upon him the urgency of her quest so that he would stop hindering her. "I have heard the cursed scream, Mr. Fennell." Her words tumbled out before she could retrieve them. "And I believe that I know who is the next target for violence."

There was a flicker of surprise in the gentleman's eyes. "How utterly . . . extraordinary."

"Oh, I know it sounds absurd, but it is true. Lord Taredell knows of it, as does Lady Serena. Surely in your position here you must have heard of the curse as well." Penelope looked beseechingly up at him. "Mr. Fennell, pray do not delay me further. You *must* see why it is imperative that I speak with Lord Taredell."

"Indeed I do, Miss Childe. I shall naturally accompany you at once to the study and lend whatever credence I can to this bizarre happening," said Mr. Fennell.

"*Thank* you, sir," Penelope said gratefully, and thus it was that she and Mr. Fennell entered the study together.

With the notable exceptions of Lady Serena and Percival Holland, all the other family members had already assembled. Colonel Caldar was also missing, but Penelope scarcely wondered at that since the gentleman had expressed himself not to have any interest in the proceedings. His only function had been to escort his sister and her children to Holybrooke.

Penelope at once looked for that individual she was most desirous of seeing, and her heart gave a leap of relief when she saw the viscount. Lord Taredell was speaking quietly to a small bent gentleman attired in a bagwig and a somber frock coat, who was undoubtedly the solicitor.

"My lord!" Penelope took a hasty step in the viscount's direction, but Mr. Fennell proved an unexpected obstacle as he still had hold of her elbow. She wondered with vague irritation at the gentleman's obtuseness.

Lord Taredell looked around. "Miss Childe; Edward. We are now all present, I think. As I was just explaining to Mr. Tweeks, Lady Serena indicated some days previously that she preferred not to participate in the reading of the will. So I think, Mr. Tweeks, that we may as well proceed."

"My lord, forgive me, but I must speak with you at once—privately!"

Lord Taredell raised his brows. His voice was gently reproving. "Truly, Miss Childe? Whatever you have to convey to me that is of such moment can surely be put off until we have finished with our business here."

"She has heard the curse," said Mr. Fennell. There was a gasp from Mrs. Holland, but Mr. Fennell's eyes did not stray to her. He continued to address the viscount. "She also claims to know who is next to meet with foul murder."

"Good Lord!" Lord Watersham stared disapprovingly at Penelope. "I had thought Miss Childe to be a sensible young woman. She has been listening to my mother too much of late, I suppose."

"You have always been a fool, Ambrose! You have never believed in anything that you did not see or hear for yourself," exclaimed Mrs. Holland sharply. "My dear husband told me of the traditions of this house, and upon becoming acquainted with the earl I could readily appreciate how such things could be true.''

"Madam, such disrespect has no place here," uttered Mr. Tweeks.

"Mama, no one knows where Percy is," whispered Gunieveve. Her eyes were huge and her face had whitened.

Mrs. Holland glanced quickly at her daughter's expression, and her own face took on the color of putty. "Oh, dear Lord, it is true! Percy is gone." Her hand went to her throat in a gesture that should have been theatrical but was not.

"It is not Percy!" exclaimed Penelope. "My lord, pray—I must speak with you!"

Mr. Fennell regarded the Holland ladies for a moment before he turned his gaze on Lord Taredell. Almost conversationally he asked, "Where is Percival?"

"He is quite . . . beyond your reach, Edward."

At the viscount's words, Penelope felt the tightening of Mr. Fennell's fingers on her elbow. She did not glance up at him in remonstrance, however, for her gaze was fixed on the face of her betrothed.

Lord Taredell wore an expression that she had never before seen. It was terrible to behold. There was cold calculation in his half-hooded eyes and a frightening ruthlessness about the set of his mouth.

"You fiend! You have killed him! You have murdered my son!"

Mrs. Holland flew shrieking at the viscount, her clawed fingers striking at his face.

Lord Taredell caught and held the hysterical woman at bay. "The devil take you, Aurelia, and be damned! Of course I have not murdered Percy. Dear God, Ambrose, take charge of her."

"Yes—of course! At once, dear fellow." On the words, Lord Watersham awkwardly pinned Mrs. Holland's arms to her sides and pulled her away.

As though she understood the futility of struggling, Mrs. Holland collapsed in a flood of noisy tears. The most ludicrous expression of dismay came over Lord Watersham's face at finding himself in such straits, but he rose manfully to the occasion. Murmuring awkward words of comfort, he gently guided the weeping woman to the settee.

Meanwhile Lord Taredell had turned back to Penelope and Mr. Fennell. He started toward them, but stopped short when Mr. Fennell brought his free hand out of his coat pocket, bearing in his grasp a pistol.

"That is near enough, Taredell," said Mr. Fennell pleasantly.

Penelope gasped at sight of the deadly weapon. She tried to draw away, but Mr. Fennell pulled her close against his side.

"I think not, Miss Childe."

Penelope's eyes flew to meet those of Lord Taredell. What she saw in their depths would have set her heart hammering with gladness under other circumstance.

After that one singular glance, the viscount did not waver in his attention to Mr. Fennell. His voice was neutral. "Unhand the lady, Edward. You have no need of her."

Mr. Fennell smiled slowly, thoughtfully. "Do I not, Taredell? It will give me the greatest pleasure to think of you lying tortured by thoughts of what I am doing to her."

Later, Penelope was never certain what took place next. She knew that the viscount leaped forward, accompanied by her own shouted warning ringing in her ears. There was a deafening roar and a thin billow of acrid smoke; screams and Lord Watersham's bellowed curses.

Then she was dragged back by an arm of steel, by fingers tight about her throat. She knew that she struggled but she was utterly powerless against that merciless grip and the inexorable progress toward the door.

All the while her horrified gaze was riveted upon the form of the viscount lying half sprawled over the desk, a dark patch of swiftly spreading blood high up on his coat. She screamed in protest, but the nightmare did not dissolve.

Lord Taredell struggled up, with the aid of Mr. Tweeks and Guineveve. Lord Watersham could offer naught but shouted encouragement to the viscount. Mrs. Holland had fainted dead away upon Lord Watersham's bosom and he was trapped on the settee by her weight. He was struggling at once to keep Mrs. Holland from sliding onto the floor and trying to push her over upon the settee.

Penelope's frozen mind registered the scene. Then she was knocked heavily to one side and the punishing grip on her throat fell away. Penelope fell hard against the edge of a marble-topped console table and would have fallen to the floor if she had not clutched it.

She heard scuffling and black curses. Dazed, she looked up.

Colonel Caldar and Mr. Fennell were engaged in a savage fight. Penelope saw the flash of a wicked dagger and sobbed an incoherent warning. The men's bodies shifted so that she could no longer see the blade. They strained together for heart-stopping moments. Then Colonel Caldar staggered back, clutching his side.

Mr. Fennell swiftly followed up his advantage, the bloodied dagger already striking downward.

Penelope watched in disbelieving horror.

Suddenly Lord Taredell lunged past her. She had a fleeting impression of a deadly short sword before the length of steel was plunged through Mr. Fennell from back to front.

Mr. Fennell stiffened, a horrible cry breaking from his lips. He started a slow turn, but nerveless fingers suddenly let go of the dagger. He fell forward, already dead.

Lord Taredell reached out to touch Penelope on the shoulder, a question in his eyes, and she nodded mutely. He then staggered forward to fall on his knees beside Colonel Caldar. He tore off his neckcloth, his movements awkward because of his wounded shoulder.

Penelope flew to his side. "I shall do it, my lord." She took the neckcloth from his clumsy fingers and competently formed a pad to press against Colonel Caldar's wound.

The viscount slumped against the wall, spent.

Penelope's eyes rose quickly to his haggard face. "My lord!"

"If you are about to inquire after my health, my dearest lady, I shall be compelled to give you a setdown," Lord Taredell enunciated.

Penelope smiled at him, her concern somewhat assuaged by his asperity. "I was only going to remark that I am happy to see that you will live."

"I shall undoubtedly live," said Lord Taredell with

a grimace of pain as he shifted to a more comfortable position.

A faint laugh came from Colonel Caldar from where he lay. "Aye, so shall we both."

The exigencies of the moment had excited Lord Watersham's mental capabilities. For once his grasp was swift and sure. With a muttered apology he had let Mrs. Holland's supine form roll to the floor and leaped over her to yank open the door. He set up a bellow for assistance that brought the household running. He spluttered orders—for the sending of a physician, for wine, for blankets, for bandages—in short, for anything that could conceivably be of comfort to the wounded men. Then he toed Mr. Fennell's body. "And get this poor madman out. Lay him in his bed until the magistrate has been in."

Guinevere had gone back to her mother, who had murmured a sigh but had not yet opened her eyes. Matter-of-factly, Guinevere placed a pillow under Mrs. Holland's head, retrieved the lady's smelling salts, and began to wave them under her nose.

Lord Watersham directed the footmen in their removal of Mr. Fennell's body, and as they exited with their burden, he was startled by an appearance he had not expected. "Mama! You should not be here to witness this upsetting scene."

Lady Serena did not acknowledge his lordship's exclamation of concern, nor his detaining hand on her arm. She stood immobile in the open door, supported on her far side by a white-faced Percival Holland.

As did the others, Guinevere looked up. When she saw her brother, she abandoned her mother and flew across the room. "Percy!" He caught her as she threw herself against him and they clung to one another.

Lord Taredell met Lady Serena's level gaze. He said quietly, "The curse is fulfilled once more. I have killed my brother, ma'am."

Mr. Tweeks had been straightening the papers that had been scattered when the viscount had fallen across the wide desk. He looked up. "I do not think you will be held in the least accountable, my lord. I shall myself testify in your defense."

Neither Lord Taredell nor Lady Serena appeared to hear the solicitor's measured reassurance.

Lady Serena inclined her head in sorrow. "It was inevitable, perhaps. Edward was a tortured soul. My brother saw to that. I suspect that he taunted poor Edward unbearably over his ignoble birth."

"Yes. My father delighted in subtle cruelties. He had Edward educated as a gentleman and acknowledged him as his by-blow, but he never extended either his name or his protection to ease Edward's lot," said Lord Taredell grimly.

Penelope had a flash of insight. "Is that why Mr. Fennell said once that your championship was at times more hindrance than otherwise, my lord?"

Lord Taredell gave a short, bitter laugh. "Edward was my father's firstborn, and despite his illegitimate birth, I felt that he deserved as much as I or my younger brother were entitled to. My father and I quarreled often over his contemptuous treatment of Edward. I see now that perhaps it would have been better if I had not tried so hard to plead his case."

Lady Serena gestured with her hand. "You are not to hold yourself to blame, John. The seeds were sown before your birth. My brother was uncaring of consequences, delighting instead in the misery of others. I do not think, however, that he ever foresaw that Edward would inherit a measure of his own madness and that it would in the end turn on him.''

"My lord, how did you know that it was Mr. Fennell who—who murdered the earl?'' asked Penelope.

"I did not know, not until you came dashing into the study with him and he asked me where Percy was. I knew then, of course, for there was no reason in the world that he should specifically turn to me, unless he had guessed that it was I who had spirited Percy away.''

Penelope looked from Lord Taredell to Percival Holland, who had set aside his sister and gone to help the reviving Mrs. Holland up. ''But I do not understand.''

Percival looked around as he settled his mother on the settee. "It was Lord Taredell's opinion that the earl had been murdered for the sole purpose of throwing suspicion upon me. He hoped to flush the murderer by my disappearance.''

Mrs. Holland put a wavering hand to her head. "I knew that Taredell was the author of your disappearance! But I cannot conceive how you came to agree to his outrageous suggestion, Percival.''

Percival exchanged a glance with the viscount. A smile tugged at his mouth. "My uncle's messenger was very . . . persuasive.''

"*That* was why I could not find you!'' exclaimed Guineveve, her eyes wide.

"You unutterable beast, Taredell! How you must have suffered at his hands, my son!''

"Pray desist, Aurelia. Your performance is not necessary, I assure you. Percival is safe, as is his inheritance,'' said Lord Taredell tiredly.

Mrs. Holland stared at the viscount, then rose

abruptly from the settee. "I shall not remain in the same room with his lordship. Mr. Tweeks, I assume that the will reading will be delayed?"

The solicitor regarded the lady with disapproval. "Indeed, madam."

Mrs. Holland nodded. She swept toward the door. "Guinevere, Percival, you shall come with me. There is nothing more of interest here this day."

Stalwart footmen had carefully picked up Colonel Caldar and were gently carrying him out of the study. He called out cordially, "Do go, Aurelia, by all means. I am touched by your sisterly concern, but I assure you that I will survive despite it."

"I shall see to my uncle, Mama," said Percival quietly. "And Guinevere will go with me."

Mrs. Holland looked at her offspring, offended. "Very well, do as you wish. I shall be resting in my rooms until dinner."

When the Hollands had left, Lord Watersham looked down on the viscount. "One does not wish to presume judgment, but I shouldn't wonder at it if that woman doesn't end in a bad way."

Lord Taredell laughed. "Go away, cousin, and take Mr. Tweeks with you. I am certain the gentleman would be appreciative of a glass of refreshment in more benign surroundings."

Lord Watersham peered about the study in a bewildered fashion. "Heh? I don't see why we couldn't make ourselves quite comfortable—"

Lady Serena firmly took his lordship's arm. "Come, Ambrose. Mr. Tweeks, if you please." She ushered the gentlemen out.

The door closed gently. Penelope looked over at the viscount. When he held his hand out to her, she joined him, slipping down beside him where he still reclined against the wall.

A crude bandage had been tied over the wound in his shoulder and he appeared pale, but there was all the original alertness in his gaze. For some reason she felt the heat rise in her face.

"Does it hurt horribly?" she asked.

"A ball lodged in one's shoulder is bound to, dear Miss Childe. That is not what concerns me at the moment, however." His hand came up under her chin and his eyes searched her face. "I have reflected deeply upon you in past hours, Miss Childe. When you appeared at the door during those terrible moments, your hair tumbled over your shoulders and horror in your eyes, it was as though I suffered a blow. I cannot adequately describe to you what I felt then, nor again when Edward threatened you."

Penelope managed to smile, though tears had unaccountably stung her eyes. "Surely it was not much different from what my own heart bespoke when I saw you fall."

"We have not been particularly cordial to one another these past few days. Perhaps . . . we might begin anew, Miss Childe?"

"I have no particular objection to it, my lord," said Penelope. The smile trembled on her lips.

"Dare I hope that you do not dislike me quite so adamantly?"

"I do not," she whispered.

"No?"

She shook her head mutely. She did not stiffen when he placed his good arm around her, instead willingly allowing him to draw her closer.

Lord Taredell regarded her intently from this interesting vantage point. He asked softly, "Would you object were I to take liberties with you, Miss Childe?"

"One must expect such from one's betrothed," she said primly, but with a flutter of laughter.

Her breathless amusement was silenced when his lips sought hers.

Through the lovely haze that surrounded her, Penelope felt an odd sensation of being under observation. She opened her eyes, and drew back from Lord Taredell to stare past him.

The courtier in Tudor costume bowed as though in farewell before sauntering through the solid wall.

"What is it, dearest lady?"

Penelope shook her head as she settled once more into Lord Taredell's embrace. "It was naught of importance, my lord." She smiled up at him rather shyly. "Dare I suggest further liberties, sir?"

The viscount answered her as only a wise man would have done.

Deceiving Appearances

by

Patricia Rice

ADMIRING THE IMAGE in the shop window of the well-dressed gentleman in gray top hat and velvet-collared cloak, Peter Denning straightened his broad shoulders, and when the image did the same, he smiled, cocked the hat to a rakish angle, and proceeded onward.

The absurd silk scarf dangling about his neck swung as he walked despite the expensive tiepin, and he felt a trifle foolish tucking a bit of stick beneath his arm as the other gentlemen on the street were wont to do, but his side-whiskers were neatly groomed and his Wellingtons gleamed and he was satisfied that he had perfected the image of the perfect gentleman that he had set out to portray. The knowledge that he was no such thing was keenly imprinted in his mind, but there was no need for the world to know that.

It was not that he meant to defraud the society in which he walked. He had as much wealth and more as the young gentlemen in the club to which he turned his feet now. Unfortunately, that wealth had not come about from the opportune demise of one of his relatives. His mother had been a lady's maid who had never seen two coins to rub together in all her life. His father had had the courtesy to marry her before dis-

295

appearing from their lives, but that had been the extent of his involvement in Peter's affairs. No, the wealth that paid for a well-appointed apartment in Mayfair, a valet who had naught better to do than see to his master's newly acquired wardrobe, and a rig and four that ate their worth in expensive feed had come from hard toil.

Not to mention a certain shipping venture that had uncovered unexpected profits. Denning grinned to himself as he pushed open the elaborately carved door, and a servant who had shirked his duties came rushing forward filled with apology, bowing and scraping as Peter handed him his cane and hat. After all those years on the sea in the company of men who ate, slept, and breathed in their own filth, he was finding it exceedingly pleasant to return to the cultured confines of an orderly society, one that he had only been able to admire from afar before he went to sea.

He was learning to conquer these outer appearances very well. He had grown up on the estate of a wealthy lord, listening to the speech of his betters, cultivating their accents even more than his mother had. His mother had encouraged him, hoping one day he would find a position in the household for himself and so secure his future. But Peter had grown into a great strapping lad with ideas of his own, and bowing and scraping before effeminate lords and their vain ladies had not been among them.

But he'd had his stomach full of sea now, and it was time to turn his mind to new pursuits. He had every confidence that he could achieve whatever goal he set himself, but the time this particular pursuit was taking seemed to be dragging out to tedious lengths and prospects weren't looking good.

Denning sighed as he took his usual table, acknowledged the salutes of several of the younger gentlemen with whom he had spent time, and ordered his meal. He knew he would be joined shortly by several of the young idlers, and before the evening ended, he would have tried his hand at cards, downed a bottle of port, and no doubt toured one or more of the brothels near Haymarket. The gentlemen considered him a rare good sport, a dab hand at all the rigs, and an easy touch for a bit of the ready when needed. He could whistle the days away in idleness forever more if he wished.

But he hadn't been bred for idleness, and as entertaining as the company might be, it didn't ease the ache of loneliness Denning had felt since returning to England to discover his mother dead and himself alone. He had spent years at sea imagining a cozy cottage in England with his mother keeping warm by the fire and a laughing maid in the doorway waiting for his return, with curly-haired children at her knee. He hadn't thought it would be difficult to find the woman of his choice once he had a home and a bit of savings to offer. He had never imagined returning with great wealth and the complications that would ensue.

Sipping at his first glass of port of the day and cutting into his beefsteak, Peter attempted to avoid the ennui that had begun to haunt him with greater frequency, but he could not find a successful diversion for his thoughts. Great wealth should have opened all the doors that had been closed to him in the past, but he was quickly discovering that there were doors behind doors and that breaching them was tedious business.

The gentlemen accepted him for what he was as long as he had the coins to keep up with their play, but the

ladies were entirely another story. He was caught between two worlds with this charade he acted, and he
was beginning to doubt that he had set the right course
when he had donned his expensive clothes and knocked
on the doors of society. Coins opened that first set of
doors and appearance allowed him to remain in those
outer circles, but to reach the inner sanctums where
the ladies waited seemed impossible without the right
credentials, and he couldn't manufacture those as he
had his image.

At the same time, he had no real dealings with the
layers of society to which he had been born. His
wealth, appearance, and speech placed him outside
their world, and any female servant would only look
at him with suspicion did he ask to call. It was an
awkward situation at best, one that Peter felt certain
he would conquer with time, but it left him restless
and alone while he sought the solution.

As he finished his meal and his second glass of port,
Peter was joined by two younger gentlemen eager to
attend a prizefight on the outskirts of town. His tilbury
was required to carry the lightskirts they meant to accompany them, and they gallantly offered to acquire a
third for Peter's use. Contemplating that evening of
entertainment, he shook his head and bowed out with
an excuse of other plans.

It wasn't a complete lie. The plan he had in mind
didn't include the tilbury or horses or loose women.
The plan he had included a warm study, a good book,
and the painting he had acquired last week. The more
he thought about it, the more eager he became to seek
that source of comfort.

Setting out on foot for his apartment, Peter conjured
up the image of his first artistic acquisition with sat-

isfaction. Had he been told while lying in his bunk at sea that one of the first things he would do upon obtaining riches was to buy a piece of oil and canvas, he would have laughed himself to the floor.

But that painting had called to him from the first moment he had set eyes on it. He was well aware that the great houses of the land had such paintings scattered haphazardly across their walls and stacked in their attics and buried in closets, and few were paid any attention no matter what their resting place. He couldn't describe a single one of the oils that had adorned the house where he had attained maturity. But this painting hanging in a shop window had leapt out at him, caught his eye in such a fashion that he had to return the next day to be certain it was still there.

And he had returned again the day after that. He had never set foot inside a gallery of art in all his life. He hadn't even been certain one could buy a piece of artwork like that or if it had just been hung for the appreciation of all. But on the third day, he had pushed open the gallery door and walked in.

He had acquired the canvas at an amazingly low price for the amount of satisfaction it brought him. He knew nothing about the cost of art. In all likelihood they had named an absurd price in hopes of obtaining half that, but Peter had merely signed the bill and walked out with the package and not questioned the cost in the days since. For all the money he had thrown away in gambling and drinking and whoring, not one cent had brought him the contentment of that painting.

Arriving at his apartment, Peter dismissed his valet for the evening, and retiring with a bottle of wine to the study he had purchased complete with books, he settled into his desk chair to admire the framed canvas on the wall before him.

The lamp lit below it cast the oils in murky shadows, but he knew every line and color by heart by now. Not that there was a wide range of colors to know. Almost the entirety of the background was filled with the broad gray walls of stone of some substantial country mansion. The walls could only be seen from behind a forest of trees and shrubbery and climbing vines, but the darker colors of these seemed to blend into the very nature of the building until, after a while, it became difficult to detect where nature ended and man's work began. Peter delighted in discerning new and previously unnoticed quirks in the house's exterior: the griffin on the lintel, a child's toy in a window, a shutter painted with a rose in the corner.

But the artwork he appreciated most in the picture had naught to do with house or grounds and all to do with a fleeing fairy figure in the forefront. In broad daylight the figure all but disappeared into the landscape of trees and overgrown shrubbery, but by night, with the lamp at just the right angle, she flew wild and free through that landscape, moonlit hair streaming in long cascades down a back as slender and feminine as any he had ever seen.

That figure fascinated him. She held her arms up in glorious embrace of the night, head flung back, face turned toward the moon that couldn't be seen anywhere in the portrait. And the face! Peter moved from his desk to the wall to better observe the delicate features of that face. She shimmered with moonlight even from this proximity. Her skin seemed to sparkle with silver. Large, almond-shaped eyes danced with a darkness that made his blood shiver. Perfectly formed rosebud lips turned upward in a smile of welcome that stripped him of all pretense and left him longing for more. He ached to reach out and touch her, to know the warmth of that welcome, to feel at home in that house with rosebuds on the shutters and toys in the windows.

How just one painting could bring him so much happiness and so much misery was beyond Peter's ability to reason. It represented everything he wanted while disguising it all in shadows and mockery. There were times when he had drunk enough that he thought it might be best to destroy the canvas, to slash it from top to bottom and heave it from the window into the night. And there were other times, like now, when he only wished he could step inside the painting and became a part of it.

Imagining being another shadowy figure in that forest of trees, one toward whom the lady was running, Peter smiled and lifted the canvas from the wall. He was not only growing maudlin, but fanciful.

Perhaps the painting was a sign that he had chosen the wrong place from which to make his entrance into society. The country house and the trees called to him. He had always enjoyed the country as a boy. He could remember fishing in wide ponds, hunting in rolling fields, tumbling down snowbanks in the winter. The country was a good place to raise children. Perhaps the women were easier to meet and less arrogant in their requirements in a solitary place such as the one in the painting.

Setting aside his whimsical fantasies, Peter pried at the back of the painting with his pocket knife. Perhaps he could find some clue as to the house's origins. Much of everything in this world was for sale. It would be amusing to locate this place and see if anyone would accept an offer for it.

The protective backing peeled off without a great deal of trouble, revealing a blank canvas and some spidery writing in one corner. Peter carried it to the lamp on the desk and tilted the frame until the light caught on the words and played them back to him:

> *Lady Honora Chelmsby, Rosebud Cottage,*
> *near High Wycombe*

Peter sat down in his chair and stared at the words with a sense of satisfaction. Perhaps he had just found a home.

Several days later, Peter was pulling the collar of his redingote up against the drenching downpour of steady rain and cursing his moment of whimsy. He didn't think it snowed in October in England, but the sharp chill of the wind certainly made it seem a possibility. He was beginning to think his soaked gloves and coat might even be a little warmer should they freeze into solid walls.

And currently, he didn't give a damn where Rosebud Cottage might be or even High Wycombe. He would settle for a warm inn and a cozy fire and a return to London in the morning.

His fancy city horses objected thoroughly to the rutted roads and muddy puddles of this rural outpost. The leather seats of his expensive tilbury would no doubt rot into tatters before the night was over, if the delicately balanced wheels did not fall off first. He would not only return to London as soon as he could find a road that might lead in that direction, he would sell the damned painting at the first break of dawn. Imagine a grown man falling in love with a bit of oil and canvas! He had to be out of his bloody mind.

Thinking he saw a gleam of light further ahead, he urged the horses faster, and as if they sensed a dry stable and grain, they surged forward with a jerk, their long legs breaking into the matched strides for which they were famous.

A second later, they were squealing in terror and raising up on their hind legs in frantic disobedience, and the light carriage went skidding off the muddy road, hitting a stone and breaking a wheel, throwing its occupant head over heels into the hedgerow as the wind howled gleefully through the trees.

"Shhh, Hodges, you'll wake him," the slight figure beside the bed warned as the manservant entered with a steaming kettle of water.

"Don't b'lieve the wrath of God would wake him right now," Hodges grumbled as he poured some of the water into the basin, mixing it with the cold already there. "If I'm any judge of head knots, that one's going to be sleeping for a while. You'd best get some rest and let him be."

Cecily used the warm water to remove more of the grime from the stranger's mud-splattered face. Now that she could see his features she thought them very nice, if a trifle out of the ordinary. Drying now, his thick black hair was springing up in unruly curls. His short side-whiskers framed a square face with a determined chin that had just a touch of a cleft to it. His eyelashes were short and blunt, as were the fingers on the hands beneath his soaked gloves once they were removed. But it was the slight scar on one side of his mouth that drew his lips up in a perpetual half-smile that fascinated her. Combined with the weathered lines around his eyes and the exotic bronze of his skin, that half-smile gave him a rakish appearance that she had only seen in books.

"Do you think we ought to add more coals to the fire? He still feels chilled." She took the heated cloth to his hands to stir the blood there. He had rough hands, a workman's hands, for all that he had been dressed in the best of London fashion. She smiled as his fingers curled reflexively beneath her touch.

Hodges gave the unconscious stranger a grumpy glare and turned to toss another piece or two on the grate. "Them animals of his are like to eat us out of house and home, and now you'll have us using the last of the fuel to keep him warm. I say we check his purse to see if he will be properly appreciative."

Cecily sent the man an admonishing look. "Now, Hodges, we are not so desperate that we must resort to thievery. I'm certain the gentleman will be happy to reimburse us once he recovers."

"Well, he's not likely to be paying you for your time in fretting over him. I'll linger a whit and you get some rest. I'll come fetch you should he wake."

Cecily smiled at that, and Hodges admired the increasingly infrequent sight. When she smiled, her thin little face lit up from within, and any fool could see that she was a beauty. But puddles of worry still lingered in her eyes, and the smile slipped away as quickly as it had appeared. He cursed the world in general as she once more became the brown little wren fussing over the blanket covers and wringing at the wash cloth.

"If rest were all it took, I would rival the Toast of

the Season. I've had naught but rest for too long now. I'll sleep a little here and wait for him to wake. You'll have to rise first thing in the morning to see if the river is down enough to fetch the physician. So go on with you. I'll be fine.''

Hodges gave the overtly masculine stranger a look of suspicion, then returned his glance to the young woman beside the bed. In the drab brown round gown with her hair pulled beneath a cap and held with pins, she looked like some frumpy old-maid servant. He growled at the thought, but he supposed she was safe enough. The blighter wasn't likely to rise from that bed anytime soon.

Cecily breathed a sigh of relief as the manservant left, then settled back in the comfortable chair and studied the stranger once again before she closed her eyes. Living alone as she did, she was given to odd fantasies, but none was so odd as this. Even her imagination had never conjured up a handsome, wealthy stranger practically crashing into her doorstep. If only she had some fairy dust . . .

Peter suppressed a groan at the pounding in his head when he tried to move. He couldn't remember ever drinking enough port to give him a head like this one. There had been a time in Antigua when he had entered into a little altercation with a sailor twice his size. . . .

He tried to find his hand to raise it to his head to see if it could be moved by other means. The motion stirred thin sheets and a cotton blanket that had no place in his memory. Worst of all, it brought about the realization that he was wearing a shirt with arms longer than his. Had he shrunk overnight?

Not daring to contemplate that possibility or the alternative that there was a man somewhere nearby who was bigger than he, Peter found his hand and carried it to his aching head, pushing it sideways to determine if there might be some light to give him some indication as to where he might be. Once he discovered that he had his eyelids squeezed closed, he recovered from the shock of total darkness and pried them open. The first sight of his new abode included a flickering candle and a slender maid curled in the corner of an overlarge chair.

That wasn't so terrible a sight. Relaxing, Peter closed his eyes again to relieve the pain and let the scene play along his eyelids. His mind's eye found a maid's prim white cap, a glimpse of soft brown hair, and an almost painfully thin face innocent with sleep. Raised as he had been, he was familiar with households that believed their servants could live on bones and gruel. It irked him that he was in the hands of such mean-spirited people, but he was in no condition to reprimand them right now.

Succumbing to the pain, he blotted out any image at all and returned to the realms of sleep.

The room seemed noticeably warmer, and Peter struggled against the blankets before coming awake enough to remember his surroundings. Perspiration formed on his brow as he fought for a breath, then opened his eyes to the still night air. This time he didn't need candlelight to see the slim white figure hovering over him.

Odd, but he had thought his keeper wore brown. He closed his eyes and opened them again, but the pale figure remained, leaning over him with some concern. Delicate moonlight tresses streamed over her shoulder with the movement, and Peter felt a shock of recognition.

The image in the portrait. His head pounded and his breathing was strangely weak, but he managed to search the lovely features he had memorized from the painting. The dancing eyes lit with laughter at his perusal, and she moved away, her thin gown flowing enticingly around her as she stepped from reach and almost out of his range of vision.

He tried to speak, but his voice was a hoarse rasp, and she was gone before he could get the words out.

When next he woke, it was to the tender ministrations of the little maid. A cool cloth cleansed his fevered brow, and Peter sighed his appreciation. She gasped and nearly whipped him with the wet cloth at the sound, but when he opened his eyes, she had serenely composed herself again.

"Good morning. Would you care for a cup of broth?"

He rather thought being pitched into a snowbank might be more enjoyable, but the croak that came out didn't deny or confirm her question. Frustrated, he glared at her, and she solemnly looked back.

"Hodges has gone to find a physician. I don't doubt that you'll have a most virulent cold from your experience. I don't know how long you lay in the hedgerow before we found you, but you were quite thoroughly chilled. I think a little broth will do you good."

As his body began to register the demands of the wine he had drunk with his last meal, Peter could only nod in hopes that she would quickly leave in search of the promised soup. She gave him a suspicious frown, then bustled out, leaving him blessedly alone to search for the chamber pot.

By the time she returned, Peter's head felt as if it would fall from his shoulders, and the raggedness of his breathing warned that her dire predictions had come true, but his lower regions were vastly relieved. He struggled with the lengths of shirtsleeves covering his hands and wondered at the size of the monster that must once have inhabited this garment, but he managed to find a reclining position that kept his head relatively intact. When the maid returned, he even attempted a smile.

She didn't smile back but efficiently made a place for herself at the side of the bed and held a spoon of broth to his lips. "You must drink this all down. When Uncle Quincy had the pleurisy, the physician said he must have lots of liquids. And the meat juices will make you stronger."

Peter made a face as she inserted the spoon when he opened his mouth to protest. Since he could produce few sounds other than grunts and groans and croaks, he surrendered the battle and allowed the admittedly tasty broth to go down.

"You must tell us if there is someone we might notify of your accident. I would not have anyone worrying about your whereabouts."

As Peter shook his head to indicate there was no one, he felt a momentary return of depression. He could have died out there on that road, and there would have been no one to care. All that grand wealth he had accumulated would disappear into the pockets of some lawyer or government official in vain attempts to locate his heirs. It made one feel exceedingly small.

Instead, he concentrated on the determined young woman forcing liquids down his throat. Her accent bothered him until he began putting two and two together. Although her accent had the polish of his, her clothes were too drab and out of fashion to belong to a lady of quality. Yet they were of good cloth, and her hands bore none of the signs of physical labor. A kitchen or upstairs maid would have work-roughened hands, and even in the best of houses she would not wear clothes of this fashion or speak in polished accents. But a lady's maid wearing the cast-offs of her mistress and with no chore more difficult than laundering her employer's linens could very well bear these qualities.

Satisfied he had solved the mystery, Peter reached to squeeze the maid's hand when she set the bowl aside. She looked shocked at first, then offered a brief, haunting smile as she smoothed a cool hand over his fevered brow.

"You're quite welcome, sir. Now you must get some sleep until the doctor arrives. He might have some medicine to ease the aching in your head."

Well, so much for his attempt at seduction. Closing his eyes and insanely smiling to himself, Peter followed her instructions.

When next he woke, it was to the shadows of twilight and the sight of a giant monster stalking the little maid. With a throat-wrenching cry, Peter swung back the blankets and tried to leap to the rescue, only to discover he hadn't the strength to stand. Grabbing the bed for support before he could collapse into a humiliating heap on the floor, Peter watched through bleary eyes as the little maid gave a cry of concern and ran to his side, while the monster merely glared at him.

He had at least diverted the creature's attention, Peter thought grimly as he allowed the slender woman to boss him back into bed while the giant lingered in the shadows, forcing obedience with his presence. Perhaps he would be flung back into the hedgerow if he refused the maid's orders. This certainly was an unusual household, but he was in no position to complain.

"Whatever made you leap up like that?" More shaken than she would admit by the stranger's sudden transformation from bed-ridden patient to large man in a thin nightshirt, Cecily fussed over the covers and ignored Hodges' glowering visage behind her. "Are you hallucinating? I understand people with high fevers suffer from deliriums. Would you like a cool cloth for your brow?"

The stranger grimaced as if in pain when Cecily touched her fingers to his forehead. He really was quite warm. She had the oddest notion that he had meant to come to her when he leapt from the bed. She really had been alone too long with her books if she could think such a thing, she mused ruefully. A tentative smile crept across her lips as his eyes opened and she finally saw that they were gray.

"Ask him what made the carriage crash." Hodges remained in the shadows, but his voice was deep and husky and penetrated the gloom with the sound of thunder.

Their patient turned his head to follow this sound, then attempted to rise to a sitting position. He shook his head in denial when Cecily tried to help him, and frowning, Hodges stepped forward and lifted the man's shoulders and shoved pillows behind him.

The stranger didn't look properly appreciative, but after sipping from a cup of water Cecily offered him, he attempted some reply. "Spooked," was the only croak that came out.

That one word seemed to explain everything to this odd pair Peter noted as they exchanged glances over his head. He thought he heard the monster whisper "the lady," but the maid shook her head in warning.

"That is only superstition, Hodges. A rabbit no doubt ran across the road. You said the horses were high-strung expensive animals."

Peter watched in amazement as the giant's expression turned mulish, but he did no more than step back beneath the young maid's rebuke. The man called Hodges could have picked her up and swung her through the air without any effort, yet he seemed to regard the slender young woman with respect. The lady had to be powerful indeed if her maid could command that much authority.

"He's here 'cause of the lady, there ain't no doubt in my mind," was all the giant manservant said in reply before retreating toward the door.

The maid ignored this parting retort and reached for the cloth in the wash basin. Peter meant to halt her, but the feel of the cool cloth against his brow was better than he had expected, and he closed his eyes and relaxed beneath her gentle hands.

"Name?" he croaked, straining his sore throat to do so.

He opened his eyes in time to see the shy smile in hers.

"Cecily," she replied. "And yours?"

"Denning." There, it was out, his ignominious ancestry. He didn't suppose there was a Denning anywhere in the history of British bluebloods. Stripped of his clothes, he couldn't even pretend to be what he was not. The maid would in all likelihood report his commonness to her ladyship and he would be out on his ear by morning.

Instead, she merely reapplied the cold cloth and in that solemn owl-like way of hers—although he thought he saw the dance of laughter behind her blue eyes—and asked, "Denning who? Or is it which Denning? Ought I to know the name?"

Incredible. Peter relaxed and tentatively stretched his long legs beneath the covers. It just might be possible that he would live to see the day again. "Peter," he supplied with alacrity.

"Very good, Mr. Denning. Are you certain there is no one you might wish to notify of your mishap? Surely someone is expecting you?"

He knew better than to shake his head in reply this time. With increasing ease, he replied, "No one."

"Well, I'd best not make you talk too much. Hodges says the physician was out, but he has left a message for him to call. I don't like him very much," she whispered conspiratorially, as if fearful the manservant would hear her. "He's always wanting to apply leeches, loathsome creatures." She shivered and made a face. "But I wouldn't want you to be dreadfully ill because we didn't do everything to help you."

Peter caught her slender wrist and forced her to meet his eyes. "No leeches!"

The worried expression settling between her eyes instantly cleared, replaced by a reassuring look of agreement. "I'll not let him bring them into the house."

Satisfied, Peter drank the cup of broth she handed him and fell asleep before he could discover more about this odd establishment.

When he woke next, it was the middle of the night.

The candle on the stand had guttered out, and he could discern little but the stream of moonlight coming in through the uncovered windows. The cursed clouds must finally have cleared away, he decided as he tried to determine what had made him wake.

It was then that he saw the movement, the elusive shimmer of silver followed by the scent of roses that he suddenly remembered from the previous night. Eagerly, Peter turned toward the movement, and she appeared before him, even more beautiful than he recalled.

She was tall and slender, with a winsome smile that made a man want to fall at her feet. Her hair was caught in smooth ropes and held by strings of pearls tonight, and he wished she had left it flowing as before. He wanted to reach for her, but he was quite certain this was the lady of the house, and he had no right to offend her.

''Hello,'' he managed to whisper, then cursed himself for such an uninspired greeting.

She nodded pleasantly, then glanced at the slight figure sleeping soundly in the chair beside the bed. Peter turned and noted the young maid then, and he smiled fondly at the thin face so innocent in sleep. There was nothing of the owl to her now. She was almost pretty in repose without that solemn look of concern imprinted upon her brow. He turned his gaze back to the lady, and she smiled approvingly. Then, tugging at his bedcovers to smooth them, she stole around the end of the bed and disappeared into the shadows behind Cecily where the door was located.

Oddly disappointed that she did not speak, Peter again glanced at the maid, and feeling unexpectedly tender at her constant watchfulness, he relaxed and slipped back toward sleep.

"Hodges, you are making entirely too much out of nothing." Garbed today in a gray wool with just a touch of black banding to frame her pale face, Cecily took the breakfast tray from the servant's hands and placed it on the bedside stand.

"It was the lady what spooked them horses and brought him here, and you can't say nothing to make me feel different." Stubbornly, Hodges remained where he was. "He's the one what will save the house. Just see if he ain't. The lady wouldn't fail us."

"Oh, Hodges." Cecily pushed a straying strand of hair back from her face, revealing the lines of worry upon her brow. "The painting is gone. There is nothing else we can do. It was our last hope, and even if I didn't want to sell it, I would have. It's too late now. I think fate is telling us that this is the end. I'll have to go to see the estate agent when the roads clear."

"Chelmsbys have owned this house since it was built. The lady won't let it go. You know that as well as I do. You go to that agent and we're like to find the place in flames before you return."

Having woken to the thunder of Hodges' last words, Peter looked from one stubborn expression to the other and wondered if now was the time to intervene. His fever had receded enough to enable him to realize the giant was a man and not a monster, but he still seemed terrifyingly dangerous to the slip of a female who defied him so persistently.

"Where is the lady?" he threw into the breech before Cecily's angry reply could leave her tongue.

Both stubborn faces turned toward him, and Peter

nearly laughed at the conflicting emotions hurriedly replacing their earlier anger.

"You saw her!" Hodges responded triumphantly.

"She's not here," Cecily answered at the same time.

The two glared at each other like brother and sister, and Peter had to pound his own pillows into an upright position.

"Who is she?" he asked affably, as long as they were providing answers of a sort.

"Lady Honora," Hodges answered defiantly.

"Well, she is here. I saw her last night." Peter lifted a challenging brow to the young maid, who slapped the breakfast tray down before him.

"You couldn't have. I was here all night and didn't see a thing. Now eat and stop this nonsense."

"You were sleeping," Peter politely pointed out. But the coffee smelled too fragrant to resist, and his interest in this quite insane argument was beginning to wane. For all he knew, he was ensconced in a house full of Bedlamites. There was no need to starve while they argued.

"You were delirious." Cecily's curt tones ended the argument.

Peter couldn't resist giving her a challenging look. "Am I so beneath the lady's notice that she wouldn't show curiosity in my appearance on her doorstep?"

That sent her into a fluster and Hodges almost grinned. "Lady Honora knows everything that goes on," he said when it became apparent that Cecily wouldn't deign to give a reply. "You be sure to tell her how good we took care of you the next time you see her."

Cecily threw him a black look for that and stalked out. Peter was sorry she had gone. Now that his head felt more its normal size and his throat worked again, he would have liked to spend more time talking with her. It had been a long time since he had enjoyed the company of a well-brought-up young woman, even if she were only a lady's maid. The good Lord knew he had no reason to look askance at conversing with a lady's maid.

"They don't feed her enough," Peter said conversationally when the dour Hodges offered no further insights.

"She's been ill." Hodges flung some more coals on the fire and stirred the embers. "Another winter like the last and she'll not likely survive."

That startled Peter into looking up. But before he could question further, the servant was lumbering for the door, and the forbidding lines of his face warned against any interference.

As he ate his breakfast, Peter heard the sound of children playing on the lawn, and his heart felt a little lighter. Perhaps this wasn't so strange a household as he had thought. Sun poured in the large windows, illuminating the mellowed wax of the old rosewood furniture. Better able to appreciate his surroundings today, he admired the coziness of the old-fashioned wallpaper and the delicate Queen Anne styles. An embroidered tapestry of a rose garden hung on one wall, and it was almost as good as looking out on a bright spring day. If he had to near break his neck and chill himself to the bone to arrive here, it was worth it to be inside a home again.

He looked up eagerly at the recognizable patter of Cecily's feet in the hall. He hoped she wasn't too angry at their earlier disagreement, if it could be called that. She was an intriguing little thing, and he would like to know her better.

She seemed to have returned to her normal self when she joined him, if this unsmiling owl-like creature was her normal self. Peter gave her a smile and she seemed startled, but there was a ghost of a smile on her lips as she bent to remove his tray.

"I heard the children on the lawn. How many people are in the household?" Peter inquired by way of making conversation.

The tray slipped and nearly dumped the empty coffee cup to his lap before Cecily righted it. Nervously, she moved the tray back to the stand and tried to wipe up small spills with the cloth from the wash bowl.

"Children? You heard children?" Not waiting for him to answer, she hurriedly continued, "There used to be many. Brothers and sisters and cousins, all laughing and playing when they weren't fighting and screaming. You know how children are. But everyone's gone now. It seems quite odd to be the last."

Peter stared at her in growing horror. She was mad. She had to be. Was that the illness Hodges had spoken of? Such a lovely young woman, and quite out of her head. He had just heard the children on the lawn and wondered about them, but she spoke as if they were all dead or blown to the four corners of the earth. He watched her nervously as she moved toward the window overlooking the lawn.

"Where did they all go?" he asked cautiously.

"To war," she answered sadly. "One way or another, war and violence were responsible. Why must men always fight? What makes them think it is a grand and glorious deed they do when they march off to kill other men? Have they no notion of what they do to themselves and those they leave at home?''

Thinking of his own escapades and the mother he had left behind, Peter shook his head. ''No, they don't. Men think that everything will stay as they had left it. It isn't real until you're in the midst of it and suddenly realize that you may never see home again.''

Cecily swung around and stared at him. In the morning light, his square, blunt face wasn't exceedingly handsome, but his eyes were wide and honest and filled with a pain similar to her own. Hodges' old nightshirt looked ridiculous on him, but somehow he had a stature to overcome that flaw. She had seen his fancy frock coat and waistcoat and frilled shirt and knew he would pass as a gentleman of means on any street in London once he was dressed. Like this, though, she could see that he was a gentleman of character as well.

''I don't understand how they can be so blind. Surely they must know that bullets kill and swords maim. Do they think their deaths won't matter to those of us at home?''

Peter wasn't at all certain what this conversation was about, but he could tell the topic was one that she had brooded about for a long time. There wasn't anything he could say to relieve her mind, though.

''They think they are protecting their way of life. I wasn't in India or Afghan, but I understand the enemies' armies weren't exactly polite to those they conquered. Men fought to keep their women and their homes from suffering that fate.''

She looked impatient. ''Forgive me if I find that utter nonsense. The Sikhs didn't fight to protect their women. They fought to gain power. The army fought to regain that power. Men can give a thousand pretty reasons for war, but it always comes back to the same thing. I've studied the wars of history, and they all have the same basic motive. One man thinks he's better than another and tries to prove it by breaking the other man's neck.''

A well-read lady's maid. How unusual. And exciting. Peter regarded her with approval. "And how would women do it differently? If someone threatens to come over and steal your chickens and take over your house, how would you stop them?''

A half-smile tilted her lips as she contemplated this question. "I think I would be inclined to let them. When they grow tired of arguing with Hodges and tracking down chickens that won't roost and patching crumbling walls, they will beg me to take it back.''

Peter laughed in appreciation and held out his hand to gesture her into a chair. "Stay, and help me solve the rest of the world's problems.''

She withdrew suddenly inside herself again, shaking her head and starting for the door. "You must rest. I have been selfish in taking up your time. Hodges will come fetch your tray.''

She was gone before he could protest. The sound of the children was gone too, and the sunshine had somehow dimmed. It was damned depressing talking to a ghost that wouldn't light for more than a minute. Maybe he ought to go in search of the elusive Lady Honora.

That thought lasted only long enough for Peter to rise and try to find the chamber pot. His legs were like wet noodles, and he had to grasp the bed and pull himself back into it when Hodges barged through the doorway.

The manservant gave him a glance of disapproval, flung back the covers so Peter could climb back between them, and reached for the tray without saying a word.

Determined to find out more about this household, Peter stopped him before he could make good his escape. "Where are my clothes, Hodges?"

The giant gave him a wary look. "You just proved you ain't in no shape to get up. They'll come back when you're ready."

"I want them near in case I am ready and there's no one around," Peter insisted.

"I'll bring up your bag. You could use a shave."

With that curt dismissal, the giant strode out.

Cursing his helplessness, Peter wished he had a book, only to discover someone had thoughtfully left one on the chair beside the bed. Determined to overcome his weakness, he once more tackled the task of standing up and reaching, this time falling back to the bed with the coveted book in his hand.

He was sound asleep before he could read more than the title: *The Family History of the Chelmsbys*.

When he woke next, the book was gone, and from the tight-lipped frown on the little maid's face, Peter could surmise who had taken it. He was quite certain now that he had somehow stumbled across the Rosebud Cottage of his painting, but there were still moments when he thought he might have hit his head too hard and be dreaming. He hadn't expected Rosebud Cottage to still exist. He'd had the impression that the painting was quite old. Only whimsy and melancholy had sent him searching for a memory. But the book and the lady's name almost proved he had woken up inside the painting. Perhaps he ought to begin wondering if he could ever get out.

He found his overnight bag with his change of clothing on the chair and his razor and shaving soaps neatly laid out on the stand waiting for him. He sent Cecily a wary look as she bustled about with a feather duster, but he wasn't about to perform his ablutions with a female in the room, even if he did suddenly realize he must bear a close resemblance to a hedgehog.

"Hodges tells me you've been ill."

She looked startled, but whether at the fact that he addressed her or the mode of that address, Peter couldn't tell. He watched in satisfaction as she stopped her dusting and turned in his direction. He might have little experience in talking to the gentler sex, but he was learning.

"That was last winter. I'm very well now, thank you."

He looked at her peaked face and the shadows under her eyes and wondered how she must have looked when she was ill. As it was, he could see vestiges of prettiness—especially when she smiled—but little more than the glimmer of blue in her eyes or the occasional blush of pink on her cheeks. He shook his head in disagreement.

"You need to be resting, not working night and day. And you should be the one eating good stout broths, not me. Your lady is no friend to allow you to work yourself into nothing."

She almost smiled at that and came to test his head with her cool hand. "I have all the rest I need, whenever I want. I'll be fine, thank you. You're the one still running a fever. I don't know what became of the physician. Should I send Hodges after him again?"

The touch of her soft fingers brought back memories of childhood, of warm beds and fevered nights and his mother's tender hands caressing his brow. Peter hadn't thought of those days in years, but this place was returning it all. He would have to speak with Lady Honora one way or another. It didn't seem likely that she would part with the cottage, but he could at least sound her out. And then he would hire her lady's maid and feed her until she was well again.

"It's just a cold. I'll be fine without any quack hovering over me. Is there any chance that I might see Lady Honora and thank her for her hospitality before I go?"

Amusement danced in Cecily's eyes as she removed her hand to straighten the bed covers. "I'm certain she'll stop by if she's interested. She's a very fickle lady."

That slander caused Peter's eyebrows to raise, but he wasn't in a position to argue. She could quite possibly be right; he just preferred to think of the lady as perfect. "I'm sure she's quite busy," he answered agreeably. "Is she a widow?" That would explain the children and the lack of any mention of a gentleman on the property.

"Yes, how did you know?" Laying aside any pretense of dusting, Cecily perched in the window seat, enjoying the heat of the afternoon sunshine.

"I've not heard a man about the house, and with the children and all . . ." Peter admired the picture she made in the window. She wore a pale blue gown today, and though she was still too slender to be healthy, she possessed a feminine delicacy that he could appreciate. Still, she was no match for the Lady Honora. And if the lady was a widow with a ready-made family, all the better for him. There had to be some way he could come to know the lady better.

"Ahh, yes, the children." Cecily nodded knowingly. "This house was made for children. Lady Honora believed they ought to be brought up in the country, and she had her husband build this cottage just so she could be with the children as much as possible, even when she accompanied the earl to London on business. The attic is littered with rocking horses and toy soldiers and dolls. The cottage is a child's heaven."

An earl. So much for his prospective hopes. The widow of an earl wasn't going to spend time in his company, although she had certainly seemed friendly enough those times he had seen her. But a woman who loved children undoubtedly would be kind to injured strangers. Peter struggled between desire and common sense.

"I would like to see more of the house. If the rest is as charming as this room, it must be lovely. Will you take me on a tour sometime?"

He wasn't certain if he imagined it or not, but a bleak shadow seemed to cross Cecily's face. A moment later she was rising from the seat and picking up her duster. "There is little more to see. You must rest for now. Uncle Quincy's pleurisy got worse when he tried to rise from bed too soon."

He wasn't Uncle Quincy, but he was in no hurry to be thrown from this extremely pleasant situation, either. Peter nodded obediently. "Might I have something to occupy my mind if you will not linger to talk with me? The book that was here earlier, perhaps?"

"Lady Honora must have dropped it," Cecily stated flatly. "I cannot imagine why else it would have been here; it's extremely dull reading. I'll see if there isn't something more to a man's tastes.''

Peter could think of any number of things more to a man's tastes than a book, but he rather thought it might be impolitic to mention them. That wouldn't stop him thinking about them, though, and planning some means to put them into action.

Once Cecily had returned with a tome on the hunting activities of Sussex and left again with a busy air, Peter swung himself from the bed and sought his land legs again. After months at sea it had felt much like this to walk on land again. He hadn't realized a meager knot on the head and a fever could drain a man's stamina so. His breathing was still ragged, but whatever miracle brew the little maid had been feeding him seemed to be working. He could manage to stand without collapsing, and with a little effort, he could reach the window and look out.

There was little to be seen from this viewpoint. The sun had disappeared behind a cloud bank, and the children had evidently disappeared with it. The stretch of grassy lawn before the dense wilderness of trees seemed rather brown and neglected, but it was October, and he supposed by October lawns must don a wintry appearance. He had little experience of nature save for the sea, and it had been a long time since he had been in England in the fall. Still, the signs of neglect caused him to wonder along another angle.

Quite often noble houses had few funds to support them. Running a half-dozen estates and a high lifestyle depleted cash reserves rapidly. Could it be that the earl had died leaving his widow without the funds necessary to support their children and various households? That could explain the seeming lack of other servants besides Cecily and Hodges, the lawn's neglect, and even the parsimony of meals.

That might even explain to some extent Cecily's inexplicable tirade on men and wars. Perhaps the earl's heir had gone off to war and died and his estates had been left to a distant relative. Only this cottage might not have been entailed. It was an intriguing possibility, one he would like to explore further.

He returned to bed with dreams of wooing and winning the Lady Honora, his mind circling the multitude of means to accomplish his heart's desire. He was a determined man, one who seldom let go of a goal without accomplishing it. A little lack of experience didn't deter him any.

Before he could open the pages of the book that Cecily had brought to him, Peter closed his eyes and fell asleep with a myriad of ideas dancing though his head.

When next he woke, Peter had the distinct impression that it was late afternoon. The room had grown dimmer with the winter light fading into the west, but it was still light enough to discern the shapes of furniture and the presence of a shadow flitting about the far side of the bed. He felt groggy from the nap, but any presence at all was of interest to him, and he turned eagerly in hopes of meeting the lady of his dreams again.

She didn't disappoint. She was always lovelier than he remembered, her smile soft and welcoming, her face a portrait of moonlight as she leaned forward and caressed his hair. He didn't feel the same sense of home as he had when Cecily touched him, only a mere ruffling of his hair, but it was enough to satisfy him for the moment.

"Lady Honora, I've been eager to meet you." Peter struggled to right himself in the bed while still preserving some sense of modesty. He remembered he hadn't taken advantage of his shaving kit, and he cursed himself vividly.

She held a finger to her lips and gave him a wickedly mischievous smile.

Peter glanced toward the doorway, half expecting Cecily and Hodges to appear, but he didn't hear a sound in the hall. Still, he understood her warning. Whatever was going on in this household, the Lady Honora wasn't supposed to be here.

"I'd like to thank you more properly for my care than I can from a bed. May I call on you once I am up and about?" he whispered.

She clasped her hands in evident delight, then blew him a kiss. Picking up her skirts, she glided toward the doorway. Reluctant to let her go, Peter called after her, "Can't you stay a little longer?"

The forlorn smile she offered when she turned back to him nearly broke his heart, and then she was gone, and he was alone again.

Punching his pillows into place and reaching for a candle, Peter cursed his own inadequacy in dealing with ladies and the unfairness of life to keep this one from his quarters. He knew that she was all a man could ask for in a woman. Somehow, he would have to set his sights on acquiring her.

And that meant getting up from this bed. It was all very well and good to lie about and pretend to be an invalid just for the pleasure of being pampered, but he obviously wasn't going to accomplish anything more by it. He needed to find out all he could about the

Chelmsbys and Rosebud Cottage and Lady Honora. With the right information, he could set his course.

When Cecily next entered their patient's chambers, Peter was sitting in the chair by the window wearing garments retrieved from his bags and fully shaved for the first time in days. She gave a gasp when he turned at her entrance. She had not imagined him quite so . . . She was at a loss for words as she met the steady glow of gray eyes and noted the chin set with determination. He was a large man, dwarfing the delicate chintz chair in which he rested. She was used to Hodges, but this was somehow different, and she feared to approach him.

"You should not be out of bed yet," she scolded mildly, setting his tea tray on the table by the bed, carefully avoiding any physical contact. Just the overt masculinity of his presence was disturbing to an unfathomable degree.

Peter glanced at Cecily and felt this painting-world he inhabited slip to a different angle. He had never tried to imagine the inhabitants of the stone cottage in the oil. He supposed he would never have tried to picture the servants if he had. And he definitely would never have pictured one like this. He would have imagined them all to be a jolly, healthy lot, laughing and carefree, perhaps. Lady Honora had much to explain when he finally had a chance to pin her down. He had the insane urge to pull Cecily into his lap and cradle her in his arms and promise her everything would be all right.

"I would like to see the house, if you would not mind," was all he said.

Cecily wiped her hands on the apron she had donned

before carrying the tray up the stairs. "I don't think you're strong enough yet. Perhaps tomorrow."

Peter's gaze was deliberately devoid of all emotion as he met hers. "I will need to leave on the morrow. Are my horses in good repair?"

Did he mistake, or did disappointment flicker somewhere behind the shadowed blue of her eyes? If so, she hid it quickly in her nervous fussing with her apron.

"They are quite well, and Hodges has had your wheel fixed, but you will find you are not strong enough to manage a rig. You will damage your health and possibly the animals if you try to take them out on the morrow. Is there some pressing engagement that you must leave so abruptly?"

"I believe I have something that belongs here. I would like to fetch it and return it."

Startled, Cecily dropped the apron and turned her full attention on him. "Something that belongs here? How is that possible?"

"I cannot say. Perhaps you can tell me." That seemed almost an accusation, and Peter was surprised by his own words. He hadn't meant to say any of that at all. To mention the painting was to give it up, and he was strangely reluctant to do so. But matters had come to a standstill, and he was desperate for some means to shake himself free from this dream world and progress on with the real one. "If I go outside, shall I find a griffin on the lintel and a rose on the shutters? It is too late in the season for roses on the south wall, I suppose, and it would be too much to ask to find toys in the window. . . ."

Cecily dropped to the bed and stared at him as if he

had taken leave of his senses. "The painting. You have the painting. How can you?"

"By walking into an art gallery and purchasing it."

"But we never sold it."

Her words sounded as much an accusation as his. Her incredulity was almost an insult. Peter wished he had the strength to rise and shake the truth from her, but his best weapon now was surprise. He had certainly accomplished that much, but her defenses were excellent. Accusing blue eyes focused on him, and he felt compelled to defend himself.

"Nevertheless, I bought it. If you do not care to give me a tour before I go, I shall request it of Lady Honora when I return. I can't say why, but the house fascinates me. I came out this way just to find it."

Cecily rose with an almost frightened expression as she stared at him. "The lady. Oh, no, that can't be. It's not possible. There is a very sensible explanation for all this. I'm certain it was the appraiser. It had to be the appraiser. He saw the painting and found some way to steal it. That's all there is to it. We must go to the magistrate and report him. I'll find Hodges. He'll ride into town . . ."

Peter stood up and tried to halt her as she walked toward the doorway in a daze, but he merely succeeded in causing her to turn to him with eyes like bruised violets that made him flinch at his audacity. He wanted to gather her into his arms and reassure her that everything was all right, but he couldn't see that anything was wrong. If the painting had been stolen, he meant to return it. What was there in that to cause fear?

"If the painting was stolen, I shall report it when I return to town. If you are concerned that I'll not return it, I shall give you my direction. You may send the law after me if I do not return immediately. There is no need to trouble Hodges.''

Cecily stared at him as if he were a total stranger. ''I cannot believe you have the painting,'' she murmured before hurrying from the room.

She repeated those words to Hodges when he rushed to her side to inquire if something were wrong when she came down the stairs in a state of shock. It took a moment before her words sank in, but though he looked equally stunned, he recovered quickly with a happy grin.

''The lady came through, she did. A wealthy nob he must be. I'll go up and get his direction. We can't sit about idle and wait for the lady to do all the work. You might ought to find one of those pretty frocks of yours. The lady means him for you, no doubt.''

Cecily's horror widened her eyes until she saw the humor in it, and her eyes crinkled with laughter. ''Oh, Hodges, you cannot mean it! Wouldn't poor Mr. Denning be terrified if he knew your plans! You said yourself he must be rich as Croesus to own thoroughbreds like those. Why would he saddle himself with a disintegrating cottage in the country and a sickly invalid when he could have his choice of any home or lady in the world?''

Hodges frowned his disapproval. ''This is not just any cottage and you're not just any lady. He should be honored to be chosen. Perhaps I ought to break one of his legs so he has to stay long enough to appreciate what he will be gaining.''

Cecily broke into gales of mirth, steadying herself against the kitchen table and finally collapsing into a chair when she took another look at the fearsome frown on Hodges' rugged visage. "Oh, you dear man, whatever would I do without you? I cannot remember laughing so in ages." She wiped her eyes on the corner of her apron. "Break his leg, indeed! I doubt that even Lady Honora would consider that. Although if it was indeed she who caused the accident, she came quite close. Ahhh, Hodges, if only fairy tales came true, I could kiss him and he would turn into a prince and carry me away to his palace, or he would wake me and I'd find I was living in one. But I'm all grown up now, sir, and I know fairy tales are for children. So if you'll forgive me, I'll make his royal majesty his supper and we will hope that he does have the painting and is honest enough to return it. If the appraiser is correct, it should bring enough to mend the roof and still leave enough to live on for a little while longer."

Hodges puffed up into an irate caricature of himself as he heard this heresy. "That's just exactly the kind of thinking that brought all this down on us. The lady don't want us to sell the painting. Don't you see that? She brought you a rich nabob so you won't have to. He's a right enough fellow. It wouldn't hurt you none to turn him up sweet."

Still laughing, Cecily rose and bobbed a simple curtsy. "Yes, sir, right away, sir. The way to a man's heart is through his stomach, is it not? Let me fetch him one of my fabulous stews, and all will be well."

Hodges frowned as he heard her chuckles floating through the hall as she headed toward the cellar. He supposed it was a good sign that she was laughing again, but he wasn't one to sit and wait for something to happen. Somehow, he had to take matters into his own hands.

* * *

Peter was pleasantly surprised by the differences in the maid's appearance when she returned with his evening meal. She was smiling, and the laughter lit her eyes to a glorious blue as she set his tray beside the chair. She had changed into a simple frock of striped challis with traces of lace about the bodice and hem that he heartily approved of. He didn't know much about women's fashions, but this gown was feminine enough to catch his eye and hold it long enough to discover that the little maid had a handsome figure.

But he wasn't one for dallying with the servants, and he kept his hands to himself as she lingered for a while in his presence, questioning him about London and his family. Her voice was soft and cultured and somehow soothing, and he was quite certain he would be content to listen to it all day were he not impatient to get on with his plans.

" 'Tis a pity you did not come in a grand carriage," she said almost mockingly at one point. "You could take Hodges and me into town with you to retrieve the painting and save yourself having to return."

"I will be happy to take Hodges with me on the morrow if you are concerned about the painting, but I have every intention of returning," he replied stiffly.

"A busy gentleman such as yourself cannot have much interest in a country cottage once you have seen it. When you are strong enough, Hodges will take you about. That should satisfy your curiosity."

"It is not just curiosity." Peter wondered at this, but he trod boldly on. "Is there some reason why I cannot make the acquaintance of Lady Honora before I go?"

"Lady Honora knows where you are," Cecily answered airily. "She will find you if she wishes. But I contend that you are not strong enough to take the stairs yet. You may as well resign yourself to a few more days' rest."

Irritated but not quite knowing why, Peter set aside his empty plate and rose to his full height. Cecily was not really diminutive but seemed frail in comparison to himself, yet she did not flinch when he came to stand before her. She met his eyes boldly, almost with defiance, and before he quite knew what he was doing, Peter found himself reaching for her.

Her lips were warm and sweet beneath his, almost intoxicatingly so. Peter shifted her slender weight closer and Cecily swayed easily with his will, blending into his arms as if she belonged there. Her kiss pierced him with a longing so deep he almost forgot himself. When her hands crept hesitantly to his shirt, Peter was jarred back to the present by a very real and pressing desire, and he was thankful he had thought to dress for supper. It would have been most embarrassing to have this encounter wearing only Hodges' nightshirt.

But remembering where and who he was, Peter reluctantly set Cecily back from him, although he could not quite bring himself to release her waist. His hands easily encompassed her slimness, and he realized how terribly frail she truly was. Yet the eyes that stared back at him were not afraid. They searched his with a wonder that made his insides shake.

"I am sorry. I did not mean to insult you." He was the one ill at ease. He supposed in his younger days before he left home that he had kissed a few maids, but since then his encounters with females had mainly been of the commercial sort. He wasn't certain what was expected of him with the gently bred kind even if she were naught but a servant. He knew what his body wanted, but he was horrified at even considering treating her that way.

"I am sure there was no insult intended," Cecily whispered before stepping out of his hands and toward the door. "I had better go now. Hodges will be up later to see if you need anything."

"Wait . . ." But she was gone before Peter could halt her.

He supposed that was the way it should be. If he had persuaded her to give him a tour of the cottage there would have been more opportunities, more dark corners and beckoning nooks where he would be tempted to put his hands on her. Perhaps the ladies of society were quite right in barring him from their doors. He wasn't quite civilized yet. He hadn't realized it would be this difficult to keep from offending innocent women.

Yet she hadn't seemed offended. That gave him enough confidence to meet Hodges' suspicious glare with equanimity when he returned later for the supper tray. Peter was quite certain the little maid had liked his kiss, and he grinned blindingly at the manservant. It was good to know his uncivilized ways weren't entirely unattractive. Now if only he could track down the elusive Lady Honora. . . .

He waited patiently until he was certain the house's inhabitants had all gone to their beds. He had slept for days now and felt no need of sleep as he sat beside the lamp and listened for any signs of life. Convinced that all was well for his midnight explorations, Peter checked the wick of the lamp and set out to explore.

His legs were weak, but they held him steady enough as he touched the dark walls and started down the hallway to his right. This wasn't how he wanted to see the cottage, but he felt compelled to show his ability to do so. Lying in bed having dreams of living inside a painting was somewhat disconcerting. He meant to prove that he was in a real house with real people, that he had somehow stumbled across Rosebud Cottage by accident and not fallen into delirium.

Kissing Cecily had certainly proved her reality. Peter wanted to try it again, almost hoped he would somehow stumble across her room as he had so fortuitously discovered the cottage, but he knew that would be beyond the bounds of proper behavior. He remembered well the rich scoundrels who had seduced the maids in his former home, leaving them with dreams of grandeur and babes in their bellies. He'd be damned certain his intentions were honorable before he touched any innocent, be she maid or lady.

The door to the next room was wide open, and he thoughtfully lifted his lamp to inspect it. A massive bed of Elizabethan proportions dominated the room. He could see little of the draperies other than that they must once have been velvet. They appeared a trifle moth-eaten in this light, and there seemed to be no other furniture to add to the room's doubtful comfort. Peter suspected the bed remained only because it was too large to move.

Almost unwillingly, his feet carried him onward. He wanted the house in his painting to be filled with light and laughter and carefree happiness. But every sign indicated that this place was falling into disrepair. A piece of plaster crumbled in his hand as he rested against the wall, and his toe caught and tripped in a bare place in the carpet. The next room was draped in holland covers, but it appeared to be a nursery. The rocking horse in one corner was covered with dust when he touched it, and it sent up a mournful squeak when he set it to rocking.

Peter didn't want to see this. He brushed a cobweb from a shelf of children's books and stared at the titles with tears in his eyes. He was a grown man, a rough sailor who had seen the worst the world had to give but he remembered a schoolroom with books like these and his envy of the children who had owned them. His own children would someday have every book that money could buy. But he wanted the children in this house to delight in these volumes. Why didn't they?

Jerking himself from the contemplation of children he did not know, Peter returned to the hall. He wasn't certain what he had proved to himself, but there seemed little point in going on. He was beginning to feel like an intruder. There was obviously something odd about this place, but he couldn't be certain how much of it had to do with his fevered dreams and his fanciful desires. If this truly were reality, he was be-having unforgivably. He turned his feet in the direction of his room.

That was when she appeared. Caught by surprise, Peter could do little more than stare as the lady hurried from a room at the far end of the hall and started downward. There was something in her haste to give the impression of fear, but her expression was implac-able as she lifted her skirts and started down the stairs. In the dim light he could be certain of her features but little more. She seemed to carry the light of the moon with her, for she had no lamp or candle, and the rest of her was lost in shadow.

Feeling her fear as if transmitted through the air, Peter hurried after her. The congestion in his chest was clearing now, but he was still short of breath by the time he traversed the entire hall and reached the stairs. He just caught a wisp of white going through a doorway at the far end of the downstairs hall as he set himself after her.

He could not imagine what would cause terror in the middle of the night when all else was asleep. Perhaps one of the children had become ill, but already he was dismissing his fantasy of laughing children inhabiting these halls. They must have been neighboring children he had heard. That this house was empty he realized as he rushed in the direction where Lady Honora had disappeared.

The musty stillness of the night enveloped Peter as he gasped for breath at the bottom of the stairs and forced himself to run on. He needed to cough, but the sound would no doubt bring the plaster crumbling down around him. He half expected to run into cobwebs and perhaps large rats, but the hall was amazingly unencumbered. The plank floor beneath his feet rattled slightly and groaned upon occasion, but he was moving too swiftly for it to sound too loud.

Raising his lamp, Peter burst into the front room where he had seen the lady enter, only to discover Cecily standing wide-eyed and frightened in the circle of light from his lantern and hers. Her hair tumbled around her white-clad shoulders in a cascade of chestnut curls that matched the intensity of her enormous blue eyes, and he was aware of the slenderness of the frail shoulders beneath the nightdress. His gaze fell to the shape of her thinly covered breasts and he felt the same shock of desire he had experienced earlier. But before he could act on impulse, she raised the book in her hands to her breast as if in protection, and Peter was returned sharply to reality.

"Where is she?" he demanded.

Cecily stared at this figment of her imagination that she had conjured up with her dreaming. He was more than she remembered, more than she dared dream after the kiss they had shared, and the restlessness that had brought her down here stirred. His dark curls covered his collar in a most ungentlemanly fashion, and she longed to touch them. She noted that his shoulders strained at his coat in a manner even the best Bond Street tailors could not contrive. His weathered face was almost fierce as he faced her, but she had seen the laughing tenderness there, and she was not afraid.

"Who?" she asked simply. She wasn't certain that she dared risk testing his forehead for fever under these circumstances, with the tension rippling between them, but she greatly feared his illness had returned with the overexertion of the day.

"Her ladyship, of course. She came in here. Something must have frightened her. Surely you saw her?" Peter was beginning to doubt his senses as Cecily stared back at him with incomprehension.

"I . . . I just came in." She ought to say something more, but his expression was so intent that Cecily began to sense some of his fear. Perhaps something was wrong. Something was always wrong. She shivered slightly and watched him for some signal as to how to proceed.

Peter was searching the corners of the room with his light, finding the various doors and windows and frowning. It was a room made for openness, as if it had no secrets to hide. But the number of draped exits made it easy to conceal a hasty departure. He turned his lamp back to Cecily.

"Something frightened her, I'm certain of it. I want to search the rest of the house, starting with the outside. I don't want to leave you here alone. Let me take you back to your room and you can lock your door."

That seemed like quite a sensible thing to do if this madman meant to roam the house in search of the invisible. Cecily obediently lifted her nightskirt and hastened toward the door to the hall.

There was something in her gesture that struck Peter as frighteningly familiar, but he didn't have time to dissect the feeling now. He could almost sense an air of panic in the house, as if it waited for him to discover the menace. Catching Cecily by the waist when she didn't leave swiftly enough, he nearly carried her up the stairs, the urgency preventing him from enjoying the sudden closeness of her supple form.

She was breathless from the force of Peter's arm around her by the time they reached the top. Unhesitantly, she turned in the direction of the room at the top of the stairs, only to find him holding her back and staring at her questioningly.

"This room?" He held the lamp up at her nod and threw open the door. The pale light revealed a femininely appointed room of elegant proportions, obviously that of the lady of the house. The covers of the bed were turned down as if someone had just departed from it. The light caught on a small bed in a far nook, and he nodded in understanding. The maid slept with her mistress.

"Lock the door. Do not open it unless you hear me or the lady. One of us will come to tell you when everything is all right. Where is Hodges?"

She told him. Peter waited until she shut and locked the door before he returned to the stairs. He wouldn't find the manservant yet. He sensed whatever was wrong was outside the house, and it would be better if Hodges was indoors with the women.

He wished he could be certain that both women were inside the house. Lady Honora seemed to be amazingly capricious. If she was afraid of something, why would she seek it alone? It did not bode at all well. Could the lady be mad? Was that why Cecily looked at him strangely whenever he mentioned her mistress? He had the ominous feeling that he was treading too close to the truth.

Unbarring the door, Peter stepped out into the still night air. No wind tripped the treetops or howled about the chimneys. The rain of his arrival had left the ground damp and soft, and an autumn chill permeated his bones as he advanced further onto the lawn. Turning around, he could scarcely see the shadow of the house, but he knew it was the same one as in the painting. He had memorized those rambling lines down to the last detail, and now he had stepped outside of it.

Oddly enough, he didn't feel the cold as he stared up at the steep tiled roof, finding the tiny dormer with the circular window, tracing the curve of the rounded chimney down to the bend of the roof over the upper line of windows. The toy had sat in that one on the left, and he greatly suspected that was the same room where he had been earlier, the one with the rocking horse, and the dust-covered books. His gaze drifted to the ornamental lintels, but in the darkness he couldn't find the griffin. But there were traces of rose canes scraping against the stone on the side wall and shutters that would undoubtedly reveal rosebuds were he to run his hands over them. The picture had showed them as being painted, but he was quite certain they were carved as well.

That certainty depressed him. He was in grave danger of losing his mind in this place. The air was as calm and peaceful as it was in the painting. Peter half expected the moon to come out and reveal the laughing lady running through the woods with her arms held out. No wonder Cecily had looked at him as if he were losing his senses. He no doubt was.

But he had seen the lady and known her fear. It was as simple and as complicated as that. If he could only find the wretched witch, he could satisfy himself that he wasn't totally moonstruck. But there wasn't any sign of her in the gardens or on the lawn, and he was certain that he wouldn't find her again this night.

Reassuring himself that no thieves lingered in the shadows and no smoke drifted from any windows, Peter returned to the house. His strength was waning, but he made himself methodically go through the downstairs rooms, throwing open doors and checking windows. He couldn't hear any snores from Hodges' room off the kitchen, but he left the man alone. There was no point in making a fool of himself in front of everyone in the house.

For it was becoming increasingly obvious that Cecily and Hodges and the lady were the only ones in the cottage. Not a curious head peered out of any of the rooms he threw open. Not a peep was heard from overhead as he rattled about, making enough noise to wake the dead. Had there been children, Peter felt certain they would have been down about his feet by now. The children were gone, just as Cecily had said.

The melancholy that had driven Peter to the reckless

dash across the countryside in search of this place now descended upon him again full force as he climbed the stairs. All he had succeeded in doing in his impetuous escapade was to unhinge his mind and endanger his health. He coughed, a great racking cough that threatened to tear up his insides and spew them to the floor.

The door at the top of the stairs flew open and a creature in white flew out. For a moment, he thought it was the lady again, but Cecily's slender shoulders were soon beneath his arm, and she was leading him back to his chamber. He smiled at the feel of soft tresses beneath his rough hand. Daringly, he ran his fingers up and down her arm, showing her he didn't need this support but thanking her anyway. She gave him a slanted look that warned of her disapproval, but Peter only grinned and lurched toward his bed.

"Perhaps I'll wait a day or two before I leave, after all," he murmured as he fell into the soft protection of the featherbed.

"I'll send Hodges to help you undress," she replied unsympathetically.

"No, don't disturb him. I'll manage. Get yourself out of here, *cara mía,* and lock your door before I do something we'll both regret."

Cecily gave him an uncertain glance, but he was grinning faintly. She didn't think he possessed the strength to do anything untoward, but she resisted the urge to lean over and brush the curls back from his brow. She had the quite unreasoning fear she might kiss his cheek while doing so. She backed toward the door without asking him what *"cara mía"* meant.

Coughing wretchedly, Peter forced himself from the bed next morning before Hodges could appear with his morning water. He hadn't bothered to strip off more than his coat and waistcoat the previous night before surrendering to sleep, and he was well aware of his wrinkled appearance when the manservant entered with the pitcher.

Hodges poured hot water into the bowl and began stropping the razor, giving Peter a meaningful look as he did.

Feeling his collar tighten around his throat, Peter sank into the nearest chair before he realized he wasn't wearing a collar. His cravat still lay in pristine condition in his bag where he had left it yesterday.

He submitted gracefully when Hodges did no more than approach him with a shaving brush and soap. The huge man was amazingly deft, and Peter was contemplating offering him the position of valet in place of the whining creature he presently paid when the giant rumbled something that made Peter's muscles knot.

"You'd best not be already married if you know what's good for you."

The razor stroked upward beneath his chin, and Peter tried not to gulp.

"What has that to do with you?" he asked with a bravery he wasn't certain he felt.

"You've been fooling around with my Cecily, and I won't have it."

The razor scraped carefully over his jaw and Peter managed to unclench it long enough to ask with surprise, "She's your daughter?"

The giant stepped back and stared at him with incredulity. "Are you daft, man?" Then, frowning, he returned to his work. "You just keep your hands off'n her lest you got a vicar with you."

That wasn't a half-bad idea if Peter gave much

thought to it, but the image of a silvered figure in the moonlight kept haunting him, and he couldn't forget the mischievous laughter on her lips and the bold welcome of her eyes. The idea of Lady Honora of Rosebud Cottage still obsessed him, even after the prior night's debacle.

"I'll try to remember that," he replied affably. He felt the increase of pressure against his skin and knew he was tempting the man, but Peter wasn't one to run scared. He meant to stand and fight for what he wanted.

Sensing that, Hodges returned to his work with efficient precision. When he was done, he cleaned off the utensils and left without another word of warning or anything else.

Rubbing his hand over his smooth-shaven chin, Peter decided it was time to leave whether he felt like it or not.

When Cecily arrived with his breakfast tray, he had succeeded in tying his cravat and donning his waistcoat and almost appeared a proper gentleman once again. She watched him warily as he reached for his coat, but when he made no move toward her, she advanced into the room to set the tray on the table.

"I thought you were going to wait a day or two."

He almost imagined wistfulness in her voice, but her expression was as serene and determined as the lady's had been the night before when he was certain she was quite frightened out of her mind.

"I think it would be wiser if I left now. I'll be back, you know. Shall I bring a magistrate with me so you may discuss the theft of the painting?"

She looked at him askance, then returned to arranging objects on the tray to her satisfaction. "Inquiries should be made, I suppose. If the painting is the one that is missing, I shall report its return to the local magistrate. You needn't trouble yourself.''

''Cecily.'' Peter came up behind her and caught her when she swung around too rapidly and unbalanced herself. He gripped her arms and studied her face before releasing her. ''I must talk with Lady Honora. Just once. I ask for no more than that. Can you not arrange it for me?''

Disappointment followed by brief disdain flicked across her eyes and was gone. ''I am not a magician. Return to London and your wealthy friends. If you purchased the painting, I suppose you have no real obligation to return it, but I would ask, in return for the favors we have done you, that you do so. I trust you'll have a safe journey.''

She turned around and was gone before he discovered the courage to stop her. He had handled things very badly, Peter decided as he pushed the food around on his tray, but he wasn't at all certain where he had gone wrong. Should he not have had the presumption to ask to see the lady of the house? But he was quite certain she had encouraged him to call again. What was wrong with bidding her farewell?

There was no use in worrying about it now. He wanted to see the cottage in the broad light of day. He wanted to make certain that this wasn't all a dream. And then he wanted to return to London for the painting and a little more information about the Chelmsbys of Rosebud Cottage. Primed with that ammunition, he could return and find some way to make his offer.

For despite its ramshackle condition, he fully intended to buy the cottage and make it his home.

* * *

Peter found his horses and gig waiting for him late that afternoon as he carried his bag outside. He gazed back at the house in the sunlight, admiring the simple angles and curves and the whimsical eccentricities that so delighted him. A shadow flickered in an upper-story window and he waved, uncertain who was watching but hoping it was her ladyship. He longed to see her again, but that would have to wait now. Perhaps he could arrange to be dreadfully ill again upon his return. He rather enjoyed the pampering attention of the ladies of Rosebud Cottage.

He set the horses briskly to their paces, but he wasn't long in discovering that Cecily was closer to right than he cared to admit. The cool wind burned his aching lungs and his arms grew weak much faster than he had thought possible.

Disgusted with himself, he halted at an inn and promised himself he would arrive in London in time to make inquiries at his club on the morrow.

But when the next day came, he was stiff and sore, and the final leg of the journey was an excruciating experience that brought him to his bed and kept him there when he finally reached his own lodgings. His whining valet was of little or no use as a nurse, and Peter tossed and turned restlessly with the return of the fever and visions of the ladies of Rosebud Cottage.

The painting haunted him. He continued to see the stark terror on the lady's face as she raced down the stairs to some unknown disaster. The quiet panic of the disintegrating household stayed with him. Enormous blue eyes in a frail face beseeched him, and he couldn't sleep, couldn't rest, while the mystery remained unsolved.

Still weak some days later, Peter stumbled from his

bed, certain that he would never recover until he returned the painting to the cottage. The fever had dissipated and he was stronger, but there were still things to be done before he could leave.

With grim determination, he set out to meet with some of his friends from the club, gaining the use of the contents of their extensive libraries. With perseverance, he tracked down family histories until he discovered the one he wanted: *The Family History of the Chemlsbys*.

When he was done, he was thoroughly confused. Staring at his Wellingtons, Peter tried to put together the book's contents with the facts he knew, but the gap between seemed wide and unbreachable. True, the book was written in a prior generation and there was no mention of the present generation. And there was an earl with a wife with the name of Honora—during Cromwell's time. Rosebud Cottage itself dated back to that century. But although there seemed to be enormous numbers of descendants, and even an earl or two among them, no female descendant had ever been named Honora afterward.

Peter studied the date of the publication and attempted to guess the lady's birth date. There had been no mention of the cottage in the last generation discussed. The Chelmsbys had seemingly gone on to other things, dispersed across three continents. It did mention some descendants still living in High Wycombe, none of them with the name of Honora. The last mention of the cottage was during the Rebellion of '45 when the resident at that time had hidden an escaped soldier and later went on to marry him. A similar incident was briefly hinted at in a later period, but the gentleman involved was a highwayman and the book provokingly passed over him. It was a romantic history, but offered no explanations of the current residents.

Returning the book to the shelf and thanking his host, Peter set out for his own lodgings—to find a man in uniform waiting for him.

Peter stared at the hostile soldier in disbelief, turned to his sneering valet, and returned his questioning gaze to the intruder. The man was as large as himself and heavily armed. The rigid disapproval in his expression did not foretell easy explanations.

"Peter Aloysius Denning?" the statue inquired. At Peter's nod, he continued, "Only son of Matilda Brown Denning, late of Lord Embry's household?" At his second nod, the soldier announced, "You are under arrest."

That made about as much sense as anything else he had encountered this last week. Gesturing toward his study, Peter suggested, "Perhaps we could sit down and discuss this? I wasn't aware there was any reason for my arrest."

The soldier produced a notebook and scanned the pages. "Theft of a valuable painting. Suspicion of robbery. Suspicion of other unspecified criminal acts. The county magistrate wishes you brought forward to explain the charges."

Lady Honora. Peter pinched his eyes closed and hoped that he was dreaming. When he opened them again, he knew he was not. Impatience had begun to appear in the soldier's expression.

"The painting and the receipt for it are in my study. If you would be so good as to accompany me, we can retrieve them and return to High Wycombe with explanations. The other charges will have to be clarified.

I cannot remember stealing anything more valuable than a kiss.''

His nonchalant attitude as he led the soldier to the painting left the man momentarily nonplussed. Peter's ability to remain calm in the midst of a storm had saved his life more than once over the years. He strained to retain it now, although anger was a harder emotion to control than fear. Ordering the insolent valet to remove the painting from the wall, Peter opened his desk and rifled through the papers until he found what he wanted. The fact that a soldier stood over him with a gun in his hand and a sword at his side did not ease his fury.

"Let us go at once, then," Peter said arrogantly, pocketing the paper and indicating with a nod of his head that the soldier was to take the framed canvas. The confusion on the man's face gave Peter some satisfaction. He was accustomed to giving orders and the soldier was accustomed to taking them. The man carrying the warrant for his arrest obediently took the burden under his arm.

When it became apparent the man had arrived by mail coach and meant to return to the country by the same means, Peter balked and ordered his rig brought around. He had no intention of being transported like a common criminal. He meant to arrive in High Wycombe as a gentleman and face down Lady Honora with the same high-handedness that she had used to obtain his arrest.

Once his captor became convinced that Peter was coming willingly, the man relaxed enough to divulge some of the incidents leading to the arrest. To Peter's disgust, he learned the soldier was no more than the son of the magistrate, currently home from duty and called into service by his father. The tale of the stolen painting from Rosebud Cottage had led to suspicion about other recent thefts in the area. The final blow had come when the magistrate himself had been held up by a highway robber the night before Peter had left the cottage. The coincidence was somewhat damning, but Peter was confident he could put an end to the charges—until the man mentioned the quite thorough investigation his father had already conducted.

Peter bit his tongue and urged the horses to a faster pace as the soldier revealed the lingering questions about his prisoner's past and mysteriously acquired fortune. So much for ever acquiring Lady Honora and Rosebud Cottage. He would be a condemned criminal in the eyes of those people for the rest of his life simply because of his birth. Damn, but he might as well never have come home.

Night was upon them before they reached the outskirts of High Wycombe. Ignoring any suggestion that they stop for the evening, Peter whipped his horses into a faster stride, sending them flying down paths he scarcely remembered from his last visit. Let them scorn his birth and his means of rising above it, but he wasn't going to linger under suspicion for one moment longer than was necessary. He'd start tearing their house of cards apart as soon as he produced the painting, and he would stomp upon the debris before the night was over.

What hurt most was that the inhabitants of Rosebud Cottage could turn against him this way. For the first time in years he had felt as if he were home, as if he had found friends and family. It had been a foolish notion, but sufficient to make him want to return for more. Returning as their prisoner hadn't been what he'd had in mind.

Rather than following his captor's directions to the magistrate, Peter lashed the horses down the drive he remembered to Rosebud Cottage. The dark shadows of trees laced both sides of the road, and the heavy clouds above kept anything but an occasional peek of the full harvest moon from slipping through the darkness. He was only thankful that it wasn't raining as a cold wind pierced his coat and caught his hat, almost tumbling it to the ground. He didn't need any more accidents like that last one.

Despite his knowledge of the danger of the road, Peter was almost caught by surprise again by the figure running through the woods. He could see it darting among the trees, dodging shadows, picking up slivers of moonlight as it ran directly toward the path his horses were taking. He caught his breath and began to haul on the reins, his heart suddenly pounding as he recognized the illusion. Lady Honora.

Just as in the painting she was fleeing through the woods, her flimsy gown flowing in the cold autumn breeze, her face silver with the moonlight. Only this time there wasn't welcome in her eyes, but fear. It didn't make sense, but Peter responded immediately, halting the horses and leaping to the ground to the furious shouts of the man who was to hold him prisoner.

Peter vaulted the hedgerow and ran in the direction where he had last seen the elusive image. A bullet whined over his head, but he ignored it, forcing his boots to find a path through the neglected grounds. He felt none of the weakness of his illness, only the panic that seemed to permeate the air as he raced toward the woman who in all probability had sent to have him arrested.

He barely had time to open his arms and catch her when she collided against his chest, her breath coming in short pants as she shivered and clung to him for support while she gathered her strength.

"Peter! They're waiting for you back at the house. You've got to run. They think you're a highwayman. Please, don't dawdle! Run."

She lifted her face to his, her long hair streaming in a cascade down her back, her blue eyes wide with terror as they met his. Her blue eyes. Cecily.

Feeling his breath catch in his throat, Peter crushed her against him. She had come to warn him. That was all that mattered now. Forgetting all else, he gathered her shivering body close, warming her with his own. Feeling her slender frailty in his arms, he couldn't fight the overwhelming sensation of coming home, and protectiveness swept over him. Bending his head, Peter found Cecily's lips with his, and he filled with joy as she responded passionately.

But then she tore away, and stared at him with fear. "There isn't time! Please, you have to leave. I've tried explaining to them, but they won't listen."

The magistrate's son found them then, a formidable frown on his wide brow as he stepped through the underbrush, gun raised and sword sparkling in the moonlight. "Miss Chelmsby," he remarked with surprise as Cecily darted in front of Peter, protecting him with her back and her widespread arms.

The name sent a ripple of shock through Peter, but he merely encircled her waist with his arm and lifted her to his side. It had been Lady Honora running through those bushes; he would swear it. But it was

Cecily he held in his arms, would continue holding in his arms if she would let him. Sending her delicate but thoroughly outraged face a bemused look, he returned to the matter at hand.

"I don't like ambushes, Acton." It had taken some time to persuade the soldier's name from him, but Peter employed it with purpose now. "I'm not your highwayman and I'm not a thief. I'd suggest we ride quietly to the house and that you stay in front of me to prevent any hasty actions. I'll not have the lady endangered by some overwrought farmer looking to be a hero."

He spoke as if he were the one carrying gun and sword and not the man who wielded them. The young man looked from Peter to Cecily in confusion, then nodded reluctantly. "We'd best walk, then. Hodges can fetch the rig."

They marched up to the front door in procession, Acton in the lead, Peter following, pushing Cecily behind him when the first man appeared out of the shrubbery. He sensed the presence of others, heard the nervous whinnies of horses, and cursed the audience. He wanted Cecily to himself, to hear her explanations, but it was far too late for that.

The men suddenly filling the empty corridor of Rosebud Cottage carried ancient weapons, but deadly for all that. Peter moved among them with assurance. He had grown up among men like these, lived among them as a sailor. Fear was the only thing to fear at such times. Finding Hodges, he glared at the man angrily.

"See Miss Chelmsby to her room, then fetch my rig. You'll find the damned painting in there." He turned curtly to the soldier. "Now, where is your father? I'll have some explanations of this mob frightening an innocent young woman in her own home.''

Even though all must know he was not of the aristocracy, they bowed to his commands as if he were. Peter had learned in childhood that appearance was everything at times. He knew how to wield his well.

But once faced with Lord Acton, appearances didn't matter at all. Hair still dark despite his years, his lined face reflecting weather more than age, he came to his feet and met Peter's eyes on an equal level. Piercing eyes looked Peter over ruthlessly, then returned to focus on his face with determination.

''I thought you might persuade my son, Charles, to come here first. Using Miss Chelmsby as a front for your unlawful actions is the work of a blackguard, sir. Stealing her most valuable possession is the work of an animal without a conscience. I'd see you hanged now were it not my duty to uphold the law. Charles, lock him up. We'll see to his trial in the morning.''

Before Peter could speak, a soft hand circled his arm, and Cecily was beside him. He meant to push her aside, but she dug her fingers in and spoke before he could do more.

''It is all a mistake, Lord Acton. He has returned my painting, just as promised. Hodges was hasty in reporting its theft. And it is only your desire to catch a thief that makes you claim Mr. Denning is the highwayman. He could not have possibly been the man to rob you. He was with me that night.''

A gasp went up around the room, and even Peter narrowed his eyes and gazed down into her innocent expression. ''Cecily, I'll wring your neck for this,'' he murmured, pushing her aside before turning back to the magistrate.

"She is lying to protect me. I would prefer to prove my innocence in some other manner. If you will guarantee that I will see a fair trial, I will be happy to accompany you. But there will be need to call other witnesses and obtain statements from my former employers, and these things will take time. If you mean to hold the trial in the morning, then you may as well go ahead and hang me tonight."

A hint of admiration appeared in the older man's eyes as he gazed at the man determinedly shaking off the woman clinging to his arm. "I would have hanged you for stealing the lady's painting, but if she is prepared to drop those charges, I will have to spend some time investigating the others. However, I don't feel it is appropriate for you to remain here while I do so. Miss Chelmsby, I will take the gentleman with me, but you can be assured that he will be safe until such time as the charges against him can be proven."

"Lord Acton, if you do not have these men removed from my house at once, I cannot guarantee their safety. You know how these old houses are." Cecily gave a chillingly sweet smile and the men who saw it moved nervously, glancing about. "And Mr. Denning has not yet recovered from his illness. I see no reason for him to go out again in the cold night air. He will remain here, with me. Unless you are prepared to press charges, I don't think you have a choice in this matter."

A shutter slammed against a wall, making everyone jump. The various lanterns around the room flickered in a wayward breeze from out of nowhere. Cecily continued to smile, clinging to Peter's arm, while the men scattered through the room began shifting from foot to foot, making mumbling noises. Even Lord Acton appeared untowardly perturbed.

"Cecily, I have known you since you were a child. You aren't going to frighten me with your ghost stories. In memory of your parents, I cannot in all good conscience allow you to remain alone in this house with any man, let alone one who could be a thief and a murderer."

There was a thud and a scream from the hall, but Cecily remained unmoved. "That was just the brass urn on the sideboard. When the wind blows in a certain direction, it falls over," she explained calmly to Peter, who was beginning to look amused. Turning back to the magistrate, she continued their conversation. "I think you overlook the fact that he has spent nearly a week with me already. I can only be ruined once, I believe."

That was the last straw. Peter wrapped one arm around her waist and placed his other hand over her mouth, looking to the startled magistrate as he did so. "I rather suspect she's something of a witch, my lord, and as this is All Hallows' Eve, she probably needs to be restrained, but if appearances are all that concern you, I can assure you I mean to do the right thing by her as soon as possible. Otherwise, I rather suspect that painting will land on my head and break my neck before I can get back to the city."

Cecily had begun to struggle against his side, and Acton looked torn between rescuing her and gladly handing her over to any madman who could hold her down. Another sudden gust of wind doused half the lanterns and sent the iron chandelier overhead to squeaking ominously. Even Acton glanced upward, and said nothing as the men around him began to edge out of the room.

Hodges loomed in the doorway, painting in hand, glancing scornfully around as men dodged past his towering frame.

"Miss Chelmsby is a lady of breeding. I will not see her seduced and shackled by a common sailor and a possible criminal." Lord Acton remained firmly in place beneath the swinging chandelier.

Peter felt the nip of Cecily's teeth beneath his palm, but this was his argument, and he didn't give her the opportunity to speak. The word or two he meant to exchange with the lady would happen in private. With a wry nod, he indicated his wiggling captive. "Does this look like seduction to you? The lady and I have our disagreements, but I will do nothing against her will. *Nothing,*" he emphasized. "My name and reputation are honest ones, or were until you came along. I came by my wealth through hard work and good fortune, and if you object to that I am sorry, but it is not you whom I wish to marry. That choice is the lady's."

Peter winced as the lady's sharp teeth bit into the base of his palm. Two of the many salon doors slammed shut, sending all the remaining men in the room scuttling for the hall except for Lord Acton. That gentleman began to look exceedingly uncertain as he watched the irate flash of Cecily's eyes and the young man's calm authority in controlling her. With most of the lamps and lanterns doused, the room had descended into shadows, and the squeaks of the chandelier and shrieks of old wood rocking in the increasing wind seemed louder.

Peter merely adjusted his grip more comfortably. "Stop biting me, Cecily, or I will hand you over to

Hodges.'' He gave that gentleman a warning look that meant a meaningful discussion would follow. Then he looked up as if just noticing that the house seemed ready to explode around them and turned a nonchalant gaze to the magistrate. "I'll no doubt have to fight Miss Chelmsby's ghosts and goblins until I can persuade her, but you are welcome to stay and chaperone if you wish.''

The urn apparently toppled from the sideboard again, and Peter grinned as the magistrate jumped uncomfortably. Even Cecily ceased wriggling and turned her head to give him a suspicious glare. Only Hodges seemed to find the abnormal sounds unsurprising. Lord Acton's son appeared in the doorway, a worried expression on his normally stoic square face as he waited for his father to leave.

The magistrate cleared his throat, looked to Hodges and his son, then questioned Cecily directly. "Are you sure you would not prefer to come home with me, Miss Chelmsby? I had not realized this place had become so unsafe.''

She waited for Peter to uncover her mouth and then replied quite clearly, "The cottage has been here a few hundred years, it will stand a few hundred more. You need not worry on my account.''

The wind already seemed to be dying down. Hodges lit a branch of candles, and they flickered and grew brighter, revealing a well-worn but inviting salon. Acton looked around and nodded, then gave Peter a stern stare. "If I find out those charges are true, I'll see you hang, young man.''

"No doubt someone deserves to, but not me. Please call again in the morning and I will give you a list of witnesses and references. You will see that I was too

weak to even manage my cattle halfway to London."
Peter flung Hodges a cold look. "If someone had just
had a little patience, none of this would have happened."

Beginning to understand the inference, Acton also
turned a cold glare to the manservant. Then, with a
few lingering formalities, he departed with his son,
leaving the trio in the old house to their own confron-
tation.

Peter released Cecily and she practically leapt from
his arms, placing her hands on her hips and glaring
from one man to the other. "You're both insufferable.
I have half a mind to sell this place and find myself
some nice little modern house somewhere peaceful,
where I don't have to put up with insufferable servants
and guests."

The wind gave one final shriek through the gables
then settled into a gentle rustling through the heavy
draperies. Peter pinned Hodges with a look. "Out,"
he ordered, "or she'll have the house splintering
around us."

The giant nodded as if fully understanding the warning. "I'll not apologize. It's been a week or better."

"I was sick in bed, you fool." Peter's tone wasn't
as harsh as his words. When Cecily gave him one of
her "I told you so" looks and started around him,
Peter caught her arm and jerked his head at Hodges.
"You'd better find some way of getting those valuables
back to their owners. You won't be needing them any
longer."

Cecily gasped, but Hodges nodded and walked out,
leaving the pair of them to fight it out alone.

"Hodges wouldn't do something like that!" she protested at once, moving away from Peter and toward the dying embers of the fire.

"For you, he would do anything." Peter followed her, taking the poker from her hand and throwing a handful of coal on the ashes. "Tell me about Lady Honora."

That startled her. Instead of moving away nervously, she stepped forward to feel his forehead. "You are not feverish."

Peter caught her hand and held it gently between his, gazing down at her searchingly. Her eyes were almost feverishly bright, and a hint of color stained her cheeks, but otherwise she appeared the same docile nurse who had lightened so many of his days. "No, I am not feverish. Actually, I believe I have just come to my senses these last hours. Will you find it very difficult to think of me as a husband?"

Cecily turned her head away and answered the easier question. "I told you that Lady Honora was the one who had this cottage built for her children, so they could be closer to their father when he was in London. It was a long time ago, back before Cromwell's reign. They were Catholics, you see."

Peter led her to the chair nearest the fire, sat down, and pulled her into his lap. The feel of her small rump against his thighs stirred more primitive desires, but he persisted. "Go on."

Cecily sent him a strange look, but seeing the determination in his jaw, she settled against his shoulder and continued. "The earl fought against Cromwell's armies. You know your history. It was a lost cause. The earl was seriously wounded in battle, but he escaped and returned here. Unfortunately, there were soldiers following him." Cecily suddenly pulled from

Peter's arms and leapt up to go to the huge, faded carpet in the room's center.

Before Peter knew what she was doing, she jerked back a corner of the carpet, revealing a sagging square of floorboard beneath. Even in the dim light he could see that one section was different from the other.

"She hid him down there. It had been obvious for a long time that such a hiding place might be necessary, and Lady Honora had it built with the cottage. Family history has it that she had just pulled the carpet back in place and gone upstairs to comfort the children when the soldiers arrived. Not knowing the earl had returned, the servants had them wait in here while they sent upstairs for her."

Peter could still see the hauntingly vivid image of the woman floating down those stairs, her expression calm but panic flowing from her like perfume. That had been what Lady Honora must have looked like, but he still couldn't make himself believe he had seen a ghost. She was too vibrantly alive to be dead.

Cecily threw the carpet back down and settled herself in a chair beside him. "The story says that she greeted the soldiers, told them she had been informed of her husband's death, and when they refused to believe her and threatened to burn the house down around her, she merely asked if she might get the children and servants out first. I've tried to imagine what it must have been like, knowing your husband was lying injured and possibly dying beneath your feet, while you invite an army to burn the house down around his head. She must have been an incredible woman. Had to have been, because the soldiers believed her and walked out, leaving the cottage and everyone in it unscathed."

As she talked, Peter had the feeling that the Chelmsby family must have included a number of incredible women through the years. He remembered the tale of the woman who had hidden the soldier in '45. And the one who had hidden the highwayman. Now he understood how they had done it. And Cecily, delicate, fragile Cecily, had raced to keep him from encountering Acton and his ambush. Even more, she had managed to keep this crumbling cottage together on her own, from sheer willpower alone, he suspected.

"Do the Chelmsby women make it a practice to hide their loved ones from the law?" he asked when she fell silent.

Cecily's lips tilted slightly in amusement as she read his meaning and met his eyes. "History has it that Lady Honora protects those who will protect her home."

"But you don't believe in ghosts," he stated flatly.

"I don't believe in ghosts." She stood up, forcing him to do so also. "And now I believe it is time to get some rest. I am sorry you had to suffer the humiliation of Acton's arrest on my account. I had no idea that he would take the reported theft so far. I will not blame Hodges for reporting it. He is extremely loyal and thought you were taking advantage of me. I shouldn't think he was guilty of highway robbery, though."

"He was not in his bed that night," Peter informed her gently. When she still seemed rebelliously intent on leaving, Peter stopped her escape by the simple expedient of standing in front of her. "Cecily, I meant what I said earlier. I have no background, but I have an honest name and enough wealth to keep you comfortably. I hope you can bring yourself to consider my suit.''

Cecily flushed as she observed the sincerity in Peter's eyes, then looked away again. ''You are only saying that because you feel obligated. We both know that is nonsense. Do not press me on the matter anymore.''

Peter wanted to catch her in his arms and persuade her with kisses, but he could see the excitement had drained her, and he would not heap more distress upon her; he moved aside to let her pass. The moon broke through the clouds as she drifted from the room, and she walked through a patch of moonlight from the window as she left. He could see quite plainly that she wasn't the silvered shadow from the painting, but a flesh-and-blood woman with a haunting beauty he was just learning to recognize. He didn't want to think of a future without her in it.

But Peter let her go without protest. Quietly, he checked the latches on the windows and doors, noted that the brass urn seemed to be quite securely attached to the sideboard, and went up to the room he had used the prior week.

Despite the furious emotions of the day and the physical exhaustion that usually made it impossible for him to relax, Peter fell asleep quickly upon hitting the soft pillow of his bed. After only a week in this place, he felt at home here. Perhaps someone who hadn't known a true home in years found it easy to adopt any semblance of permanence. And Rosebud Cottage provided more than a semblance of permanence. Centuries-old timber creaked over his head as he drifted into sleep, and he thought of the sounds as music to his ears.

He wasn't at all certain what woke him later. The

wind had died and the moon had fallen lower in the sky, sending pale shadows through the uncurtained window. Peter woke with a start and gazed around, suddenly certain that someone was in the room with him.

He found her waiting in the corner, watching him with a fond smile. He still couldn't believe that she was a ghost. He couldn't quite make out the pattern of her dress, but he knew nothing of women's fashions anyway. Whatever she wore suited her; she moved with the same gentle grace as Cecily did as she went out the opened door.

He was quite certain he had closed that door before he retired, but the doors in old houses were notorious for not fastening tightly. Jerking on his trousers hastily, Peter followed Lady Honora into the hallway. There was no panic in her tonight. Even as the house rested quietly, so did she seem calm and at peace. She seemed quite alive to him, beckoning him with a smile that made his throat dry and his loins tight. He could easily follow a woman like that to the ends of the earth.

Instead, he followed her to the doorway at the end of the hall, the one he had once carried Cecily through. The door fell open silently, but when Peter thought he had caught up with her, the lady was gone. To his astonishment, he found himself standing before the draped bed where Cecily slept, and even as he watched, her eyes fluttered open to find him there.

It was then that he understood. He didn't know how he understood, but he did. The same look that had been in the lady's eyes was in Cecily's now as she looked up at him and made no protest at his appearance. When he sat down on the bed's edge and reached for her, she came to him easily, sliding into his arms as if she belonged there. Her kisses were inexperienced, but her passions were not. Peter groaned and clutched her against his naked chest, resting his chin against her head to keep from dishonoring her further.

"One of your names must be Honora," he murmured against her hair, trying not to feel the pounding of her heart through the thin nightdress. She was slender, but not as fragile in his arms as he had imagined. He could feel the strength in her embrace as she wrapped her arms around him.

Cecily looked up then, studying the square line of his jaw, trying not to flush at the sight of his wholly improper state of undress. "How did you know?"

"A lady told me." Unable to resist any longer, Peter returned his mouth to the parted surprise of hers and placed his claim.

Cecily never noticed when the covers between them tumbled to the floor. The dream she had been having for so many long nights had finally come true, and she felt more alive than she had for her entire life as she felt the solidity of Peter's warm flesh against hers. Tomorrow, she would wonder what had drawn him here. Tonight, she would take what he had to give. She shuddered with rapture as the warmth of his fingers closed over her breasts. It was as if she had always known it would be like this, and her hands reached eagerly to caress his hair and hold him in her arms as their bodies learned what their souls already knew.

And the old house sighed and chuckled and settled contentedly on its foundations as the lovers discovered each other and themselves. The moon drifted to bed, leaving the warmth of darkness to cover them.